BLACKEST
RED *In the Shadows*
PART 3

a billionaire SEAL story

BLACKEST RED

In the Shadows
PART 3

by P.T. MICHELLE

COPYRIGHT 2015
by P.T. MICHELLE

ISBN-10: 1939672244
ISBN-13: 9781939672247

Interior designed and formatted by E.M. Tippetts Book Designs
www.emtippettsbookdesigns.com

To stay informed when the next **P.T. Michelle** book will be released,
join P.T. Michelle's free newsletter http://bit.ly/11tqAQN

BLACKEST RED
In the Shadows
PART 3

by P.T. MICHELLE

No matter how hard I've tried to let go of Mister Black, the memories of us together torture me. They're an unforgettable reminder of a life I can't have for many reasons.

Burying myself in work mostly keeps thoughts of him to a screaming minimum, until he's thrust into my life under circumstances beyond my control. Despite my need for his protection, this time I'm not sure if I'm strong enough to survive with my heart intact.

He is Black: a fierce protector and irresistible charmer.

I am Red: a trouble magnet and rainbow weaver.

Together we ignite. Explosive colors merging at the hottest melting point.

NOTE: BLACKEST RED is meant for readers 18+ due to mature content. This is part 3 in the IN THE SHADOWS series. The series must be read in the following order: MISTER BLACK (part 1), SCARLETT RED (part 2), and BLACKEST RED (part 3).

WHEN BLACK AND RED COLLIDE

Talia

*W**hy* is my editor calling me to Midtown Central *Publishing the day before Blindside's promo tour? After all the hype and push they've put behind this book, are they going to cancel the tour?* Tension throbs through my shoulder blades, and I squeeze the paper cup a little tighter as I enter the senior editor and publisher, William Macken's, top floor office in Midtown. The thought makes my stomach roil, considering the fact I've put my own life on hiatus these past six months, working crazy (read: *insane*) hours to get this standalone novel written in record time right behind turning in the last book in my trilogy.

My fingers dig even deeper into the cup. Of course the lid pops off, but I'm not quick enough to snap it back into place before coffee sloshes over the edge and onto my hand. Wincing against the burning pain, I make sure the lid's secure and follow William's assistant editor, Jared, as he gestures for me to sit in the leather chair in front of William's desk.

Leaning against the desk in front of me, he crosses his arms and smiles. "William is running a bit behind. His last meeting ran over, but he'll be here in five."

I find it amusing that Jared refers to his boss so formally. Like I don't know he's William's son. The resemblance between the two is eerily uncanny. Whenever I'm in the same room with them, I feel like I'm standing in a time warp staring at the same person at two different points in his life.

The only physical difference between father and son, other than the obvious age, is that William's light brown hair is more a grown-out and finger-combed look. The longer style does an excellent job covering up the bit of gray at his temples. In contrast, his son's hair is short on the sides, leaving only bedhead-styled hair on the top. Whereas William prefers designer khakis and Merino wool sweaters, Jared wears a suit and tie. William calls Jared "son" every so often, but Jared always tenses when he does it and only addresses his father as William. Then again, who am I to judge how people label each other; I don't call the woman who raised me "Mom". If Aunt Vanessa minds, she has never mentioned it.

I hold Jared's light green gaze. "Do you know why William called this meeting? He was very vague on the phone. He's not cancelling the promo tour is he?" I say in a teasing, upbeat voice, then take a sip of my coffee to stop myself from blurting out other bad scenarios that might be behind this meeting. I can accept a cancelled several-day, city-wide book tour; I'll just take those few well-needed days off before heading into work at the Tribune instead. *But what if my publisher decided not to do the extra print run they mentioned last Thursday?* Less books will mean that Blindside's chances of being picked up by more bookstores will drop considerably.

Jared smiles smugly, the slight cleft in his chin disappearing. "On the contrary, we've hyped Blindside's fictionalized version of you being stalked by a serial killer so well since its release last Tuesday that we're just taking extra precautions."

I furrow my brow. "What precaut—"

"Talia!" William calls from the doorway, a warm smile on his face as he walks straight to his desk and sits down. "Thank you for coming."

I instantly straighten. "I'm not exactly sure why I'm here, William, but Jared says you'll enlighten me."

Shuffling paperwork on his desk, William snaps the papers upright and straightens them. "Due to the increased media interest in Blindside's release, we've received another letter and thought it best to make sure there's plenty of security during your promo tour this week."

I quickly set my coffee cup down on the edge of his desk. "I've received another threatening letter not to promote the book?"

He nods, but immediately holds up his hand. "Now, the last thing we want you to do is worry."

"Should we get the police involved?" Why didn't I realize just how much media attention this book would generate? Considering Tommy's unsolved murders had started here in New York, I should've known better. But I really thought that pitching my book as a fictional story based on true events would keep me out of the media-frenzied spotlight. Apparently that wasn't the case.

The thing is…I couldn't *not* write it. After pitching the one paragraph summary to my editor, before I ever got his feedback, the story just poured out of me. Of course I changed people's names, and left out Tommy's connection to my past and the entire romance between Sebastian and myself, but apparently a fictional story based on true events is just as newsworthy as the fact the killer had been revealed and killed.

"We've taken care of it," Jared cuts in as he picks up my coffee and hands it back to me. "Don't worry."

"How have you taken care of it?"

William nods and pushes a button on his desk phone. "Cindy, send him in please."

When Sebastian walks into the room, dressed in a slate gray suit and a deep blue tie, I force my shocked gaze away to address my editor, but William is already on his feet and stepping toward Sebastian, his hand outstretched. "Welcome, Mr. Black. We were just assuring Miss Lone that she'll be in good hands with your security business for the duration of her book's promo tour."

Good hands? That's what I'm afraid of. "Surely this is overkill." I set my cup back down and stand, trying to ignore my heart slamming against my chest. I haven't seen Sebastian since I slipped out of his room at the Hawthorne resort in Martha's Vineyard six months ago.

When I first got back to New York, he tried to get in

touch with me, but I knew that the only way to protect my heart from being completely shredded to bits was to avoid all contact with him. To not let myself get pulled in deeper. Whenever he touches me, he's like a drug I can't get enough of, and yet he'd made it perfectly clear he doesn't *do* relationships, certainly not anything lasting. Why would I open myself up to that kind of devastating heartache? So I kept my head down and buried myself in my writing deadlines and work for the Tribune instead.

Sebastian shakes William's hand, then shifts his brilliant blue gaze my way, his tone crisp and to-the-point. "I assure you, my presence isn't unnecessary, Miss Lone. I've read the letters. Someone out there doesn't want you speaking about this book to the public. I've been hired to keep you safe and that's exactly what I intend to do."

I quickly shake my head. "I think this is way too much. I don't need a security detail."

Jared approaches and clasps my tightly clenched hands between his. "Mr. Black is highly trained, Natalia. He will be sure to blend in at the signings, media interviews, and evening events we have planned this week. He won't stand out as your bodyguard, but he'll be there, giving Midtown Central Publishing peace of mind."

"But Mr. Black isn't even his..." I pause and glance over at Sebastian who raises a dark eyebrow, a mocking challenge in his eyes. *Are you really going to say my name isn't Mr. Black?*

Jared releases me as William walks over to rest a reassuring hand on my shoulder. "It'll run smoothly, you'll see. The authors' event tonight will make a great dry run before Blindside's promo tour officially kicks off tomorrow. We've taken the liberty of booking you a room at the Regent for the evening, since the event will run late. Please make sure to be downstairs in the Imperial ballroom an hour before it starts. I hope you're ready for all the attention, Miss Lone." Before I can respond, he squeezes my shoulder. "Now, if you'll excuse me, I need to go over a few things with Mr. Black."

"I'd like to see the letters, please."

William nods to Sebastian. "His company is a security firm. They're investigating as we speak."

"Do we know if they're even from the same person?" I ask, directing my gaze to Sebastian.

He nods. "They are."

"And?" I raise my eyebrows, frustrated that he's so non-committal.

"When we have something to share, we will. Just know that more than one veiled threat has been made about the release of Blindside. It's not extreme to assume you might be specifically targeted."

I throw my hands up. "This is crazy."

"Come on, I'll take you to lunch," Jared says, clearly trying to calm me down. "I have some PR business to discuss with you anyway."

Yes, it worries me to think someone might be after me, all because I wrote a book, but what bothers me more at the moment is being kept in the dark. Not to mention, Sebastian's presence is setting me on edge. I can't decide how I feel about the fact he's acting like we barely know each other. Does Midtown Central know *he's* Aaron White from my book? I don't buy for one minute my publisher just happened to pick *his* company out of the abundance of security firms out there. Straightening my spine, I narrow my gaze on Jared. "I want to see the letters."

Jared sighs. "I have them scanned on my phone. You can see them during lunch."

Nodding, I let him escort me out of the room with every intention of grilling him about BLACK Security's involvement during lunch.

As Jared and I walk into the restaurant, a text pings on my phone.

> *Unknown: Make sure Ivy-League Junior doesn't get in my way this week. You will follow my instructions, not his. Got it, **Natalia**?*

My face flames with indignant fury. Even though Jared and I haven't stepped beyond a business relationship, the tone of Sebastian's text seems to imply there's more between us. It doesn't matter that Jared's been moving toward a romantic relationship the last few business meals we've had together. I resist the urge to blast Sebastian with a "mind your own damn business" text while Jared asks the hostess for a table. Instead, I address the bigger issue.

> *Me: How did you get my number? You'd BETTER not still be tracking my phone.*
>
> *Unknown: William. Add me to your contacts.*

His abrupt order makes me set my jaw. The man doesn't ask for anything. He demands.

Me: Why?

*Unknown: So my stubborn client will know it's
me texting her.*

I ignore the unbidden fluttering in my stomach and
grudgingly add him to my contacts. I've just saved his info
on my phone when another message comes through.

*PainInMyAss: This isn't up for negotiation. Is
it done?*

Smirking, I send him a screenshot of his last text to me.
While the waitress leads us to our table, another text
comes through.

*PainInMyAss: Begging me already? A blistering
shade of red on that sweet ass of yours sounds
perfect to me.*

The thought of his low, sexy voice whispering that in
my ear makes my insides burn. *Arrogant ass!* I shake my
head and shut off my phone, annoyed that he turned my
intended dig into some kind of kinky come-on.

CHAPTER ONE

Talia

"What did the police say?" I ask Cass as she walks into my hotel room with my suitcase and her bigger one in tow. "I'm sorry I couldn't come home. Jared sprung back-to-back PR meetings on me right when we got back from lunch."

Cass pushes her long dark hair over her shoulder and sits down on the bed, adjusting the slit on her black formal dress. "No worries. The police came and did their thing. Just in case…" Pausing, she hands me a key. "I had the locks changed. The doorman's going to keep an eye on our place, but I'm glad you're listening to me about staying at the hotel all week. I'll feel better knowing you won't be at home alone at night. Whoever broke in didn't steal anything that I could tell, but they went through your bedroom. Opening drawers, your closet, your jewelry

box, your toiletries. It was beyond creepy to see what all
had been touched."

I shake off the shiver that crawls up my spine.
"Answering the police's questions via speakerphone
while signing a stack of books felt so awkward. Did they
get anything useful?"

Cass nods. "Fingerprints all over the place. Obviously
the person didn't care that they left them behind. Once the
police eliminate yours, hopefully the person's prints will
be on file somewhere. Oh, by the way, on my way in I saw
your aunt and Charlie downstairs."

Tensing, I hold her gaze. "Do me a favor and don't
tell Aunt Vanessa about the break-in. She's already on
me about not doing the tour after I made the mistake of
telling her about the threatening letters." The two letters
that Jared showed me at lunch had been very vague. They
had both supposedly come via the regular mail. Both had
been typed out on a computer and had just said that if
I promoted Blindside, I would regret it. "I don't want to
give my aunt another reason to worry."

Cass nods. "She didn't see me. I noticed her leaving the
restaurant as I walked past."

I laugh as I lift the suitcase Cass brought for me onto
the bed to unzip it. "I think it's Aunt Vanessa's new
personal goal to make sure she tries every restaurant.
Now that she's got her friend, Charlie-the-foodie to hang
with, I don't think she has cooked a single meal the past
six months. I'm surprised Charlie's husband doesn't get
jealous of all the time they spend together."

"It's not like she's going to steal him away." As Cass
snickers, she lets her gaze scan the opulent bed and

expensive furnishings in the room. "This has to be one of the most exclusive hotels I've ever been in."

"You're welcome to stay and keep me company this week instead of trotting off to Spain. I'll even sweeten the deal by offering to pay for a mani-pedi and a massage."

Her eyes widen, then she twists her lips, expelling a grunt of frustration. "You are so wickedly cruel, Talia. But this is Spain! You know how much I've been dying to do a shoot there."

I sigh, knowing I won't get her to change her mind. When it comes to her photography business Cass is obsessed. Her crazy long hours are the only reason I was able to work so much these past few months. Otherwise, my best friend would've staged an intervention. And truthfully, once I'd turned my Sly Fox club article in to the Tribune, even I knew something had to give. At least with Blindside's release, I'll be able to breathe again. Pulling my formal gown from my suitcase, I shake it out. "Ah well, I tried. At least you can be here tonight to help me celebrate the tour kick off tomorrow. Thank you for coming and being a buffer when Nathan shows up."

Cass shakes her head. "You'd think after this much time, he'd get the hint you really aren't going to take him back."

I shrug and lift more clothes out of my suitcase. "He hasn't been too happy with me ever since I ditched him while working on the Sly Fox club piece."

Pressing her lips together, Cass' gaze narrows. "I didn't like that you sent him home. He might be annoying as hell, but we both know he'd have your back while you worked undercover at the club."

I hold a pair of three-inch heels up beside a strappy pair and raise my eyebrow. When Cass points to the strappy ones, I say, "Nathan's a great researcher, but he didn't blend in enough. I was worried he'd blow my cover. Plus, the new bouncer, Theo, took me under his wing. He might've come across as laidback, but that brute of a man wasn't letting anyone mess with me. Did I tell you he even walked me to my car each night?"

Shaking her head, Cass exhales. "I know you felt it was a second chance to finally bust that human trafficking ring, but I've never been so glad when you told me you were finally done with that piece."

I smile. "It *was* something I needed to finish. Not to mention it bought me tons of good cred at the Tribune."

"I know, I know." Cass nods. "Though you may not need me to help with Nathan. It sounds like that assistant editor of yours is more than interested. Bet he'll Velcro himself to you tonight."

I shrug out of my clothes and step into my dress. "I seriously doubt that. Along with his father, Jared will be hosting this event. He'll be very busy schmoozing it up with all the authors and industry people, not to mention the media who've been invited."

"Then a buffer I'll be," Cass says, grinning. Curling a strand of her long, straight dark hair around her finger, she bats her lashes at me. "You, uh, do realize I will be doing a bit of my own stalking tonight. Mr. Osslander is still coming, isn't he?"

I snicker, knowing all too well her love for the playboy mystery writer. "Yes, Clive is supposed to be here. Though, I don't know why you wouldn't rather meet David Sharp.

At least he's not eighteen years older than you."

"David doesn't write with Clive's sharp wit. I love that man's style. It's classic and sexy all rolled into one. Age difference, *pffft!* You'd better introduce me."

"Fine. You'll get your introduction. Just keep in mind Clive has a reputation with the ladies, especially ones half his age."

Her light brown eyes narrow into pleased slits. "I'm counting on it." Clapping her hands excitedly, Cass stands. "Okay, let's get you dressed. You need to be downstairs in an hour."

Once Cass adjusts the spaghetti strap on my fitted black velvet tea-length dress and I slip on my diamond stud earrings, a knock sounds at the door. "Miss Lone. It's time to head downstairs," Sebastian calls through the thick wood.

Cass taps my collarbone, excitement glittering in her eyes. "I have a necklace for you to wear." Meeting my gaze in the mirror, she lowers her voice. "His deep voice sounds divine. How hot is your bodyguard? Would I want him to guard *my* body?"

All Cass knows about my involvement with the Hawthorne resort's pilot this past summer was that it happened, and that he'd saved my life. I never told her he was the Robin Hood from that masked party that she and I had attended three years before. I hadn't planned to tell her anything, but Sebastian sent a package to my apartment the day after I'd returned to New York from Martha's Vineyard, so Cass quickly learned that what transpired between myself and the pilot was more than a fling.

Once I opened the slim package to see the gorgeous strand of black pearls I'd left behind and a note penned in his bold script that simply said, *"Per your request, a clean slate. Have dinner with me,"* Cass had squealed with delight and instantly grabbed up the necklace. "Oh my God. You didn't say your pilot was loaded, Talia."

I shrugged. "It's a strand of pearls, not crown jewels."

"Not just any pearls." Carrying the necklace over to the light, she inspected them, then glanced my way. "Do you have any idea how rare these pearls are?"

"What do you mean?" I asked, confused.

She held the necklace up. "These are Tahitian rainbow pearls, Talia. The dark color isn't a dye. It's formed naturally, and because of the iridescent rainbow hue it takes on, that means putting a matching necklace together would take combing through thousands of pearls. With this longer length and the uniformity of each pearl, I'll bet this strand is worth at least twenty grand."

"How do you know so much about pearls?" I'd asked, trying to sound casual. While she went on about how her mom had started collecting different kinds of pearls once her dad's career took off, my mind stayed locked on one aspect of what she'd said.

Rainbow pearls?

My heart clung to the word. Did Sebastian know that when he bought them? *Of course he knew.* Everything he does is with purpose. Why did he have to be so freaking perfect in all the ways I wanted him to be but the one that mattered most? His confession that he wouldn't stick around was pretty much a deal breaker, no matter how layered his gift appeared. Learning the necklace most likely had an intimate meaning specific to us only made my heart hurt more. I quietly took the strand from Cass, closed it in its box, and then put it away. Cass could tell by my expression that I didn't want to talk about it, so she let it go. I've never been more thankful for my friend's silent understanding than I was that day, because I couldn't bring myself to look at the necklace again after that.

Sebastian knocks on the door once more, pulling me out of my musings, his tone sharper. "Miss Lone, we need to get moving."

Cass scrunches her nose and whispers, "Is he always that bossy?"

I snort. "You don't know the half of it." I have no plans to tell her that my bodyguard and the pilot are the same man. She'd demand answers. And honestly, I don't have any to give her that don't involve cutting open a vein and bleeding out my conflicted feelings. It's bad enough that she's already given me a hard time about Blindside's straight mystery storyline, saying, "I can't believe you totally denied your readers some good smexy-times." Why give her more fuel to tease me with?

"We'll be out in a sec," I call to Sebastian just as Cass clasps a necklace around my neck.

A dime-sized filigree white gold design decorates the Y on the delicate lariat style chain, while a single pear-shaped black pearl dangles at the bottom of the Y. The pearl stops just at my cleavage that's currently pushed up by my dress' fitted bodice. "This is gorgeous, Cass. Where did you get it?" I ask, leaning toward the mirror to inspect the unusual swirled pattern in the filigree.

Before she can answer, the door opens and Sebastian

scowls at us. "Ladies, we need to leave now."

"Holy hot-damn!" Cass spouts out, then grins unrepentantly at Sebastian. "If Talia gives you a hard time tonight, I'll be happy to let you guard *my* body."

A slight smirk breaks Sebastian's stoic expression. "You must be the roommate, Cass."

I roll my eyes. Of course he's done his homework. "Cass, meet my guard for the week, Mr. Black."

"Ah, so Talia has told you about me. That's interesting..." Pausing, she cuts a suspicious gaze my way. "Because she'd told me nothing about you."

"For the record, I told him *nothing* about you," I say, giving her a cheesy smile.

Huffing, she glares. "We are so going to have a talk when I get back."

I slide my phone into my clutch purse, then snap it shut. "You'll have to stay home long enough."

"Ugh, you're so exasperating!" Tossing her long hair over her shoulder, Cass grabs her purse and precedes me into the hall, but not before she stops briefly in front of Sebastian. "Talia definitely needs guarding, and if she gives you a hard time at all tonight, let me know. I'll be sure to kick her ass for you so she flies straight the rest of the week."

Ignoring Sebastian's low, "I'll keep that in mind," comment, I follow my well-meaning friend down the hall.

Once Cass and I step into the elevator, I turn to her while Sebastian pushes the button for the lobby. "Where did you get this necklace? Did you borrow it from your mom?"

"No silly." She quickly opens her purse and pulls out

a small white card. "It came this morning, along with this. Since your name wasn't on the package, I opened it." Handing me the card, she says, "Is this Jared's way of wooing you?"

As soon as I see the bold script I know it's from Sebastian. Cass never saw his note in the first package he sent me, so she had no way of knowing this is from him. I work hard to keep my hand from shaking as I focus on one sentence on the stark white card.

To favorite places.

I feel Sebastian's gaze on me as Cass continues, "It's a gorgeous necklace. I think the pearl sits a little low, but you can easily have that adjusted. So, did you two walk past a jewelry store and he saw you admiring it? Is that what the card means? What a romantic gesture. Well played. But why doesn't the guy just freaking ask you out already?"

My gaze strays to the black pearl practically kissing the hollow between my breasts and my body heats all over at the memory of Sebastian holding my breasts and running his nose along my cleavage. He'd inhaled deeply and told me it was his second favorite place on my body. I refuse to look up when Sebastian says in a curt tone, "The necklace is perfect as is."

Cass chuckles, sliding her gaze to my chest. "Well, it's certainly sexy."

Just then the elevator pings and a couple people get on, separating us from Sebastian. I glance up briefly to see his jaw muscle working as the elevator doors close. When the elevator slows to the next floor and a few more people dressed in formalwear squeeze in, I quickly whisper in Cass' ear, "Mr. Black *is* my pilot, Cass. No more talk about the necklace, okay!"

While Cass gapes at me, Sebastian maneuvers fluidly through the crowd to stand on my right, cutting off her chance to ask the myriad of questions written all over her face. The general hubbub in the elevator goes up as the group of people—obviously there to meet their favorite authors and rub elbows with big wigs from the oldest and biggest publishing house in New York—discuss the upcoming event.

"I can't wait to meet David Sharp," a middle-aged woman says.

"I'm dying to see Carolyn Rivers. I hear she looks nothing like her picture on her book," another woman pipes in with a smirk.

"Have you heard Clive Osslander speak? Did you know he narrates his own audio books? His voice is so riveting."

I suppress a chuckle when I see Cass nodding with the others about Clive.

"I got an advance copy of Blindside to review for our magazine," a preppy guy in his mid-twenties says from the opposite corner of the elevator. "It's based on true events and ties back to a string of serial killings that happened right here in New York. It's a damn good story."

"Who's the author?"

He smiles down at the petite blonde woman next to him. "Her name is T.A. Lone. I'm definitely looking forward to meeting her."

"I'll bet Blindside is nothing but a bunch of lies loosely based on an ounce of truth," a bearded man with slumped shoulders grumbles directly in front of me.

Cass stiffens, and when she opens her mouth to say something, I squeeze her arm and shake my head.

We arrive on the lobby floor, and once everyone walks out and Cass follows, Sebastian glances down at me, his expression hard to read. "Ready to face the wolves, Miss Lone?"

I raise my eyebrow as we walk out together, twisting my lips into a smirk. "With a deviously cunning raven keeping an eagle eye on me, I know I'll be just fine."

Amusement at my reference to something from our past briefly flashes in his eyes before his intensity returns. "Don't even think about returning that necklace. I meant what I said..." His gaze strays to my breasts then snaps to my face once more. "Pure perfection."

How does he manage to make two simple words sound like the most bone-melting compliment? I honestly can't figure him out. He had been so cold in William's office. Then later, he'd been almost angry, but definitely bossy in his texts while I was at lunch with Jared. And now I can feel the heat in his eyes as they slide over my skin. Is he the type of man who only goes after someone if she's conveniently in his face? But otherwise, he can easily forget the woman the moment she leaves his sight? Before I can say anything about the necklace one way or the other, Jared approaches us, looking very formal in his double-breasted tuxedo and bow tie.

"There you are, Miss Lone." Clasping my hand, he wraps it around the crook of his arm. "Mr. Black," he says in a business-like tone before he pulls me along and whispers in my ear, "Tons of people have been waiting to meet you."

I don't look back at Sebastian, but I feel better knowing his solid presence is in the background watching and observing. I know he won't miss a thing. Despite my bravado with Cass and while I talked to the police earlier today, knowing that someone broke into our apartment and pawed through my things is unsettling. No matter what transpires between Sebastian and me as individuals, I know he'll do everything he can to keep me safe. That knowledge helps me hold my head high and meet the crowd of people in the ballroom with confidence.

CHAPTER TWO

Talia

My aunt and Charlie approach not long after I walk into the room. "You look stunning in that dress, my dear," Aunt Vanessa says as I hug her.

I pull back and smile, looking over her formal gown. "And so do you. Teal really is your color. Have you lost weight?"

"I have," my aunt says, cutting a look Charlie's way. "Thank you for noticing."

Leaning down from his barrel-chested, six-two height, Charlie kisses my cheek, his white hair tickling my temple. When he straightens, his black eyebrows are raised, amusement dancing in his dark eyes. "She didn't like it when I commented on her weight loss, but when you do, it's apparently a compliment."

While my aunt sputters at him and fluffs her salt-and-pepper styled bob, I smile. "That's the benefit of blood. We get a free pass." I turn to Jared, who's gone quiet beside me, and introduce him to my aunt. "Jared, meet Vanessa Granger, my aunt, and her good friend Charlie Hamilton.

Shaking Aunt Vanessa's hand, Jared smiles. "You have a very talented niece, Mrs. Granger. We're going to make her a household name yet."

My aunt clasps his hand and says in a firm tone, "Nice to meet you, Jared. I understand you're management at Midtown Central. You make sure to take good care of my niece this week."

"Aunt Vanessa!" I say, embarrassed by her comment.

Jared wraps her hand in both of his, sincerity in his gaze. "We've hired the best to keep her safe. Don't worry."

When my aunt snorts as if she doesn't trust him, I'm thankful Jared didn't notice as he waves to a man snapping pictures of authors posing with their editors. "Let's get a nice family photo of you two ladies for the company newsletter. Shall we?"

Midtown Central's photographer isn't the only one who takes pictures though. Suddenly the crowd around us grows until it feels like a hundred flashbulbs are going off at once while we smile for the cameras.

After the initial barrage of snapshots, the reporters turn to Jared and ask him questions. My attention stays focused on my aunt as she blinks repeatedly and presses her fingers to her temples, saying, "Oh God, how do you do that? I feel a headache coming on."

Charlie takes Aunt Vanessa's hand and folds it around his arm. "Come on, Vanessa. I'll take you home." When I start to apologize, he smiles. "Don't worry. Bright lights give her migraines every so often."

"Really?" *Since when?* "I'm sorry, Aunt Vanessa. I didn't know."

She squeezes my hand. "I'll be fine, Talia. I'll call you tomorrow, okay? Let's go have lunch together."

I mentally grimace, knowing I'll be swamped with tour stuff the next several days. "I can't this week, but once the tour is over, let's definitely have lunch."

My aunt sighs her disappointment, then lifts her eyebrows, an expectant look in her eyes. "Rudi's at noon next Wednesday. I'd like to make lunch a weekly thing, dear."

"Um, but I have to work—"

"To make up for all the times you've missed while working so much the past few months," she says, her dark eyes searching mine.

I glance at Charlie, who's frowning slightly as his gaze shifts to my aunt. *Great. I'm feeling bombarded with guilt.* "I'll figure a schedule out."

A genuine smile spreads across her face as she pats my cheek. "That's my girl. Be very alert this week. I want you to stay safe. Enjoy the rest of your evening."

I nod my agreement, but don't get a chance to watch them walk away because Jared pulls me into the conversation, introducing me to the magazine and newspaper people. When they start asking me pointed questions about the serial killer, Tommy Slawson, Jared interrupts and provides the dates of Blindside's launch this week, including the two media Q&A time slots.

When a few people ask to be included in the first Q&A session, Jared calls over a dark-haired girl in her early twenties to add their names to the schedule. I let my gaze quickly scan the crowd and I catch a glimpse of Sebastian standing not more than seven feet away, his back is to the wall. Broad shoulders pushed back, his expression is serious as he surveys the people throughout the room.

Sebastian was right in his assumption about Jared. My assistant editor wants more between us. Jared asked me to dinner during lunch yesterday for the fourth time. This is after he confirmed my suspicion that BLACK Security had contacted them, pitching their high-profile company for the job opportunity that had gone out to a few smaller security firms to provide security for me.

I've considered going to dinner with Jared. He's smart and definitely driven to succeed like his father, but I certainly wouldn't do it if he could ever potentially become my official editor. That's currently his father's role and I know he wants it. Jared just assists right now.

Technically, that means I can say "yes" to dinner, but I've held off on answering him, claiming a need to get through the release of Blindside. My gaze strays to Sebastian, and I can't help but compare the two men. Jared is a little over six feet. He's well-built and looks fantastic in his tux tonight. Sebastian is the definition of fit, bulked in all the right places, yet he looks perfect in a suit. Instead of a tux, he'd opted for a custom black suit and a striking blue tie that matches his eyes.

As Jared speaks to the crowd that has started to gather around about how they came to buy my book, his voice an interesting blend of confidence and storytelling, I have to smile. Jared's all about grandstanding, whereas his father is currently walking through the crowd, shaking hands with as many people as possible.

William is wearing a traditional tux, his longer hair newly trimmed and set with gel to give him a polished look. I mentally shake my head at the differences between their styles, but there's no doubt they make a powerful team. Hence the reason their publishing house is number one. Jared is the type who commits to everything he does. I've seen it in his work ethic, his desire to be seen as his father's equal despite the family ties. One of the secretaries let it slip that his last relationship lasted five years and everyone assumed he'd marry her, but then she got a job across the country. Jared's attractive, attentive, and admirable. He represents stability.

My gaze strays to my bodyguard and despite my efforts to remain detached, my heart jerks to attention. Sebastian represents something else entirely. He exudes an alluring, indescribable intensity. We have an edgy connection that I can't deny, but he definitely represents heartbreak, and potential all-out devastation if I let myself get sucked in even deeper this time. Maybe the three women who've approached him the last forty minutes have picked up on his I'm-fucking-good-in-bed vibe, but did they not also notice the way he can so easily detach himself from everyone in the room? Or maybe they don't care.

I don't know if it's Sebastian's domineering bearing or the way he carries his six-four height, but I've noticed people glancing his way and whispering. They wonder who the striking man is. Their gazes are drawn to him, the women's raking over him with devouring eyes, and the men's with covetous scowls. He commands attention even when he's trying to blend into the background. I barely resist rolling my eyes when yet another woman approaches him. It would be almost comical to watch if it didn't make me grind my teeth. This time I look away.

My gaze settles on Cass who's standing very close to Clive across the room. She sees me looking at her and gives me a cheesy grin and a thumbs up while he's signing a woman's book. Once he's done, Cass says something, and when he touches my roomie's lower back as he bends close to hear what she's saying, I smile. No introduction necessary.

"Congratulations, Talia." A familiar voice to my right draws my attention.

Nathan tucks his hands in his pants' pockets. This suit looks far more expensive than the ones I remember. Apparently he's upgraded. "Thank you, Nathan. I appreciate you coming to support me."

He nods. "Though I'll admit to be glad it's almost over. Now that you're finished with the Sly Fox club piece, you should be back to normal working hours. I've missed working together."

"What's this about the Sly Fox club?" Jared turns his attention to Nathan as his assistant draws the gaggle of newspaper and magazine people away. "I'm Jared Mackens. And you are?"

Nathan puts out his hand. "Nathan Brentford. Talia and I work together at the Tribune." Rocking on his heels, Nathan nods. "She didn't tell you about her stint as a stripper..."

When he stops there and leaves the rest hanging, Jared raises an eyebrow and looks at me with a new light in his eyes. "Really? A stripper, Natalia?"

"Yeah, she went by Simone," Nathan says, grinning.

I put my hands up before Nathan can dangle the juicy tidbit any longer. "Enough, Nathan. Tell him the rest."

Chuckling, Nathan continues, pride reflected in his brown eyes. "While she wrote two books for your publishing house, Talia also worked undercover at a strip joint where she helped shut down a human trafficking ring."

"Wow, that's pretty gutsy," Jared says, though his enthusiasm doesn't quite reach his eyes. "I'm glad you were successful, but I'm equally glad I didn't know."

I smirk and translate for Nathan. "Jared's all about protecting Midtown Central's investment. Getting caught might've put a wrench in my tight deadlines."

Nathan frowns at my joke, then cuts his gaze to Jared. "I'm just glad it's over."

Pulling his brows together, Jared clasps my hand. "I meant that I would've been worried for your safety."

My phone buzzes in my clutch purse, saving me from responding. I look up to see Cass standing by the doorway. When my gaze locks with hers, she mouths, "Bathroom."

I nod and quickly excuse myself from the guys, then weave my way through the crowd and dodge past a waiter carrying a platter of mini éclairs, then almost run into a blonde waitress holding a tray filled with glasses of complimentary wine.

"Excuse me," I mumble to the wide-eyed girl in the process of righting her tray.

I exhale a sigh of relief once I exit through the doors into the quiet hall.

Cass is applying a new coat of lipstick when I walk into

the bathroom. "You looked like you needed rescuing," she addresses my reflection in the long vanity mirror, before smacking her lips together.

I sigh and lean against the counter, thankful for the reprieve. The last thing I want to talk about is how awkward it felt standing between my ex-boyfriend, who still thinks we'll get back together, and the other guy who hopes I'll finally say "yes" to his dinner requests. "The air felt thick around me, that's for sure. How are things going with Clive?" I tease.

"Very well!" Cass finger combs her hair, teasing it at the scalp to give it some lift. "That's one of the reasons I called you in here. I'm going to the bar for drinks with him after the event, so it'll be late when I get back to the room."

"Don't forget you have an eight am flight tomorrow."

"I won't forget. Why do you think I brought my cameras with me? It'll save me time in the morning." Pausing, she faces me. "Then again, set your alarm for five-thirty just to make sure I get up."

"Five-thirty? You don't need to get up *that* early."

"Oh, yes, I do. That way I'll have time to grill you about why you didn't tell me who your bodyguard was."

When I open my mouth to argue, she holds up her hand. "As much as I want to give you hell about it, I can't right now. Clive is waiting for me. He wants to introduce me to some of the other authors."

I grin, folding my arms. "Looks like you found a perfect source to help feed your fangirl needs."

"Don't you know it!" Laughing, she steps close, her expression turning serious. "Are you okay with this man having your back? I got the feeling he had really hurt you or something."

I shake my head. "It's more the 'or something' part. He's a good man, bluntly honest to a fault and protective of people he's close to. I guess the simplest way to put it is that we want different things in a relationship."

Cass touches the pearl on my chest, then meets my gaze. "Sometimes the heart doesn't know how to say what it really wants, Talia. That's when actions really do speak louder than words."

I give a half-smile and hook my finger with hers, lifting it off my chest. "How'd you get so philosophical?"

She squeezes my finger and snickers. "What else am I going to do on all those long plane flights but take quizzes in magazines others have left behind. I can psychoanalyze the shit out of just about anyone now." When I laugh, she continues. "You've got two handsome men out there, one vying for your attention and the other who seems to hold it. There's nothing that says you have to decide right away. Right now the odds are in your favor, and personally, I like having options."

"Spoken from a girl who has one guy sneaking out her window while the other one is knocking at the door."

"To be fair, that only happened once," she says on a pout. Cass hugs me, then wags her finger as she starts to walk away. "Now remember to set your alarm."

I roll my eyes. "I'll make sure you get up in time. Have fun with Clive."

After I use the facilities, I'm drying my hands on a paper towel when I hear my phone go off with another text.

Curious why Cass would be texting me already, I pull

up the message as I walk out of the bathroom.

PainInMyAss: Never leave the room again without telling me.

I stop walking when I see Sebastian leaning against the wall outside the bathroom, his arms crossed, a deep scowl on his face.

"Sorry, I'm not used to having to report my whereabouts," I say, dropping my phone into my purse before snapping it shut. "I just had to use the ladies' room."

Sebastian pushes off the wall and steps into my personal space, scowling. "Why the hell didn't you tell me about the break-in at your apartment?"

I take a step back and frown. "The police have already taken care of it. It's done."

"Done?" An incredulous look crosses his face. "That break-in just made the threat on you personal. How can you not see that?"

I stiffen my spine. "It's probably not even related to the letters Midtown Central received—"

"That's for me to rule out," he cuts me off. "What was the officer's name you spoke to?"

I blink at him. "How do you even know about the break-in?"

"Cass just told me. It's good you're staying at the hotel this week. I would've insisted on it anyway. His name, *Natalia*."

Natalia? It ticks me off that he's now calling me by my formal name and putting emphasis on it. Is he mocking

Jared? "That's *Miss Lone* to you, Mr. Black" I reply, then walk back toward the ballroom.

"His *name*," Sebastian demands in a low tone a couple steps behind me.

"Officer James Hogan," I say over my shoulder and keep on walking.

When I get back, I mingle on my own for a good half hour, then Jared walks me around, introducing me to so many authors and editors from Midtown Central that I lose track of their names. Then we move on to the highlight of my evening; a receiving line of sorts, where I get to meet the reviewers who have already read Blindside and want me to sign their copies.

As each person approaches, Jared introduces them, telling me which industry magazine, newspaper or bookstore they work for. While signing each book, I take the time to chat with the person, thanking him or her for their review. Once I sign the last reviewer's book and she wanders off to talk with another author, Jared looks at me.

"Would you like a drink now? I sure could use one."

I stare into his green eyes. He has seemed a bit off. I can't really put my finger on when his demeanor shifted, but I sense it. "Is everything okay?" When his mouth twitches in a subtle tightening, I frown. "What's wrong?"

He slides his hands into his pants' pockets and rolls his head from one shoulder to the other. He appears to be stretching his neck, but I know what he's doing. He doesn't want to voice what's bothering him.

"Jared, if we're going to work together, you need to say what's on your mind."

He glances my way, clearly needing to get the gorilla

off his chest.

"What is it?" I keep my voice calm even though I want to shake the answer out of him.

He releases a slow breath. "The whole stripper thing was interesting in an edgy, dangerous sort of way, but to find out you used to deal drugs when you were younger does make me wonder if you did them too. Did you, Natalia?"

The blood drains from my face, then heat instantly shoots up my cheeks, tingling all the way to my scalp. It takes major effort to keep my expression perfectly composed. "Are you asking me as the man who asked me on a date just yesterday, or as the assistant editor of Midtown Central?"

His eyes widen slightly. Apparently my question throws him. "I'm not judging you. There's just so much I don't know about you…and I'd like to."

"Really? Because it sounds like you were completely judging me."

"That's not it, Natalia, I—"

"Actually—" I hold my hand up to stop him. "I will take that drink now. A glass of Chablis."

Jared opens his mouth, then closes it. "I'll be right back."

The second he walks away, my hands shake while I quickly send a text message to Sebastian.

Me: Hallway. Now.

Across the room, I see him pull his cell out of his pants'

pocket.

> *PainInMyAss: Is that code for another bathroom break?*

> *Me: You're fired.*

As soon as I hit send, he jerks his dark head up and narrows his gaze.

Sebastian meets me in the hall, but doesn't stop. Instead, he grips my elbow and escorts me across the hall into another ballroom.

Once the door closes behind us, shrouding us in the dim glow of the low lights above, I jerk my arm from his grasp and step back from his imposing height.

Sebastian moves in front of the door and crosses his arms. "Tell me, Miss Lone, what exactly am I being fired for?"

I hold his suspicious gaze with a determined one. "I don't want someone watching my back that I can't trust."

He lowers his arms, his expression changing from annoyed to full-out pissed. "What the hell are you talking about? How have I betrayed your trust?"

"You are the only one who knows about my past. The only person I've told that I got pulled into the drug dealing business when I was a teen. Jared just asked me about it. I swear the guy stopped short of asking if I'm a recovering *addict.*"

His tone shifts to icy sarcasm. "Are you worried your lover's sensibilities might be offended at the possibility?"

My back goes ramrod straight even as my heart sinks.

"That's none of your business. Why did you tell him? What were you hoping to accomplish?"

Sebastian slices his hand toward the ground, his voice dropping to a menacing growl. "I haven't said anything to that pompous prick. And the fact that you'd think I would betray your confidence is fucking insulting as hell. You should know me better than that."

I did. Or at least I thought I did. The moment Jared asked me about it, I was more upset at the idea Sebastian would divulge something I'd told him in confidence than what Jared thought of me. Just when I start to apologize, Sebastian continues in a less forceful tone, "I might be the only one you told, but I'm obviously not the only one who *knows*."

As my mind tries to wrap around who else could possibly know, my phone buzzes in my purse.

Sebastian crosses his arms once more and leans against the door. "Now that you're no longer out for my blood, why don't you *share* what prompted you to tell your boyfriend about our past tonight? Was your goal to discredit me?"

"Stop calling Jared my boyfriend," I snap while trying to ignore the realization Jared now knows about Sebastian and me. Ugh. Even though I didn't write about any romance between the pilot, Aaron White, and my main character, Sophia, in my book, every reviewer who read Blindside commented on their great chemistry tonight. No wonder Jared acted so out-of-sorts. "I'm not the one who told Jared you're the pilot in Blindside. Obviously someone else did."

His brow furrows. "No one else knows but us."

We stare at each other in thought for a couple seconds,

and just as my phone buzzes again, realization hits.

"Nathan!" We both spit his name like a curse.

While I set my jaw at my ex-boyfriend's attempt to put a wedge in my working relationship with Jared—Nathan must've seen Sebastian follow me out of the ballroom earlier—Sebastian's gaze slices into me with determined precision.

"For the record, you can't fire me. My contract is with Midtown Central Publishing, not you. I will fulfill it, even with your boyfriend's bullshit addendum."

I ignore the boyfriend comment this time, knowing he's saying it to rile me. "What addendum?"

Sebastian pulls out his phone and turns it for me to read a new document with today's date and his company signature at the bottom: **BLACK Security**.

> *Addendum A: In the best interest of the client's safety and well-being, the contracted bodyguard is prohibited from any form of fraternization or BLACK Security's services will be immediately terminated.*

I meet Sebastian's gaze, completely conflicted in my amusement and annoyance. "I can't freaking believe he did that. He totally cock—"

"Don't say it—" Sebastian cuts me off, his features darkening.

"—blocked you," I finish with a snicker.

"You're enjoying this too fucking much," he grates out, clearly irritated.

"I doubt you've remained celibate these past six months. Maybe some non-fraternization time will help sharpen your 'personal security' skills."

His gaze slits. "My skills are always on point, Miss Lone. Rest assured."

My phone buzzes yet again, and this time I retrieve it from my purse. Great. Three texts in a row from Jared.

Jared: Where are you?

Jared: I'm getting worried.

Jared: I'm going to fire that overgrown bodyguard.

Glancing up at Sebastian, I say, "I don't appreciate Jared meddling, but Midtown Central *is* footing the bill. Plus, isn't a fraternization policy a standard clause in most personal security contracts?"

"Only when guarding government officials."

As soon as he finishes speaking, Sebastian's gaze holds mine for several seconds, then slowly lowers to my chest. As the tension grows thick between us, I work to keep my breathing even. I know he's looking at the necklace, thinking about our time together.

When his gaze snags mine, hot lust smolders in the blue depths. I can read it in his eyes; he's mentally tracing his tongue along the necklace, kissing his way to the pearl and my cleavage beyond. I can't let him draw me in again. I want more than he's ever going to give. Flushing with heat from my own imaginative thoughts, I adopt a lighthearted tone to diffuse the palpable chemistry sparking between us. "Thank you for the gift. You give good rainbow, Mr Black."

"I give the fucking *best* rainbow, Miss Lone," he says in a low, taut tone.

My comment had been my way of acknowledging the deeper meaning behind the pearl, but the rough rumble in his voice and aroused intensity in his stare tells me he meant something else entirely.

He takes a step closer and my stomach turns upside down. I don't move, but my fingers cinch around the phone so tight I can feel my pulse throbbing along my fingertips against the cool metal.

Another step and the tips of his shoes almost touch mine. Just as I look up at him, the phone buzzes again, instantly jarring me back to reality.

I exhale a shaky breath and turn the text screen toward Sebastian, holding it between us like a protective shield. "We need to get back so he doesn't fire your overgrown ass."

CHAPTER THREE

Talia

After I get back to the ballroom, Jared never says a word about Sebastian. As a matter of fact, once I murmur that I was in the restroom, sheer relief scrolls across his face. Like he's genuinely worried for me. Clasping my hand, he leads me over to meet his dark-haired assistant who had helped him out with scheduling earlier.

"Natalia, I'd like you to meet Kayla. We've assigned her as your handler. She will attend all of the functions with you this week. Her job is to assist you in any way she can, from getting you coffee, water, food, to making sure that your signing table is set up the way it should be. She'll open books to the right page, take the pictures of you with fans and make sure readers abide by the one book per customer parameters we've set. Trust me, your hand will be glad we instituted that rule. That way everything will run smoothly."

As Kayla leans over to shake my hand, it feels like I'm trying to hold onto a limp noodle. But I do get a great view of her boobs on full display in her red dress. Eh, at least the color matches the red bottoms of her designer shoes. We all need to accessorize, right? Hmm, long black wavy hair, a tight dress that leaves nothing to the imagination, mile-high designer heels, and perfectly manicured nails. *And this girl is willing to gofer for me for the next few days? Maybe if I looked like Sebastian.* "It's nice to meet you, Kayla."

A wide smile on her face, she dips her head in a slight bow. "It'll be my honor to help you in any way I can, Miss Lone."

When she gazes up at me, her light brown eyes full of sincerity, I suddenly feel like a royal bitch making snap judgments about her. Questionable business attire and wimpy handshake aside, once she starts talking about tomorrow's event and how the schedule will work, I kind of warm up to her.

The rest of the evening, Jared is so attentive he never leaves my side. His constant companionship annoys Nathan so much—I can tell my ex wants to get me alone—that I end up laughing and grinning at anything my assistant editor says just to irritate Nathan more. What is the point in bringing up what he did? I'm sure in his mind he was protecting me somehow by telling Jared about Sebastian and me. Truthfully, acting cheerful and upbeat isn't that easy, because I still don't have any idea who told Jared about my drug dealing past. That's one of many things from my past Nathan doesn't know. Since Jared doesn't bring it up again, I'm not going to remind him that I never answered his question.

By the time midnight rolls around, I can't wait to head up to my room for some peace and quiet. I practically run for the elevator.

"I'll secure your room," Sebastian says as the elevator doors slide open on my floor.

"That won't be necessary, my room's fifteen feet away. You can go on to your room now." I'm mentally and physically exhausted as I step off the elevator. Of course Sebastian ignores me. He's so close, he might as well be my shadow. To his credit, he'd been the perfect bodyguard throughout the event, staying out of sight but always in the background.

Walking down the silent hall after hours of loud conversation is music to my ears. If it weren't so late, I'd have a glass of wine, but as it is, I'm going to wash my face and collapse into bed. I reach my door and pull my keycard from my purse, sliding it into the lock. If tonight is a precursor of how the tour will go, I will definitely need some vacation time once it's over. Making sure I say the right thing and smile at the right time around industry types is exhausting. And I have at least two more promo-based events to go. Book signings are pure pleasure. For readers, it's all about the story. No politics, no agendas, just book talk. I love that.

I frown when I try for the second time and the red light on the door flashes at me again.

Sebastian quietly reaches over my shoulder and turns the keycard around in my hand. Refusing to inhale his amazing masculine scent, I silently roll my eyes at myself and start to slide the key into the lock for the third time when the door pulls open.

"Did you de-magnetize your key—" Cass starts to say, toothbrush in hand. Standing there in an old football jersey hitting her mid-thigh, her hair pulled up in a messy bun that she only wears when she's getting ready to take a shower before bed, she shifts her attention from me to Sebastian. "Good evening, Mr. Black. Did my roomie give you a hard time tonight?"

"No more than usual," he murmurs.

I glance at him over my shoulder. "As you can see, my room has been Cass-secured. I'll see you tomorrow after lunch."

His gaze lasers into me. "I will secure your room for the night." Before I can say another word, he steps in front of me and says to Cass, "Excuse me."

"By all means," she says in a perky tone, stepping into the bathroom doorway to let him pass.

When I frown at her, she steps farther into the bathroom and calls out, "Don't mind me. I'm just going to take a shower."

"You don't have to rush—" She flashes me a secret smile and shuts the door in my face. Two seconds later the shower turns on.

Sighing, I follow Sebastian into our room to see him sliding a key into a deadbolt lock at the top of the door that apparently leads to an adjoining room. "What are you doing?"

He opens the door to check if it's unlocked, then shuts it before turning his bright blue gaze my way. "You will leave this unlocked."

"I don't think so," I say, holding my hand out for the

key.

Sebastian slips the key in his pocket and steps closer, his expression inflexible. "I won't come in unless you're in danger or I'm invited. But the damned door stays unlocked between us, Natalia."

"Stop calling me that," I snap.

His face hardens. "You prefer Miss Lone even when we're alone?" When I look away, his tone loses its bite. "Your protection takes precedence over us."

I meet his gaze, my words softening. "Thank you for protecting me. I know no one is better qualified, but there is no *us*."

"And why is that exactly?" He touches my chin to keep me from turning away. "Why didn't you respond to my note when I sent you the pearl necklace six months ago?"

My back stiffens. "I had two deadlines and a project to complete for work."

"*Bullshit.*" He traces his finger along my bottom lip. "You were running."

I pull my chin from his grasp, finally letting my anger, hurt, and disappointment rise to the surface. "What could I have possibly been running from? You made it perfectly clear our time at the resort was just that, a weekend. That you wouldn't always be there." I turn my back to him so he can't see the hurt I feel reflected in my expression. "I just made things easier. Drawn-out goodbyes aren't my thing."

He steps so close I feel the heat of his body from my shoulders to my butt. Even though he's close enough to touch me, he doesn't. "I'm here." His tone softens to a tender caress. "When you need me most. I'm here, Little

Red."

Hearing his nickname for me spoken in that husky voice he only uses in the bedroom feels like a knife slicing across my skin; its sharpness releasing bittersweet pain. *But you're not here in the way I need you. Not in* that *way, Sebastian.* I close my eyes and fight the mist gathering. "Don't call me that," I say sharply.

"Why? Because it turns you on? Good. I want you turned on. I fucking want you, period."

As much as his words ignite flames of hope in my chest, I tense and snuff them out, refusing to be drawn in yet again. "Well, you're not fucking getting me."

Sebastian grasps my hips and pulls me fully against him as he bends to purr in my ear, "You and I are tied at the hip and have been since we were kids. There's a reason we can't seem to stay away from each other."

"Oh yeah?" I'm furious at his familiarity with my body, that he knows exactly what to do to stir the blood in my veins to a roiling boil. Coupled with the aroused frustration in his voice that echoes my own, it takes all my concentration not to let myself meld into his hard frame. It would be as easy as taking a breath. "And why is that?"

He slides a hand to my belly and presses me closer so I can feel how much he wants me. "I haven't a fucking clue, sweetheart, but this time I'm not letting you go until we're both worn the hell out."

Yanking from his hold, I whirl to face him. "I really appreciate you being here to protect me, Sebastian, but that's as far as our *relationship* extends. I think I'll pass on your suggestion of 'let's pick up where we left off for old time's sake.' It's leaving me cold."

"The last thing you feel around me is cold, *Natalia*." His sharp expression melts into a cocksure smile. "I'll bet editor boy leaves you as dry as the Sahara. And that I'm the one you're thinking about when you're sexually frustrated and need to get yourself off."

Cass turns the water off at the exact moment my hand connects with his face, making the slap sound even louder in the suddenly quiet room. My palm stings like hell as I hiss in a low voice, "You arrogant bastard!"

Sebastian rubs his jaw, his gaze reflecting surprised admiration. "No woman has ever been brave enough to hit me before."

Common sense says I should feel a twinge of apprehension that he could easily use his deadly SEAL skills against me, but I'm too pissed to care. "You've probably never insulted any of them enough. Get the hell out of my room." I point toward the main door, my back teeth locked together. I cling to my outrage, while shaking on the inside with worry that he'll learn the true depth of my feelings for him.

He turns to open the connecting door and steps through, but before he pulls it closed he meets my gaze, his own flashing with smug satisfaction. "Your reaction was the exact opposite of cold, Little Red."

"Out!" I pick up the first thing I can find, and just as I lob the can of hairspray at his head, he closes the door.

When it clatters loudly against the thick wood, Cass comes running into the room, a towel quickly tugged around her wet body. "What in God's name is going on?"

I shrug and bend down to toss her dented hairspray in the trash. "Sorry. This went flying when I tossed my purse onto the bed."

Cass' eyes slit suspiciously. "Did your purse have bricks in it? Otherwise, nope, I'm not buying it."

"A ghost then," I suggest as I step out of my heels.

She smirks and crosses her arms. "Unless a ghost can take what sounded like a prize worthy slap, I'd say you have some 'splaining to do."

I wince. "So you heard it?"

"Like a shot in the night. But I couldn't hear what was said. So…" she pauses and twirls her hand rapidly. When I shrug and shake my head, she sighs and holds her hands up in defeat. "Really?"

"Why don't you tell me why you're in the room before three?" I say, hoping to distract her. The last thing I want to talk about is my argument with Sebastian. I don't even understand what just happened. Other than he royally pissed me off. "Tell me why Clive got the boot," I say, following Cass back into the bathroom.

Cass tucks the towel around her boobs and picks up a comb. Running it through her wet hair, she meets my gaze in the mirror and shrugs. "I'm all for playing the field—you know I don't judge—but this dude likes to play it at the same time."

"Ah, he was flirting with other women while you were at the bar?"

She snorts and picks up the hairdryer. "Try ordering drinks for other women while he's sitting there with me."

"Ouch," I say, wincing.

She turns on the hairdryer and calls over the loud noise. "It's no biggie. Just means I'll get to bed at a decent hour, you don't have to be my mom in the morning, and

I won't wake up with a hangover. I call that a win for the evening."

I don't miss that she's not meeting my gaze in the mirror anymore as she talks, so I reach out and take the comb from her. "What's really bothering you?"

She turns off the hair dryer and looks at me. "I guess I'm disappointed that the image I'd built up about him was destroyed, you know? I'd kind of rather have gone on thinking he was almost omnipotent, than to learn his goal is to spread his potent parts around to anyone with a vagina under twenty-five."

Snickering at her metaphor, I nod. "I understand. Sebastian—Mr. Black—was like that for me. Bigger than life, and the dream guy I've had in my thoughts since I was a little girl. My knight in shining armor."

"Metaphorically speaking of course," she says winking.

"No, actually. I mean that quite literally. Sebastian and I have crossed paths several times in our lives, and each time he's protected me. The first time is when I was thirteen and running away from a horrible situation, the second was at the masked party—yes, he was the Robin Hood who rescued me from Gavin getting too suspicious about me."

"Are you effin' serious?" Her eyes widen and she sets the hairdryer down. Facing me, she clasps my hand. "I want to ask about the party, but more importantly what happened to make you run away? You have never told me about your past before."

I shake my head. I really don't want to talk about that part of it. "It doesn't matter. My point is that because he'd been there for me in my past, I'd built him up to be the 'one', but I'm just another one of many to him. I don't think he has it in him to commit."

Squeezing my hand tight, she dips her head until her eyes lock with mine. "I might not know jack about my own love life, but I have never seen you like this, Talia. With other guys you've always been go-with-the-flow. Laidback even. But with the sexy Mr. Black, you seem to be in constant control. That man is a walking, talking sex magnet and I couldn't understand how you could remain so detached over the pearl necklace six months ago or the one you're wearing now, especially once I learned he was your fling back in the summer. But now it all makes sense. Is that why you won't let your inner-slut free with him? Because you're afraid he'll break your heart?"

When I nod, she pulls me into a hug. While she squeezes me, she says, "Then you need to figure out how to make him open up, because the chemistry between you guys is unlike anything I've ever seen between two people. It's so sizzling I can *feel* the pheromones in the air, and it makes me so freaking jealous I can't see straight. Poor Jared must hate his guts with the heat of a thousand suns."

I pull back and roll my eyes at her exaggeration. "But it's not healthy, Cass. I want more. Sebastian shares very little of himself with me. As for Jared, he made Sebastian sign a 'no fraternization' addendum to my bodyguard contract tonight once he learned from Nathan that Sebastian and I have a past."

"Nathan!" She spats my ex's name, twisting her lips. "Now that's a man who deserves a true bitch slap. When I saw him having a low, heated conversation with one of the servers at the event tonight, my palm started itching to smack him. He looked irritated as hell. You'd think the girl had stolen his favorite toy the way he appeared to be dressing her down."

"She probably spilled something on his new suit," I say, snickering.

Cass shrugs. "At least someone is annoying *him* for once."

"Nathan has had his slap-worthy moments for sure, but trust me, Sebastian totally asked for it."

She smirks, eyes twinkling. "You'll have to keep me updated on everything while I'm gone."

I purse my lips. "So glad the threat on my life amuses you."

A horrified look crosses her face and she sputters, "You know I'm worried about you. That's why I told Mr. Black—Sebastian—about the break-in—"

I burst out laughing, unable to keep a straight face any longer. "I'm just teasing, Cass. I know you love and worry about me. Speaking of blabbing to Sebastian about the break-in, did you know he insisted on coming *into* the restroom the last time I went."

She gapes. "And you let him?"

"Hell no! I let him check all the stalls, then made him leave. Though I'm pretty sure he blocked anyone from coming in while I was in there. I got some angry glares from the two ladies waiting outside."

Cass lets out a belly laugh. "You are going to have to figure out a balance with him before you two explode. The fact he can't touch you now should make things even more interesting." Putting her hands together, she gives me her best pouty face. "I so hope you find a way to embrace your inner-slut. That man's gorgeousness should not go to waste."

I scowl. "That's a terrible idea. No inner-slut embracing will be happening." *But reminding him he signed the addendum isn't such a bad idea. His code of honor is very strong.*

Picking her hairbrush up, she sighs and points it at me. "Regardless of what you do about Sebastian, make sure you let Jared down easy. William might be your boss, but you know how nepotism works. You still want a working relationship with your publisher." Pausing, she grins evilly. "All this is so popcorn worthy. I hate that I'm having to go out of town."

I give a rueful smile. "So happy to be a source of pure entertainment for you."

She giggles unapologetically. "Right now, your life is better than fiction, girl."

CHAPTER FOUR

Talia

"*Up* and at 'em, Miss Lone." The deep voice is quickly followed by my covers ripping off me.

"What the hell!" I bolt upright, chill bumps spreading across my exposed skin as I glare at Sebastian standing over my bed.

Freshly dressed in an impeccable charcoal business suit and deep purple tie, he has a stoic, all-business expression on his face. "If you'd like time for breakfast, I suggest you get moving. I need to grab some paperwork from the business office."

Noting the time is barely eight, I pull the covers over my white boy shorts and matching tank top. I glance at the door, knowing I'd pushed the lock button on the doorknob before I went to bed. "How did you get in here?"

His face hardens. "I told you not to lock the door."

"A hairspray can thrown at your head should tell you what I think of your *order*," I snap before rolling back onto my stomach and pulling the covers over my head. "I don't have to be up for another two hours. Go run your errand."

The covers are yanked off me again, followed by a resounding smack on my ass. Before I can react beyond gritting out, "I'm going to kill you," he quickly presses his hand to the center of my back as he bends close to my ear.

"Apparently that sounded like a request, so let me rephrase. If you don't get your sweet ass out of this bed and in the shower in the next five seconds, I'll strip you down and put you in there myself."

"Ugh! Why are you being such an ass—?"

He puts his cell phone in front of my face, his voice a harsh command. "Read."

As he removes his hand from my back, I cut my narrowed gaze from his face to the typed words on the screen.

Blindside is nothing but lies. I will make you suffer for everything you've done and then the truth will be revealed

My attention jerks to Sebastian, my heart thudding hard. The other two notes didn't directly threaten me. "When did you get this?"

He straightens and slides his phone into his inside jacket pocket. "This is a scanned copy of the letter that arrived at the Midtown Central offices this morning. Someone from my team has already confirmed it's from a different printer."

My eyes widen. "This is someone else? Not the original person escalating?"

"No this is someone new. The pattern of the words is different." His gaze focuses on mine. "Is there anything you'd like to share? Any reason someone would think you're lying about what happened at Hawthorne with Tommy Slawson?"

I furrow my brow. "It sounds far more personal, doesn't it?"

When he nods solemnly, I shake my head. "I don't have a clue. I told the truth as it happened."

He scowls. "Who would think you're not telling the truth?"

I shrug. "An angry family member who doesn't want me to ruin the Slawson family name?"

"Tommy didn't have any family. His mother is dead, and there aren't any other living relatives."

"Are you sure?"

When he gives me an insulted look, I wrack my brain trying to come up with an alternative. "Don't serial killers sometimes have followers? Maybe it's someone who believes Tommy was innocent of the other murders or somehow justified in his murderous rampage?"

Sebastian's expression shuts down. "We've been checking on all leads, message boards that mention Tommy and any cult-like followers who've made comment about you. So far, nothing on that front. One thing we have going for us is that this letter was printed in red, which should help us narrow it down to the actual printer that was used."

"Why does that matter?"

He raises an eyebrow. "Get your shower and I'll tell you on the way down to the lobby."

As we walk toward the elevator, Sebastian's gaze skims over my black suit jacket, emerald silk shirt, then to my pencil skirt and black pumps. "You could've changed into your signing clothes later."

"What?" I button my jacket closed, then push the down key on the wall. "You don't approve of my look?"

His gaze moves in a predatory glide from my head to my toes, then back to my face, his eyes turning a deeper crystal blue. "My preferences in your attire haven't changed, Miss Lone."

My stomach flip-flops and my face flames as I remember his last words as to what he preferred seeing me wear: Him. *Wrapped around me. On me. In me.*

God, help me. Cass would love this! I clear my throat to shove her pleased giggling out of my head. "You were going to tell me about the letter and how a color copy matters."

The elevator arrives and he holds the door for me to enter, then follows me inside. As we slowly descend, Sebastian says, "Every color printer since 2002 now puts a unique set of invisible dots on any color copies made. It's invisible to the eye, but can be seen under blue light. Each set of dots identifies a specific printer, which will then allow us to trace who purchased it."

"Why are printer companies putting spy dots in their color copiers?"

He shrugs. "Those 'spy dots' are one way to help our government combat against counterfeiters."

I nod my understanding, then mumble, "How Big Brother-ish."

"Be glad or we'd have nowhere to start looking for the culprit."

I sigh. "Point taken. So after you pick up what you need to in the business office, I'd like to go for a bagel. I saw a bagel/coffee stand a block away." *And along the way, I'll get to see the Christmas decorations. I bet they're amazing in this area.*

"Not a good idea. You'll eat here in the restaurant."

Straightening my spine, I lift my chin. "Oh, did that sound like a request? Let me rephrase. I'm going to get a bagel once you're done picking up your paperwork. You can either come with or not."

Sebastian scowls. "Your stubbornness puts you at risk."

"And here I thought you'd said my stubbornness is what saved my life the last time it was threatened."

He turns to face me, a deep frown bracketing his mouth. "To be clear, I saved your life back then. Same as I'm doing now. And why is it that you're, yet again, in someone's crosshairs?" He quickly scans my face, his assessment detached, methodically calculating. "Is that gorgeous face hiding layers I've yet to uncover?"

My stomach bottoms out; he hasn't mentioned my past and I'd foolishly hoped he'd leave it alone. I'm not the person I was back then. My gut response is to instantly defend myself, but knowing Sebastian, he'll drill in on anything I say. The man doesn't miss a thing. Redirecting him is best. "What's so important about this paperwork you need?"

He holds my gaze for a split second longer, then

answers, "It's a ballistics report from my mom's case."

My eyebrows elevate. "That wasn't already in the police file you had on your mom?"

Sebastian's jaw tenses. "I told you they thought she was involved in drugs. Why bother looking for her killer? I'm sure they shoved the paperwork aside and moved on to the next case. It took me five months to convince one of the officers to have the ballistics run on the bullets that killed her. No one wants to admit to making a mistake, especially on a case almost twelve years old. The officer who asked for the report is retiring in a month, so he had nothing to lose by helping me. The guy's old-school and insisted on faxing me the results."

"I'm sorry, Sebastian. I hope the report gives you more to go on."

He nods briskly. "It's a step forward on a case that went nowhere."

The lobby is quiet as we walk through it toward the business office. A few businessmen are checking out at the main desk, and a couple of middle-aged ladies are checking in with two massive suitcases. Cars are starting to line up out front, where the valets are blowing on their hands, their breath pluming in the brisk December air.

"Wait here," Sebastian says, gesturing to an arrangement of cushioned chairs next to the main desk.

Once his broad shoulders disappear behind the business office door, I don't bother to sit down. He didn't sound like he'd be long.

While I watch the two ladies bickering with the front desk about their room not being ready, even though they're checking in before eleven, a tall man dressed in a nice suit steps up beside me and says in a cultured accent, "Do you have any meetings you must attend soon, Miss Lone?"

"Not for a couple hours," I say, taking in the striking combination of his dark skin and light brown eyes, set off by amazing bone structure. Even his close-shaved hair adds to his arresting features. His accent sounds a bit different, not exactly British, more like New Zealand maybe? When I realize he's not wearing the hotel's discrete gold bar on his lapel, I stop trying to place his accent. "Excuse me, who are you?"

"I work for Adam Blake. He'd like a word with you in private. If you'll come with me please."

The only thing multibillionaire Adam Blake and I have in common is his estranged, illegitimate son, Sebastian. I glance back at the door where I expect Sebastian to walk through any moment. "Please tell Mr. Blake I'll be happy to make an appointment with him next week—"

"I'm afraid he insists on today, Miss Lone. It's a matter of utmost importance to him."

How did he even know to find me here? Probably because of Sebastian. *Does Mr. Blake think I have something to do with Sebastian deciding to throw away his inheritance by taking the Blake family name?* There's obviously no stuffing *that* cat back in the bag. But what else could Adam Blake possibly want with me?

Once I nod, I expect the tall guy to lead me to a quiet boardroom somewhere in the hotel. Instead, he quickly escorts me outside and into a sleek black car with dark tinted windows.

When he slides in beside me and calls to the driver, "Blake Tower," I glance his way as we pull away from the curb.

"I can't go directly there. I have a stop to make along the way."

"That wasn't Mr. Blake's directive."

I ignore his comment. "If Mr. Blake wants me to come when I'm called, like an obedient dog, then he's going to have to accommodate my schedule. Give your driver this address, please."

"That's on the Lower East Side," he says, concern creasing his brow.

"Yes, it is. I'll need you to walk me inside the building too. Hope you're packing."

When his eyes widen, I can't help but grin. "I'm just teasing. You shouldn't need a weapon, but I would like your very intimidating height standing behind me while I ask the building manager a few questions if you don't mind."

He lets out a deep laugh. "That I can handle, Miss Lone. I'm Dennet, but you may call me Den."

"I'm Talia," I say, smiling. "Where are you from, Den? At first I thought England, but I can't quite place your accent."

A quick smile spreads across his face. "You're partially right. I was born and raised in London. My father is from Kenya and my mother is Irish."

Ah, that's where your light eyes came from. I start to ask what brought him from London to the U.S., but my phone buzzes with a text from Sebastian.

PainInMyAss: One simple request and you can't

even follow that.

Me: How do you know that I haven't been kidnapped?

PainInMyAss: Because you're texting. Tell me where you are.

Me: I need to run this errand on my own.

PainInMyAss: Where are you? I'M NOT FUCKING AROUND!

Me: I have backup. Don't worry.

PainInMyAss: A Taser in your purse isn't backup.

How does he know about the Taser? I press my lips together, then realize he must've gone through my whole purse that night he bugged my phone at the Hawthorne resort. At least he'd kept his word about not bugging it this time or he wouldn't be asking where I am. I'd left the Taser at home. It's certainly wasn't going to fit in my evening clutch purse. Shaking my head, I type my response.

Me: THIS backup is the living, breathing kind. And I won't be anywhere near a bookstore, books, or tour-related stuff.

PainInMyAss: I don't trust anyone else to watch over you. WHERE!

"Who is that?"

Den can't see my screen, but he knows I'm responding to someone. "My bodyguard flipping out."

He frowns, his gaze snapping to mine. "Why do you need a bodyguard?"

I eye him in surprise. Then it hits me that Adam Blake wouldn't know about my author drama. Though he apparently knows I *am* an author, since Den had called me by my penname earlier. Now I'm even more intrigued by this out-of-the-blue summons.

Den points to my phone and says in a gruff tone, "Send him your safe word."

My eyes widen. There's no way he can possibly know about Sebastian and my sex life—correction, *past* sex life. "Safe word?" I squeak.

He nods. "Your bodyguard must've discussed that if you were ever separated, you should include a word if you rang him, or some other signal in a text to confirm that you aren't being coerced."

Relief quickly washes through me. "Oh, *that* word," I say, like Sebastian and I had totally set up the protocol he's talking about. Then again…hadn't we?

Me: I'll be back in two hours tops. Promise. #Rainbow.

A few seconds later, Sebastian responds.

PainInMyAss: Can't-Sit-For-A-Week,   fire engine red. Promise.

If he's firing off innuendo punishment texts, he has stopped freaking out and is just royally pissed. That I can deal with. I don't want to think what a rampaging Sebastian would be like. His normal domineering demeanor is intense enough.

As we enter the Lower East End, Den glances at my purse. "You turned it off, right?"

"My phone?"

He nods. "If you don't want your guard to follow you, you need to turn it completely off. If he's worth what you're paying for his services, he's already pinging its location."

Damn it. I'm sure Sebastian is hot on my trail. "Oh, I didn't even think about it." I hesitate before I turn it off. *What if I'm being played, and this guy's taking me straight to my stalker?* Then again, no one knows my connection to the Blake family except me. There's nothing on-line, no paper trail to follow. There's *no way* anyone other than a Blake could know that their name alone would be enough to convince me to agree to this meeting. Feeling assured, I switch my phone off.

Den gives the sorry, dilapidated apartment building we've pulled up to a disapproving look, his accent becoming more pronounced. "Is this the proper address?"

I nod and start to open the door on my side, when he says, "Exit this way and I'll escort you in. You weren't exaggerating about needing backup."

Smirking at him, I follow his line of sight to the trio of rough-looking teens who've stopped talking while sitting on the hood of a car down the street to stare at us getting out of the sleek car.

"Keep your attention sharp, the doors locked, and the engine running," Den says curtly to the driver before he grips my elbow in a protective manner. "Lead the way, Miss Lone."

I stare at the building as I approach. It doesn't look any different than the one I lived in with my aunt, Amelia, and Walt. Same dreary, pollution-coated brick. Same cracked cement stairs leading to a broken buzzer at the main entrance door. The only difference was that our building had been dingy brown brick instead of red. And ironically resided just seven or so blocks from this one.

I knock on the building manager's door. His name is Mr. Snitch, according to the scratched-through sign next to the main door. Den never lets his golden eyes rest, his muscular neck craning upward at the sudden sounds of a couple fighting a floor above us.

Just as I start to knock again, the door rips open. A balding, middle-aged man, sporting a pink bathrobe and a raised metal baseball bat, growls from the doorway, "What!"

Den instantly steps in front of me, scowling. He doesn't have to say a word; his menacing expression is enough to make the man stumble back a little. Screwing up his face, the building manager holds the bat higher. "Back off Zulu Warrior or I'll take this to you."

"Excuse me." I barely resist rolling my eyes at the man's ignorance as I nudge Den to the side. "I just want to ask you a couple of questions about some past tenants, Mr. Snitch. How long have you worked here?"

"That's Fritch. Assholes keep marking up my sign," he spits angrily, then gives me a wary look. "I've been here fifteen years. Nobody's gonna do a better job collecting rent from these shit-for-tenants, so tell Mr. Harmon I said to fuck off. No one's getting my job."

"Mr. Fritch. I'm not here on Mr. Harmon's behalf. I'm here for my own purpose."

He tilts his head. "And what might that be? You sure as hell—" The fighting couple above us have gotten so loud, the manager pauses to hit the bat three times on the ceiling. "Pipe down or I'm calling the cops!" Turning back to me, he continues as if he'd never stopped talking, "—don't look like you belong here." His gaze skims from my silk blouse down to my heels. "Those fancy clothes probably cost more than my rent."

I take a breath and ignore his resentful comment. "I'd just like to know if you remember a couple of tenants, a woman named Brenna Slawson and her son Tommy?"

"Nope, don't remember." He starts to close the door, but Den puts his leather shoe out to block it at the same time he rips the bat from the man's hand.

"Answer the lady's question truthfully, or I'll happily demonstrate what an S.I.S.-trained *Brit* can do with this bat."

Fritch glares at Den, then shifts his squirrely gaze to me. "Yeah, I remember the scrawny kid and his bitch of a mother. Why?"

My stomach tenses. At least I'm getting somewhere. "Do you know if they had any relatives?"

"What do I look like, a family reunion rep? How the hell should I know?" His gaze narrows suspiciously. "Are you some kind of reporter? I heard the kid turned out to be a freaking serial killer. That true?"

I shrug. "I'm not here about that. I'm just doing some research for a project I'm working on. So no one else lived with them?"

"Bet he's the one who killed his mom all those years ago. Left a fucking bloody mess, whoever did it," he murmurs, then waves his hand, answering my question dismissively. "Just her freeloader boyfriend."

I latch onto the possible lead. "Can you tell me the boyfriend's name?"

"Asshole," he deadpans, then snorts as he digs spindly fingers into his armpit, his nails leaving trails against the robe's velour nap. "The lease was in her name, so I didn't give a damn who else stayed there as long as she paid. Though, now that I think of it, he stopped coming around after a while."

I suppress a sigh of frustration. "Can you at least tell me what he looked like?"

Fritch holds his hand a couple inches above my heeled height of five-nine. "He was about here. Average height for a guy. Brown-ish hair, regular build. Constant scowl. That pretty much covers it."

"No tattoos or anything else that stands out?"

He shakes his head. "Nope. Like I said. Just your average, clompy Joe-Asshole. I couldn't pick him out of a crowd if I tried."

"Clompy?"

"Yeah, I sure as hell don't miss hearing his footfalls dragging up the stairs at one in the morning. Bastard always woke me up."

Picking out a heavy walker in a crowd won't be easy either. I sigh inwardly. "Thanks for your help."

The second Den removes his foot from the doorway, Fritch grunts and slams the door in our faces.

Once we drive away from Tommy's apartment, I give Den another address. "Please have the driver take us here. It's on the way and should only take a few minutes."

Den shakes his head. "We've delayed enough. We're going straight to Blake Towers."

"Have you ever had something you needed to do?" I say to Den. He unlocks his gaze from the driver's in the rearview mirror to look at me. "Something you've avoided because it was too painful?"

When sadness briefly scrolls across his features, I say softly just for his ears, "This is my 'thing', Den."

He slowly nods, then tells the driver to head to the address I gave him.

Once we arrive at the address, Den steps out of the car to allow me to exit. I put my hand on his chest when he starts to follow. "Stay here. I'm not going inside."

He glances around the sketchy neighborhood and his gaze zeros in on a couple of teens tagging a car parked on top of the curb further down the street. "Not a good idea, Miss Lone."

Light drizzle pings my face, the chill reaching all the way to my bones. Or maybe it's just being here that makes me feel cold and numb. I told myself I would never return after the explosion put a huge hole in our apartment, yet here I am, quaking on the inside. I hold myself perfectly still as I look at Den's towering height. I'm pretty sure he has a couple inches on Sebastian. Clenching my teeth to keep them from chattering, I finally speak as I point to the alley beside the drab building. "I'll be fine. I'm just going there."

He scowls, a displeased look forming on his sharply defined features. "Alleys are unacceptable."

I shrug and wrap my arms around myself so I won't visibly shiver. "Check it out if you must."

He grunts, then shrugs out of his jacket. Before I can say anything, he drops the suit coat over my shoulders. "Put this on then to keep you warm."

His suit jacket is so big it hits midway down my thighs and the sleeves cover my fingers. Even though his shoulder harness and gun are now completely exposed, I can't help but smile a little as I follow behind him while he walks ahead of me to check the alley. A gentleman with a gun. Obviously Mr. Blake hires more than muscle.

After he's certain the space is empty, Den moves to the top of the alley and refuses by a terse jerk of his head to leave me alone all together. My heart races as I walk over a shredded bike wheel, a baby doll head with its hair lopped off, and a garbage can's worth of trash strewn about, my gaze scanning for the one place on the brick wall I'm looking for. It takes me a few minutes, since someone had moved the Dumpster from its old place against the opposite wall, but just past the Dumpster I find it.

A place on the wall where the brick looks slightly off.

The Dumpster blocks me from Den's view as I hold my breath and pull the loose brick out. Reaching inside the hole, my fingers scrape for something I'd hidden in the spot over eleven years ago. I quickly pull it out, bittersweet relief flooding through me.

Hunching my shoulders to protect the crisp paper from the light rain, I open the paper and remember the last time

I spoke to my little sister, Amelia.

"*Draw with me, Talia,*" she demands, dropping her little hands on her hips like she's seen me do a million times.

I sigh and set my math book on the table. "I can't Amelia. I have to study. I have a test coming up."

"*Pleeeeeze,*" she begs. And just for effect she tilts her blond head to the side and pouts.

I can't help but laugh at her curls flopping to one side of her head with her exaggerated movements. She really is very cherubic and adorable when she wants to be.

"Okay, fine. But this time. I get to pick what we draw."

"Uh." *Amelia folds her arms, totally not okay with that suggestion.*

I grin. "Go get your markers and a piece of paper. You'll like this one."

Squealing, she retrieves the requested items, then quickly climbs into my lap at the kitchen table. "Draw something magical, like a unicorn."

When I start to write out her name across the paper in black ink, she quickly interrupts. "That's not magical. That's just my name."

Snickering, I nod. She can't read, but knows the alphabet and now recognizes her name. "I know, but you have to watch for the magic."

She bobs her head, wiggling on my thighs.

Then I write my name under hers. "This is how my name is spelled. Talia. Do you see the magic yet?"

Amelia looks up at me, her eyes bright. She shakes her head, but she's totally trusting I'm going to deliver on my promise.

I put down the black marker and pick up the red one, then draw a heart around the last three letters in our names. "Do you *see it now?"*

Her eyes light up like it's Christmas and she claps her hands. "Our names have the same letters!"

"Yep," I chuckle and then write, "The 2 Lias!" across the top of the page.

Giggling in delight, Amelia picks up the hot pink magic marker and thrusts her tongue past her lips as she attempts to trace her heart around the outside of the heart I've drawn. Hers is jagged and shaky and looks more like an oval than a heart, but she's proud by the time she's done, announcing excitedly, "Two Lias, two hearts."

I smile, thinking about the two floating hearts on my necklace. One for me and one for her when she gets older. "Yep, two Lias, two hearts. How'd you get so smart?"

Giving my neck a big squeeze, she says, "You," then jumps down and runs off toward her room, her new artwork floating behind her like a kite.

My heart clenching, I tuck the paper into my purse, then continue toward the end of the alley. With each step I take, the years strip the confidence I'd gained, slowly cracking and peeling it away, like a chameleon's skin sloughing off.

I finally reach the back corner of the building and stare up at the fire escape.

Throughout my young years I saw that metal platform as a way out of my world. All I had to do was climb down its ladder to freedom. "I was so naïve," I murmur.

Thoughts of the night I fled, the night Amelia died, rush back. While we were together in Martha's Vineyard, I told Sebastian what Hayes did to me, but I didn't tell him everything...

Walt had been locked in the adjoining apartment with Hayes and Jimmy for hours, which was fine by me. I needed quiet time to study for my math test, so after I drew the "2 Lias" picture for Amelia, I settled her on the couch with her favorite doll in front of the TV and turned on the one program I knew would keep her enthralled until it ended.

Fifteen minutes into my study time, Walt stumbles into the small kitchen and sits down in one of the extra chairs we have pushed against the sidewall a few feet away from the table. We only pull it up to the table when we're all eating at once.

"Make me some eggs and toast, Talia," he slurs, his eyes half-mast.

I'm ticked. It's the first time I've seen him coming down from a high right in front of me. In the past he at least tried to hide it. I heard him being hyperactive earlier, laughing and talking extra loud next door. I knew that he had started using the Ecstasy he helps Hayes package, but he's taking more now. I can tell by the crazy hours he's keeping, the excessive sweating, and sudden bouts of extreme exhaustion. How he's hidden his habit from my aunt is beyond me. I really hate that she's pulling a double shift and won't be home for several hours. Does that mean she's making enough money now that we can leave? A part of me thinks Walt might actually be relieved if we took Amelia with us, that he'd never even notice she was gone or bother to report her missing. No way I'm leaving without her. At least Amelia's occupied in the other room and won't see him like this. "Why don't you go sleep it off," I say in a low, sarcastic tone.

"I said for you to cook me something," he grates, waving his arm.

Maybe if I cook him some food, he'll decide to take a nap. I get up and by the time I set the pan on the stove, he's slumped over in the chair snoring.

Ugh! Rolling my eyes, I sit back down at the table and try to focus on my math once more.

I'm so focused on my homework that I don't hear Hayes step through the door connecting our apartments until his hot breath rushes across my neck.

"What are you working on, Talia?" Before I can respond, he straightens and kicks Walt's outstretched foot, and when Walt slumps over even more in the chair, he lets out a low laugh.

I tense when he turns back to me and bends over my shoulder, his closeness and creepy voice sending a shiver of revulsion down my spine. Heart racing, I glance at Walt, then snap, "I'm trying to concentrate and you're not helping."

Hayes' hand lands on my notebook, covering it completely as he leans over me. "How about you concentrate on me for once."

He smells of smoke and beer. I want to hold my breath, but panic mode overrules. "Walt…" I call out in a warning voice.

Hayes is blocking me in, and at this point with Walt not responding, I'm just done. "I'll study somewhere else," I say in a snotty tone. Slamming my book closed with an annoyed huff, I stand, then push the chair hard under the table.

Before I can pick up my book, Hayes grabs my arm and yanks it behind my back. Hooking his other hand on the crook of my neck, he shoves me over the back of the chair and presses my cheek against the table.

"After today, you're never going to talk to me like that again," he grates in my ear. Releasing my neck, he twists my wrist even more. His tone is hard and angry, his actions the most violent he's ever been toward me.

As soon as I hear him yanking at his belt buckle and then the zipper of his pants coming undone, I call Walt's name again. I stare at his slack face, hoping the panic in my voice will rouse *him. I don't care about Hayes' earlier threats concerning Walt's future. All I care about is what's happening right here and now.*

"Shut up if you don't want the brat wandering in here," Hayes says, his breathing changing to ragged pants.

I'd forgotten about Amelia in my haze of fear. His comment is sobering, and it takes everything inside me not to scream as he grabs my other hand and yanks it behind my back too. When he folds my fingers around his erection, disgust rolls through me. He lets out a deep groan and grinds his hips against my butt.

Bile rises in my throat and I gag. I try to pull my hand free of him, but his fingers are locked around mine, holding his cock in a vise hold. "Don't you dare let go," he warns, as he rolls his hips and moans deeper.

All I can do is lay there as the bastard uses my hand to jerk himself off along the back of my jeans while Walt sits right there next to us, completely oblivious. When he's done, he smacks my ass, then rubs his cum along my jean-covered butt and then down between my legs. Grabbing my crotch, he fists his other hand around my pinned-up bun and yanks hard as he leans over to pant in my ear, anticipation in his satisfied tone. "You're going to be the best fuck. I can't wait to have you."

Hayes casually walks over to the sink and washes his cum off his hands before he strolls past me, saying, "I'll be back later. Better be on your best behavior, Talia."

As soon as he walks out, I clench my jaw and swallow the words I want to scream in Walt's ear. He wouldn't hear them right now anyway. Silent tears stain my cheeks as I race upstairs and strip out of my clothes, stuffing them in an old grocery store bag I find in the corner of my room. Tomorrow I'll burn the whole thing in the alley and let ashes take my prayers up. Maybe someone will hear. I'm too embarrassed to tell anyone, especially not my aunt.

I can't get in the shower fast enough or make the water hot enough. I use the entire bottle of liquid soap and scrub my skin raw, trying to wash away the disgusting memory. I want to stay in the shower forever, but I can't leave Amelia alone much longer. Her show is almost over.

Choking back a sob, I dry my hair, braid and re-pin it, then step into clean clothes and tiptoe back downstairs. Once I sit down at the table like I'd been before, I kick the hell out of Walt's foot, which sends him flying off the chair and onto the cheap linoleum floor.

"What the fuck?" he roars, jerking upright with his fists clenched.

"You fell asleep," I say tightly, flipping my pencil toward the chair he'd been passed out on.

Rolling to his feet, he stumbles a little as he straightens, then directs his annoyance at me, his tone accusatory. "My foot hurts, like I was kicked."

I shrug and look down at my book, my tone snarky to cover the raging anger inside. "Probably slept on it wrong. You're the one who passed out on a chair."

"Watch your mouth," he snaps. Glancing around, he looks at the stove. "What happened to my eggs and toast?"

"You fell asleep." You failed ME.

"Daddy!" Amelia squeals and comes running into the kitchen, the picture I'd drawn earlier clutched in her hand. "Look what Talia drew. Two Lias! Does your name have those letters too?"

Walt winces and puts his hands to his head. I narrow my gaze and hope it hurts like hell, but the last thing I expect is for him to sweep his hand out and shove Amelia back, growling,

"Quit that shrieking."

As soon as I see Amelia stumble and lose her footing, I jump up to catch her, but I'm not fast enough. She slips past my fingers and hits the side of her head on the table on her way down.

"You're such an asshole!" I yell at Walt as I bend over Amelia crumpled on the floor, my stomach knotting at the bit of blood I'd seen on the table. When I tilt her chin, I see she's split her head open. "Are you okay, Amelia? Talk to me." But she doesn't flutter her eyes or move at all.

"Is-is she okay?" Walt says from behind me, his voice a bit panicky. "You know I didn't mean to hurt her. It was an accident."

Warm blood coats my hand as I touch her head and then her cheek, trying to wake her up. "Amelia, you're going to be okay, sweetie," I say and wonder how fast an ambulance can get to our apartment. But the second I touch her chest, and realize it's not moving up and down, my own breathing halts. My hands shake as I quickly check for a pulse at her throat. Nothing. A wail escapes my lips and my burning lungs finally force me to breathe, but my heart starts to crumble as everything inside me goes numb.

I slowly stand, tingling everywhere at once. I feel like I'm in a slow-moving nightmare. Clenching my hands by my sides, I hammer a fist against my thigh to wake myself up, but all I feel is pain. I turn to Walt and spew my anger. "She's not breathing!"

"No." He shakes his head back and forth, his eyes wide as he falls to his knees beside Amelia. "It was an accident. You saw."

"We need to call an ambulance. Maybe there is something they can do." I'm shocked by my calm tone, when all I want to do is scream and cry until my throat is raw. I know in my heart that she's gone. That she's never going to wake up and smile at *me again.*

"Not yet." Walt jerks his gaze to me, and when I realize that I see fear in his eyes and not remorse, unimaginable fury whips inside me. While Walt leans over Amelia and fruitlessly tries to shake her awake, I run into the room next door and grab one of the two plastic containers of Ecstasy sitting on the counter, waiting to be packaged. It's the largest supply I'd ever seen and the sight of it sickens me.

Returning to the kitchen, I shut the door and scream at Walt as I dump the whole container over his head. "She's dead. All because you got mixed up with this stuff!"

"What the fuck have you done?" Walt rails, his face turning bright red. Rage engulfs his entire body. He tries to stand, but the pills slide under his feet, making him trip and fall back to his knees.

As he growls his anger, I yell at him, too angry to be fearful. "You're so weak! You were supposed to cherish and protect her. You promised to protect us," I finish in a lower hiss.

"Protect you? You little bitch. I don't even think I can protect you now. Do you have any idea how much money you just destroyed?" He huffs out at the same time he grabs the edge of the table.

"Like you ever protected me. And now I've just lost my sister because of these stupid drugs. When the police test your blood, at least someone will finally know the truth and—" My voice cracks but I force myself to continue. "At least Amelia's death won't have been for nothing."

Shaking with fury, Walt slits his gaze, his voice low and deadly. "You're going to help me clean all this shit up and get rid of it. And then we'll tell the police that Amelia getting hurt was an accident...which it was."

I lift my chin higher. "I'm going to tell them to test your blood for drugs."

When he takes an unsteady step toward me, his foot sliding on the pills, the murderous anger in his eyes finally registers in my brain. I quickly run to the desk in the hallway where I saw him hide a handgun for protection not long after he started working with Hayes.

Grabbing the gun, I hold it up as he approaches, my hands shaking. "Don't come anywhere near me."

"You're not going to shoot me. You're the one who's weak," *he sneers.* "You'll do as I say and tell the police what I want you to. Not one thing more! And...then—" *he glances around frantically before his gaze snaps back to me, full of clarity.* "We'll kick open the other apartment door, and I'll tell Hayes someone broke in and got away with half the drugs before I could stop them."

"Don't you even care that she's gone?" *My voice quivers as tears blur my vision. I angrily blink them away and tighten my grip on the gun.*

"I didn't mean to hurt Amelia." *He tenses for all of a second, then hardens his jaw, refusing to look down at his daughter.* "We're all dead unless I fix this. Now give me that goddamn gun."

The moment he lunges and grabs my hands, the gun goes off.

I watch in horror as Walt stumbles back, then falls to his knees, his hands gripping his chest, blood oozing past his fingers from the gaping wound.

As the gunshot continues to reverberate in a shrill high pitch in my ears, Walt collapses on the floor on his side, sightlessly staring at me. Oh God! I killed him. *I drop the gun and take a step back, shocked by what just happened. Did I really pull the trigger? I look down and my stomach heaves at the sight of Walt's blood splattered on my sweatshirt and hands.*

Proof of my guilt.

I can't stay. What if Hayes comes back before my aunt? The thought of facing her is hard enough—she'll probably hate me for letting something happen to Amelia—but Hayes... I start to shake. He'll kill me with his bare hands. My gaze lands on the drawing that had slipped from Amelia's hand when she fell. My shoes slide in Walt's quickly pooling blood as I step around him and bend down to kiss Amelia's sweet forehead one last time. Holding back my sobs, I shake the pills off the drawing and carefully fold it.

"Hey, lady. You planning to do some parkour or something?"

The sarcastic comment yanks me back to the present. A young dark-haired teen is standing on the fire escape a floor above my old apartment, staring at me like I'm crazy.

I blink away the sleet on my lashes. I hadn't even noticed the cold drizzle had switched over. "The ladder can stick. Jiggle it to the right and it'll slide all the way down." I don't acknowledge his surprised look before I turn and head back down the alley.

My gaze snags on the brick I'd pulled out earlier to retrieve my drawing. It's crooked. That night as I climbed down the fire escape, the sky opened up. I put the drawing behind the brick to keep it dry. Stepping up to the wall beside the Dumpster, I reset the brick more firmly in place. This hiding spot has kept a happy memory safe for me all these years. What I wouldn't give to be able to shove all the bad memories inside that same hole and lock them away forever.

I glance across the alley and close my eyes, my stomach churning. I try not to think about everything that happened that night, but the guilt rises up regardless. That hole isn't large enough for my sins. There's a twisted part of me Sebastian has never seen, and as far as I'm concerned he never will.

Opening my eyes, I take a breath and pat the brick once more, then walk back up the alley. "I'm ready to go now, Den."

"Did you get what you came for?" he asks softly, seemingly unaffected by the cold.

I slide out of his coat and hand it to him. "Thank you. Yes, I got what I came for." *And I relived memories I wish I hadn't.*

When Den settles into the seat beside me and we drive off, I watch the building fade in the distance. Over the years I'd convinced myself that all the good I'd done had meant something. That I'm not really a bad person. Coming back was a gut-wrenching reminder that my past actions can never be overridden. Like dust under a rug, they'll remain hidden but always present. But having someone else there quietly in the background—who won't pressure me for answers—gave me the courage to finally face my demons. The memories still hurt like hell, but it was worth it to retrieve a physical reminder of Amelia when she was happy. I hate that her features are fading from my memory. At least now I'll have something of hers to hold onto and remember her by.

CHAPTER FIVE

Sebastian

"What do you mean you lost the signal?" I bark into my phone, then wave at the cab driver to keep going when he asks, "Are we still heading to the Lower East Side then?"

"It's gone, Sebastian," Elijah says, the sound of keyboard keys tapping in the background. "I'm pinging her cell off all the towers in the area, but it just dropped. She must've turned her phone off."

When my phone beeps with an incoming call, I tell him to keep trying and then click over. "Talk to me, Connelly."

"I struck out at Windsor Middle School. Only a P.O. Box is listed for her address. Got that from her college info, but not much else. The Middle School did have an address listed that was a co-worker of her aunt's. They stayed there temporarily when she was thirteen after a fire took out their apartment."

"A fire?" I watch the newly refurbished buildings whiz by as the cab moves into the area of the Lower East Side that hasn't been "revitalized" by the city.

"Yeah, according to the lady they stayed with, it was some kind of explosion. She lost touch with Talia and her aunt once they moved to their own place."

"Find out where the aunt and this woman worked together. The employer must've had an address on file. Hopefully we'll get lucky and the employer didn't erase the old address from their records once Talia found a permanent home."

"They worked together as nurses at Memorial. Headed there now. Oh, and Bash?"

"Yeah?"

"What are you going to do with this information? I thought you only wanted to go so far back into her past. I got the impression she likes to keep to herself."

Bear's protective soft spot for Talia is starting to piss me off. "That was before someone started threatening her life, Connelly. The serial killer, Tommy Slawson, had a connection to her past. And since there's no one from *his* past left to care about this book coming out, I just want to make sure there aren't any other connections from *Talia's* past that we're unaware of. Now get over to that hospital."

"Whatever you say, *Boss*."

His obvious sarcasm makes me grind my teeth. I do what's best for the people who matter to me. Period. I make no excuses or apologies for it. The big guy's so wrapped around Talia's little finger, now he's insisting I call him Theo—her nickname for him. His fucking name has been Bear ever since our BUD/S (Basic Underwater Demolition/SEAL) training. At least he's answering to his last name. Next he'll be telling me to call him Teddy. Fuck that. From now on, if anyone from BLACK Security has to interact with Talia, I'll call Elijah in. My tech guy doesn't have an empathetic bone in his body. There's no way she'll reel him in like she did Bear.

Talia. She both arouses and infuriates me. The moment our gazes locked in William's office, I got kicked in the gut. I know I pushed her too far last night. But watching her so easily pretend we'd never met, and then hearing her spout that "we can work together but nothing more" bullshit when the pull between us in that ballroom felt like a fucking vertical G-force and vortex rolled into one, I didn't give a damn if I stepped over the line. The fact she refused to acknowledge our attraction when she never had before brought out my ruthless side.

If she wants to battle, she needs to know I go for the kill every time. She shocked the hell out of me when she slapped me, but the more I think about it, the more I fucking love it. It means the passion is still there. Now I just need to get her to show it. I sure as hell can't stop thinking about what we were like together. I miss her smell and the feel of her soft body against mine. I crave her taste and the sensation of her hair spread across my chest. We work well together, both in and out of the bed. No matter how much she tries to deny it, she knows it's true.

And yet the first chance she gets, she ditches me. What errand could be so important? With the hours she kept while working two jobs since she got back from Martha's Vineyard, she made it impossible for me to reconnect with her. When she didn't respond to the note I included with the pearl necklace I returned to her, I focused on things I could control.

While we were together in Martha's Vineyard, she gave me very little to go on. The names Walt and Amelia didn't help. Without their last names, I couldn't make the connection to this Hayes guy. The apartment building where I'd dropped her off when we were teens turned out to be a dead end. Either that or the lease wasn't in her aunt's maiden name, Murphy. Hopefully something Bear comes up with now can help with Talia's current threat situation. And as a side benefit he might uncover more info that will help me find that bastard Hayes.

Just before I put my phone away, I receive a text from Elijah.

> *Elijah: You hung up before I could update you. I tracked down the copier that was used to print that threatening letter. Some college student made the copy using his copy card. A guy in sunglasses and a hoodie paid him fifty bucks to do it, but he never got a good look at his face.*
>
> *Me: Age, height, body-build?*
>
> *Elijah: Late-thirties to mid-forties. Average height, muscular build. Hoodie guy told the college kid he was paid to make the copy, but he didn't have a card to the machines, so he waited for someone who did.*

Fuck. I need to ID the person *behind* the threat.

Me: Hoodie guy is still a lead. See if any security cameras around there caught his face.

Elijah: On it.

Once I put my phone away, I give the cab driver an address. The new information in that ballistics report about my mom clawed at my gut. Heading to this side of town would've been my first priority once the tour was over and I knew Talia was safe, but now that I'm close and have at least an hour to kill, I'm not passing up the opportunity while I'm here.

"This the place?" the cab driver says, pulling up to a house just around the block from the apartment I grew up in. A dingy sofa sits to the right side of a sparse lawn currently littered with liquor bottles and beer cans. A couple of guys walk out and stare from the front porch. I don't know the younger guy in his mid-twenties dressed in baggy pants and a parka, but I instantly recognize the scrappy shorter one sporting spiked dark hair and a flannel shirt. Paulo, Banks' second.

Familiar spikes of heat and anger crawl along my spine. I might've walked out of that house beholden to no one when I was sixteen, but I'd still gotten the shit kicked out of me. It took weeks for all the cuts and bruises to heal. I had to lie to Mom, telling her I'd gotten mugged on the way to school. "Wait for me," I say in a curt tone as I hand him a couple Franklins. In a neighborhood like this, I know it'll take at least that for him to agree.

"Well, damn if it ain't Blackie himself," Paulo gives my

suit a smug once over. "I heard you'd moved up in the world. Gone and gotten all soft, huh?"

"Don't believe everything you hear, Paulo. I need to see Banks."

Hooking his hands on the open lapels of his flannel shirt, Paulo rubs his knuckles on the white T-shirt beneath as he rocks on his heels, his dark gaze full of suspicion. "What business could you possibly have with Banks?"

I narrow a steely gaze on him. "Tell him I'm here."

Grunting, he jerks his chin to the guy next to him, silently telling him to convey the message.

While the guy's inside, Paulo folds his arms and tucks his hands in his armpits, remaining silent. At least he knows when to keep his mouth shut. Maybe he remembers what my fist felt like splitting his lip wide open all those years ago.

Banks opens the door himself, a look of smug curiosity on his face. "You're the last person I ever expected to see here again."

"I need to talk to you," I say, knowing all eyes are on us.

He looks me up and down. "Why do I get the feeling you're not here to stay?"

"You inviting me in or not?"

Waving, he turns and I follow him inside to the living room with ten or so guys lounging on sofas and the floor playing video games and watching TV. Machine gun battles rage on the high-end surround sound speakers. Stolen. Like most of the nice things the guys have in their house. Even the old tattered sofas have been replaced with leather.

Banks' crew isn't technically a gang, but they were unofficially known as the BBs around the neighborhood, short for Banks' Boys.

"And what do I owe the honor of your visit, Blackie?" Banks says as he rests his two hundred-and-forty pound bulk on the sofa's arm. He's feigning a relaxed pose, but I know better. Just like I know the six guys playing video games and the other four watching the wall-mounted TV are keeping one eye on me.

Time hasn't been kind to their leader. Sporting a goatee and a scalp buzz cut, he's put on a good fifty pounds since he beat the hell out of me that day in this very room. I remember every punch and kick; Banks' way of trying to convince me to start rolling with his crew.

A scar slashes across his forehead and over his left eye, ending halfway down his cheek. The scar is so deep it's a wonder he still has his eye. That scar definitely overshadows the small one I gave him along his chin. I was fighting for my life back then; my freedom to choose where I went and what I did. I didn't hold back, and I can tell by the way he's rubbing that tiny scar, he remembers it too.

"I'm here for some information."

Banks snorts. "What kind of information would a trust fund type from the Upper East Side want from little 'ole me?"

I tense. "The tabloids are mostly fiction, Banks."

He hitches his jaw. "So you're not a billionaire's bastard?"

"That part's true," I admit in a dry tone.

"Always did act like you were better than the rest of

us," Banks snarls, his beefy hand clenching into a fist on his jean-covered thigh.

I shrug. "Just smarter."

When two muscular guys jump up from the sofa, growling their offense, Banks puts out a calming hand. "Settle, boys. I want to hear what Blackie has to say."

I'm aware three men have entered the room behind me. I feel their ready-to-pounce presence. Paulo has moved to stand in front of the door, blocking my exit. Four guys on the sofa have put down their gaming controllers. The situation is escalating. Then again, I've never been one to back down from a fight.

"I want to know if you had anything to do with my mother's murder," I say in a low, steady tone.

Five guys stand at once, hands curled into fists, but Banks just barks out a laugh. "You've got great big elephant balls, Blackie. That hasn't changed about you one bit."

Tension fills the room. His men wait for his cue and I'm watching to see if someone is packing. So far I haven't seen a gun, but the last thing I need is to get shot.

Folding his arms, Banks' gaze shifts from amusement to slitted anger. "I know you're the one who stole those electronics I had stored at Brewsky's. You know how I know? 'Cause I know every fucking thing that goes on in *my* neighborhood."

Fury ripples, tightening my tense muscles. I speak calmly to maintain my focus. "Since you claim to know everything, maybe you can shed some light on how bullets pulled out of my mom's dead body happen to match a gun used in a crime committed by Parker Johnson? Did you send him in retaliation?"

"I'm not saying shit!" Banks spits.

"And I'm not leaving without an answer. Since Parker's dead, I'm asking you."

Banks glares at me, then his expression turns calculating. "Tell you what, Blackie. Show me you haven't gone soft living the high life—"

"Mr. Moneybags should give us a huge donation—" A knife suddenly embedded in the door next to Paulo cuts him off.

I raise an eyebrow in respect for Banks' fast reflexes. The thick guy moved faster than I thought he could.

Grunting his annoyance at Paulo, Banks turns his attention back to me. "Show me, Blackie. If you lose, I get that watch you're flashing. I can get ten grand for it, easy. You win, I'll answer your question."

The fact that he wants my watch only pisses me off more. I've been wearing the one my father gave me for a while now. "No weapons," I say in a curt tone as I unbutton my suit jacket and lay it on the TV stand.

Banks nods his agreement.

"Four of your best," I continue while rolling up my shirtsleeves.

He raises an eyebrow, then counters with a cold smile. "Six."

Other than SEAL training, height is my second advantage. Only one guy in the crowd is close to mine. Thankfully I have at least thirty percent muscle mass on him. I slowly nod, then hold my hands up in a battle stance as several guys begin to surround me in a wide circle, fists clenched and leers of anticipatory aggression on their faces.

When some five-foot-nothing kid jumps on my back like a tree frog and sucker punches me in the chest, I'm quickly reminded just how dirty Banks' scrappers fight. Ignoring the pain in my chest, I capture his swinging fist as it flies in for another punch aimed at my jaw.

With a growl of fury, I fling him into three guys, mowing them down like bowling pins, before I pivot toward the other two men rushing at me with blood lust in their eyes.

They never even get a punch in before I lay them flat with two quick jabs, leaving one knocked out cold and the other gasping to regain his breath.

"Did I forget to mention I'm a SEAL?" I say in a casual tone as I face the three who've just shoved the little guy off them and are scrambling to their feet, fists raised and ready to rumble.

"As in the fucking military?" Paulo says incredulously, jerking his gaze to Banks to make a judgment.

Banks lets out a belly laugh and waves the rest of his crew into the fray.

When three more guys pound the floor toward me, and I see the flashing metal of brass around their knuckles, for a split second I question my sanity. But adrenaline takes over and deep thinking shuts down as my body goes into survival mode.

Just as the last guy falls and I start to turn to Banks, someone sucker punches me in the jaw, sending my head snapping sideways.

"That's for thinking you could steal from me, you fucker!" Banks growls as he straightens and rubs his knuckles in his open palm.

Clenching my hands, I jerk a furious gaze back to Banks

and see Paulo fanning his fingers underneath his chin in the background, warning me not to retaliate.

I exhale to calm my rage and straighten to my full height. Stepping over the battered guys, I move to stand directly in front of Banks. Even though I'm seething inside, I ask the question that has plagued me with guilt and remorse since I saw my mother murdered before my eyes. "I held up my end. Now it's your turn. Did you send someone after me because of what I did?"

Banks eyes me for a second as if contemplating not answering, then shrugs. "Nah, I knew why you did it. I'd heard your mother was sick and that she was having trouble paying bills." Turning away, he helps two of his guys to their feet. "A man came around, asking about you. Wanted to know where you lived."

Every muscle tenses as I reach for my coat. That's the last thing I expected to hear. I'd always thought Banks was somehow behind it. Shrugging into my suit jacket, I button it. "Did he say what he wanted?"

Banks shakes his head. "No, and I didn't give a damn. Told him to fuck off. I don't rat people out in my hood. Even you, asshole."

Nodding my reluctant appreciation, I ask, "Do you remember what he looked like?"

"White guy. Looked to be in his late thirties."

"Anything else? Hair color? Height?"

"Jesus, that was what…twelve or so years ago? I was on the porch. He was on the ground. How the hell should I know how tall he was?" He pauses and rubs his goatee. "The guy looked shifty though. Can't say about hair color. He was wearing a black knit cap. I remember 'cause it wasn't cold enough for one yet."

That black cap was probably the ski mask the murdering bastard wore that night. Why was he looking for me? Who the hell ratted me out, and how did he get Parker's gun? "Thanks for the info."

Nodding, Banks' gaze locks on my wrist as I straighten my cuff. "You sure you don't want to donate that watch?"

"Fuck off, Banks," I grumble and walk out of the house, his booming laughter trailing behind me.

The cab driver steps on the gas the second I close the backdoor. "I didn't know if I'd ever see you again," he says with a breath of relief, tugging on the bill of his cap.

I exhale a grunt and rub my sore jaw. "Could've gone to hell, that's for sure."

Snorting, he turns out of the neighborhood, then holds a piece of paper over his shoulder. "Was told to give you this once we were out of sight of the house."

I take the folded note and dial the number scratched on the paper.

"Hold a sec," the guy on the other end says. The sound of a door opening, then closing comes across the line. "That's not how it went down."

I'm surprised it's Paulo. "How'd you know what I came for?"

"Made an educated guess."

I grip the phone tighter. "Why are you telling me?"

"If you hadn't punched me, I would've continued to defend you back then. I realize now you were trying to protect me from myself."

"And your way of thanking me is to make sure I had to fight every guy in that room?" I snap, letting my sarcasm flow.

"No, this is. Banks lied. Not about the part where the guy asked if we knew where to find you, that part was true. Banks gave him your address. Then the guy wanted to know where he could buy a gun. Banks told him he didn't deal in guns. Now you know why Banks didn't come after you for stealing from him. He figured you were going to get yours soon enough."

"That guy unloaded half a clip into my mother, Paulo," I growl. "Do you know how the bastard got Parker's gun?"

"Parker was in a bad way back then, needing cash to get out from under some debt. He was there when the guy came to Banks asking about you. My guess is he sold his gun to him on the side. One other thing, the man who asked about you...his eyebrows were brown. Means his hair under that cap probably was too, right?"

"It's a high probability. Thanks for the info." I end the call, my jaw clenched in fury. *Banks, that lying motherfucker.* Anger simmering, I dial the number of one of my police contacts who works the Lower East Side. "Hey, Phil. Thought you might want to check out Brewsky's abandoned warehouse. Might find some stuff of interest there."

CHAPTER SIX

Talia

"*I appreciate* you coming to Blake Towers, Miss Lone." Buttoning his custom suit jacket, one of the country's wealthiest men steps around his massive mahogany desk as I walk into his luxurious top floor office. Adam Blake nods to his uptight secretary standing behind me, his deep voice full of authority, "That'll be all, Ms. Shaw. Please shut the door behind you."

Ms. Sourpuss—who'd already snipped at Den and me for being over an hour late—gives me an annoyed look before she shuts the door.

Mr. Blake gestures to the expensive leather chair in front of his desk, his tone all business. "Ms. Shaw knows everything that goes on around here. She doesn't like not knowing what this appointment is about."

As I take a seat, I notice that Adam's eyes are a deeper

shade of blue and his dark hair is just starting to pepper with gray, but I can't believe how much Sebastian really does favor his father. I can really see it now that I've spent some time with Sebastian. Adam's bearing is intense, his presence dominant, and if he wasn't staring at me with such a serious gaze, I imagine he probably has a charming side, just like his son. "Your secretary's not the only one baffled by this meeting, Mr. Blake. Why *have* you called me here?"

Sliding his hands into his pockets, he settles his serious gaze on me. "I'm curious, do you always make it a habit of taking advantage of those around you?"

"Excuse me?" I instantly straighten in my seat, my jaw tensing. "What are you talking—"

"Driving around town in my car doesn't endear you to me one bit," he continues, talking over me in an autocratic tone.

"Ordering me to your office as if I have nothing better to do with my time doesn't endear you to me either, so thanks for the lift earlier and I'll call us even on that score." Folding my hands around my purse, I elevate my chin. "I have somewhere I need to be in less than a half hour, Mr. Blake. If you wouldn't mind, please enlighten me as to why I've been summoned."

His gaze briefly narrows. "It seems you've successfully managed to manipulate your way into the Blake family this time, Miss Murphy." He smirks when my eyes widen at his mention of my real name. "Yes, I know who you are. I remember you trying to finagle your way into seeing my daughter three-and-a-half years ago when she was at her weakest." Waving at me dismissively, he continues, "And yet again, I find you preying on my daughter's current circumstance with what I can only assume is another self-serving agenda. Mina doesn't have many friends, but the few she does have should be ones she can trust. I want you to cease whatever endgame you're working toward and quietly end your involvement in my daughter's life."

Ever since I left the hotel, I assumed he wanted to talk about Sebastian. "You called me here because of Mina?" I quietly ask while resentful rage festers in my chest. Yes, I'd spoken to Mina a few times since I returned from Martha's Vineyard. She video conferenced to thank me for the baby gift I sent her. And a month after her daughter was born, she pinged me to introduce little Josi to me. And then later, she videoed to thank me for the books and toys I'd sent Josi. The last we spoke was a couple weeks ago when she heard about my new book's upcoming tour. She called to congratulate me and we talked about Josi and her new life as a mom. So what current circumstances is he referring to? The fact Mina's a new mother? She's handling it like a pro. "What exactly are you accusing me of?"

"I believe I was pretty clear. I don't trust your motives," he says in a cold tone.

Standing, I grip my purse by my side so tight I can't feel my fingers. "I'm not perfect, not at all, but to be accused of evil intent toward the sweetest girl I've ever known is beyond insulting. I've spoken to your daughter briefly via video chat all of four times in the last six months. How in the world could I possibly be concocting some kind of nefarious plan under those conditions?"

"Four times?" Surprise flickers in his expression, then he looks away, mumbling, "This makes even less sense."

I fold my arms, tucking my purse tight against me. "I know one thing that does make sense. If this is how Mina's treated by those around her, being judged for her choices without reason or cause, then I can understand why she might look for friendship outside her normal circle."

Mina's father visibly bristles. "My daughter has had the same two best friends since childhood, so yes, I'm questioning why she would choose *you* as her child's godmother over one of them, Miss Murphy."

I gulp back my surprise. "Go—godmother?"

His dark eyebrows elevate. "You didn't know?"

"This is the first I'm hearing of it."

Furrowing his brow, he steps forward and gestures to the chair once more, his tone more conciliatory. "Please, have a seat."

I sit down only because my legs suddenly won't hold me. I can't believe this. *Why would Mina want me to be little Josi's godmother?*

"I hope you understand the position I'm in, Miss Murphy," Mr. Blake says once he's seated behind his desk. "Mina's mother is beside herself with concern for Mina and Josephine's well-being. My daughter's friends were so distraught that Mina didn't choose either of them, they came to my wife and me for answers. Considering my first introduction to you was far from positive, I don't understand my daughter befriending you, let alone this choice she's made. But if you're saying that being Josephine's godmother isn't a responsibility you would accept anyway, that will save everyone a lot of undue stress."

I jerk my head up and meet his gaze head on. He has

no idea what I sacrificed to keep Mina's name out of the school paper when I wrote that article. "Mina's obviously a better judge of character. That's all I'll say about the past. As for her choosing me, all I said is that I'm surprised. And I'm honored she would consider me."

His eyes narrow slightly. "So you're saying you plan to accept if she asks you?"

I match his slitted gaze. "I'm saying that I'm fully capable of the responsibility, nothing more. At this point, I haven't even been asked. If I am, my answer will be to Mina, not you."

"My granddaughter stands to inherit a lot of money, Miss Murphy. You can understand my position. It's my job to protect that at all costs."

I openly roll my eyes and stand. "This conversation is over. You're back to veiled accusations and my defensive hackles are rising. Focus on taking care of your daughter's happiness, Mr. Blake. All the money in the world can't buy that."

As I start to walk away from his desk, I realize I'll probably never get another chance to speak with this man so frankly again. I've burned the hell out of this bridge, might as well yank the flaming thing down. Pausing, I turn back to him. "And another thing, that watch that you gave Sebastian…"

When surprise flickers in his eyes, I nod. "Apparently I've been *plaguing* your family a lot longer than you realize. Sebastian gave that watch to me when I was thirteen and in a very bad place in my life. He didn't do it to get back at you. He did it because that's the kind of seventeen-year-old boy he was, headstrong and protective, even in his kindness to a total stranger. He never saw the inscription you had engraved on the back until recently when I returned the watch to him. Did he tell you that?"

Mr. Blake slowly shakes his head, regret reflected in his unguarded gaze. "My son and I aren't very close."

"Sebastian's a proud man, so I doubt he'll ever tell you how much you hurt him. If you want the kind of relationship your brother had with him, words on the back of a watch only get you so far. Tell him what he means to you."

"Do you think he'll listen?" he asks, his expression shuttered.

"It's a start to mending old wounds." I nod, then walk toward the door.

"Miss Murphy," he calls out and I glance back at him.

"It appears I've misjudged you. I don't know what transpired in the past, but I can see you've gotten to know Sebastian and Mina well enough to have their best interests at heart. I would appreciate it if you would keep this meeting between us. Mina will be very upset if she finds out I contacted you."

I offer a half-smile, enjoying the peek into his softer side. He might be a rich and powerful man, but family matters to him. That's exactly how Sebastian operates. Family above all else. He's more like his father than he realizes. "What meeting?"

Mr. Blake smiles. "Thank you for your discretion."

"Did your meeting go well?" Den asks as the driver pulls away from Blake Towers.

"Yes," I say, then frown at the slight smirk on his lips. "I hope I didn't get you in trouble, Den."

He laughs. "Miss Talia—"

"Just Talia," I correct.

Nodding, his laugh settles to a chuckle. "Talia, it was my pleasure. Truly." He pulls a business card out of his jacket pocket and hands it to me. "If you ever need my help, I'm only a ring away."

"Thank you, Den. And maybe next time around you'll tell me why you left the S.I.S.?" I say as I start to take the card.

He holds fast to it, a challenge in his eyes. "Only if you tell me what you pulled from the brick behind the Dumpster."

I gape. "You couldn't have seen that. I know the Dumpster blocked your view."

Releasing the card, he taps his temple. "I observe everything."

When I eye him suspiciously, he shrugs. "I noticed the brick didn't line up with the others when I checked the alley for you."

"Ah, well, in that case." I tuck the card in my purse, and then slide the folded drawing out to show it to him.

His gaze moves over the drawing and then flicks to me, questions in his eyes.

I touch the hearts, my chest squeezing a little. "I wanted a good memory to overshadow the ones I want to forget."

He gently takes the paper and folds it neatly before handing it back to me. "Put it in a safe place. Memories like those should be cherished."

I want to remind him it's his turn to share, but I can tell by his expression, he won't. "One day?" I ask, looking at him hopefully.

"Perhaps. We'll be at your hotel in five minutes."

"Oh, then I should probably turn on my phone."

As soon as I hit the power button, my phone pings with several incoming texts.

> *PainInMyAss: Your two hours are up.*
>
> *PainInMyAss: Where the hell are you?*
>
> *PainInMyAss: You'd better be here in the next five minutes, or so help me I'll handcuff you to me. How do you think your readers will like that?*

The last text had been sent only a minute before.

> *Me: My readers would find that amusing and ask why I don't use them in my books. I'm a couple minutes away.*
>
> *PainInMyAss: Junior's here, annoying the front desk looking for you. Use the entrance on the North side of the building. I'll be there waiting.*

I look up at Den. "Can you drop me off on the North side. I need to go in that entrance."

Thankfully the sleet had stopped while I was visiting Blake Towers, but it feels even colder now, so I slide out of the car and walk along the newly salted sidewalk to the big glass door with quick steps. Sebastian is standing inside, a few feet back from the door, his arms folded. His gaze locks with mine, an annoyed look stamped on his face.

Warm air blasts me as soon as I step past the sliding glass door and keep my pace at a brisk clip across the red foyer carpet.

When Sebastian lowers his arms and takes three fast steps forward, I pause for a second just before a secondary inner glass door slides out of my way.

"What?" I say, glancing up at him.

He exhales sharply and grips my arm in a firm hold, muttering, "I thought you were going to *pigeon it.*" Turning to the left, he leads me along a side hallway. "This will take us to the lobby where your boyfriend's waiting for you. The hotel staff had to move your interview to the Royal meeting room. The change has delayed the start of your media interview by fifteen minutes."

As soon as we enter the lobby, Sebastian releases me. We've only just passed the main desk when Jared turns and sees me. "Thank, God, Natalia!" he says, his wool coat flapping around his suit pants as he briskly walks over to clasp my hands. "You're so cold." Rubbing my hands between his warm ones, he frowns at Sebastian. "Why didn't you answer any of my texts?"

"I was hired to watch over Miss Lone, not check texts," Sebastian says in a curt tone.

I pull my hands free of Jared's. "I'm fine. I just had to run a couple errands."

Sighing, he glances over his shoulder to his assistant, who's walking in the main doors. "Kayla has your schedule for today. At least moving rooms gives you time to go upstairs and fix your hair."

"My hair?" I immediately reach up and feel the waves the sleet has brought out. Great. So much for my blow-drying effort this morning. "Um, yeah, I guess I'd better go fix it."

He smiles and nods. "A sleeker style always looks better on camera. I wish I could stay, but I've got a meeting in thirty minutes. I should go before the sleet starts up again. You can tell me how it all went at dinner tonight, but in the meantime, I wanted to come and wish you well. And for luck…"

Before I can react, he clasps my face and presses his lips to mine. I'm so stunned, I freeze. Just as I start to pull back, Jared lifts his head and cuts an angry gaze to Sebastian, his hands falling away. "When did you start wearing cologne?"

Damn, I didn't think about Den's jacket leaving his cologne behind. Ignoring the kiss Jared just laid on me, I lift my blouse's collar and sniff. "You think it smells like cologne? I tried a sample while I was out earlier. Thought it was one of those unisex scents."

He tucks his hands in his jacket, visibly relaxing. "I like your floral perfume better."

I refuse to look Sebastian's way. Jared sounds exactly like a boyfriend, but right now I don't have time to set the guy straight. I nod and force a smile. "The camera's not going to care what I smell like, but I do need to run upstairs and fix my hair. Thank you for the well wishes."

Kayla waves to me from a chair in the lobby as I walk past, calling out, "See you in a few, Miss Lone. I'll be in the meeting room, making sure everything is set up properly."

I smile my appreciation, and then turn into the elevator with Sebastian by my side.

As soon as the elevator doors shut, I lean against the

wall and Sebastian does the same against the opposite wall.

His expression is back to the intensely annoyed one he had right when I entered the building a few minutes ago. But something he'd muttered after I walked in finally hits me, and I start giggling. "Pigeon it?"

Maybe the reason I'm laughing like a loon is because his witty comment briefly overshadowed his usual intensity, showing a rare side to him I don't often get to see. Humor. Or maybe it's because I don't want him to grill me about that freaking kiss. All I know is, I can't stop giggling.

Sebastian gives a half-smile. "Yeah, *splat*. You were moving so fast, I wondered if you saw that second glass door."

He chuckles along with me, and for those brief few seconds while we zip up to my floor my heart feels light. With him looking at me like that, I feel like I could tell him anything and he would understand. When our laughter settles and his blue eyes are still alight with amusement, I realize that even if we can't be lovers, I still want his friendship. I want the kind of loyalty he reserves for family. I want that very much. He was right about us. I feel connected to him in ways I can't explain. If he ever needed me, I would be there for him, no matter what.

The elevator pings, interrupting my thoughts. I start to step forward, but Sebastian puts his arm across the doorway. All amusement is gone and he stares at me with laser sharp scrutiny. "Where the hell did you go, *Natalia?*"

CHAPTER SEVEN

Talia

And just like that, Sebastian blows through my inner calm with his sarcastic use of my name. "If you must know, I chased down a lead."

He lowers his arm, his brow creasing. "What lead?"

Brushing past him, I wait until I'm a few feet away before I call over my shoulder, "I went to Tommy's old apartment to speak to the building manager."

"You *what?*"

I wince at the anger in his voice, but I keep on walking. He's by my side, fuming with fury by the time I insert the keycard in my door. "I told you I had backup."

As soon as the door closes behind him, he steps into my personal space and inhales next to my neck. Standing straight, his eyes shift to a darker blue as he glares down at me. "I'm your fucking security, Talia. You should never have gone there without me."

I shrug. "You'd already dismissed the fact that Tommy didn't have any more relatives. So I knew you wouldn't let me go."

"Of course I wouldn't," he snaps.

I sigh and walk into the bathroom, shutting the door behind me. Once I use the facilities, Sebastian calls through the door, "Did you learn anything helpful?"

I start to answer him, then pause and open the door. I'm not having a whole conversation through a piece of wood. Sebastian's gaze is expectant, eyebrows raised when I step into the room.

"I learned that Tommy's mother had a boyfriend." I unbutton my jacket and slide it off. Draping it across the back of the desk chair, I continue, "He stopped coming around several years ago."

Sebastian grunts and folds his arms. "Did the boyfriend have a name?"

I shake my head. "No. The manager didn't know it. He just said that the guy was a heavy walker. That's it."

"You risked going to the Lower East Side for that?" he says, incredulous.

I shrug and walk past him, entering the bathroom. "I wouldn't have known for sure unless I went, Sebastian. I'm back safe and sound. No worries."

As I pick up my hairbrush, he settles his shoulder against the doorjamb, disapproval clearly stamped on his face. "Who went with you?"

"A friend took me."

"How many fucking boyfriends do you have?" he rumbles in a low growl.

I snap my gaze to his. "I don't have a boyfriend. I've been too busy working. Did you learn where the latest threatening letter was printed?"

He holds my gaze for a long second, then unbuttons his jacket to tuck his hands in his pants pockets. "Not the person who sent it. My guy's trying to track the one lead we have to find the source."

"Looks like we both struck out," I say while trying to smooth my hair with my brush. When it becomes apparent that the unruly waves aren't going to cooperate, I dig through my makeup bag for some bobby pins.

Just as I start to lift my hair up into a French twist, Sebastian pulls my hand free of my hair. As the twist falls and the waves bounce around my shoulders once more, he says in a quiet tone, "It's what you are on the inside that matters, Talia."

Hearing him say my name the way he did six months ago—with a lover's intonation—turns me inside out. I hold his steady gaze in the mirror, and as my heart races, it hits me how foolish I was to dream about sharing any of my ugly past with him. When he looks at me, he sees a good person. I want to be worthy. I don't ever want to see his belief in me dim in his eyes. All I can do is strive to be deserving of his respect going forward.

Nodding, I run my fingers through my hair, then add some mousse to smooth the frizz. Once I'm done, I snicker at the crazy waves. "I guess I may as well enjoy what only nature can create. Fluffing my hair once more, I step out of the bathroom, then slide my suit jacket back on. "This is called the 'standing in sleet' wavy look. What do you think?"

As I button my jacket, Sebastian steps close and tilts my chin up, his gaze scanning over my hair. "It reminds me of you standing on the boat in Martha's Vineyard, the sea air turning your hair wavy. You looked carefree."

For that brief time with him, I felt carefree. I'd let myself forget about my past. He does that to me—makes all that darkness feel like remnants of a fading nightmare. But I know when the light shines the brightest, that's when the shadows grow bigger and longer. No matter where I turn, they're always there, waiting to swallow me up.

As I stare at him, I tilt my head and study his jawline. "Where'd you get that bruise?" When he waves like its nothing, I frown. "Seriously, what happen—"

His kiss cuts me off, but unlike Jared's kiss that stunned me into immobility, Sebastian's lips claiming mine devastate me. As I inhale his arousing masculine smell, I want nothing more than to yank him close and fully absorb the heat of his mouth pressing against mine. But I know what a bad idea that would be. When I flatten my palm on his chest to push him back, Sebastian's hand slides through my hair. As if he knows I'm ready to bolt, his fingers curl around the back of my head to hold me in place, while his tongue teases the seam of my mouth, demanding entrance.

A mewl of fierce desire claws in my chest, racing to my brain and telling me to accept his kiss. My breasts swell and my center aches with want. *I can't let this happen. He will crush my heart.*

Just when my palm applies pressure against his chest, his other hand grips my hip and he yanks me closer, growling low in his throat. It's a primal "don't fucking deny me" warning, and yet the frustration I feel in his hold tears right through my defenses.

My lips part on their own and just as my fingers begin to curl against his jacket, Sebastian lifts his head and holds my gaze.

I blink in confusion at his smirk, then push on his chest and take a step back. "What the hell was that?"

"Your good luck kiss."

"I didn't ask for one," I say, flinging my hands out to my side in exasperation.

His eyes narrow, all amusement gone. "You didn't ask your non-boyfriend for one either. And since you've made it clear you and I are nothing more than colleagues, then you should have the best fucking, non-boyfriend good luck kiss possible. Never say I don't take my job seeing to your well-being seriously."

The fact he kissed me to prove some kind of point about my relationship with Jared sends angry heat shooting across my cheeks. I pick up my purse and meet his bold, unapologetic gaze. "Your *job* also includes an addendum you signed, restricting you from fraternizing. I know for a fact you're a man of your word. You would never go against what you agreed upon, right?"

He stiffens, looking insulted. I turn and start to walk out, but his stern command makes me pause in the doorway. "Don't ever leave me again, Talia."

With my back to him, I close my eyes for a brief second and fantasize that he means more than me taking off earlier today.

"We're not done." His voice, low and on edge, is directly behind me. "There's still the matter of you defying me.

That sweet ass of yours is begging for a good tanning."

My eyes snap open and my chest aches that my fantasy was just that. I lift my chin and square my shoulders. "The last place you'll see me is across your knees," I say breezily before I head down the hall for the elevator.

Sebastian joins me in the elevator and pushes the down button. As the doors sweep shut, he says in an even tone, "We *will* talk about this. You owe me that much."

I meet his hard, unyielding gaze. He doesn't know that I was well protected. I need to set his mind at ease without disclosing whom I was with, so I nod. "I wasn't trying to make your job harder. I just had to see for myself—"

"You will do what I say, when I say it. Are we clear?" His body might appear calm, but the tense set of his jaw says differently.

I want to yell at him for being so infuriatingly overbearing, but he doesn't have all the facts, and since I promised Mr. Blake I wouldn't discuss our meeting, I just nod.

He shakes his head once in a fast jerk. "Say it. Then I'll know you'll keep your word."

God, he's hitting my stubborn meter big time. "Okay."

He narrows his piercing blue gaze. "The words."

Keeping my eyes locked on his, I bow slightly. "I will do what you say, when you say it, *Master Black*."

His jaw muscle jumps, but my answer seems to placate him, because he grunts and looks away the second the doors slide open.

"Miss Lone, right this way." Kayla leads me past rows of chairs starting to fill up with media and news people to the front of the ballroom.

Once I step behind the podium with her, I try not to think about how goofy my hair is going to look on camera. Sebastian had me so wound up, I didn't have time to dwell on it much while I was in my room. Normally I'm not so insecure about my looks, but seeing all the men standing in the back of the room with their big news cameras resting on their shoulders or on tripods, I can't help but feel like my face being displayed in Hi-Definition would never be good enough, no matter what my hair looks like. The last time I was interviewed on TV it was for one local channel. This time around, I'm pretty sure every news channel in town is here.

Not that any of the men or women in this room care about my looks or my book for that matter. The real "story" is about the fact a serial killer has been stopped.

I wince when Kayla adjusts the mic at the podium a certain way and the feedback shrills throughout the room.

"Sorry," she whispers, then turns the mic off while she lifts it up to my height.

As my nerves continue to wind tight, I find myself seeking Sebastian's location. He's standing ten feet away to my right, his back against the wall. His expression remains neutral, while his blue eyes slowly scan the crowd filling the room.

The critical evaluation in his stare and the taut readiness of his stance drills his reason for being here home far more effectively than anything he'd said to me before now. Apparently six months isn't enough time for me to separate my emotions from rational thought when it comes to Sebastian. Looking at him in his element, it's obvious that his bossy dominance is an extension of his defender instincts. As reassuring as that is from a protection standpoint, it's also a kick in the gut. A part of me secretly hoped he'd been acting so extreme the past couple of days because I meant more to him than a convenient piece of ass.

The general murmur building in the room draws my attention to the reporters who are currently filling the seats in front of the podium, waiting to ask me questions. With news cameras rolling, this event will really paint a big fat bulls-eye on me. Someone has threatened to hurt me for telling the truth. Could that person be among the men and women staring at me right now?

Kayla turns the mic on and as she picks it up, the mic's echo sounding through the room makes my palms suddenly tingle with thousands of tiny pinpricks. I fold my fingers inward and scrape my nails across my palms, trying to scrub away the tension ebbing through me.

"Good afternoon, everyone. Midtown Central would like to thank you all for coming out in the frigid weather for this exclusive interview. I'd like to introduce bestselling author, T.A. Lone, who's here today to discuss her book *Blindside* with you. And now I'll hand this over to Miss Lone to answer your questions during this Q&A session."

Stepping away from me, Kayla pours a cup of water from the carafe on the table next to the podium, then moves over to Sebastian's side. When she touches his arm and bats her lashes while quietly offering it to him, I turn away as he bends down to hear what she's saying. Grinding my back teeth, I focus my attention on the thin guy with a smoker's voice asking a question from the front row.

"Miss Lone, I'm Mitchel Riker from The Sun News.

What was it like being stalked by a serial killer?"

"Actually..." I pause when my voice booms and pull back from the mic. "I didn't know I was being stalked until it was almost too late. Facing down someone as unbalanced as Tommy Slawson was beyond scary. He had me trapped, so all I could do was keep him talking."

"Sandra Hale from The Globe," a woman in a sharp suit says as she stands. "But then he attacked you, right?"

Phantom aches twinge in my hip and thigh as the memory of Tommy hitting me with his belt streams through my mind. I blink while the cameras' flashes temporarily blind me and grip the podium to ground myself in the here and now. "Yes, before he physically hit me. Thankfully, I was rescued before he could inflict too much damage." *To my body. I still have nightmares about that day, but at least they're happening less often now.*

"How does it feel being responsible for helping bring down one of the most notorious serial killers New York has ever encountered?" the same woman talks over someone else trying to ask a question.

I shake my head. "I was investigating a completely different case that happened to be tied to Tommy's due to his obsession with me. I wasn't actively investigating the serial killer who'd killed all those women. That was Aaron White's role."

"Hailey Jones from The Sentinel. Are we going to get to meet the real Aaron White during your tour this week?" a blonde woman in the front row asks, her bright eyes alive with interest.

"Yeah, the pilot at the Martha's Vineyard resort, Trevor, claims he's not your Aaron White," a raspy voice in the back corner of the room asks.

When I meet the grizzled older man's gaze, he belatedly says, "Jim Meecham from Midtown News."

So he figured out which resort I stayed at. I'd changed the name of the resort to protect Hawthorne's reputation, but with the Internet, finding the news about Tommy's death would only be a few clicks away. I know I can trust Mr. Hawthorne's people not to reveal Sebastian's identity. And I'm really glad the details of this case aren't a matter of public record. "That's correct, Mr. Mccham. That pilot is not Aaron White."

Hailey huffs as if disappointed, then throws out another question. "We know Blindside is considered a standalone book due to its true-facts origin, but the storyline was very compelling. Do you plan to write more books in that vein?"

I breathe out a low chuckle. "I certainly don't want to be stalked anymore just for story material, that's for sure."

While the group laughs, the first blonde, Sandra, follows up. "What about Sophia and Aaron? They had great chemistry while working together in your story. How much of that was real?"

I can tell by her expression she asked just to see my reaction. I hold her curious gaze and answer with a light tone. "The imagination a fictional story elicits is always better than real life."

As the crowd rumbles in amusement, agreeing with my quipped response, Jim's raspy voice pierces through. "You mentioned you weren't actively trying to catch a serial killer, but you don't just write mysteries, you investigate real life mysteries, too, through your job at the Tribune.

That was a nice piece you wrote on helping bring down that trafficking ring run out of the Sly Fox club."

The man's praise surprises me. He seems the kind to pick apart every little nugget in a story. Just as I start to thank him, he continues, "So, how hard will it be for you to focus on this book tour while someone's threatening your life over it?"

At the sudden silence in the room, a smug smile spreads across his weathered face. "At least that's the rumor. And if it's true, I'm sure you're itching to discover who's behind the threats."

Jared was supposedly keeping the threats in-house. I wish I knew who at Midtown Central blabbed. "I guess that's—" The power goes out, and voices rise at once in the darkness.

CHAPTER EIGHT

Talia

I freeze, unsure what to do in the black, windowless room. When I hear Kayla call out, "What should we do, Mr. Black?" And his clipped reply, "Stay calm," my mind instantly pictures her clinging to his arm and pressing her overabundant breasts against him.

I jump when Sebastian's hand suddenly grips mine. His gruff "I've got you" whispered in my ear is all I need to let him lead me away. He tugs me along, his stride assured, like he knows exactly where he's going in the darkness. As we head in the opposite direction of the podium, people are shuffling around, and a couple of curses rise above the din of anxious voices. Probably hitting their shins on the chairs. When the floor behind us vibrates, Sebastian tenses and quickly yanks me in front of him. Shadowing my back, he pushes me forward a few more feet, then leans around my shoulder to open a door to an equally dark hall.

"Why are we out here?" I ask as he quietly shuts the door behind us.

Sebastian texts a message to someone, then sets his phone on a nearby chair to light the darkened seating area. Leaning his shoulder against the door, he shrugs. "Until I know the power failure wasn't engineered, you're safer here."

"You think someone did that on purpose?" The thought didn't even occur to me.

"I'm not discounting the possibility."

Silence descends between us, but when I hear Kayla's voice inside, calling out in a loud-whisper, "Miss Lone? Mr. Black? Are you over here?" I can't help but smirk a little. "You know, you really should put her out of her misery before the girl gets too wound up over you."

He frowns. "Pardon?"

I wave toward the door. "That no fraternization addendum you signed. Poor Kayla's going to be devastated she can't have a piece of Mr. Black."

The door makes a clicking sound as if someone's about to come through it. Sebastian stiffens, then points to a door diagonally across the lobby area, saying in a low tone, "Go in there."

"Really?"

When he scowls, I sigh and quickly walk across the area toward the door. Just as I open it, Sebastian's right behind me, ushering me inside.

"Why are we in a supply closet?" I whisper as men's voices rumble in the hallway discussing the possibility that the ice outside caused the power to fail.

Sebastian sets his lit up phone on the shelf next to a stack of tablecloths. "Once my guy confirms with the hotel staff that the storm did cause the power outage, we'll head back to the ballroom. I want you away from people for now. The darkness makes you an easy target otherwise."

When I nod my understanding, his tense shoulders relax and he rubs his jaw, giving me a contemplative look. "As for the addendum, it only applies to Natalia. Everyone else is open season."

Natalia. Now he's talking about me in formal third person. Annoyed, I fold my arms and snort. "How convenient for you, but I think it might be a good idea for you to keep Kayla's wandering hands out of your pants while you're working this week."

An arrogant smile tilts his lips. "I'm an excellent multi-tasker. If you'd like references to put your mind at ease, I'll be happy to provide them."

Is he really suggesting he'll give me a list of his conquests while on the job? "Well then, have at it," I snap and brush past him, but just as I reach for the door handle, he clasps my other hand. "Would you like me to *break* the rules, Little Red?"

He's close enough that his appealing smell wraps around me. I'm immobilized by his fingers intimately sliding between mine, lacing our hands together, but when his thumb slowly runs from the heel of my hand to the middle of my palm and then back up again, I close my eyes and swallow as he stokes the flames, building my desire through the sensitive spots along my skin.

Bending close, his deep voice is a rasp of pure carnal temptation next to my ear. "Do you want me to *fraternize* you senseless?"

Yes! No. Argh! *Don't give me a choice, Sebastian. I'm happiest when you take control and you damn well know it.* I'm afraid to say the words, terrified to go down that path with him again. My feelings are too deeply rooted in wishes of forever with him. I don't know if I'll be able to pick myself up when he decides to move on.

Stepping fully against me, Sebastian presses his impressive erection along my rear, his voice a husky rasp. "As you can see, my pants are rather full at the moment. Not much room for anyone else."

When I exhale a quiet gasp of relief, he releases my hand and grips my waist, his warm breath brushing my neck. "I've read Blindside, and the readers' imaginations can't possibly fathom the depth of the explosive chemistry between us." His mouth traces up my neck and along my cheek, his low tone vibrating against my skin in an intimate caress. "You and I both know that real life is far more pleasurably satisfying than fiction will ever be."

"Real life moments are fleeting. Fiction lasts forever," I breathe out, trying to sound unaffected.

"And yet there were moments between us that felt like time was suspended," he counters as he slides his hands to my hips, his possessive grip almost bruising. Tilting my pelvis so my back arches slightly, he wedges the length of his erection between my cheeks, his words guttural with want. "You have no idea how many times I've thought of your sweet ass turned up just like this." He presses deeper so I feel his hard thickness from tip to base along my ass. "Your body's perfectly aligned to mine, *fucking made for me.* It's doing my head in just thinking about your sweet pussy dripping down my cock, begging me to take you like this." He touches his lips to my hair, his voice hoarse with need while his hands glide to my thighs, my skirt hiking in his tense grip. "Tell me you want this as much as I do."

My heart thumps and my breasts are so sensitive even my bra is chaffing them. I am a lump of clay, waiting to be molded by his skillful hands. When he touches me, I form to him perfectly. He makes me feel like priceless art: beautiful, coveted, and cherished. Like I'm the only woman for him, even though I know that isn't true.

God, what happened to keeping my distance?

I try to maintain even breathing, but I've never throbbed so much in my life. As my chest rises and falls, my body trembles inside with the need for him to claim me all over again. But this time, I need him to *want* to keep me for good.

I put my hands over his on my thighs. "Sebastian—"

He spreads his fingers, locking them around mine, holding me in place, his tone on edge. "Anything other than *yes* is a lie."

Sebastian's phone starts ringing at the same time the florescent lights bloom to life in the closet.

"Unfuckingbelievable," he grates out, dropping his head to my shoulder.

I let out a half-laugh, relieved by the reprieve. I'm honestly not sure who my biggest weakness is: Sebastian or myself. If he had pushed me, I don't know if I would've been able to resist him. But I *need* to be strong. I laid it on the line for him earlier and he didn't step-up beyond suggesting we hook up. Nothing has changed.

As soon as he picks up his phone, I open the door and slip out of the room to wait for him in the hall where everyone's attention is focused on the people spilling from the ballroom.

Thankfully I don't have to try and salvage the Q&A. Kayla's already on top of it. Standing at the ballroom door, she's speaking to all the reporters who've filled the hall. "We're sorry the Q&A session was interrupted by the ice storm. Midtown Central thanks you all for coming, but Miss Lone has a signing to attend shortly, so that'll be all the questions for today. There will be one more Q&A at the end of the tour. If you'd like to sign up to attend that one for any questions you didn't get to ask, you can do that at the hotel's front desk before you leave."

I have to admit, the girl can run an event. Jared was right to assign me an assistant. If she'd just stop openly flirting with Sebastian, I could really appreciate her.

As the older reporter, Jim from Midtown News, passes me in the hall on his way out, he stops and eyes Sebastian, who's watching me with one eye while he's talking on the phone. "Is he your bodyguard?"

"Yes, why?"

"Keep him close."

I furrow my brow, confused by his comment. "Why do you say that? It was just a power outage."

He nods toward the ballroom. "Unless you pulled the podium down yourself, how did it end up on its side exactly where you were standing?" When my eyebrows elevate, he pats my shoulder and nods. "Watch your back, Miss Lone. You may have the makings for another novel yet."

CHAPTER NINE

Talia

"*Time* to go," Sebastian says, walking into my room at a brisk pace.

I quickly close the leather room-service menu over the "2 Lias" drawing. I'd taken it out to reminisce for a couple minutes, but apparently Mr. Never-Late decided to leave five minutes early. "Okay, let me use the bathroom first."

Once our original plans derail, I quickly follow Sebastian down the subway stairs. "I don't understand why we didn't just take that cab."

"The one that just happened to drive up just as we discover the car waiting to take us to the signing has a flat?" He cuts me a sideways look. "I don't believe in convenient coincidences."

"So now the cab driver's a stalker?" When he grunts and turns down a tunnel to our left, I throw my hands up and follow him. "You've been on edge ever since I told you what that reporter said. You heard people bumping into things in the dark. It's more likely that someone accidently knocked that podium over."

He faces me on the subway platform. "After the staff set the podium back up, I lifted it. That thing weighed at least forty pounds. I doubt a person bumping into it would've knocked it over."

"Okay, so that's a little concerning, but are you really worried about a seventy-year-old cab driver?"

The train arrives and we get on with the press of people around us. A huge group of college-age guys rush on at the last second just before the doors close. In the packed car, Sebastian wraps an arm around my waist and pulls me against him, speaking low in my ear. "Hate and vengeance are ageless. I've seen a seventy-year-old mow down a group of innocents without batting an eye, while a ten-year-old gleefully loads the next gun for him. Never underestimate motivation."

I can tell his hold is more protective than sexual, and my heart twists that this is the first time he's spoken about his military experiences, so I show my appreciation of his perspective by relaxing against his hard frame. He doesn't have to know I'm also soaking in his irresistible masculine smell for as long as the ride lasts.

All too soon the subway cars start slowing. Just as the doors slide open, Sebastian's fingers flex on my hip, the roughness in his voice sending chill bumps scattering across my skin. "When it comes to you, I always operate in the extreme."

Unsure of his meaning, I don't get a chance to respond as we're swept up in the mass of people moving into the subway tunnels.

The last person I expect to see at the Brownstone bookstore is my editor standing with my agent Pauline. William is practically bouncing on his toes when Sebastian and I walk in. "Welcome, Miss Lone." After Pauline hugs me in a cloud of chic perfume and wispy dark hair, William grins. "Right this way."

Pauline always dresses sharp, and today's eggplant business suit and plum lipstick are no exception. William's wearing a business suit too, which is a surprising change from his normal everyday attire. They escort me over to the signing table, where stacks of Blindside are piled, and Kayla and a middle-aged woman are waiting with huge smiles.

"Welcome to the Brownstone, Miss Lone. I'm Eden Shaw, the owner," the pint-sized lady with soft eyes and a gray pixie haircut says, clasping my hand. "We're thrilled to host your first signing for the tour."

I shake her hand and smile. "Thank you for having me, Ms. Shaw."

"Please, call me Eden."

While Kayla whispers excitedly, "This is the biggest signing turn out I've seen in a while," as she takes my coat, Eden gestures to the long line of people behind a cordoned off rope.

"Your fans are ready whenever you are."

I take in the crowd snaking through the bookstore and disappearing behind a row of bookshelves. Holding my trilogy books in their hands and wearing expectant expressions on their faces, they chatter amongst themselves. I smile at the few I make eye contact with.

Sebastian has taken up a position against the wall a few feet behind me. Of course he scrutinizes the people in line before shifting his gaze to the layout of the bookstore, making sure he as a clear view to the main door.

Glancing Pauline and William's way, Eden says to my editor, "The readers have been told your book signing rule of one personal book beyond today's purchase of Blindside, Mr. Mackens."

William moves over to my left and claps his hands. "Wonderful!" Addressing the crowd, he says, "Are you ready, everyone?"

As they all cheer, he grins and rubs his hands together, his light green eyes full of mischief as he holds their rapt attention. "I just have one announcement to make before the signing begins." Spreading his hands, he raises his voice to make sure it travels throughout the store. "I'm aware how many of you really enjoyed the romance subplot in Miss Lone's previous trilogy. As you know Blindside *is* a mystery—" When groans of disappointment interrupt him, he grins. "But today I've got a surprise you weren't expecting. Not only do you get to meet Miss Lone today, but the man who saved her life. In *my* book, nothing could be more romantic." Turning to Sebastian, he waves him forward. "Mr. Black, would you please come to the table."

Sebastian looks as surprised as Pauline, Eden, Kayla, and me. Once he steps to William's left, my editor clasps his thick shoulder. "Meet the pilot from Blindside. That's right, ladies and gents, Aaron White is here in the flesh."

When a cheer rises up among the readers and Pauline joins in clapping enthusiastically, I manage to swallow the lump of surprise in my throat and smile at my fans—

who seem genuinely thrilled as they stare at Sebastian. There's no way I'll look at him right now. Instead, I turn to William and act like he didn't just drop a bomb in my lap. "Thank you for the introduction, William." Gesturing to William and then Pauline, I tell my readers, "Meet my editor, William Mackens and my agent Pauline Grayson."

William beams as the crowd applauds, then leans to his right and whispers in my ear. "Now *that's* how we appease readers about the lack of romance in your book. They'll spread the word. Have a wonderful signing. I'll see you tonight at dinner, where I have another special announcement to make."

Waving to the crowd, he walks over and hooks his arm with Pauline's, saying, "We're leaving things in Eden's capable hands." And as soon as he and Pauline walk out the door, the owner quickly takes charge. Unhooking the rope, Eden says to the fans, "If you'd like a picture, you'll only be allowed one to keep the line moving. All we ask is that you have your phone or camera ready for Miss Lone's assistant when you come up to the table."

While Eden reiterates the "one personal book" rule, the readers are eyeballing Sebastian with fascination. Great. The man's head will be so swollen, he won't be able to fit through the doorway. I have a feeling Jared's going to be royally ticked over his father's off-the-cuff marketing angle, but I don't have time to ponder beyond that as the line of readers move to my table.

The first few readers are shy and quickly get their books signed and move on, but the next group of four women who approach can't keep their eyes off Sebastian. Once I sign the first lady's copy of Blindside, she quickly turns to Sebastian and holds her pen out to him. "Will you sign it too, please?"

While I pretend I'm not annoyed that she's asking him to sign and move on to her friend's copy of Blindside, Sebastian sets the lady's book on the table to my left and signs in a bold flourish.

When she makes a swooning sound and turns to show it to her friend, I catch a glimpse of his signature. Underneath my T.A. Lone signature, he put an ampersand and Aaron White. Sheesh, all that's missing is a heart around our names.

I quickly cut a suspicious gaze his way. He's looking down signing the second reader's book, but I don't miss his slight smirk. If I hadn't seen the surprised look on his face when William called him over, I would think he engineered this whole scenario.

Before the next set of readers approach, I realize how subdued Kayla is. She'd been bubbly and excited when we first arrived, but now her smiles seem forced. Maybe seeing the readers romanticize my past with Mr. Black puts a wrench in her "seduce the sexy bodyguard" plans.

Trying not to grin too widely at that thought, I reach for the whole trilogy set held out by the blond middle-aged man in front of me, and Kayla puts her hand on the stack. "Excuse me, sir, but there is a one book policy."

"But I'm a huge fan," he says as he lifts a new copy of Blindside off the stack and sets it down for me to sign too.

Kayla purses her lips and pushes the stack back to him. "Choose one, please."

When he sighs and hands me the first book, I give an apologetic smile. "Who should I make it out to?"

"Kenneth McAdams," he says, holding my gaze.

I smile, and when I turn to the front page, he slides the other two books forward once more. "I really am your biggest fan. Would you mind, please?"

Just as I nod and reach for the two books in front of me, Kayla turns from talking to the reader behind him. "Excuse me, sir. I just told you—"

"She said it's fine," he says in a tense tone as he starts to reach in his jacket's inside pocket.

Sebastian's on him in a flash, clamping a restraining hand on his shoulder. "I think it's time for you to move on."

While the women gasp excitedly, the man pulls out a pen, disappointment spreading across his face. "But I'm here. Why can't she just—"

"It's fine. I'll sign his books," I say to Sebastian in a calm tone, holding my hand out for the man's pen.

Sebastian grunts, then releases him, moving back in to position beside me.

Once I've signed his books, the man collects the stack and beams. "I've always wanted to be a writer, but I just don't have the patience to stick with it. I read Blindside as soon as the eBook released. I think it's your best work yet."

I grin my appreciation. "Thank you, Kenneth. I'm thrilled you enjoyed it."

He starts to say something else, but a short lady in a knit cap and a calf-length down parka clears her throat and says in a raspy voice, "I'm burning up in here. Can you please move along?"

After he walks over to the register, the parka lady slides

her Blindside book forward at the same time she hands her camera to Kayla. "I'd like a picture of Miss Lone with Mr. White, please."

Before I can suggest that she stand in the picture with us, Sebastian clasps my free hand and pulls me to my feet, then nods to Kayla. "We're ready when you are."

While Kayla asks the lady about adjusting the zoom, I glance at him and grumble, "You're enjoying this entirely too much."

His lips curl in a ruthless smile and he says just low enough for my ears, "I think it's hilarious that Junior disclosing our past to get that damned addendum added to the contract had to be what gave William this marketing idea." Bright blue eyes dancing with merciless triumph, Sebastian pulls me against his side. "Smile for the camera, Miss Lone."

I adjust the ribbon tie on my black wraparound sweater, making sure the red bow lays flat on my hip. Smoothing my knee-length black skirt underneath my rear, I take a seat beside Jared at Midtown Central's senior staff table. Dressed more casually for this evening's Christmas party, William steps behind the podium at the front of Regent's Imperial ballroom to the applause of his employees.

Once their applause slows, William grins and begins speaking. "It has been a fantastic year at Midtown Central Publishing and I'm happy you're here to celebrate our successes during this holiday party."

"You really don't have a clue who might've leaked the

information about the threatening letters?" I whisper to Jared, trying to draw him out. He's been unusually quiet ever since he met me at the ballroom doorway. It's nice to see him without a tie for once. He looks more relaxed dressed in black slacks and a light blue V-neck sweater. His choice makes me glad I toned down the fitted strappy black dress Cass had packed for me with the crossover sweater. At least I have an excuse to wear my new red heels. With a small red bow at my hip the only color to my black outfit, the shoes add just enough Christmas pop to tie it all together.

Jared doesn't take his eyes off his father as he shakes his head. "No clue. My father questioned everyone that knew anything about it, but no one's admitting anything." Turning to me, he clasps my hand resting on the table. "It's going to be okay. We'll work out the security thing."

I furrow my brow. "I'm not worried about security. My bodyguard is more than capable. I'm just curious why someone would tell the media about the letters."

Tension brackets around his mouth. "I don't think it's in your best interest to have a bodyguard who knows you personally."

"Is this about your father's announcement at the book signing today?" When he doesn't answer, I shake my head, annoyed. Kayla must've told him. "I don't want you to dismiss Sebastian for such a silly reason."

His eyebrows pull down. "So it's Sebastian now?"

I roll my eyes. "There's no point in calling him Mr. Black when I know the guy."

"Which leaves me wondering why you didn't mention that fact on the day we hired him."

I shrug. "He's a professional. I didn't want our knowing each other to impact your decision after the fact." It's on the tip of my tongue to say something about the addendum being proof I was right to stay quiet, but when his green gaze narrows slightly, I realize we really need to have that discussion. "Jared, we need to talk about—"

He holds his hand up. "You have to hear this part."

Other than myself, only two other authors are at this party tonight, so I turn my focus to William.

"We're very proud of all our authors' accomplishments, so right now I'd like to recognize the editors who've had an especially fantastic year."

I listen while he rattles off the plethora of acquisitions each editor has accumulated as well as the many awards their authors' books have won and list rankings they've reached. My stomach starts to knot when I realize that I've been so anxious about the threats and book tour this week that I haven't thought at all about how well my book's sales have done. Normally I'm checking my on-line rankings daily or bugging my agent for my numbers. Just goes to show how idle minds really can get all worked up. From now on, during a release week I'm going to make sure I'm too busy doing something else to worry about rankings, sales, and hitting lists.

William saying my penname jerks me out of my thoughts. My editor is clapping, a huge smile on his face. "Congratulations on hitting the New York Times at number seven and the USA Today at nineteen, Miss Lone. I'm looking forward to many more from you."

Blindside hit the lists? Why didn't my agent tell me? I blink in shock, my cheeks flushing with heat. Every single person is looking at me. Smiling, I gesture toward William. Once the applause and attention moves away from me and back to him, I finally allow myself to breathe.

At the same time I exhale a calming breath, Jared's hand squeezes my bare knee just below my dress' hem, pulling my gaze to his. "Congratulations, Natalia. I asked your agent not to spoil the surprise tonight. We knew this book was special, and I'm glad everyone else has seen what my father and I did in it."

Just as I clasp Jared's hand to remove it from my knee, he surprises me further by snapping a half-inch wide, diamond cut bangle bracelet closed around my wrist. Untying the festive silver-threaded red bow, he slides the ribbon off the white gold bracelet, smiling. "This is your Merry Christmas slash 'Congratulations on Hitting the Lists' gift from me."

"Thank you for the thoughtful gift, Jared." The bangle shifts against the table when I move his hand from my knee and set our hands on the table next to my clutch purse. Releasing him, I say, "It's a lovely gift, but it's too much." I haven't had a chance to talk to him about that kiss. And now this? Is Sebastian's presence making him move so fast? As I try to unsnap the stubborn locking mechanism on the bracelet, I continue, "I consider you a colleague and it just doesn't seem appropriate—"

He covers his hand over mine and shakes his head. "Please accept my gift, Natalia. I'm willing to wait until the end of the tour to have dinner with you, but I saw the bracelet and couldn't resist. I've never seen you wear one before, which is a shame…" He traces his thumb across the fine bones on my wrist. "You have such beautiful wrists, I wanted to decorate one."

Well, shit this just escalated. How do I let him down easy without ruining my working relationship with him? Just as William ends his speech and applause erupts around us, the table vibrates under my purse. Untangling my hand from Jared's, I murmur, "Sorry, I need to get this."

Pauline Grayson: Congrats on hitting the lists, lady! I'm so excited for you. Hope you have fun celebrating tonight. I've sent your gift to your apartment. Be sure and save me a signed copy with Aaron White's signature. He is one fine bodyguard!

"It's from my agent," I say to Jared as people begin to disperse from the tables to mingle and chat with others.

When he smiles and takes a sip of his scotch, I type her a message. Just as I hit send, another message comes through.

PainInMyAss: Hallway. Now.

I look to where Sebastian was standing earlier, but he's already by the doorway waiting for me.

Does he have new information about the stalker?

Putting my phone away, I stand. "I'm going to the ladies' room before it gets too crowded."

Jared quickly follows suit. "I'll escort you."

"Go mingle." I wave him on. "I'll be right back."

Sebastian follows me through the ballroom's main door. As soon as we're in the hallway, he clasps my elbow, his tone curt. "We need to talk."

"Have you found out who's stalking me?"

He doesn't answer, but tugs me to the nearest door before escorting me inside.

"What is it with you and closets?" I say as he sets his lighted phone on an old speaker. Apparently this closet is a catch-all. Beyond the Valentines, Halloween, and Thanksgiving decorations stuffed against the back wall, it's obvious by the clothes' rods and empty hangers above our heads on either side of the narrow space, that it was used as a coat-check room at some point.

Sebastian takes my purse and sets it on the speaker. Lifting my wrist up between us, his gaze lasers in on the bracelet. "You won't wear what I gave you, but you'll wear this?"

Earlier when he met me in the hall to escort me to the event, he commented that I should've worn my necklace. Even though he was right that the gorgeous single pearl necklace would've gone well with my outfit, wearing it would send him the wrong signal, so I remained quiet and didn't rise to the bait.

But his sharp tone raises my defenses now. I tilt my chin up. "It's a congratulatory gift."

"Did you see any one else getting a bracelet?" he grates out, stepping closer.

His nearness is unnerving. I back up to put space between us. "Not that it's any of your business, but I tried to give it back. I don't want anyone to think Jared's playing favorites with me." Raising my wrist once more, I twist the bangle around and squint at the latch. "The release clasp seems to be stuck."

"Let me see it," he rumbles and grasps the bangle. When he pushes the release button and the bracelet doesn't pop open, his blue gaze snaps to mine. "It's locked on you like some kind of damned shackle."

Rolling my eyes, I pull away and try to unhook it once more. "I'm sure it's just stuck." Nothing budges.

Sebastian grunts and captures my hands just as I give up.

When he lifts my arms and sets my hands—one on top of the other on the rod a few inches above me—my voice pitches higher. "What are you doing?"

Curling my fingers on the back side of the cool metal pole, he folds his large hand on top of mine, locking me in place. "I'm reminding you what *us* feels like."

If he starts working his magic, I'm a goner. I should never have let him lead me in here in the first place. *Idiot.* Panic sets in and I try to tug free, but his hand only curls tighter around mine.

"Be still and listen." Pressing his other hand against the wall behind me, he leans in, his warm breath tickling my ear. "I saw that prick put his hand on your knee. No one touches you but me."

His steely tone slams my heart against my chest at a crazed pace. I need a good offense before his possessive dominance robs me of all common sense. "Right now there's a contract that says different," I remind him.

His head snaps up and a knowing smile tilts his lips.

"Actually, I'm following the letter of my contract. It's my job to protect you from outside threats."

"Threats *to* me or to your claim *on* me?" I counter, eyebrow raised.

His smile turns darkly savage. "I claimed you three years ago."

"And you think that gives you squatters' rights?"

When I snort, he bites out, "You're *mine*."

I hold his determined gaze, my heart leaping, daring to hope. "You can't say you want me, but then claim not to do relationships." I lay it out there, then hold my breath.

He scowls. "You're the one who didn't show up at that coffee shop."

"Actually, I did. I came to bring you the watch. You'd helped me in the past. I wanted to return the favor, but then I overheard you on the phone. You were leaving, so I left and gave it to Mina instead."

His gaze searches mine, surprise lurking in the blue depths. "You came?"

I nod and let the tension ease out of my words. "You were there when I needed you. I'll always be here for you if you need me, Sebastian."

"I don't want to be your obligation." His jaw tightens. "I want to be your fucking obsession."

You've dominated my thoughts since I was thirteen. I'd say that's pretty damn obsessed! I want to scream at him. Obsession is *not* love, nor does it imply commitment, so why should I expose my heart for him to toy with?

I don't get a chance to say anything as his furious tone turns brutal yet silky. "But I'll take *obligation* for now." He steps close and his words vibrate in a sensual bass along my temple. "I need you."

The yearning in his declaration clenches my insides. God, I crave his touch too, but I tilt my head back. "Not like that."

His brows pull down. "Why not?"

"Because the word 'relationship' isn't in your vocabulary."

He shakes his head, frustration in his gaze. "I'll always tell you the truth. I'm *incapable* of being more for you. I'm broken and will never be whole again."

What happened to make him feel like this? Whoever said, "the truth hurts" wasn't fucking kidding. I swallow back disappointment and grumble, "Like I'm a poster child for the perfect upbringing."

His gaze holds mine, full of self-deprecating awareness. "I've destroyed every relationship I've ever had. I won't let that be an option for us, because I *will* fuck it up. There's a difference."

I press my lips together. "Not to me there isn't."

His jaw muscle twitches. "So you're just going to walk away. You can turn us off that easily?" he asks as he clasps the inside of my thigh.

I bite my cheek, using the pain to distract me from the seductive warmth of his touch as my skirt lifts with the slide of his hand up my thigh. Jerking my chin up, I tug to free my hands from his vise grip, but can't bring myself to twist my hips away. While conflict rages between my head and heart, blood seeps onto my tongue as I hold his gaze with a steady one. "Yes."

His eyes narrow. "Liar. And since you refuse to speak the truth, why don't you let your body say it for you?"

My pulse thrums as he slowly turns his hand and traces his thumb down my silky underwear, spearing through the bit of hair. When his thumb hits my clit, I can't hold back the gasp. He presses down, his tone cocky and assured. "Go ahead. Pull away from me. Show me that you don't want me to make you come. If you can do that, then I'll walk out of this closet and we'll never discuss this again."

When I slit my gaze on him, but hold myself still, he gives a dark smile and presses deeper, driving me to the edge of my sanity. "Tell me that you're not aching for me to take you."

No matter how hard I try, I can't stop myself from wanting the bliss he's offering. The woodsy notes of his cologne wrap around me, drawing me in, heightening my senses. My body craves the sensation of his hard frame pressing against mine. I miss that so much. The second I realize I'm reacting and my hips have started to roll, I stiffen and hold myself still. I grind my teeth and resist my need for arousing friction. Closing my eyes, I lower my head so he doesn't hear my shallow breathing. *Keep it together, Talia.*

"If I move…" His voice is next to my ear now, his breath sensually inviting, warming my skin. "Will you shatter for me? Nothing is more beautiful then seeing you come apart under my touch. Show me that you feel as intensely as I do, damn it!"

I whimper and my arms shake while I try to remain perfectly still and not let my hips rock the way they want to.

Sebastian rolls his thumb over my clit twice more

before he pulls my underwear to the side and flattens his fingers against my sex. "For someone who doesn't want, you're pretty fucking wet, Little Red."

When he pulls away, I jerk my head up, ready to blast him for his smug arrogance, but I'm struck speechless by the look of pure pleasure on his face. Eyes closed, his cheeks are hollowed as he sucks his two fingers clean.

Releasing a low groan, Sebastian's brilliant blue eyes snap open at the same time he pulls sopping fingers from his mouth. I barely have a chance to wonder why they're so wet as he quickly slides them deep inside me.

I gasp at the pleasurable invasion, and my walls instinctively clamp around his fingers as my hips start to move on their own. With a primal grunt, he yanks his fingers forward, pulling me up on my toes and fully against his body. Holding me still, he bends close until we're nose-to-nose, his tone possessively fierce. "I want to pee a goddamn circle around you so it's clear to everyone that you're mine, but at least you'll be walking out of here with a part of me in you." Moving his lips to my ear, his voice drops to a rougher husk. "Next time, I'm staking my claim so *no one* questions it."

He releases my hands at the same time he pulls his fingers from me, merciless determination on his face.

Furious that I can't control my physical responses around him, I ignore the edgy tension in his stance and shove him back. "That was just shitty. There won't be a next time."

"What's shitty is you denying us both what we obviously want. Don't let him touch you any more."

"Fuck you!" I grab the doorknob, my hand shaking as

I try to ignore the sexual frustration vibrating through me. "Talia."

His tone is calmer. I turn back, hoping he's going to apologize, since he's not calling me Natalia.

Arms folded, challenge flickers in his eyes. "Any time you're ready."

CHAPTER TEN

Talia

Music is playing by the time I walk into the ballroom. When Jared looks up from chatting with a group across the room and sees me setting my purse on the table, his eyes light up. I barely have a chance to see that Cass has sent me a text in response to the rambling "I want to kill my body guard" text I'd sent her on my way back to the ballroom, before Jared's by my side, holding out his hand. "Come dance with me."

I let him tug me to the dance floor, partly because I need a distraction and partly because I'm so ticked at Sebastian for trying to dictate who I spend my time with. He says that sex is all he has to offer, but no matter how freaking fantastic I know the sex is between us, I have to stay away from him.

Jared and I dance in the crowd for an hour to all the

latest pop songs with some Christmas songs mixed in. Apparently the Midtown Central group is fun and boisterous when an open bar and music is added to the mix. At least a hundred people are out on the dance floor enjoying themselves.

For most of the hour we dance in big groups, and I smile at Kayla when I see her dancing a bit closer to Jared. I can't help but wonder why he hasn't gone for her. When she lifts her brown eyes up to him and I see the adoration he seems oblivious to, I think I understand why. She doesn't represent a challenge. I glance around and watch the single guys in the firm doing their best to break through the group of ladies dancing together in the middle.

With all of humanity's progress, men are still hunters, even when it comes to women. What's the fun in hunting the prey if it'll lie down and offer up its neck in two seconds flat?

My gaze swings back to Jared when he grabs my hand and quickly twirls me around, singing the song's lyrics to "All I Want for Christmas is You".

What he lacks in singing skills, he makes up for it in his enthusiasm, so I grin and let him spin me. Twirling me once more, he tugs me close and stops singing. "Do you know why I keep asking you to dinner?"

I nod. "Because I haven't said 'yes.'"

Laughing, he clasps my waist and spins us in a circle, his gaze sliding appreciatively over my face. "No, it's because you're beautiful, intelligent, talented, and have so much potential."

His compliment spreads warmth across my cheeks, but as he folds his arm around me and starts to tug my body against his, the pleasant sensation of being held by him doesn't hold any of the heat that zings all the way to my core when Sebastian just looks at me.

And then it suddenly hits me what Sebastian meant by his "you'll walk around with a part of me in you" comment. His spit-soaked fingers had been his primal way of not just marking me, but also showing me what he really wanted to do to me in that closet.

An unbidden memory of his hard body pressing against me as his erection slides deep inside me sends heat shooting across my cheeks. I instantly push against Jared's chest, needing space. *Damn that infuriating man!* "I um... it's hot in here. I need to get some water."

"Sure, let's get you something." When Jared grins, then clasps my hand and starts to pull me through the crowd, I belatedly realize he thinks my comment was about him.

I quickly follow behind him, but then twist my hand free of his, saying, "Speaking of dinner, I've been meaning to talk to you."

He stops on the edge of the dance floor and turns to clasp my shoulders. "You said you wanted to wait until the tour is over. I'm respecting that."

I shake my head. "No, you don't understand. I think it's best if we remain colleagues. I don't want to lose our great working relationship."

Frustration flickers across his face briefly, then he smiles. "A tour like this is always stressful. Add in the threatening letters and I'm sure it has you on edge."

"But—"

His fingers flex against me and he shakes his head. "We'll talk about it next week when things have settled down." Turning, he heads for the bar, leaving me little choice but to drop the discussion for now.

A little later, William approaches Jared and me while we're sipping on drinks. "Congratulations, young lady. You're a rising star."

I set my empty glass on the table and start to shake his hand, but he laughs and tugs me into a hug. "We're family here at Midtown Central." Pulling back, he drops an arm across my shoulders. "I can't wait to see what you come up with next."

I grin up at him. "I've got a few ideas."

"Then have Pauline send them on so we can discuss." Shifting his gaze to his son, he continues, "I'm going to have to steal Jared away for a bit."

"That's fine. I need to call it a night since I have an early day tomorrow." I glance Jared's way. "How about breakfast in the morning?" I really can't delay settling things between us any longer. The bracelet pretty much pushed the issue.

Jared's light brown eyebrows elevate. "Don't you have something at ten?"

"I do, but we can meet at eight in the hotel restaurant."

"A meal with my favorite author? How can I refuse? Kayla has my phone." He glances around the crowded room looking for her. "Once I get it back, I'll make sure I don't have an early meeting and text you."

Nodding, I shoo the Mackens men on. "Go talk business."

I check the text from Cass before I head out of the ballroom.

Cass: Wow, I really need me a Mr. Black. He sounds deliciously raw.

I quickly send her a response back.

Me: That's all I get? No thoughts? Advice? I don't think I'll have to worry about the stalker anymore, this man just might be the end of me. He's so controlled and yet he plays me like some kind of sex virtuoso.

Cass: Remind me again why this is a BAD thing?

Me: He's made it clear he just wants sex. He says he's not capable of a relationship.

Cass: That's a load of crap. The one thing you have going for you is that he wants you. Use that to your advantage. Make him want you MORE so he loses control.

Me: I can't do that. I just told him there won't BE a next time.

Cass: If you want him, then put on your big girl panties and show him he's not the only one with seduction skills. Let your inner-slut free, then leave him hanging. Later…if you decide to go for it, all that sex time together might be what makes him rethink his "no relationship" rule."

Me: Not sure if I can handle that.

Cass: It sounds like he's worth the risk. Broken

hearts mend. Regrets fester; make sure you don't have any.

Me: Ugh.

Cass: Keep me updated. *noms the popcorn*

Me: Right now he's probably pissed at me since I danced with Jared.

Cass: Ooh, you do like playing with fire, don't you, girl.

Me: He ticked me off.

Cass: *noms more popcorn*

Me: And this ends your soap opera fix for the day.

Cass: *pouts*

I'm thankful for the short elderly couple who get on the elevator at the same time Sebastian and I do. My heart sinks when the husband hits the button for the second floor. Sebastian's steely gaze holds mine across the tops of their silver hair. I don't miss that they're whispering to each other and snickering like a couple of teens. Any other time I would've thought it was sweet. Right now it just points out how far away Sebastian and I are, and I don't just mean because we're standing on opposite sides of the elevator.

When the couple shuffles off the elevator and the doors slide closed once more, for once the absence of the Christmas music floating through the speakers is noticeable in the thick silence.

"You openly defied me."

Sebastian's voice is rough and tight, the low bass vibrating through me.

I hold his gaze and refuse to let his intensity get to me. "What are you going to do? Spank me?"

His nostrils flare and his hand clenches. "Are you trying to set me off, 'cause it's fucking working," he grates out. "You're two steps away from needing that safe word."

All I can think about is him thrusting his fingers deep inside me, then hauling me against him with just that intimate hold. God, the man's so primal. Chill bumps spread across my skin, but I keep my expression neutral. "You deliberately left me hanging." I shrug and lift my chin. "I guess that makes us even."

His stare turns icy. "I left you wanting what I'm willing to give. You gave him what I fucking *want*."

His ferocity surprises me. "Dancing isn't sex."

"Depends on who's dancing."

The sudden heat in his gaze reminds me of the look in the men's eyes as they watched the girls dancing at the Sly Fox club. Their gazes were full of lust and lascivious thoughts. Okay, so he has a point. Dancing can be sexual. "Dancing isn't *having* sex," I clarify.

His jaw tightens. "Care to place a wager on that?"

I mentally snicker. He's so going to crash and burn on this one. "Are you saying you want me to dance with you?"

Striking blue eyes travel up my body, sliding along my curves, lingering on my neck before locking on my face, full of possessive intent. "If that's what you want to call it."

Cass' plea for me to let go of my inner-slut gives me the perfect idea. "I'll give you one *dance*." When he takes a step toward me, victory written on his face, I hold my hand up. "On my terms."

His dark eyebrows pull down. "Equal terms."

The elevator pings, letting us know we've reached the floor. I straighten my spine, then step off the elevator. "One term each."

"Three," he counters, walking briskly beside me.

Unlocking my door, I glance his way. "Fine. Mine will be non-negotiable."

He flashes a dangerous smile. "That's the only way I operate."

Once Sebastian shuts my door and we're alone in my room, I almost lose my nerve. My stomach is fluttering like crazy, twisting into knots, but I force myself to buck up. When Sebastian steps close to me once more, I point to the straight back chair by the desk. "Have a seat."

He looks like he's about to say something, but I shake my head. "My term."

I watch him shrug out of his suit jacket, then loosen his tie and unbutton his collar before he pulls the chair closer and sits in it facing me.

The heat of Sebastian's piercing gaze follows my every move as I retrieve my phone from my purse, and then riffle through my suitcase looking for the extra long charging cord. My skin prickles from the intensity of his stare. To distract myself, I say in a conversational tone, "I learned a lot while I worked undercover at the Sly Fox club."

Out of the corner of my eye, I see Sebastian sit a little

straighter. I turn away for a second so he doesn't see me smile. "Did you read the article I wrote about it?" I ask, glancing at him.

He nods. "I did. I was very proud of you when I saw it in the paper. Your story balanced the business investigation with the human aspects as they related to trafficking very well. It's what you said you wanted to do. Help people. That was some excellent undercover work."

I didn't expect such a thorough evaluation from him, but his words wash over me like an invigorating shower. It feels good to be appreciated. He'd just said more to me about my contribution to that article than my own editor did. After the first week, my boss, Stan, complained, constantly asking how much longer my investigation would take. I thought gathering all the information that I did, then having the follow-up interviews with the authorities after they raided the place—all within three weeks time—was pretty damn good.

"Thank you," I say quietly. Fiddling nervously with the cord, I hold Sebastian's gaze as he nods. I want so badly to ask him what he's been doing the last six months, but I'm pretty sure that probably involved more than one woman I don't want to know about, so I keep my question professional as I plug the charger into the wall. "Have you expanded your security business any more?"

He watches me, his attention unwavering. "I want to bring Calder into the business, but I have to find him first."

I glance up while I set the phone on the end of the bed. "I thought you and Calder were like brothers. Why don't you know where he is?"

Sebastian rubs the evening beard on his jawline, his

expression darkening. "Cald didn't handle his dad's death well. After Jack died, he threw himself into mission after mission, never taking a break. I heard he left the Navy six months ago, but he hasn't returned home. His father's house just sits there, unoccupied."

The grooves around Sebastian's mouth show his worry about his cousin. "He'll come home when he's ready," I tell him. "He still has family here who cares about him."

Sebastian lifts his shoulders, but doesn't say anything else. He obviously doesn't want to talk about it, so I scroll through the songs on my phone and cue one up.

Holding his gaze, I untie the crossover sweater, then lay it on my bed next to the phone. "The deal was one dance, so you're going to benefit from my time at the Sly Fox." As a sexy grin spreads across his face, I shake my head. "This will be a traditional lap dance. My term: no touching."

When he grunts his disapproval, I *tsk*. "We can't have you breaking the terms of your contract, now can we?"

His eyes narrow and a smile curves his lips. "My term: Come here."

I'm immediately suspicious. "No touching," I remind him.

He pulls at his tie, unraveling the knot. "I won't touch you." As I step in front of him, he adds, "Unless you ask me to."

If he touches me, all bets are off. I'm surprised he's taking my lap dance offer so well considering he thought he'd be wrapping his arms around me the second we walked into my room.

"Give me your wrists," he orders quietly.

I glance at the tie lying loosely in his hands and lift my wrists toward him. "That will make it harder for me to dance."

As he wraps the cloth around my wrists, he pauses, his lips thinning to a straight line. Looping the tie just behind the bangle on my wrist, he says in a low tone while he binds my wrists together. "I would never give you a bracelet like that."

The fluttering in my stomach from the sensation of his fingers lightly brushing against my skin ceases. "Why?"

He concentrates on my hands while he spins the tie around and then knots it under my wrists. "Because whatever gift I give you, I'd want you to be able to wear all the time. You're a writer and on your laptop constantly. A clunky bracelet would get in the way." Draping the trailing ends of his tie over my hands like he's tying a bow on a cherished present, he lifts his gaze to mine. "Congratulations on hitting the New York Times. I had no doubt you'd get there."

With just a few simple words, he shreds my heart. How can he pay attention to the smallest things concerning me but not want more for us? It's baffling and heartbreaking and so damn frustrating I want to shake him, then throw myself into his arms. Instead, I say softly, "Thank you," while determination gathers in my chest in a rising wave, giving me the nerve to go through with this dance. I have to find a way to break past his tightly held control.

Picking up my phone, I start to click on a specific song that Yvonne, a dancer at the Sly Fox, used to teach me her moves, but Sebastian shakes his head. "If I just get one dance, I choose the song."

I might not plan on having sex, but I'm sure going to enjoy making Sebastian wish he *was* having it. When I start to refuse, he says. "My term. Phone's in my jacket."

I blow out a breath and retrieve his phone, then raise my eyebrow and wait for him to tell me the title.

"Scroll to your name in my contacts."

Heart thumping, I start scrolling. My excitement sinks as I pass dozens of female names. More than I want to count. More than I want to know about. By the time I reach my name, my jaw is clenched so tight I almost don't click on it, but then curiosity has me tapping on Talia. In the notes, Sebastian had typed one phrase, *Closer:NIN.*

Holy Shit! My gaze jerks to his, pulse spiking. The Nine Inch Nails song might be twenty years old, but it's still one of the rawest primal sex songs to date.

"Play it, Talia," he commands, his gaze smoldering with intensity. "And dance for me."

CHAPTER ELEVEN

Talia

*S*ebastian may have tied my hands, but I'm going to use what he likes seeing most—the idea of me bound and under his control—to drive him insane with want. When the music starts and the heavy, sensual beat begins to thump through me, I quickly set the toe of my right shoe on the seat between Sebastian's thighs to throw him off. To his credit, he doesn't flinch, but instead his dark eyebrow elevates in appreciation.

Emboldened by the heat in his gaze, I trace my bound hands sensually over my knee and along my inner thigh, sliding my skirt halfway up.

As the music's first few lyrics slide out of the speakers like a raw, erotic whisper vibrating along my skin, my breathing ramps and I take a step back, offering Sebastian the full view of the long lines the sexy heels give my legs.

Resting my bound wrists against my right hip, I begin to move my pelvis in a seductive sexual roll.

The left corner of Sebastian's mouth quirks. His thoughts are written all over his face; *I want to fuck you. Primal and hard. Come closer and let me show you.*

Thankful I wore my hair down, I look over my shoulder through the red curtain as I pivot in a slow, undulating circle, moving my hips and body to the arousing bass.

Once my back is to him, I grasp the trailing ends of his tie in my hand and snap it against the outside of my upper thigh.

When Sebastian's nostrils flare and his hands clamp onto his thighs, I mentally celebrate the feeling of triumph that rushes across my skin, flushing my cheeks with warmth. It makes me brave and I move closer. Swaying my hips in moves worthy of a belly dancer, I gyrate my ass just over his thighs.

My stomach flutters with arousing desire as he unclenches his fingers and rests them, palms up just under my rear. A beat, then he's quickly gripping the chair under him. He wants so badly to touch me; I mentally cheer that I'm working this lap dance routine like a pro.

Holding this position isn't easy, considering I'm only using stomach and thigh muscles, so I quickly stand between his thighs and face him. While the song's build up is spiraling, I raise my bound wrists above my head, throw my head back, and writhe and roll my hips like I'm in the full throes of the best orgasm of my life. Smiling at his half-mast gaze and the obvious bulge in his pants, I begin to dance around his chair. Brushing my hip along his shoulder, I bend close and let my hair tickle the back of his neck.

Once I make my way around to his right side, my mind parses out the song's mental segues from its physical descriptions. Music can be interpreted many ways, and as the lyrics overlay sinful thoughts and actions, other emotions come racing through: despair, self-loathing, desire, yearning, need, and hopeful acceptance. Realization pulls at my heart, shifting my goal from sexually arousing Sebastian to learning if he attributes any of those emotions to himself and us.

Just as the music ends, I lower my arms and meet his gaze, asking quietly, "Why do you want me?" The music starts up again, and the fact it's on a repeat loop makes me even more desperate to know his answer. "Why, Sebastian?"

He gestures to his lap, his tone low and on edge. "Sit." When I start to lower my butt cheek to his right thigh, he shakes his head. "My term. Sit in front, facing me."

Doing so will put me squarely in his intimate space, but I need to know. My own emotions clogging my throat, I stand and rest my bound hands on his shoulder for balance, then slide my right foot across his lap. Sebastian closes his eyes and releases a low groan as my body slides down his until I'm straddling his thighs.

The sensual beat of the song thumps in the background, and when Sebastian opens his eyes, I try not to react to the lust turning the bright blue a turquoise shade. To his credit he hasn't touched me. I'm impressed that he's honoring his word by holding onto the bottom of the chair.

"The song is still going, which means you should be dancing," he says in a matter-of-fact tone.

"I'm on your lap," I huff and pretend I can't feel the heat of him just a couple inches from me.

He leans close and speaks next to my ear, his husky voice igniting every nerve ending. "If you want me to answer, put your arms around my neck and dance."

Moving my body with my legs spread across his muscular thighs is near impossible without holding onto him, so I sigh and lower my bound wrists over his head. As I begin to slowly roll my hips to the song, Sebastian takes advantage of my binding preventing me from pulling back and slides his nose up my neck. Inhaling near my jaw, he quietly says, "Take your shoes off."

I'm thrown by his request, but fine with shucking my shoes. Doing so gives me a chance to separate our bodies a bit.

The second I kick my heels off, Sebastian commands, "Tuck your legs behind you and hook your feet on my knees." When I hesitate, he smirks. "I know how limber you are."

I try not to pant as I do as he asks, but as soon as my second foot is hooked, I realize too late that this position thrusts my body forward and aligns my sex with his erection perfectly.

When I start to unhook my feet, he growls along my jaw. "My term. Stay put."

"That's your third," I exhale in a whisper just as he lowers his nose to my cleavage and breathes me in, rumbling his approval.

"Why have you stopped dancing?" He says in a casual tone as he begins to move his hips in a slow, arousing rock.

His action slides his erection with jaw-grinding

pressure along my sex. "I—I can't dance like this," I say, my voice suddenly raspy with want.

"Yes, you can. Move your hips with mine."

I realize I'm not even trying. My body is moving on its own, a counter to his gyrations.

"Fuck, you feel good."

His voice is gravelly with desire, and the sheer heat of his body and muscular hardness under my legs and along my sex is making it very hard to focus. "Tell me, Sebastian," I remind him. My voice is barely a whisper. I'm trying so hard to keep my composure, while his movements turn more aggressive. Each time he moves, he's hitting my clit just enough to make my insides feel barren and empty, aching to be filled.

His lips graze my ear. "Should I tell you all the flowery things women want to hear?"

Ironically, in the background, the singer is explicitly saying what he wants to do to the girl…and I want that too. I want Sebastian raw and at his dirtiest. "No, that's not you."

He exhales a harsh snort. "Damn straight. Look at me, Talia."

When I meet his gaze, he holds mine with magnetic intensity. "Animalistic doesn't begin to describe the many ways I want to take your sweet body. I want to possess every part of you. My mouth waters at the thought of licking you raw, then making you wet for me all over again. I can't stop thinking about the feel of you under me, your pussy dripping with want while you beg me to let you come."

He still hasn't told me why. Is this his reason, pure sex?

"Tell me to touch you," he commands as he slowly begins to move to the music again, his movements grinding into me, showing me what he wants.

Did I read so much more into that song than he meant?

My body clenches at his sexual stimuli and even as my hips move instinctively with him, my body absorbing his arousing friction against my center, I shake my head. "No touching."

His jaw sets and he quickly reaches behind him, yanking down on the tie dangling from my wrists. I'm instantly pulled forward, my chest crashing against his hard one. "What the fuck is this then?" he growls, grinding his cock aggressively against me.

I gasp and close my eyes as my body clenches in stimulated response. *Shit, if he keeps this up I won't last.* My mind is yelling for me to tell him to stop, but my body is clamping my mouth closed, keeping me from speaking. It feels so good being pressed against him like this, his warmth and smell spreading through me with each breath I take.

"Do you really think a contract covers us?" he grates, lifting his pelvis off the chair. His hard abs ripple against me, and his next movement presses his cock just inside my entrance. Only his clothes and my underwear are separating our mutual desire to connect in the way we both desperately want. The tease nearly sends me over, making it hard for me to think past my own cravings. "Sebastian, we can't—"

"What we have is indefinable; it can't be bound by words on a fucking page," he says as he grasps my hips and stands.

Taking the few steps to the bed, he ducks his head out of my arms and drops me onto the mattress. He's on his knees and sliding my dress up my thighs on my first bounce. Yanking me to the end of the bed, he shreds my underwear in one sharp tug and before I can move, his mouth is pressed against my wet entrance, his tongue thrusting inside me.

I scream out and arch against the bed; the feel of his hands spreading my thighs wide, his hot mouth devouring me, is an arousing jolt to the electric need zinging through my body. He's never gone down on me like a starving man before. He's always controlled the pace, teasing me until I'm begging for it.

I'm shocked by his aggressive savageness, but also so turned on all I can do is let him pillage me, his lips tugging and teasing mercilessly while his tongue flicks and sucks every sensitive crevice. As he groans his approval, he doesn't leave a part of me unplundered, and my body reacts to his thorough possession, flooding with the desire to be taken. I dig my fingers into his thick black hair, not to push him away, but to yank him closer.

"You taste like the fruit you ate earlier," he murmurs against me. It's a lover's comment, one of a man who pays attention. "I'm going to lap up every last ounce from your pussy tonight," he growls, his fingers gripping my ass and tilting me to give him better access.

Chill bumps scatter across my skin. I'm connected to him at this moment. Every suckle, nibble, and lick sends shivers racing through me, shooting my pulse to the stratosphere. When he rumbles a primal sound, then lifts my leg over his shoulder so he can burrow closer, I moan and whimper. Letting my arms fall to the bed, I surrender fully to his mouth, rocking against him, pressing as close as I can get.

This is the Sebastian I want—out of control and ravenous.

He swallows, his deep voice vibrating against me in a rough rasp. "I can't get enough of your taste. It's making me so hard I could pound a hole through a brick wall." He glances up at me, his eyes pinning me to the bed as effectively as if he laid his body over mine. "When you come, I want you to give me all you've got. I want to fucking drown in you."

This time he dips his head and sucks my clit deep into his hot mouth. I gasp and tremble as my passion builds. My hips follow the rhythm of his mouth's unrelenting intensity, and my walls clench, yearning to be stretched and filled with his hard heat. As my mind conjures the memory of his thick cock thrusting deep inside me, his muscular body pressing my smaller one to the bed, shudders roll through me, and my breathing hitches. My orgasm rips through me in a storm of erotic, all-consuming shudders. While the sensory explosion shoots from my core to my heart, his name rushes past my lips over and over in a reverent chant.

The pressure of his mouth eases and he slides his tongue in slower, leisurely swipes along my sex as if the act alone is pleasurable to him. Tracing a sensuous path up and over my throbbing clit, his arresting eyes reflects smug arrogance mixed with simmering want as he presses a tender kiss to the tiny patch of hair between my thighs. Just as he puts his knee on the bed between my legs and leans over me, a light knock sounds at the door. "Natalia. Are you still up?"

Shit. It's Jared.

Fury floods Sebastian's features and he says in a menacing tone, "Get rid of him."

Heart racing anew, I quickly shove my bound hands against his chest and whisper, "Untie me and go to your room."

Standing, he folds his arms, his face set in determined lines, voice low. "I prefer to stay."

"Do you want to get fired?" I whisper as I quickly stand and wiggle my wrists free of his tie on my own. Glaring at him for not helping, I push his tie against his chest while tugging my dress back down with my free hand. "Please go, Sebastian."

A knocks sounds again. "Natalia?"

Sebastian takes his tie, but he doesn't move to leave. When I notice the muscle ticking in his jaw, panic rises in my chest. I really don't want him to get fired. I don't want him to leave me and walk out of my life. I'll never be ready for that, but definitely not right now. I walk over and open the door that connects our rooms. "Let me talk to him first."

Grunting, he starts to walk through without his jacket, but I quickly grab it and shove it in his arms, then shut the door behind him.

"Just a sec, Jared," I say as I glance around the room for my underwear. *Where is it?* As I get on my knees and look under the bed, it occurs to me that Cass would be laughing her ass off right now while totally giving me hell about having one guy coming in the front door while shoving the other guy out the back way.

Blowing out a breath, I put the chair back, then walk over to the door and smooth my hair before grabbing the handle. "Hey, Jared. What's up?"

His gaze drops to my chest and a smile spreads across his face. "You should've just worn that tonight. Can I come in for a sec? I don't want to discuss this in the hall."

"I was getting ready to go to bed, but sure," I say, waving him in.

As we step into my room, my gaze instantly snaps to the rumpled end of my bed and the two cell phones lying on the corner of it. Heart racing, I stand so he has to put his back to the bed to face me. "What did you want to talk to me about?"

Smiling, he rocks on his heels. "I'm able to have breakfast with you tomorrow."

"Great. So eight in the restaurant downstairs?"

Once he nods, but doesn't say anything else, I tilt my head. "Is there something else you wanted to talk about?"

He nods and takes a step closer to push my hair over my shoulder. "You really are beautiful with your hair loose and a bit mussed."

"Um, thanks," I say, then clear my throat and take a step back. I need to have that talk with him now. This can't wait until tomorrow. "Jared, what I—"

"I want to discuss your security," he interrupts, his tone breezy, turning to business. "I'm going to change it, hire another firm."

I quickly shake my head. "No, I don't want you to. I'm comfortable with Sebastian."

His mouth tightens. "Well, I'm not. The way he watches

you makes me want to punch him."

I snort and fold my arms. "It's his *job* to watch me."

"Not like *he* does," he says briskly, his lips thinning. "The man looks at you like something he covets. Did you have a relationship with him in the past?"

I don't know what to call what Sebastian and I have, but I'm definitely not defining it for Jared. "My past relationships are private. I'm not discussing them with you. Just like I haven't asked you about yours."

"I would tell you if you asked," he says, his tone softening.

I rub my hands on my arms to erase the sudden chill and shake my head. "I can't do this, Jared."

Worry creases his brow. "What can't you do?"

"Us," I say, waving my hand between us. "I want my relationship with Midtown Central to be a long one. You've pretty much acted in editor capacity for me the past month, and one day you could be my editor. I think it's best not to go to dinner with you, except in a business capacity."

"So that's it?" he says, his tone sharper, eyes drilling into me.

I touch his sleeve. I'm sorry, Jared. I'm just not willing to jeopardize my career."

He puts his hand over mine and I'm surprised by the resolute look on his face. "You might be giving up, but I'm not."

"I think it's for the best to remain colleagues," I say, nodding.

Jared shakes his head. "You're still having breakfast with me." When I start to suggest we skip it, he continues,

"There are some things I want to go over about your agenda for the rest of the tour."

It's most likely stuff Kayla can easily convey, but I can tell Jared's feeling rejected so I just nod. "Okay. I really need to get some sleep now."

As he turns to walk to the door, his gaze strays to my bed. I'm not sure if he sees the two phones, but I pick up my pace anyway and open the door for him, saying in a light tone, "See you in the morning, bright and early."

After Jared steps outside my room, I'm relieved that he knows where I stand on us. I may as well make sure my past isn't going to be an issue. "Who told you about my past at the kick off party?"

He turns, eyebrows raised. "So it's true about the drugs then?"

I knew asking him meant he'd question me again. Squeezing the door handle, I let out a slow breath. "I didn't have a choice. I was thirteen. And no, I didn't take the drugs."

Sympathy in his gaze, he nods his understanding, then lifts his shoulders. "I have no idea, honestly. I was standing there in the crowd talking to Nathan and when I glanced down a note had been left on the plate in my hand. I asked Nathan why he didn't just tell me directly, but he was just as clueless about your past."

"It's not a part of my life I like to talk about," I say. "Goodnight, Jared."

"Thank you for trusting me enough to share," he says, smiling. "Night, Natalia."

Once he leaves, I sag against the door, frustrated that I still don't know who tried to ruin my career. Exhaling a sigh, I know I need to take Sebastian his phone, but just as I start to pick his cell up, my phone rings.

I'm surprised Mina's calling me so late, so I grab my phone and answer. "Hey, Mina. Is everything all right?"

She expels a light laugh. "Everything is great. I know you're used to me calling via video, but this time I'm hoping we can get together in person. I think we're way overdue. Would you be able to meet me for breakfast tomorrow morning?"

"I'm sorry, Mina. I just made breakfast plans—" I pause when I hear her dejected sigh. "But if you can meet me at the Regent at seven, we could have coffee in the restaurant. Would that work for you?"

"That'll be perfect," she says, perking up.

"Wonderful. And I hope you're bringing Josi. I can't wait to hold that sweet munchkin."

Mina laughs. "I don't go anywhere without her. She can't wait to meet you too."

I'm smiling when I hang up with Mina. I truly like Sebastian's little sister, and if she asks me over coffee tomorrow to be Josi's godmother, I'll be honored to accept.

My heart aches as I stare at the door separating Sebastian and me. I thought I could conjure my inner-slut, and then put her neatly back in the bottle—my feelings for Sebastian right along with her—but right now I feel raw and torn.

He makes me feel every spectrum of emotion. Yes, lust is high on that list, but he also makes me want so much more every time I'm with him. The ache in my chest hurts even more this time than when I left him sleeping in Martha's Vineyard. Obviously sex is all he wants from me. Well, it's all he's willing to give of himself at least. And I deserve more than that, because I would give the infuriating man the freaking moon if I thought he'd stick around.

As if Sebastian knows I'm thinking about him, my phone pings with a text.

> *PainInMyAss: Planning on returning my phone anytime soon?*

I frown at Sebastian's phone on the bed and type him a message.

> *Me: How are you texting me if your phone is right here?*

His phone silently vibrates on the bed a second later with my text.

> *PainInMyAss: Bring it to me and I'll tell you.*

Taking a steadying breath, I set my phone down and pick his up, then walk through the door between our rooms.

He's standing straight across from me in the dark room, leaning against the wall next to the window, his dress shirt unbuttoned and his hands tucked into his pants' pockets. I blink so my eyes adjust to the lack of light. "Why are you in the dark?"

"This feels normal to me."

It's said without humor or sarcasm. A simple statement of fact. It's true; the man lives in the shadows. I hold his phone up. "Per your request."

"Come here, Talia."

My heart thumps at his directive, but I can't stop myself from obeying. When I'm a foot away, he pulls another phone from his pants' pocket, then glances at the one in my hand. "It's cloned."

I frown even as I hand it to him. "Why have you cloned your own phone?"

"Security," he says, setting them both on the desk next to him. "If it's stolen, I can turn on the mic or camera to discover who the bastard is. If I lose it, I can remote erase the data. It's a fail safe."

I tilt my head and study him. His mood has shifted. I feel the tense vibe simmering off him. "Are you always so prepared?"

"Whenever I can be. Did you send him away?"

"Jared's gone if that's what you're asking."

"You know what I'm asking. He wants you. Did you tell him he can't fucking have you?"

"Why? Because someone else already does?" I snap, wanting to hit him upside the head. I spread my hands and glance around the room, sarcasm building. "I don't see anyone here claiming that role."

Sebastian pushes off the wall and gets right in my personal space. "I *claimed* you not less then fifteen minutes ago. The only word out of your mouth while you came was *my* name. You want me, but you're too damn stubborn to let yourself admit it. That penname you're hiding behind,

T.A. Lone…" He straightens and snorts. "I know 'A' isn't your middle initial. So does that name really represent Talia Alone, because I swear to God sometimes I think that's what you want is to be, *alone*."

His sharp words slice through me in a million tiny cuts, but I won't let him turn this around on me. "That's rich coming from a man who says he always fucks up every relationship he's ever had. Of the two of us, who do you think will be alone in the end?"

When he doesn't say anything, I turn to leave, but he grabs my hand and yanks me against him. As we fall back against the wall, I brace my free hand on his chest, ready to push away, but he cups the back of my neck, keeping me in place. "You asked me why I want you. I could say it's because you're intelligent, stubborn, and sexy as fuck." Tracing his thumb along the side of my neck, his gruff tone softens as his gaze scans my face. "But the simple truth is, I don't have a choice."

Of all the things he could've said to me, that hits my heart the hardest. I hold back the sob that threatens to erupt and feel the burn slide deep into my chest. *Why can't he let himself believe I'm worth having something real with?* I want to demand that he stop bullshitting me and tell me why, but I know the reason I haven't asked. I'm afraid his answer will tear me apart even more than not knowing, because hope for a future with Sebastian has always been what I've clung to. I was an idiot to think I could just have some fun tonight and not pay for it. Sebastian is my drug and I'm the addict. We can't keep doing this. His inability to try for something more between us will eventually shatter me.

"Then I'm making the choice for us. Jared is gunning for you. He wants to fire you and that's the last thing I want. Despite our inability to connect on a personal level, I think you and I make a good working team. I want you to remain as my security person."

Sebastian's hand clamps tighter on my neck. "We *connect* explosively on a personal level and you damn well know it."

His statement makes my stomach flip-flop, but I force myself to keep talking. "That's all I can offer, Sebastian." I know that if we have sex, my heart will hurt every time I look at him, because I'll know he won't ever truly be mine. I need to get the hell out of his room, but the last thing I want to do is leave things so tense between us. Before he can say anything, I flatten my hand on his chest. "Think of me as a partner. And one of the things partners do is maintain equal footing." He's suddenly still, his expression hard to read, so I run my hand down his abs and over his belt. Sliding my hand down, I cup his erection lightly.

He clasps my hand resting over his cock and wraps my fingers fully around him, his tone tight. "Are you suggesting a tit-for-tat?"

I hold his gaze. "It's a one-time offer. Your choice."

His jaw muscle flexes even as he moves my hand along the ridge of his erection. Pressing the heel of my palm against the tip of his cock, he says, "Then it'll be on my terms."

That's only fair. When I nod, he clasps my hips and quietly orders, "Unbuckle my pants."

When I start to look down to unbuckle his belt, he says, "Don't look down. Look at me while you do it."

He's pissed. I see it in his eyes, hear it in his tone, and feel it in the tightness of his hands clamped around my hips.

It's hard to keep my breathing even as I hold his gaze. He's not saying a word, but his eyes convey so much. He's not happy with this, but he wants me touching him, so he's staying quiet.

I unzip his pants, then push his fitted boxers down his hips, but pause when his gaze narrows on my hands. Reaching down, he slides the bangle on my wrist as far up my arm as it will go. Once it's locked high in place on my forearm, he grates, "Wrap your hand around me and feel what you could've had tonight, Talia."

I'm both frustrated and aroused by his comment, but I follow his directive and slowly fold my fingers around his hardness.

Despite his matter-of-fact manner, Sebastian groans the second I clasp him tight. Gripping the material of my dress at my hips, he starts to slide it up, but I shake my head. "This is just you."

"This *is* for me," he says tightly. "Don't deny me."

I have never been more turned on. He's so on edge; all I can do is nod. When he slides his hand down my hip, and then slips it between my legs, thrusting two fingers deep inside me, I gasp and slit my gaze, but don't say a word.

"You're *fucking* dripping for me," he growls, fury flickering across his features. When all I do is swallow, he orders, "Release me."

The second I let go of him, he pulls his fingers from my body and fists his cock. Sliding his hand from tip to base, he rubs my moisture all over himself, then commands,

"Now taste what you're denying us both."

When I start to kneel, he clasps my arm, his voice a rough rasp, "Stay standing. I want you close."

I step to the side and the second I lean over and take him into my mouth, then begin to slide my tongue around his erection, his fingers fist in my hair. "Do you taste how sweet you are? That's what I crave. Fuck—"

He cuts himself off and tilts his head back against the wall as I suck him in, then glide my mouth up and down his length. I love how I taste on him. Sweetness mixed with his musky maleness. His masculine smell surrounds me and I can't help but dig my nails into his upper thigh before I cup his sac firmly, then run my thumb down the sensitive seam, sliding it underneath.

When he groans deeper and says a few choice curse words, his hips starting to move, I internally smile. It's a heady sensation, having a sense of power over a man who normally dominates me. In this one instance, I welcome the role reversal. His breathing elevates and he grips my hair tighter, his other hand racing along my spine to cup my ass while he pushes his cock deep into my mouth. It's exhilarating to see him like this; unable to stop himself from absorbing every bit of pleasure I'm offering.

Suddenly I'm yanked off him and my back's set against the wall. Pressing his hands on the wall on either side of me, Sebastian's voice is gritty and raw. "There's nothing I want more than to have you go down on me, but that's not what I need right now. When I come, I want to be balls deep, to feel your warm pussy absorbing every last drop." He slides his hand between my thighs, his intimate hold tight and dominant. "*This* is mine, Talia. I own it, goddamn it! You know it and I know it."

I'm literally shaking from his possessive hold and arousing words. He's turned the tables on me so quickly, my insides are mush. There's no denying he ruled my world earlier and could easily do so now if he pushed me. "Sebastian—"

"No." He shakes his head in a hard jerk and quickly releases me. "A blow job will only make me want to nail you to the wall even more. You need to leave. *Now.*"

He's kicking me out? I stare into his eyes, hoping he can see how torn I feel, but even as his breathing saws in and out, his intense look doesn't waver, so I duck underneath his arm and walk away on shaky legs, my heart twisting.

Just as I reach the doorway, he calls my name. I turn, my pulse ramping at a crazy pace. He holds my gaze, his tone low and dangerous. "Lock the door tonight."

CHAPTER TWELVE

Sebastian

As soon as Talia walks out, her gorgeous red hair trailing down her back, hips swaying in that way only a woman who unknowingly possesses natural sex appeal can, I dig my fingers into my scalp and blow out a harsh breath, trying to get control over my raging need to throw her on the bed and fuck some sense into her.

Having her warm mouth moving over me felt so damn good. It would've been so easy to let her suck me off. I know it would've been heaven, but the battle of wills between us just elevated several notches. I meant what I said; until I'm coming inside her body and feeling her warm pussy clenching me tight, her hands clutching me to her, I won't feel satisfied.

I glance at the closed door, my dick throbbing, stomach

muscles flexing. Damn-it-to-hell…since when have I not been able to trust myself around a woman? Not fucking ever. But I sure as shit don't trust myself not to lose it if I follow her into her room. I could do it; I could walk in there right now and seduce her into having sex with me. I'd touch her in all the right places until she's pulling me into bed, desperate to have me inside her. I know exactly what turns her on, and God knows I can't get enough of hearing the sounds she makes when she's begging me to let her come. Talia's not a constant screamer like other lovers I've been with, but when she feels deeply, she expresses herself passionately. The moans and sighs she makes resonate through her sexy body. The arousing vibrations would bring even a deaf man to his knees. It's the ultimate turn on knowing I'm the one who brings that out in her.

I pace the room until my breathing settles and my heart returns to a normal pace, but a dull ache throbs in my stomach. At this rate, I'll have the worse case of blue balls before this week is out. One thing has become very clear to me the last few days, I crave Talia, but I want her to want me without reservation. No, damn it, *despite* them. I want her so overcome she can't control her responses. She was so close earlier.

Jared showing up gave her too much time to think. Fucking prick. I could strangle that pretentious bastard. He had to have called me right after he left Talia's room, because he wasn't gone thirty seconds before my phone rang.

"Black, this is Jared."

"Do you have more information?" I snap, annoyed at his interruption.

"No more threats. I'm calling to inform you that I've replaced you with another security detail for Natalia. Clear out your things from the hotel room before eleven tomorrow. I'll send you a check for the services you've provided so far."

I wasn't surprised by Jared's move. Honestly, I couldn't believe it took him this long. Sometime this week, he grew a pair. I eliminate threats for a living and would've bounced my ass the first day I met me. But Talia's situation wasn't about a pissing contest, so I kept my response calm. "It's not in Miss Lone's best interest to change her security detail at this late juncture, nor do I think she would approve of the change."

"Natalia has no choice in the matter. We're paying for the service. She'll adapt to her new security person."

"For someone who obviously wants to date Miss Lone, you sure as shit know nothing about her," I say before I hang up. When he tries to call me back, I ignore the call. A couple minutes later, I receive a text.

Jared: Are we going to have a problem?

I'm tempted to let Jared fail miserably with Talia—I know what her reaction to him saying she has no choice in her new security would be—but I refuse to take the risk with her safety.

Me: I no longer work for you. Miss Lone has hired me directly. Any security you procure will be

*redundant and only get in my way. Save yourself
the cost or I'll remove whomever you hire from
the premises myself. You will continue to keep me
apprised of any new developments as pertains to
Miss Lone's safety. Any failure to do so will be
met with DUE force. Am I clear?*

Jared: Are you threatening me?

Me: Just stating a fact.

As I glance over at my phones sitting on the desk
now, it occurs to me that Jared probably saw the second
phone lying near Talia's on her bed and assumed the
other belonged to me. *That's* why he called me when he
did. The bastard was testing to see if the phone was mine.
He probably stood outside Talia's door listening after he
dialed. *Asshole.*

A smile of satisfaction flickers that my phone in her
room had been on silent mode. Knowing that I one-upped
Jared's suspicion purely by accident is the final amusing
balm that helps settle my raging need for Talia. For now.

I grunt my annoyance at the Midtown Central editor.
I've never been so relieved to be out from under a contract.
Jared is such a clueless idiot that he doesn't realize he just
pissed away the only leverage he had over me: my word.
And now that I'm not being held to a contract, all bets are
off. I'm going after Talia, full force, and on my fucking
terms.

When she and I are in public, my first priority will be
getting her through this week unharmed. It's been easier
having her near in the hotel. I'll deal with her qualms when

I suggest she change location again. She won't like it, but it's necessary until I can find and eliminate this threat on her life for good. The threat could die down once the book tour is over, but I don't trust that. One thing I've discovered over the past few days is how important Talia's safety is to me. Every time we leave the hotel, my concern for her well-being is so intense, it feels like someone's stabbing me in the chest with a hot poker.

But when we're alone again, and I don't have to worry about others coming after her, she's all mine. And she'll have no idea what's going to hit her. I almost feel sorry for her. Almost. But not enough to stop myself from finally having the one thing that has made me feel the closest to being whole in a very long time. Talia leaving me hanging for six months has put a damper on my desire for anyone else. One-night stands just weren't worth the effort.

She and I feel…unresolved. I've never been with a person that left me feeling like that before. It's beyond frustrating. If we can spend time together, preferably in bed for at least a week, then maybe I can begin to feel like a normal guy who no longer obsesses about one particular redhead more than he should.

Will we be able to be friends after I inevitably fuck it all up? I don't know. I've never cared enough to bother before, but I hope so because she fascinates me as a person. For now, I'm not thinking that far ahead. When I'm not worrying about keeping her safe, my dick is doing most of the thinking. And until he's satiated, nothing else will matter.

But the idea of having her to myself for a week grows more appealing the more time we spend together. I'm going to submerge myself in Talia, drink in her feminine scent, soak up the feel of her skin, and taste every last part of her. I will wear her the hell out, so there's no room for thoughts of anyone else in that intriguing mind of hers. I might be far from perfect, but I am one unrelenting, determined bastard in bed, which will absofuckinglutely be to her benefit.

With a plan in place, I strip and fall into bed, knowing I can't let thoughts of Talia keep me up all night long. She needs me at my best and that's exactly what she's going to get, no matter how much my balls ache.

Talia

Shaking my head, I stare at my naked wrist as I wait in the hotel restaurant for Mina. After a restless night's sleep, I woke this morning to find the bangle Jared had given me laying open on the pillow beside me. I instantly narrowed my gaze on the doorknob, but the push button was still locked. Not that it apparently stops Sebastian. He has picked my lock before. This time he just bothered to lock himself out once he "unshackled" me.

Before I went to bed, I tried once more to remove it, but the thing was definitely locked on my wrist. I finally gave up, washed my face and crawled into bed, only to have erotic dreams of Sebastian bringing me to climax with his mouth, his hands, and other parts of his body but the one I wanted. I awoke in such arousing pain that I instantly headed for the shower. Anything to distract myself from thoughts of the domineering, infuriating, stubborn, autocratic, sharp-witted, sex-on-a-stick man on the other side of that door.

Once I'd showered, I tried to put the bracelet back on, but it no longer stayed clasped. Of course Sebastian made sure that was the case, which was probably for the best. It's not like I'm wearing the jewelry he gave me. Not that he knows any of this yet. I didn't bother waking him, since I'm having breakfast here in the hotel. And honestly, communicating directly with him right now would just remind me of how I woke up this morning; painfully unsatisfied.

Mina carrying an infant carrier into the restaurant sidetracks my thoughts of Sebastian, and I instantly stand and wait for her to come to my table.

She looks gorgeous; her long blond hair is slightly coated in sleet as she sets the carrier on the floor, then hugs me tight. "I'm so sorry, Talia. I just found out about my father contacting you. I'm horribly embarrassed."

I hug her and then pull back, clasping her shoulders. "I handled your father. No worries."

She smiles. "If anyone can put Adam Blake in his place, it's you."

Chuckling, I slide my hands to hers and pull her into the seat across from me. "I just didn't let him intimidate me. That's all." A sweet gurgling sound coming from the carrier draws my attention and I glance down at Josi. She's staring at me with bright green eyes and a happy smile on her face. "Well, hello, little Josi. I'm so happy to finally meet you in person," I say as I release Mina to touch the short blonde curls framing her little face. A hard lump forms in my throat. She reminds me so much of Amelia when she was tiny like this.

While I let Josi pat her hand on my wrist, Mina unstraps her from the carrier. "Would you like to hold her?"

I can't even form the words. Instead, I just nod and wait with bated breath for her to hand me her four-month-old daughter.

As soon as Josi settles in my arms, I pull her close and inhale her baby powder scent. Moments spent with Amelia flood back to me, fiercely bittersweet, but I force myself to stay in the present with Mina and Josi.

"She's beautiful, Mina."

Mina dabs at Josi's mouth with a cloth, giving her daughter a worshiping gaze. "And drooling like a champ. I have a feeling she's starting to teethe early. God help me."

I set Josi on my thigh and press her back against my body, wrapping an arm around her to hold her securely. While she coos and makes contented sounds playing with the toy her mom hands her, Mina looks up at me. "I truly am sorry. That's the last way I wanted you to find out. I could kill Regan for going to my dad."

"Who's Regan?" I ask, wondering why the name sounds vaguely familiar.

The waiter arrives, and after we place our orders for coffee and croissants, Mina answers my question. "Regan is one of my best friends that I've had since childhood," she says with a tolerant sigh. "I know it's going to seem like I'm asking you to consider being Josi's godmother at the last minute, but my family and friends have been giving me such a hard time as to who should take on the role that the whole thing is really stressing me out."

"I can only imagine," I murmur. *Regan.* Ugh, now I know why that name sounds familiar. That's the girl who brought Sebastian that box of stuff from Mina while he and I were together in Martha's Vineyard. I never saw Regan's face, but I already dislike this girl. The way she spoke to Sebastian while standing outside his room at the Hawthorne estate…she definitely wants him back. I doubt her thoughts about him have changed these past six months. He's a hard man to forget. It was clear to me that she wants an "in" with the Blake family, and being his niece's godmother is definitely a way to accomplish that. My arm folds protectively around Josi. I would never let that woman near this sweet baby.

"And with the christening happening tomorrow afternoon, I'll totally understand if you say 'no'. I know you have a lot on your plate this week and the timing couldn't be worse, but I just wanted you to know how much your friendship has come to mean to me, Talia. So—"

I put my hand on hers and squeeze so she can stop worrying. "I would be honored to be Josi's godmother, Mina. Truly. But can you tell me why you chose me? And does your husband agree? As your father pointed out, you do have two best friends whom I'm assuming Josi's father has met."

Mina leans over and touches the heart on my necklace at the same times she touches the matching one on hers. "It's because of this, Talia. You loved little Amelia so much that you never forgot her. Everything you did to help me, you were also doing it in her name." Reaching down, she clasps my hand between hers. "I haven't exactly been honest with you."

I furrow my brow. "What do you mean?"

She releases my hand to smooth her hair, then bites her bottom lip as she runs her finger lovingly down the side of Josi's face. "Derrick couldn't handle the idea of being a father. It freaked him out so much that he left a couple months before she was born. So yeah, I'm a single mom and up until a month ago, I didn't handle it well at all."

What kind of man deserts his wife and unborn child? "I don't understand, Mina. Every time we talked you said "we" love Josi so much. You seemed so put together. Why didn't you tell me you were alone and needed help?"

She looks up, a need for me to understand reflected in her gaze. "Because you were my inspiration, Talia. You somehow managed to make your life better despite a bad past that included losing your little sister. And yet, there I was, unable to handle losing my husband and being a new mom. I didn't want to look like a failure in your eyes, so yeah, when we talked all those times...I faked it. The truth is, if it weren't for Seb, I don't know how I would've handled things."

"Sebastian?" I ask, totally surprised.

Mina nods. "Yeah, when Derrick bailed, my brother swooped in like a lion. Not that my mother did a whole lot, but Sebastian took over after battling with my mom a few times. He wouldn't let her do anything. He took me to appointments, he was there when Josi was born, and he made sure I got out of the house when he saw I needed time to myself after my post partum depression got pretty bad. Because of him, I'm finally feeling like I can do this single mother thing. Even dealing with his own stuff, he's been my rock. That's why I sent him your way."

So that's what Sebastian has been doing the last six months, being the best big brother in the world. My respect for him vaults several notches. "What do you mean you sent him my way?"

She tucks a strand of hair behind her ear. "When you mentioned that first threatening letter your publisher received, I told Seb. I knew he'd protect you." She glances around, looking toward the restaurant's doorway. "I'm surprised he's not here. He's your security, right?"

I nod. "He is, but I didn't tell him I was getting up so early to meet with you, since I knew we'd stay here in the hotel. So you discussed me with your brother?" This whole conversation is throwing me off a little. In our few talks, Mina and I never talked about Sebastian. It was like an unwritten rule we both abided by.

She bites into her croissant, then wipes the crumbs from her fingers. "I didn't talk about our conversations with Sebastian, because I was so wrapped up in my own misery. But based on Seb's reaction to that letter you wrote, I knew he would want to know if you were in danger."

I furrow my brow as I lift my coffee cup. "What letter?"

"The one you left behind with the watch all those years ago." Sipping her coffee, she nods. "Once I told him what the rest of the letter said, I could tell you meant something to him."

The fact that Mina thinks I mean something to Sebastian makes my stomach flutter, even if it's her own perception. Blinking in confusion, I say, "I don't understand. Why did you have to tell him what the rest of my letter said?"

Mina turns her fork on the tablecloth several times, obviously nervous. "I'm going to tell you something that

Sebastian would kill me for revealing, but I think it's important."

"Of course," I say quickly, desperate for more insight into the enigmatic man.

"When Sebastian got hurt during that explosion, his eye color wasn't the only thing that changed. He's colorblind, Talia. The only colors he sees now are black and white and the brighter end of the red spectrum." Her gaze skims my hair and her lips quirk. "He must love looking at you. Anyway, the P.S. part of your letter was written in—"

"Green," I supply in a hushed voice, remembering that I'd added that part with another pen once my black pen ran out of ink.

She nods. "Which made it invisible to him."

That means he didn't know just how much the watch meant to me when he commented that giving it to me was a foolish mistake. "Why didn't he tell me about his eyesight?"

Mina snorts. "My brother's pride is as strong as his honor. He didn't say anything because he wouldn't want to be seen as *less*. Not by anyone. I'm the only one in our family who knows the truth about why he left the Navy, and he only told me because of your letter."

Is that what Sebastian meant about not being whole? Because he lost so much more than his color vision? Losing his military career had to be devastating. She's right. That's something he would never disclose. Not willingly. "Why are you telling me?"

She tilts her head and holds my gaze. "Because I think you care for him too and you should know the demons he deals with everyday. Can you imagine not only having to start over, but having all the color stripped from your life at the same time? Where you once took the beauty all around you for granted, and then the next day, it's just gone? My brother has pulled more into himself since he came back. The past few months, when he wasn't helping me, he focused solely on work. If anyone can get him to reengage in life, it's you."

Her revelation about Sebastian's extreme colorblindness helps me understand his inflexible attitude about us a little better. Does he really think he's somehow less? And does he think that I would see his colorblindness as a flaw? If anything it makes me admire him more. "Sebastian means a lot to me, Mina, but he has to want more for himself. There's only so much I can do."

She nods and smiles. "I know, but I have faith. Yet another reason why I'm choosing you to be Josi's godmother. Like my brother, you stand by your word. I know that if something happened to me, Josi will be well-loved and protected. The Blake name might come with money, but I know from experience wealth can't buy loyalty, not without strings attached." Her lips press together for a second before she continues. "For Josi, I want pure-of-heart devotion. You had that for Amelia."

Pausing, she clasps my hand and squeezes. "I don't just want you to say 'yes' to being Josi's godmother, Talia. I'm asking you to become a part of our lives. I so enjoyed our chats and wanted to meet you in person for drinks and dinner, but I knew you were on a crazy schedule. Now that your deadlines are behind you, I'd like to do something fun like see a chick flick, enjoy a long lunch, or have a girls' night out. I want to really *be* friends."

Her words are choking me up, and I blink back the mist in my eyes to cover just how much. Other than Cass, my aunt is the only other person in my life. Kissing the soft curls on top of Josi's head, I rub my thumb over the baby's tiny hand grasping my finger and smile at her mom. "I would love that. And thank you for keeping Amelia's memory alive. You have no idea how much that means to me."

Mina smiles. "Will your schedule allow you to come to the christening tomorrow? It's not required at such short notice, but if you can make it, I'd love for you to come. It'll be at four."

I nod. "I have a couple of signings and a media thing, but then I'm free. I wouldn't miss it for the world."

Mina's smile brightens as she lifts her barely eaten croissant. "I've got a lot to do to get ready for tomorrow. I'll text you the church's address later today."

Nodding toward her coffee and croissant, I grin. "Better fuel up. You're going to need the energy."

I'm just finishing my croissant when Sebastian stalks into the restaurant in his business suit, his blood red tie making me smile inside despite the annoyed look on his face. "Why didn't you answer any of my texts?"

"I take it you didn't get my note?" I say in a calm tone as I pull my phone out of my purse and turn it on. I'd turned it off after I got a text from Jared letting me know he had an early morning meeting he didn't know about and would have to catch up with me later. My breakfast with Mina was too important to let it be interrupted.

"What note?" Sebastian says, still towering over my table.

"The one I wrote and left on my desk for you…" I trail off when I realize the pen I grabbed from my purse was blue. *Well, shit.* Standing quickly, I say, "I'm sorry. I turned my phone off during my breakfast meeting. I thought for sure you'd see my note letting you know I was here, Mr. Lock-picker."

He scowls, clearly annoyed. "I didn't. Don't turn your phone off again."

I nod and sigh, feeling bad for inadvertently making him worry. Now that I know about his vision's limitations, I'll be more aware. "Since the signing isn't for another couple hours, will you take me to the market? I still haven't had a chance to see the Christmas decorations and vendors."

"No." He shakes his head, his mouth set in a firm line.

"Consider it your way of making up for destroying my bracelet."

His gaze sharpens and his voice lowers as he takes a step closer. "No one else is allowed to bind you, Talia. I respect the nuanced meanings behind it. Do I need to remind you of the pleasure you've experienced every time I've done so?"

My stomach flutters with excitement, but I force myself to remember his commitment phobia and take a calming breath. Shaking my head, I try a different approach. "Please, Sebastian. Christmas is my favorite time of the year. I've been so busy, I haven't even decorated my apartment, which makes me feel anxious to walk around and admire all the glitz and glamour. I still need to get a couple of gifts and I'm hoping I'll find them there."

His blue gaze searches mine for a couple of seconds before he brushes a tendril of hair back from my cheek. I can tell by the softening of the lines around his mouth that we've called a truce, for now. Sighing, he lowers his hand to his side and takes in my black slacks, white silk blouse and black blazer, then looks at his own suit. "We'll need coats. It's not snowing, but it's hovering close to thirty this morning."

I beam, giving him the full force of the excitement brimming inside me, before I run off ahead of him to get my coat.

CHAPTER THIRTEEN

Talia

Sebastian's right about the need for coats. The air is frigid as we walk the couple streets over to the Holiday market. He's quiet, his gaze scanning the cars and people bustling about. Buttoning my wool coat all the way, I inhale deeply as we enter the market area. The scent of mulled spices hangs enticingly in the air. "Smells yummy, doesn't it?" I say, my gaze scanning over the velvet red bows and bright holiday lights twinkling amongst the pine boughs framing each vendor's booth front.

Sebastian walks up to the first booth selling mulled cider and buys a cup. "May as well benefit while you're here," he says, handing me the steaming drink.

I grasp the Styrofoam cup in both hands and let the warmth soak through my skin while I inhale the spiced aroma. "Thank you. You don't want any?"

"I've already had my coffee for the day."

He sounds so regimented, I snicker. "So you're only allowed one?"

He glances down at me. "I want my hands free. Why is Christmas your favorite holiday?"

I try not to let his reminder that he's working dampen my spirit. "Because it makes me think of renewal and new beginnings." Taking a sip of the spicy cider, I turn and start to weave my way through the early morning shoppers. This close to Christmas, the place is buzzing.

Sebastian quickly follows. Just as he pulls up beside me, I say, "Look at that gorgeous wreath. I never thought non-traditional lights as Christmas-y, but with the other colored flowers, it's breathtaking."

He eyes the wreath skeptically. "How would you write an article about it, selling the non-traditional?"

I immediately open my mouth to start spouting off a description when it hits me that's exactly what Sebastian asked me to do that day on the boat. He wanted me to put into words how I saw the sunset. That's why his eyes were closed when I looked back at him after I finished describing it. He couldn't see the colors and he wanted me to tell him so he could picture it in his mind's eye. My chest aches. I can't imagine what it would be like to have color completely stripped from my daily life. Gripping his arm, I pull him away from the crowd and closer to the wreath.

"Whoever thought purple could represent Christmas? It's bright and brash and non-traditional, but pair sparkling purple lights, yellow-centered, lavender forget-me-nots, and clumps of airy baby's breath together on a teal-tinged Blue Spruce wreath, and you'll be reminded why purple is considered the color of royalty. The symbolic combination of flower choice and colors make this wreath the perfect Christmas decoration."

Sebastian chuckles and shakes his head. "I'm sold. Maybe you should write all the marketing copy for BLACK Security."

I snicker to cover how much his comment flatters me and continue on, winding my way past people until I run across a booth selling scarves in various shades and textures. Just as I start to run my fingers over a silky turquoise scarf because its shade reminds me of the color of Sebastian's eyes in a passionate moment, he says quietly, "My mom loved Christmas. Even though we could only afford to get each other a couple of small gifts, she'd spend hours decorating that fake tree she dragged in from someone's curb when I was little. Each year she'd hum Christmas tunes and hang every dumb ornament I was forced to make in school. Then I'd have to help her untangle the lights. I always hated it."

"Why would you hate it? It sounds like a fun, happy time in your life."

While he spoke about his mom, he was watching the people around us, but now he turns his gaze to me. "That damned massive tree only made my gifts look puny."

He sounds so disgruntled, I shake my head. "It's never the size that counts. I'm sure she treasured each gift."

A brief smile tilts his lips, a far away memory reflected in his eyes. "She always made a big deal over whatever I got her. When I gave her a necklace with a fake sapphire, she acted like I'd given her the Hope diamond." He shrugs off the past. "I just felt like it was never enough. That last year I couldn't get her anything. Bills kept piling up. So I bought a 'worry stone' from a street vendor with my last few bucks. I was willing to do anything to take her mind off the pain."

My heart aches for him, but I manage to keep my voice even. "Did it work?"

"Mom lied like a champ. Told me that my stone worked wonders." He snorts and glances away. "But you know how her story ended. Needless to say, I don't believe in fairytales."

"And yet you still gave me a rainbow." The fact that he had enough hope left in him to help me after what he'd gone through with his mom says a lot about Sebastian's character, whether he realizes it or not.

When his gaze snaps back to me, full of heat, I shake my head and *tsk*. "Hope, Sebastian. You gave me hope."

He touches my jaw, tracing his thumb from my lip down to my chin. "Now it's your turn, Little Red."

His comment could mean so many things. Is he asking me to say yes to a good sex romp? Or does he want me to give him true hope? All I know is, Mina's plea for me to help her brother keeps echoing in my mind. I can at least focus on that. But how am I supposed to get him to open up in other ways if he refuses to share something as simple as not being able to see color? Looking over the scarves gives me an idea.

Clearing my throat, I ask him to hold my cup. Once he takes it, I pick up an emerald scarf and a bright yellow one, then push them in front of him. "Cass is so hard to buy for.

Which color do you think would look best on her?"

Sebastian casually lowers his gaze to the scarves and rolls his shoulders. "Whichever one looks best with dark hair."

Smooth. I smirk that he manages to maneuver around answering my question so easily. Then again he's had a few years to perfect his responses. Maybe if I show him he's not alone, that no one is perfect. "My roommate travels all over the world. So getting her something unique is a challenge." As I lay the scarves down, I'm glad the vendor is busy with other customers. Picking up a pair of "Risky Business" style sunglasses, I set them on my nose. "And *this* is why the one outrageously expensive gift she brought me from Paris ended up on her face instead of mine."

He grins when I tilt my head to make the glasses look straight on my face. "Yep." I sigh as I set the glasses back on the table. "One ear is slightly higher than the other."

Sliding his hands into his pants' pockets, his voice is husky-low as he takes a step closer. "I prefer them one at a time, anyway."

Excitement curls in my belly as the sensation of him biting my earlobe during a heated moment in the past rushes forth. Every time we've been together, the man never left a part of me unbranded in some form or fashion. How have I let him distract me from my current goal so easily? Mentally shaking myself, I start to pick up another two scarves, hoping to get him to share. But a loud popping sound has him dropping the cup and grabbing my waist as he shields me with his body.

My heart racing with worry, I peer up into his face,

then around his shoulder when a three-year-old boy starts crying uncontrollably. I breathe a sigh of relief as his mother consoles him over the English Christmas Cracker he just set off by picking up the toy prize that fell along with the confetti to the ground. Sebastian grunts and moves to straighten, when a scratchy voice sounds beside us. "Perfect for some private time with the lady, yes?" The amused creases around the vendor's dark eyes deepen as he unfurls a delicate black scarf over our heads.

Sebastian and I are nose to nose, and for some reason when he looks at the vendor through the gauzy material, he smiles, his first genuine one of the morning. Pulling the silky material off, he tells the man, "We'll take it."

Once he buys the scarf, Sebastian lowers the silk around my neck, one side of his mouth tilted in a seductive half-smile. "To memories."

Is he reminiscing or asking to make new ones? "Thank you, Sebastian," I say, too wound up to voice the question out loud.

Grasping the scarf's ends, he glances down and loosely ties it around my neck, his movements turning swift and efficient. "We need to get back. I don't like how exposed you are out here."

How does he manage to arouse and exasperate me at the same time? It's a talent the man excels at without even trying. I blow out a breath of frustration and nod. "I just need to get a couple of things and we'll be own our way."

After I pick out an organic perfume for my aunt, a pair of lapis drop earrings for Cass and an extra small silver bracelet with a tiny heart on it, Sebastian quickly escorts me out of the market, his demeanor all business. When we turn down the hotel's street, he says, "I have something I need to do tomorrow afternoon that has been set for a while. Since you know my sister, I hope you don't mind coming with me. That way I can still keep an eye on you. It'll take no more than an hour."

"You're talking about Josi's christening, right? Mina invited me too. The bracelet is a gift for Josi. I'll be happy to come with you." I keep my tone casual, even though I'm surprised Sebastian apparently hasn't been told that I'm going to be Josi's godmother.

He glances my way, his gaze guarded. "I didn't realize you and my sister were that close."

Since Mina hasn't told him, maybe it's best to honor her wishes and let her tell him at the church. "She invited me. Is that a problem?"

He shifts his attention to the hotel up ahead. "No."

We arrive at the hotel with just enough time for me to drop off my purchases and head out for the signing. As I slip into the car Sebastian has waiting on the side of the building, I'm still no closer to figuring out how to get him to open up. If anything, as he gives orders to the driver to take us to the bookstore, it feels as if he has shuttered himself completely.

Three TV news vans are lined up outside the Westside Book Corner as we pull up. "Looks like you're getting extra publicity today," Sebastian says, his mouth setting in a firm line before he opens the door.

Inhaling a deep breath, I let him take my hand and escort me through the bookstore's main door. News crews quickly follow us inside, and I do my best to ignore them bustling behind us with camera equipment as the store's owner, Jameson Danvers, walks up to greet us.

Buttoning his tweed jacket, he grasps my hand and raises his bushy gray eyebrows behind black-framed glasses at the entourage that followed us in. "I can't say I'm sad to see the extra publicity for your signing, Miss Lone." Grinning, he pauses and briefly glances Sebastian's way, "And you too, *Mr. White.*"

When Sebastian pulls his annoyed gaze from the news people to acknowledge the owner, Mr. Danvers' attention pings between us. "Word of your double-signing has spread. After Miss Lone hit the New York Times, I had to order more books to accommodate the people who called at the last minute, hoping they could get a signed copy of Blindside today."

Sebastian gives a quick nod, then says in a curt tone, "Excuse me for a minute."

As he walks away, dialing his phone, Mr. Danvers chuckles. "A man of few words, I see." Patting my hand, he continues, "Congratulations on hitting the list, Miss Lone. Blindside is a riveting book."

"Thank you for hosting me, Mr. Danvers. I'm looking forward to a great signing."

Turning to glance at the signing table sitting on a raised dais area in the center of the store, he says, "Your assistant arrived early, bringing the books I ordered at the last minute. She has everything ready for you."

Kayla's long, perfectly curled dark hair is pulled forward over her shoulders for maximum appeal, a striking contrast to her form-hugging electric blue dress. When she looks up from straightening a stack of books and waves, her generous breasts bouncing, I smile. I can't fault her for being comic-book-character perfect. She made sure the extra books arrived and has been an excellent assistant so far. "I'll have to make sure her boss knows what a great job she's doing," I say, nodding my agreement.

I wave to the huge crowd of readers lined up to the left of the dais and call out, "Are you ready to be Blindsided?" As they let out a near-deafening cheer, I grin and head toward the dais.

Just as I sit down, Sebastian moves to stand behind me, but Mr. Danvers pulls out the other chair for him. "Readers will want your signature too, Mr. White."

When Sebastian looks at me, I chuckle and hand him a pen. "Your fans are waiting, Mr. White."

The second he sits down and signs the first reader's book, a sandy-haired reporter steps forward. "*Mr. White.* What made you decide to officially join the Blake family ranks six months ago? Jack Blake passed away over three years ago. Why the change of heart?"

Sebastian looks up, his blue gaze steely cold. "This event is a *Blindside* signing. Unless you're here to interview Miss Lone about her book, I'll have to ask you to leave."

While the other reporters lean in with their mics, their gazes greedy for a scoop, the first guy apparently doesn't know the kind of man he's dealing with or he would've heeded Sebastian's warning. Instead, he steps to the side of the table, holding his mic closer. "Everyone's speculating that you're really Adam Blake's son and not Jack's. Care to comment?"

The readers were already buzzing at the interruption, but the reporter's question sends an audible, collective gasp through the crowd, then they start tittering and whispering to each other.

Sebastian grabs the top of the mic and with one twist, breaks it off. "You're done." As soon as he stands to his impressive, towering height, the guy backs up a couple steps, his eyes wide as he stares at his damaged mic.

Nodding toward the doorway, Sebastian says to the three men in business suits who must've entered after I sat down, "Escort these uninvited guests out. They're disturbing the event."

Two of the tall men walk forward, their dark eyebrows pulled down as they start issuing commands for the news crews to leave. Then the third one, a blond man with linebacker shoulders, circles around the back, keeping any of the crew from trying to blend into the group of fans. Mr. Danvers looks anxiously at Sebastian. "My apologies, Mr. White. I thought they were here for the signing or I would've made them leave when they first pulled up this morning."

"It's fine, Mr. Danvers." I wave dismissively to soothe the man's obvious anxiety. "Mr. White takes his job very seriously." I turn and beckon a tall, thin woman clutching her copy of Blindside forward. She's standing on the bottom step of the dais, her eyes wide with both admiration and fear as she blinks at Sebastian behind chic glasses.

The second she sets her book in front of me, she pulls one of the chopsticks from her pinned up black hair and quickly uncaps it to reveal a pen at the same time she says in a hushed voice, "You weren't exaggerating about his intensity, were you?"

I slide a sideways look Sebastian's way. He's back in his seat now and staring at me, one black eyebrow hiked high.

When he flashes a megawatt smile and the storminess disappears from his eyes as if he's the most laidback person in the world, I snort and open the woman's book to the right page. "Not one bit."

"Are you Adam Blake's illegitimate son? The public has a right to know who might be running Blake Industries one day," a reporter screams around one of Sebastian's men holding back the crowd while we get into the car. Sebastian slams the car door shut and tells the driver to take off.

He was fine through the rest of the signing, but once we walked outside to an even bigger crowd of reporters, I could tell by his stony expression that he was pissed.

"Do you want to talk about it?" I address his stoic profile.

His icy gaze snaps to me. "Do you want me to seduce you now or later?"

"You're trying to sidetrack me." I narrow my gaze and tilt my chin up. "It won't work. Not this time—"

Before I complete my sentence, Sebastian leans over me, pushing me flat on my back. "Who says I'm not serious?" he says in a dangerously calm voice as he traces a finger from my jaw to my neck, then across the curve of my cleavage just above my blouse.

As soon as he touches the top button of my blouse, I grasp his hand. "Why is it so hard for you to share with me?"

He lets out a low arrogant laugh. "Sweetheart, I've been trying to share with you for days, but you haven't been taking deposits."

"Crudeness won't work either," I grit out and start to push his shoulders back.

He clasps my hands and presses them into the leather seat on either side of my head, his chest crushing mine as he says in an arousing rumble against my ear, "You like my dirty mouth, Little Red. Very, very much."

My body instantly reacts to his amazing smell and body heat. I tingle all over at his suggestive words. "Share with me, Sebastian. Something. Anything," I say against his jaw.

He squeezes my hands and presses his nose against my neck, inhaling deeply. A rumbling groan erupts from his throat before he lifts his head to stare into my eyes. "I can't *stop* wanting you."

The pain in his expression feels like a butcher knife twisting in my gut. "Do you want to?"

A quick head jerk. "No."

"Then I don't understand—"

"You asked me to tell you something. Are you ready?"

I nod quickly, wondering if his mercurial mood has to do with the reporters showing up and ambushing him.

Sebastian leans close once more and nips at my ear lobe. As my body tightens and heat rolls across my skin in waves of sheer want, he releases a slow, warm breath against my ear and says, "You're moving to a different room when we get back."

When he quickly straightens and pulls me upright with him, I jerk my hands free and scowl. Are these hot and cold tactics his way of distracting me from prying? "I'm not moving rooms," I huff as I straighten my jacket and blouse.

"It's not up for discussion," he says gruffly, his gaze straying to my hands as I check to make sure my blouse is still buttoned.

"You're right next door. I'll be fine."

"*You're moving,*" he says in a final tone.

Crossing my arms, I glance out the window. So much for getting him to open up. Damn, he's like Fort Knox. Why do I get the feeling the inside of his mind is just as dark as that closed-up, impenetrable vault? As the car turns, a bright ray of late afternoon sunlight shines directly in my eyes. I wince as a headache from lack of sleep begins to throb against my temples. *Great. Just what I need.* Midtown Central has set up a cocktail hour for their authors to mingle with librarians in the ballroom later tonight.

As Sebastian and I enter the hotel lobby, he stops off at the front desk. "I believe you have a package for me." Once the employee hands him a manila envelope, she turns to me. "This was left for you earlier today, Miss Lone." After handing me a white envelope, she walks off to help someone check in.

Sebastian takes the envelope from me before I get a chance to open it. I frown at him and hold my hand out. "That's meant for me."

"Were you expecting anything?"

"No, but—"

He opens it.

When his jaw clenches after he reads it, I ask, "What does it say?" and turn to read over his shoulder.

He pulls out his phone, scrolling for a number. "Nix the room change. We're moving hotels."

You didn't listen.

That's all the note says, but this time it feels even more threatening because it's handwritten in black ink.

"I'm not moving, Sebastian."

"This isn't up for—"

"Discussion, debate, argument?" I wave my hand toward the letter. "Whoever this is knows I'm in and out of this hotel all week due to all the company events here. They don't know that I'm *staying* here. I switched my reservation under the name Smith once I learned of the break-in. I'm fine."

He lifts the letter to my nose, renewed determination settling in his expression. "It smells like your perfume, Talia. You're moving. There are several hotels in the area."

My stomach dips that he knows what my perfume smells like, but the concentrated scent makes my head hurt even more. I push the letter back and rub my temple. "There's an event here tonight and my head is killing me. I need to try to sleep this off."

Sebastian lifts me from the bed like I weigh nothing. My body melts against his hard frame while my woozy vision drifts in and out. As he carries me across the room toward the open doorway, I loop my arms loosely around his neck and tuck my head into his shoulder, drawing in his amazing smell. Closing my eyes, I imagine him pulling me closer to inhale against my hair too. "You always smell so good," I mumble to dream Sebastian.

He chuckles and presses a kiss against my forehead. "I like your groggy honesty."

A sudden chill rushes across my body, and I open my eyes. We're walking into the elevator. I look up at him. "I'm not dreaming, am I?"

"No."

I stiffen in his arms, remembering that I fell asleep while he talked to one of his men about retrieving the letter and having it dusted for prints. I didn't argue when he insisted on keeping the door open between our rooms, because I found the resonance of his deep voice in the background comforting. "My suitcase."

He presses a button and as we zip upward, says, "I'll collect all your things. Tomorrow we move hotels."

Maybe I should've only taken half a sleeping pill. I'm so tired that I can't make my eyes stay open long enough to focus, let alone argue with him about switching anything, but at least my headache is gone. When he walks off the elevator, I sigh and drop my head back to his shoulder. The swaying movement of being carried only makes me want to sleep more, so I mumble, "Remind me when I wake up to rip you a new one."

His arms tense around me slightly before he presses his jaw against my cheek, locking me against him. "I *need* you close, Talia."

My lightheaded brain latches onto the emphasis in his comment, and I tighten my arms around his neck, content to let him hold me while I drift in and out of consciousness.

"I need you close too," I murmur, then finally let sleep pull me under.

I wake to a dark room, my heart racing. I was dreaming about that night I ran away. The night I killed Walt. The same night I met Sebastian and he gave me his jacket and watch, changing my world. In my dream, I'm teenage Talia, but this time I know what he will come to mean to me, and instead of pretending to punch in a fake code to an apartment building I don't live in, I turn and call out, "Wait!" Then run back down the stairs after the BMW, screaming, "Promise you'll never stop believing in rainbows!"

But the car keeps going, the red taillights fading in the distance.

I finally stop running and bend over, trying to catch my breath. Rain mixes with the tears on my cheeks as I whisper against the driving rain, "So we'll have a chance, Blackie."

As the dream fog fades and my eyes adjust to the tiny sliver of evening light coming from the closed drapes across the room, I blink. *This isn't my room.* Then I remember that Sebastian moved me. The room is so big that the light from the window only penetrates part of it, leaving shadows along the edges and in the corners.

Evening? I quickly glance at the clock, relieved to see I have a couple hours before I need to be downstairs for the cocktail.

When my line of sight lands on the edge of my suitcase sitting on the floor at the end of the bed, I immediately push the covers back and gasp at the coolness that hits my skin. All I'm wearing is the camisole and underwear

I had on under my clothes. Sebastian must've stripped me before putting me in bed. Glancing toward the closed door, which I can only assume leads to his adjoining room, I get up and quietly walk over to it. Even though I don't hear anything, I push the button lock on the doorknob, and for good measure, I also close the flip-lock at the top of the door too before I turn to my suitcase and unzip the compartment where I keep Sebastian's jacket neatly tucked inside.

Slipping it on, I lift the collar up and inhale the masculine leather scent. When flickering movement in my periphery draws my gaze to the gauzy curtains, I smile and walk over to the window to push them back away from the glass. Snow is falling heavily outside, and the sight of the fat white flakes fills my heart with peace. A torrential rain right now wouldn't have soothed me, but quiet snowfall does the trick. I know I should be worried about that latest threatening note, but oddly I'm not. And that's all due to Sebastian.

As I pull the cheap necklace Sebastian won for me at the fair in Martha's Vineyard from the coat's pocket and hook it around my neck, I question if it makes me a horrible person that a tiny part of me hopes this threat stuff continues beyond this week. It's the only way I know for sure that Sebastian will stick around. The protector in him would never leave if he thought I wasn't safe. That's one thing I can always guarantee with him.

Glancing around, I see the best chair for snow-gazing in a tall wingback near the desk. I quickly drag the chair over to the window, then stand behind it, sliding it to the left, then the right until I get it settled in the best spot.

Just as I mumble, "Perfect," Sebastian's deep voice sounds directly behind me.

"It's mine, isn't it?"

CHAPTER FOURTEEN

Talia

I freeze and dig my fingers into the cloth material on the chair. And now I can feel the warmth radiating off him. "What are you doing in here?"

"You told me you wanted me close," he says. Hooking his finger on my hair, he slides every bit of it over my right shoulder. As the heavy weight thumps against my right breast, he runs his finger slowly down my bare neck. "Why do you still have it, Talia?"

I'm exposed, and it's not just because I'm standing here in skimpy underwear and his jacket. How can I explain *this* in a way that won't leave me raw and shredded? I stare at the snow outside and think about the sense of peace I felt just a few seconds ago. "You know when you said my penname means 'alone', you were half right. The 'A' is supposed to represent Amelia and the 'T' is me, but the whole name does mean 'T Alone.' I've always been alone, Sebastian. At least…I felt that way until I ran into you."

His finger pauses at the base of my throat and when he lifts it away, my heart sinks, but I refuse to let my fear of scaring him away keep me from telling him this part at least. "Whether you meant to or not, you helped me believe I was worth more. I can't thank you enough for that."

His warm hand cups my right thigh and his chest brushes my back as his lips graze my ear. "Is that the only reason?"

My heart rate soars when he spreads his fingers along the front of my thigh. "What do you want me to say?"

"That you need me, Talia." He grips my thigh tight, his hold tense as his mouth hovers along my neck. "That you want my hands sliding along your thighs, spreading them wide, my mouth consuming every part of you." Prickles race along my skin when his lips move just behind my ear, his warm breath making my stomach swirl crazily. "I want to hear your moans of pleasure as you come while I'm deep inside you." His hand glides up the outside of my thigh to my hip, then slowly slides downward and under my panties. Just as his fingers trace the bit of hair at the juncture of my legs, his other hand smacks my ass hard.

I gasp at the dual erotic sensations, enjoying his hands arousing my body while his aggressive descriptions short-circuit my brain. My ass stings—and all I can think is how much I want him to touch me while he does it again. I'll explode in two seconds flat.

As if he knows what he's doing to me, Sebastian

slides his hands to my hips, then thumbs my panties to the middle of my ass, exposing my rear. He smacks the other cheek harder, then grabs both stinging cheeks in a possessive hold as he nips at my ear. "Spread your legs."

The commanding edge of his voice makes my heart sprint. It's beating so hard, my chest aches. I take a step to spread my legs, then gasp when he grabs the back of my underwear in his fist and yanks my hips against his. "Why won't you wear any of the jewelry I've bought you, but you willingly wear a necklace from a goddamn sideshow game?"

"Sebastian—" When I start to speak, he turns his hand and twists my underwear, pulling the material tight against my clit.

"Don't even think about lying to me, Talia," he snaps fiercely, then yanks the flimsy material completely off my body.

The rough act was just enough to put me on the brink of an orgasm. I curl my fingers into the chair's seams and take a deep breath to keep it together.

"*Why*," he demands. Ever so slowly he traces his fingers down my ass, then slides a hand between my thighs, tracing his fingertips along my dampness.

His barely-there touch is making me want to scream. I can't tell him it hurts too much to wear a piece of jewelry that was based on something I won't be able to hold onto forever. Those other gifts stemmed from him thinking of me in a sexual sense, of us together. This gift was just... because. "You won it for me, that's why," I say on a desperate exhale. My voice is hoarse, my emotions raw, while my body throbs. I ache so much to feel him inside me.

He pauses and mutters, "Simple things," as if filing the information away, and then slides his fingers along my sensitive lips. He's *so* close. I swallow to keep the yearning wail rising in my chest from escaping. I close my eyes in embarrassment when I feel my dampness dripping out of me, seeking his fingers, making them slicker.

"Christ, I don't even have to touch you, you're so fucking wet," he whispers, arrogance and strained desire in his gruff comment.

I tuck my chin to my chest to keep from panting loudly and hiss, "Then do something about it!"

"You drive me out of my goddamn mind," he grates out, then pushes two fingers aggressively deep inside me. The rough invasion feels so good, I grab the chair in a death grip and throw my head back, pressing into him, crying his name.

"It's not enough though, is it, Little Red?" he purrs in a knowing tone.

Before I can move, he quickly pulls his hand away. I can't believe he's torturing me like this. I'm about to turn and lay into him, when I hear his zipper sliding down. Instead I bite my lip and my whole body vibrates as I wait for him to take me. At this point, I'm his puppet. I need him to pull the fucking strings. And yank them hard.

"Damn right, it's not," he answers my silence and grips my hip with his right hand. The second he touches me, I arch my back, then mewl at the sensual feel of his rock hard erection sliding between my thighs. He rubs himself along my slickness, teasing my sensitized folds. When a strained groan rushes past his lips, I feel a little less like a desperate hussy and press my jaw to his mouth as he rasps against me. "I want to feel your sweet pussy clamping around my cock, Talia. Like you never want to let me go."

I don't. Ever. The length of him glides back and forth oh-so-slowly, arousing and just out of my reach. My legs start to shake when I realize he's lubricating himself with my desire for him. I'm so turned on and frustrated, but I know if I try to pull him inside me, he'll stop and tell me to put my hands back on the chair, so I hold myself perfectly still.

When his thickness finally tests the edge of my entrance, I inhale quickly and instinctively flex my lower muscles. Craving him. *God, I want him. This. Us.*

"That's it, sweetheart." He nips at my neck, while holding himself just outside of me. "Your body's telling me what you're too afraid to admit."

My heart stutters and my breath rips from my lungs. "What do you think I'm afraid to tell you?"

The fire alarm starts blaring in long, piercing bursts. As I grind my teeth at the interruption, Sebastian curses, then pulls away. A second later, he turns me around, and while he quickly zips my coat closed, he says calmly over the noise, "That we're meant to be together." *Is he saying what I think he's saying?* "Until we're both fully satisfied," he finishes with a dark, sexy smile, tucking a strand of my hair behind my ear.

Fierce burning spreads through my chest and my lungs feel like they're on fire, but I hold in the scream reverberating in my head. *Forever is all I want, Sebastian!* I've already told him that I want more than a fling. "I hate being at a stalemate," I say in a flat tone. He starts to speak, but I hold my hand up and shake my head, then walk over to my open suitcase to riffle through for underwear, jeans, socks, and my boots.

While I quickly dress, Sebastian moves to the door and flattens his palm against the wood. Glancing back, he waves me forward. "It's not a false alarm. It's faint, but I smell smoke. Grab what matters. We need to get out."

Sebastian and I stand under the awning of a restaurant across the street from our hotel, while snow falls on the crowd of guests standing outside, waiting for the firemen to clear them to go back in. Even though I don't see any visible signs of fire, I also smelled smoke when Sebastian escorted me down a back stairwell he had a special keycard to access.

I gesture to the fire truck's flashing lights. "The firemen have been in there for at least twenty minutes. I told you taking that back stairwell was overkill. This wasn't a 'diversion'. Someone pulled the fire alarm for a reason."

As Sebastian grunts his assessment and readjusts my laptop bag on his shoulder, a sudden realization hits me. Even though I know I won't find it, I open my purse and search through both zip-up sections inside, looking for the folded piece of "2 Lias" artwork.

"What's wrong?" Sebastian glances down at me, his brow furrowed.

I shrug and try not to let him see how worried I am. "Nothing."

He grasps my elbow once I fold the flap closed on my purse. "What did you leave behind?"

I count the floors to the fifth one and nod toward it. "I left something in my other room. You wouldn't have known it was there, so I know you didn't pack it for me."

His eyebrows lift. "What is it?"

"Just something I don't want to lose."

Releasing me, he nods. "When they give us the thumbs up to return to the hotel, we'll go back to your old room first. It's still in your name, so no one else should be in there."

Nodding my appreciation, I try to let the worry go.

Sebastian makes me wait until the fire trucks leave and the crowd dissipates before returning to the hotel. It has been a full hour since we left my room. At this point, I'm assuming the cocktail event has been cancelled, and even if it isn't, I'm excusing myself for tonight. Stepping onto the elevator ahead of Sebastian, I start to push number five, but a piece of paper has been taped over it that reads: See front desk.

My heart jolts and my gaze jerks to Sebastian's narrowed one. "Maybe there's something wrong with the elevator," I say, then walk back toward the lobby.

"Excuse me," I call quietly to the blonde woman working on some paperwork behind the front desk. "The fifth floor button is taped over. It says to see the front desk."

The girl nods and quickly moves to the computer to tap a few keys. "We had a small, contained fire upstairs. Everything is fine, but to make things comfortable for our guests, we've shut that floor off while we ventilate the smoke properly. If you tell me your last name, I'll let you know where we've moved you for the night. You should be able to retrieve your things tomorrow morning."

"The fire was on the fifth floor?" As my voice cracks, Sebastian puts a hand on my shoulder.

"You said the fire was contained. Where did it start?" he asks in a calm tone.

She frowns. "I'm not allowed to disclose—"

"I've been cleared," he interrupts. "Now tell us where."

Tapping on the keyboard, she looks nervously at Sebastian. "It was contained to room 529."

As the blood drains from my face, Sebastian squeezes my shoulder. "Call Bryce Sellers and get him to clear us to go up. Miss Lone left something in that room. She'd like to see if it survived the fire."

The security officer, Bryce, locks our stuff away in his office, then brings gloves and masks with him as he escorts us upstairs personally. Sliding my mask on, I rush out of the elevator and head down the hall the moment the doors open on the fifth floor.

A thin haze of smoke and the smell of burning wood hangs in the air. Tubing is hooked to huge industrial fans running at both ends of the hall to draw out the smoke. The loud noise drowns out the sound of my heart thudding in my chest and the soft thump of my feet hitting the carpet as I run down the hall.

Sebastian grabs my hand before I can enter the burned room. "Careful. We only have a few minutes. Bryce says the fumes are still strong." His warning sounds muffled behind his mask as he hands me gloves once Bryce walks up behind us.

"If a couple guests hadn't brought their fire extinguishers up from the floor below to help the sprinklers put the fire out, the flames would've made their way into the hall before the fire trucks got here."

I gape at the burned out door and scorched walls just

inside my room, and even though my heart jumps to a faster pace, I take a deep breath and nod to let Sebastian know that I'm calm.

Bryce steps in behind us. "According to the firemen, they found what smells like gasoline just under the door. They said someone must've slipped a soaked piece of paper or something underneath, then lit it. This was definitely arson. What the sprinklers couldn't put out—water rolls off gasoline—thankfully the fire extinguishers took care of."

I know the head of security is trying to sound optimistic, but I just want to tell him to shut up, because everything in the room is covered in white, sopping goop. I walk over to the desk and look for the room service binder, my eyes stinging from the remnants of smoke still hanging in the air.

It's not where I left it.

When I start to bend down, Sebastian grasps my arm to stop me, sympathy in his eyes, but I'm frantic. "I have to find it." I shake him off and get on my hands and knees. The goop soaks through my jeans as I look under the bed, lifting wet covers and pillows. When I see Bryce and Sebastian move the desk, I get up and peer behind it. Nothing.

I finally find the leather portfolio several feet from the desk. It's open on the floor near the chair. The artwork is water-smeared, and a fireman's boot print has torn the paper completely in half.

I hold the two halves up, and then let them fall back to the floor in a sopping heap.

Unshed tears make my eyes sting even more and I look

up to Sebastian. "I'm ready to move hotels now."

I don't say much to Sebastian on the way to the hotel. I think he knows I'm feeling raw inside, even if he doesn't know why. While the hot shower water rains down on me, I cry for the final loss of Amelia, angry with myself for being so afraid to return to my past before now. If I had retrieved the drawing sooner, it would be safe in my apartment, not a mangled mess on the floor of a burned hotel room. As soon as I turn off the shower, I freeze when I hear another man's voice just outside the bathroom door.

"Here are your bags."

I relax when Sebastian answers, "Thanks for bringing them, Connelly. I owe you."

"Everyone okay?" the guy asks.

I'm surprised by the concern in his question, but even more by how familiar his voice sounds. Where have I heard it before? I don't know anyone named Connelly.

"Yeah, it will be," Sebastian answers and then the door shuts.

Sebastian doesn't know that. I wish I felt his confidence. I take my time drying my hair, then I press my ear to the door to see if I hear him moving around my room.

When silence greets me, I walk out in a towel, thankful Sebastian has moved to his own room and is apparently talking on the phone. I quickly grab a pair of sleep shorts and a T-shirt from my suitcase and get dressed in the bathroom. Once I turn off the light, I stare at the door Sebastian left open. The shower's running in his room, giving me the perfect chance to shut the door without him hearing.

I worry my bottom lip, my teeth digging deep. I don't

like the idea of sleeping with my back to an open door, but I realize that Sebastian probably just wants me to feel safe, so I leave it before climbing into bed.

The shower stops, then a few minutes later the bathroom door opens and he turns off his light. My room goes dark for a second before my eyes adjust to the fresh three-inch blanket of snow reflecting outside lights into my room in a dim glow. It's completely still outside now. The snow stopped while we were looking through my old room at the Regent. Amelia loved the snow. I remember the delight in her laughter as she stuck her tongue and arms out and spun in circles, trying to capture as many flakes as possible. The sudden resurfacing of an Amelia memory is so unexpected, silent tears trickle across the bridge of my nose, hitting the pillow.

I freeze when the bed dips and Sebastian slides under the covers. "What are you doing?" I whisper and quickly brush the tears away.

"There's no way I'm leaving you alone tonight," he says, punching the pillow before he settles. "Might as well accept that you have a roommate for the evening."

His simple act of just being here for me is so sweet, my volatile emotions get the best of me. I hunch my shoulders and try my best to cry silently into my pillow.

I squeak when Sebastian's strong arm curls around my waist. Pulling my back against his hard body, he twines his muscular legs with mine. "Tell me about the drawing. Why did it mean so much to you?"

The sincerity in his voice, coupled with the pleasing smell of masculine soap and shower-warmed skin, work together to relax me. I brush the last tears away and melt into his hold. He's the only one who really knows what happened to Amelia, so I might as well tell him about the drawing.

Resting my cheek on his pillow, I take a deep breath. "That's part of the errand I ran the other day. I went to my old apartment building and retrieved the artwork. Amelia and I had drawn it together. She was so excited to learn our names had the same letters. I called it the '2 Lias' since it was our names inside two hearts. She died that same night. I just couldn't leave the drawing behind, but it started to rain as I left the apartment. I didn't want it to get ruined, so I hid it for safe keeping." I exhale a sad sigh. "How ironic that water finally destroyed it after all. It's like I was never meant to hold onto her memory."

"The sick bastard who set fire in your room is to blame." Sebastian's arm tightens around me. "I'm just glad I moved you when I did."

I cover my hand over his on my waist. "Me too."

Sebastian spreads his fingers and threads them with mine, folding our hands together. "Tell me the rest." When I don't answer, he says, "You looked so devastated. Tell me, Talia."

I swallow and nod. "I've been losing bits and pieces of Amelia from my memory. I can't picture exactly what her face looks like anymore." My voice cracks as I finish. "That artwork was the only thing I had left of her, Sebastian, the only sweet memory to hold onto. Nothing else survived the fire."

"You didn't mention a fire before," he says quietly.

A part of me wants to confess all my sins. I squeeze my eyes shut. I can't tell him everything. I just…can't, but I can tell him about the fire. "When I got back to my apartment after you dropped me off, there'd been an explosion in the building, destroying our place. We were later told it was a gas leak."

He presses a gentle kiss to the back of my head. "I'm sorry."

"I am too," I whisper. A few quiet moments of silence fill the space. It feels right, laying here in silence with him.

When a bright red alarm light shines in the shape of Sebastian's watch face on the ceiling from the nightstand, I'm instantly reminded of the inscription on the back. *I'm proud to call you son, Sebastian. Stay brave, remain loyal, and protect family above all else.* I love that his father saw those qualities in him, even when he was a rebellious teen.

"It's one-eleven," I say quietly. "Tell me why you set that alarm everyday."

Sebastian turns off the silent alarm, then wraps his arm around me once more. "I told you, it's a reminder."

"To remain 'diligent, aware, and ready.' I know, but you haven't told me why."

He sighs into my hair. "That night my mom died, I came home late. I'd been out drinking and doing something I shouldn't have." He pauses and exhales sharply as if the memory still pains him. "One-eleven is when the intruder entered our house. If I'd been fully sober, things might've turned out differently. Maybe I could've taken control of the situation and protected her."

"Is that why you don't drink?" When he remains quiet, I say, "Sober can't stop bullets, Sebastian. Your mom would be proud of the protector you've become, of the good you've done, and the people you've saved."

He squeezes my waist. "Keeping those I care about safe is how I operate."

It suddenly hits me where I've heard that other voice from earlier before. It was Theo talking to Sebastian outside my bathroom door. I should've known Sebastian would keep an eye on me. He wouldn't let me go undercover at the Sly Fox club without inserting his own level of protection. He has always watched over and protected me. "You assigned Theo to me, didn't you?"

"Yes."

I can tell by the tension in his body, he wonders if I'm mad. I sigh and rest my head on his arm. "Thank you for being my friend. The best actually. You've always been that to me."

Sebastian

Nobody surprises me like Talia does. As she burrows her soft body even closer, I keep my thoughts on task so I don't react to her sexy curves and arousing floral smell. If I get hard right now, I'll lose all the ground I've gained with her. Somehow I stay focused and find my voice. "I thought Cass was your best friend."

"She is, but even she doesn't know about my past like you do. You've always been there for me when times were the hardest." She grips my fingers tight. "Always. Promise me we won't lose that for each other. That no matter what, you won't lose faith in me."

"Never." I uncurl my fingers from hers and press the flat of my hand to her chest. Her rapid heartbeat hammers against my palm, while my heart calmly *thump, thumps* against her back. *Why is her heart beating so hard? How could she think I'd ever lose faith in her?* "I promise." Folding our hands back together, I press her closer and softly command, "Now go to sleep, Little Red. You're safe."

I'm amazed that she instantly falls asleep in my arms. *Best friends.* It's a foreign concept to me. Like love. I've never had a best friend. Calder is the closest, but he's family. And so is Mina. I would do anything for my family, but I've never once told any of them that I loved them. Losing my mom the way I did was more than my teenage mind could handle, so I shut that part of me off. Learning to control my emotions helped me make sense of the world that crumbled so completely around me. It seems that life has never stopped shifting under my feet, but Talia's been a beacon among the chaos.

I feel protective of her like family, yet that's where the similarity ends. My response to her is savage and passionate, my dominant instincts jacked to the highest level, pushing me to possess and defend every inch of her. I would take an entire clip of bullets for Talia. I don't even want to think how I'd react if something had happened to her tonight. I would be an epically scary motherfucker. "Best friends" is a tame, one-dimensional…*safe* description of us.

Talia's quietness as we made our way to the new hotel bothered me. She didn't speak as we entered her hotel room. I was thankful I'd booked our adjoining rooms this morning, so at least we could go straight up to the room. She didn't spare the room a glance, just set down her laptop and purse on the desk, then immediately walked into the bathroom and shut the door, locking it behind her.

As the shower turned on, I leaned against the wall next to her bathroom door and scrubbed my fingers through my hair. *I've never hated being so fucking right in my life.* The look on her face when she gazed up at me while holding that destroyed artwork tore me to shreds. I've seen fear, worry, sadness, anger, fury, and defiance flicker through her gorgeous eyes, but the emotion I witnessed tonight nearly brought me to my knees. I've never seen disillusionment in Talia before. In that moment, it felt like she'd lost hope. One of the things I'm in awe of is her unflappable optimism.

The sad sound of her sobs rising over the pounding water made me want to break down the fucking door, climb in there with her and hold her close, but I knew she wanted to be alone. So I stood there and listened, grinding the back of my teeth and growing more determined than ever to find the bastard responsible not just for threatening her life, but for taking that light out of her eyes.

She mumbles something unintelligible in her sleep, bringing me back to the present. While my gaze slides over her profile, my erection hardens. I ache all over for her. She'll let me be her friend, but not her lover? She claims I'm the only man she trusts, and to an extent, I believe that. But now that she won't allow herself to be with me, unless I seduce her into it, I feel torn up inside. My gut tells me she wants us just as much. What changed from the woman who gave herself over to me so freely at Martha's Vineyard? How do I convince her to want *us* again?

The snow outside reflects in the room, giving me a full view of her profile. Knowing she'd tense up if she were woken, I gently roll her toward me to stare at her gorgeous face. Without conscious thought, my fingers slide into her soft hair and I rub my thumb tenderly along her cheekbone. She's so soft and smells like heaven.

Touching her is pleasurable torture. I know I'm pushing my luck, but I can't help it. I've never craved someone as much as I do Talia. I can't stop thinking about her, wanting to touch her. I trace my thumb along her cheekbone once more, my fingers pressing into her scalp. *Mine.* She sighs and snuggles against my chest, whispering my name, like she's done it hundreds of times before.

The surprising act of unconscious trust and the sound of my name from her lips radiates through my chest, shooting straight to my cock. Does she feel more deeply for me than she lets on? I know she cares, because that's her nature, but could her unshakable trust in me as her protective friend also mean an unfettered acceptance of me as her lover? I'm not a perfect man and I might be broken in many ways, but no one arouses every part of me like she does. She makes me forget my flaws, and fucking hell, she satisfies me on every sexual level. Like she was made just for me. The unexpected realization sends warmth spreading through my chest, lifting the heaviness and letting me breathe deeper than I've been able to in a long time.

I smile in the darkness and press a kiss against her forehead, murmuring. "No more running. No more hiding your feelings from me. You are going down, Little Red."

CHAPTER FIFTEEN

Talia

*W*hen my eyes pop open in the morning, Sebastian's arm is still around me, his hand tucked intimately between my thighs. *Have we been like this all night?* A flush spreads across my skin and I slowly untangle us so I won't wake him. Grabbing clothes, I head for the bathroom. By the time I exit the bathroom fully dressed, I'm relieved that he's already in his own room doing business on the phone.

Even though I'm hungry, I don't bother with room service for breakfast. Instead, I pull out my laptop and start taking notes for a story idea that came to me while I was in the shower. Working always helps keep me focused, and in the light of day, last night's reality crashes around me hard. Someone wants me dead. Work will keep my mind off that very sobering fact.

I'm so in the zone, the sound of my phone ringing makes me jump. I quickly answer it. "Hey, Aunt Vanessa."

"Talia! Thank God you're all right. I saw the news blip about a fire at the Regent. I just wanted to check on you."

"I'm fine. I'm actually at a different hotel."

"Why did you move? They said the hotel guests' schedules wouldn't be disrupted."

"I just thought it was best. It's all good."

"Hmm, I've been keeping up with your tour. That was interesting learning about your security guard, aka, Mr. White, being a potential Blake. He didn't look pleased with the reporter at all."

"The reporter was being a jerk."

"I'll just be glad when the tour's over. All this marketing drama is a bit much, but hearing about the fire really worried me. I keep thinking about those letters. I want you to be safe. It's all I've ever wanted for you."

She's really wound up. "I know, Aunt Vanessa. We're still on for lunch at Rudi's."

"Did we make a lunch date?" she says, sounding instantly excited.

I frown. "Um yeah, don't you remember at the kick off party?"

"Oh, that's right." She laughs at herself. "Jotting it down now. I'm looking forward to it."

I hang up and stare at my phone, wondering how my aunt could've forgotten when she's the one who insisted on our lunch date.

"I'd like you to consider cancelling the rest of your tour," Sebastian says from the doorway between our rooms.

Instead of a suit, he's wearing a black cashmere v-neck sweater over a light gray dress shirt, dark jeans and black leather shoes. I'd asked him to dress a bit less formal for the last couple of signings today, since I planned to do the same. Even in casual clothes, the man could've stepped out of a fashion magazine. He's strikingly impressive and devastating to the heart no matter what he wears. I shake my head. "I'll cancel the Q&A hour scheduled with the media, but I'm doing these last two back-to-back signings today. I don't want to disappoint my readers."

Sebastian looks like he wants to argue, but then his phone rings. "Black here." He glances my way. "Yes, I want all the employees ID photos. I understand you can't give out personal data. The photos will do. If I find anything, I'll let you know. A file is fine." While he's talking, I send him a text with my email address, then just before he starts to walk out of my room, I wave to him.

When he pauses, I point to myself and mouth, "Send me a copy."

He nods curtly, then walks back into his room, still talking.

My stomach starts growling a few minutes later, making it hard to focus on my outline, but then I get an email from Sebastian with the file. I quickly open it and start scanning, looking for anyone familiar or anything that stands out about them.

Sebastian closes my laptop lid on my fingers. "Time to eat."

"Hey!" I glance at my phone to see an hour has passed. I pull my hands free, scowling at him. "I'm working."

"Did you get anything from that file I sent?"

I shake my head. "Was that every single employee at the Regent?"

"Yes, why?"

I tap my finger against my lips. "It wasn't who I saw, it's who I *didn't*. Are you sure they didn't hire extra staff for that kick off party the first night?"

Sebastian frowns. "Bryce told me it was the complete photo database, but I'll confirm with him. Who didn't you see in those ID photos?"

"There was a blonde woman serving drinks that night. I only noticed her because we almost collided. As I walked away, I remember thinking that she looked familiar."

"How familiar? Like someone you knew in the past?"

I shrug. "It's a vague recollection. I don't think I knew her. It's like she's someone I saw in passing. That's why I can't tell you more."

"I'll follow up with Bryce if there might be some temporary employees they brought in, but in the meantime, did any of the men seem familiar?"

I tilt my head. "Why are you asking specifically about the men?"

"Because the handwriting expert I had look over the letter you received yesterday is ninety percent certain a male wrote it. Even narrowing down the list of suspects to men, since there wasn't a log-in time for the note delivery, there's just too many people who came in and out on the security footage for us to figure out who might've dropped it off."

"You think I'm focusing on the wrong person?"

He holds my gaze. "I'm not ruling anything out."

The conversation makes me think too much about who

might be after me, and a chill races up my spine. It must've shown on my face, because Sebastian clasps my hand and pulls me to my feet. "For now, you're eating. No arguing. You skipped dinner last night."

He's right. I completely forgot that I didn't eat. Maybe that's why I feel so on edge. "We don't have time for a long meal," I say as I let him drag me to the door. "The car picks us up in a little over an hour for the first signing."

"I'm aware of the schedule, Miss Lone." Flashing a grin, he continues, "I know just the place. It's based on a similar restaurant in Paris."

"This is…different," I say skeptically as I eye the crowd inside the small, standing room no bigger than thirty feet wide and forty feet deep. Only a couple streets over from the hotel, the restaurant has menu placards hanging from the ceiling, depicting wines, appetizers and main courses.

Fast moving workers bustle behind the main counter, calling out orders to those in a back kitchen, while also handing baskets full of warm bread and tapas-style foods to people over other patrons' heads who're waiting to order at the counter. People are eating from their baskets, standing shoulder-to-shoulder at the one-foot wide standing-only island that breaks up the middle of the restaurant, or along the narrow ledge that lines the side walls.

It's a totally boisterous and chaotic environment, but people must really enjoy the experience of this place, if the long lines at the two different entrances are any indication. I'm not so sure I'll even get any food, let alone find a tiny corner to stand and eat it in.

"The food here is delicious," Sebastian says, grinning

at my hesitant expression.

"Bounty awaits the brave, Talia. How bold are you? Ready to dive in?" Before I can utter a word, he clasps my hand and tugs me into the mass of people.

I've never been more thankful for Sebastian's towering height. His wide shoulders cut a swath through the crowd and he quickly finds us a spot along the wall in the corner. As Sebastian waves to a guy behind the counter, I notice the body heat and fast conversation, keeps the place warm and buzzing with energy. In here, my long winter coat definitely feels unnecessary.

A few minutes later, one of the servers brings us several different baskets to try. While observing New Yorkers pass by the huge glass window beside us, Sebastian and I eat and chat about living in the city. I enjoy his witty observations about city-folk while I down every morsel of the perfectly marinated skewers of meat and vegetables, and sop up the juices with the restaurant's signature crusty bread.

When Sebastian moves on to funny stories about his BLACK security guys, I interrupt. "Wait, so Theo won't let you call him Bear any more because of me?" I snicker when Sebastian grunts his annoyance. I like seeing him relax enough to tell stories, even if he doesn't share ones about himself. I can't believe that a crowded, jostling stand-up restaurant could feel so cozy with him, but it does. The entire experience is unique and delicious, from the food to the company. It's definitely a place worth braving the mad crush of people for.

"I think you might know the staff," I tease Sebastian as I take the last bite of my bread. A bit of butter didn't quite make it to my mouth, and I laugh while unsuccessfully trying to wipe it away.

"Let's just say I've been here a few times." Sebastian's lips quirk as he swipes the drop from my chin. Watching him suck the butter off his thumb is so incredibly arousing, I can't tear my gaze away. All I can think about is his mouth on me just like that…licking me clean.

Another rush of people make it through the doorway at the same time that a couple with fresh baskets of food shoulder their way into the corner next to us.

When I'm pushed to the side and nudged against his chest in the process, Sebastian scowls and grasps my hip with one hand and my inner thigh with the other to steady me. I start to tell him I'm fine when his thumb slowly slides down the seam of my jeans.

Gasping quietly, I jerk my gaze up to see smoldering turquoise blue staring back at me. "All mine," he simply says, but the words make me shiver despite the heat in the room. Then he does it again, this time harder.

I glance around, but the place is so jammed, no one can see past my long winter coat. My gaze returns to his and my breath hikes. There's something incredibly sexy about him choosing to do this in such a public place.

"I'm waiting, Talia."

"For what?" I say in a breathy voice.

His gaze searches my face as his fingers dig possessively into my inner thigh. "For you to tell me to fraternize you senseless. To demand it, even."

Sebastian's suggestive comment reminds me of that stupid contract my brain seems to have temporarily forgotten during the inferno blazing between us right before the fire alarm went off last night. If I weren't so sexually frustrated, I'd find that hilariously ironic.

"But what about the contract?" I grasp at anything to keep him in line. Despite the simmering moments we've had, I know his signature on that paper was the only thing keeping him walking a very gray line. He's a man of his word, first and foremost.

Sebastian shrugs. "That jackass fired me two nights ago."

"Jared fired you?" I stiffen my spine, suddenly anxious. There's nothing to keep him from pushing hard on me now. Gray just shifted to full on black. "Why didn't you tell—?"

"I told him you rehired me." A ruthless smile tilts his lips. "He wasn't pleased."

I swallow my nervousness. "I'm sure that pissed him off royally. Why are you still here?"

That smile turns downright wolfish. "I'm waiting, Talia." His thumb pauses at the spot on my jeans that will rev me in no time. "I want to hear you say that you want me."

When I start to press my lips together, his thumb applies pressure, making my stomach flutter and my pulse skip in excitement.

"You say my name while you sleep," he says smugly. "You did it several times last night."

Do I really say his name in my sleep? Cheeks flaming, I reach down and try to remove his hand, but he just clamps onto me even tighter and leans close, saying against my temple, "Do you ache deep inside so much you feel nauseous? There's only one cure, and that's me giving you the kind of carnal satisfaction that hits you bone deep."

"Arrogant much?" I reply against his jaw, wrapping sarcasm around me like a bulletproof vest.

He cups the back of my neck as his lips move to my ear. "Not arrogance. Assurance. That's how you make me feel every time we've been together. Incredibly, deeply satisfied." Pulling back, he scans my face. "What we have is more than a connection based on strong attraction and raw chemistry. Call it friendship, call it mutual respect at the highest level, label it whatever the hell you want, Talia, but don't fucking ignore its existence." He tilts my chin, forcing my gaze to his. "I'm done letting you deny *us* with flimsy bullshit excuses. I want you to look me in the eyes and *say it*."

His eyes are so bright and intense my heart leaps. "I want you, Sebastian, but that's not enough."

He shakes his head in a fast jerk, his grip tensing on my jaw. "Yes, it fucking *is*."

My stomach twists, but he needs to know why, even if my answer means he'll turn away from us. "Not for me. I need—"

"Natalia!" Jared's voice sounds above the crowd. He's standing in the doorway, waving to get my attention.

As he shoulders his way through the crowd, Sebastian releases me and says on a low growl, "Per the terms of BLACK Security's contractual agreement, I see him as a threat to your well-being. If that shit so much as tries to put his hand on your lower back or touches you in any other intimate way, I'm going to protect you. Meaning… I'll break his fucking arm."

"No you won't!" I hiss.

His gaze narrows to a "watch me" stare. Mine narrows

too.

"I'm glad I found you," Jared says once he reaches us. Concern etching his brow, Jared ignores Sebastian's low, "You weren't invited," comment and grasps my hand in both of his. "Are you okay? I got a call this morning about the fire since the room was originally booked on the company card."

When Jared tries to rub his thumb across the back of my hand, I sense Sebastian stiffen. "Yeah, it was pretty intense." I pull away from his hold and pick up the empty baskets from the ledge. When I turn back and see the pleased smirk on Sebastian's face, I push the baskets into his hands and answer Jared. "I'm fine."

Jared eyes Sebastian, clearly waiting for him to take the baskets back to the counter. Holding Jared's expectant gaze, Sebastian stacks the baskets, then lifts them over his shoulder at the same time one of the servers walking past grabs them. Shaking off his annoyance at Sebastian's continued presence, Jared shifts his gaze back to me. "I was told this morning that your *security* cancelled your media interview today. I'd like you to reconsider."

"*I* cancelled it," I say to keep Jared's gaze on me. He does *not* need to see Sebastian's murderous glare drilling into the side of his head.

"It's the wrap-up of the tour, Talia. Not to mention, it'll show that you don't let anything get you down, something I admire tremendously about you."

"It'll wave a red flag in the face of the psycho who tried to kill her last night. No fucking book is worth risking her life over," Sebastian snaps.

"You're sure it was intentional?" Jared asks, his face

losing some of its color.

Sebastian crosses his arms. "The fire was set just inside her room door using gasoline as an accelerant. You can't get any more intentional than that."

Raking a hand through his hair, Jared blows out a breath. "We've never had anything escalate like this before. If we have proof, we need to call the police."

"We don't have enough proof to call the police in as a threat on Talia," Sebastian grates. "She switched the name on the room from her penname before the tour even started. Access to the credit card details is locked in the computer system, so whoever is responsible couldn't have used your publishing house's name or hers to target her. For now, the hotel is cooperating with the authorities' general arson investigation."

That must've been what Sebastian's phone calls were about this morning. I glance up at him. "Why didn't you tell me any of this?"

"I planned to fill you in on the way to the signings." Sebastian's gaze softens, telling me the rest. *I didn't want the case getting in the way of us. Again.*

"Are you okay with these last two signings, Talia?" Jared asks. "I'll understand if you want to cancel them under the circumstances."

I nod. "I'll be fine with Sebastian."

Sebastian doesn't look away from me as he addresses Jared. "Extra security measures have been put in place to keep the media out and the bookstores secure. Talia will be safe."

"I'd like to ride along to the signings today," Jared says, breaking the mesmerizing hold Sebastian has over me.

"Hell no."

"That'll be fine," I say, overriding Sebastian. "That way, you can deal with the media, and Sebastian's men can focus their energy on security." I smile when Sebastian clamps his jaw tight. He doesn't like it, but he knows I'm right.

"Sounds like a plan," Jared says, rubbing his hands together. "I'll spin it that you won't allow media interviews to take away from one-on-one time with your readers. Don't worry, I'll turn this into positive PR for you."

"You have exactly thirty minutes," Sebastian says from the doorway between our rooms.

"Could you be any more bossy?" I mumble as I kick off my shoes while opening my suitcase at the same time.

Sebastian tugs his sweater over his head, mussing his hair. "We wouldn't be having to hurry if Ivy League Junior hadn't pulled you in front of the cameras on our way out of that last signing."

I drop to my knees and dig through my suitcase, looking for my other nude heel. "He was just trying to wrap up the end of the tour on a positive note."

"What happened to *no* Q&A?"

Sebastian sounds so annoyed, I set my pumps on the bed and stand to face him. "So that's why—" My comment lodges in my throat. The sight of his muscular chest and mouthwatering abs flexing as he shrugs out of his button down shirt momentarily stuns me. *God, he's beautiful.* When he looks up and grins at me staring, I straighten my spine and lift my chin. "Why are you arguing with me when we have so little time?"

Sebastian opens his mouth, then closes it. Before he shuts the door behind him, he says, "You now have twenty-eight minutes."

Exhaling an exasperated sigh, I quickly grab my teal dress. I love its straight lines, pinched waist and fitted skirt that hits me a couple inches above the knees. But most of all, I love its versatility. If I wear pearls and nude pumps with it, the look is ultra classy. Switch out the pearls for sparkly, dangle earrings, and the pumps for black spiked heels, and the dress changes from classy to sexy. Smoothing out a wrinkle in the skirt, I slip on a pair of classic pearl earrings, then pick up my makeup bag and head into the bathroom.

After I've touched up my hair and make-up, I try to zip my dress. The one downside of the dress' tailored style is its hidden back zipper. The tiny tab makes it difficult to grasp and pull all the way up by myself. I can get it to my bra, but Cass usually helps the rest of the way.

My phone vibrates on the counter while I make strange contortions in the mirror. It would be funny if the clock wasn't ticking. I instantly answer, chuckling into the phone. "Hey, Cass, I could so use you right now. You forgot to pack yourself when you packed my teal dress for me."

"And to think I could be standing in the Regent being your personal dress maid instead of sitting on this veranda drinking a to-die-for coffee," she says, snickering.

"Actually, I'm not at the Regent any more. I moved to the Royal Grand due to a fire being set in my room."

"Oh, shit! I didn't know. Are you okay?"

"I'm fine, Cass. Sebastian is taking good care of me."

"Well, I'm seriously glad you're okay, but wait….as in *really* good care of you?" she says suggestively.

I snicker. "Not *that* kind. He's an excellent security guard."

"What happened to letting your inner-slut have some fun?"

Twisting my lips in a wry half-smile, I run the brush through my hair. "Apparently I don't possess your skills in putting my inner-slut to good use."

"Oh, Talia."

Cass sounds so disappointed, I sigh. "I know. I just suck at it."

"That's where I know you're wrong. You're just thinking too hard. You have to learn to shut your brain off, girl. Please, for me, just give yourself a night with him. And if things don't work out, and he breaks your heart, I promise to hang with you and watch sappy movies and eat buckets of ice cream until we want to bust. I'll even go out and buy you a bigger BOB if you want me to."

I can't help but laugh. She really is the best. Letting my laughter fade, I sigh. "I can't."

"Yes, you can! Everything you've ever worked for— getting into that journalism program early in college, your job at the Tribune, *twice*. Busting up that human trafficking ring at the Sly Fox club, writing two books in the time you normally write one…You've worked your tail off for every one of those accomplishments. Why would you expect someone like Sebastian to be any different?"

She has a point. Sebastian is anything but easy. But he's

also an unpredictable person, not a goal to be reached. I exhale and smile. "I'll keep that in mind. I miss you. When are you getting home?"

"In a couple of days."

"I can't wait until you get back. We'll crack open a bottle of wine, and I'll regale you with all the tour goings on, and you can tell me how brilliant your shoot went."

"Deal. See you soon. Oh, and Talia?"

"Yeah?"

"Step off the ledge. Anyone worth winning has to be worth losing your heart to in the first place."

She always makes me smile. "More magazine advice?"

"Nope. That was a one-hundred-percent, genuine Cassism. You're welcome. Now go have that hunky man take care of your zipper. I suggest down, not up."

Snickering, I tell her goodbye before she can give me any more relationship advice. Hooking my arms over my shoulder, I try to pull the zipper the rest of the way.

When I hear Sebastian walk into my room, I blow out a breath of frustration and step out of the bathroom. "Hey, do you think you can help me zip my—holy *shit*."

Yeah, I said it out loud—Cass-style—but the last thing I expect to see is Sebastian wearing formal dress blues, his black-billed white hat with gold trim tucked under his arm. There's a reason women drool over men in uniform, but Sebastian standing in my room, his dark hair perfectly combed, bright blue eyes piercing into me as his broad shoulders fill out his Navy uniform to utter perfection, is just downright cruel. *How am I supposed to resist that?*

Sebastian gives a wry smile. "Mina insisted on dress white. I argued for a suit. We compromised on dress blue.

My sister said taking on godfather duties deserves the uniform."

I knew in my heart that Mina chose Sebastian for such an important role in Josi's life, but hearing him say it drills the fact home. How will he feel when he learns I'm going to be Josi's godmother? Will it make him uncomfortable? I start to tell him, but then the look in his eyes as he sets his hat on the desk stops me. It's saying so much more. I watch him re-straighten a perfectly knotted tie and realize why he looks tense and edgy. He doesn't feel right wearing it. Why? Then it hits me...

Now that he's a civilian, he doesn't believe he deserves to wear the uniform. Knowing how he left the Navy, I can't let him think that way, so I walk right up to him and put my hand on his chest. Sliding my palm to his shoulder, I smile. "You look fantastic. I agree with Mina. It's perfect for a christening." I smirk and touch the gilt eagle button on his midnight blue, double-breasted jacket, then tap his tie. "Not to mention, those gold stripes on your sleeves will have all the ladies swooning in their seats. In a church, no less."

Sebastian clasps my waist, his expression turning serious. "There's only one woman I want to swoon, but she's too busy saying 'no,' while her body tells a different story every time I touch her."

My heart ramps and my breasts swell as his big hands wrap around my waist. I swallow and start to speak, but he quickly spins me around, then brushes my hair to the side as if he'd never said anything. "A stubborn zipper, huh?"

Trying to regain my composure, I inhale deeply and

nod, holding my hair out of the way for him. "If you wouldn't mind."

He starts to slide the zipper up, then pauses to press a warm kiss to the back of my neck. Chill bumps instantly scatter across my skin, and just as I exhale a sharp, steadying breath, he zips it the rest of the way.

Before I can move away, he slides the pads of his fingers down my arms just below the dress' capped sleeves. Tracing the raised skin, his voice is a husky rasp in my ear. "Every time I touch her."

CHAPTER SIXTEEN

Talia

I'm surprised when Sebastian opens the front passenger door for me, but then the driver gets out and Sebastian slides behind the wheel of the black Mercedes. He doesn't say anything to me the entire car ride. I can tell he has something on his mind, so I don't intrude on his thoughts.

Once he pulls into a parallel spot twenty yards back from the church, I start to open the door, but he scowls at me. Sighing, I release the handle. He sets his uniform hat on his head before he opens the passenger door and holds his hand out. I still can't get over how handsome he is in a uniform as I put my hand in his. With Mina's gift bag in my other hand, I step onto the snow cleared, newly salted sidewalk.

"At least it's not snowing," I say, glancing up at the burgeoning clouds ready to dump another four inches by the evening, according to the weather app on my phone.

Sebastian grunts his agreement and tucks my hand in the crook of his arm. I hold onto him, appreciating the support since the sidewalk has a bit of an incline.

When we approach what appears to be a patch of snow at least twenty feet long, Sebastian doesn't say a word, he just turns and scoops me into his arms.

"I could've walked across it," I say quietly, my face turning beet red when an audience of people standing outside the church start clapping.

"You're not twisting your ankle on my watch," he says in a matter of fact tone, completely ignoring the two guys who are now belting out a few lines from *An Officer and a Gentleman's* theme song.

As soon as we reach the well-salted area in front of the church, he sets me down. While Sebastian is greeted by his half-brothers, Gavin and Damien, with shoulder hand-clapping and a bit of ribbing, I look up the stairs leading to the church's massive main doors, and meet the icy, distrusting stare of a thin, blonde woman holding court by the left door. I instantly recognize Isabel from news articles about the Blake family. Standing beside her is her husband, Adam, who is shaking hands and chatting with those just arriving. She gives me one last disdainful glare, then turns away with a tilt of her nose to smile at someone reaching in to hug her. I start to move closer to Sebastian when another guy with short, light brown hair clamps on to Sebastian's shoulders, wrapping an arm tight around his neck. "Heya, bro. Long time no see."

My heart races for Sebastian. As I watch him turn and shake Calder's hand then pull him into a hug, happiness fills my chest. Calder might be his cousin by blood, but he's truly his brother. I'm so glad he came to the christening. I hope that means they'll get a chance to talk.

My hand is clasped and it's instantly tucked into the crook of another man's arm. I look up and smile at Den, who's gazing down at me from his massive height with wise eyes. "Would you allow me to escort you up the stairs, Miss Lone?"

I smile brightly at him and squeeze his arm. "That would be wonderful. Thank you, Den. And please, call me Talia."

He nods and walks me up the stairs. Without consciously realizing it, people move out of Den's way. His imposing build and height are like an invisible force field. I smile at the effect he has on everyone without even trying. "No wonder Mr. Blake hired you. This is like 'red sea' awesome."

As we move off the last step and into the crowd near the church doors, Den lets out a deep laugh. "You're so refreshing, Talia. It's my pleasure. Anytime."

When I look over and see Adam staring at Den, I release my hold on him. "Thank you for the escort. I believe Mr. Blake needs you."

Den doesn't even look Adam's way. He just gives me a slight nod and glides through the crowd toward his boss.

"Talia!" Mina calls excitedly as she weaves her way through the people, her charcoal wool coat flapping around her calves. Josi is propped on her hip wearing an adorable white dress under a fur-trimmed winter coat.

When I touch her coat's fuzzy hood and smile at Josi, Mina waves her hand. "It looks real, but it's faux. I'm so glad you're here early." Craning her neck, she turns to look for her parents. "I wanted to introduce you to my mom, but it looks like she and my father might have already gone inside. Where's Sebastian? The pastor wants Josi, me, you, and my brother to come inside now."

"He's down there talking to Calder…" I start to say, then trail off when I glance down the stairs to see a tall woman with long dark hair hugging Sebastian. Pulling back, she grins at him then swipes his hat off his head and drops it down on hers.

"Calder's here?" Mina practically squeals in my ear. Before I can ask who the woman flirting with Sebastian is, Mina's curled blonde hair is flowing behind her as she races down the stairs, excitedly saying, "Calder Blake. I can't believe you came!"

While Calder swoops she and Josi into a huge bear hug, spinning them around, my gaze stays locked on Sebastian and the brunette. She's standing in his personal space, fiddling with his lapel. He reaches for his hat, but she backs just out of his range, laughing as she holds it on her head.

"They are striking together, aren't they?" a woman's husky voice says next to me. When I look at her, Isabel turns cool blue eyes my way, her face flushed from the frigid air. "Regan should be standing up there during the ceremony, but despite my best efforts, I can't control the whims of my flighty daughter."

Regan. That's the girl who Sebastian had a semi-relationship with when he first got back from leaving the service. The girl's obvious familiarity with him makes sense, while also making me nauseous. But as much as Isabel's statement about Sebastian and Regan bothers me, it's her comment about her own child that I focus on. "Mina's not flighty, Mrs. Blake. She's had a rough time of it, so maybe instead of tearing her down, you could try to lift her up."

Isabel narrows her gaze on me, her breath coming out her nose in long, dragon-like plumes. "How dare you tell me how to be a mother, you conniving little gold-digger. You might've snowed my husband, but I'll be perfectly clear with you. You will *never* see a penny of Blake money. Your role as godmother is just window dressing."

I shake my head at her vitriol, not at all surprised by her one-track mind. No wonder Sebastian despises her so deeply. "The great thing about not being motivated by money or social status, is that I have nothing to lose. It would be wise if you steered clear of me, Mrs. Blake. I have no problem calling you out, *whenever* and *wherever* you deserve it. My only priority is Mina and Josi's well-being."

"Uncouth trash," Isabel utters before walking away in a huff, her heels clicking on the hard floor in the church's entryway.

A petite woman close to Mina's age approaches. Tucking her wavy, shoulder-length black hair behind her ear, she wrinkles her nose, a spattering of freckles showing up along her smooth light brown skin. "That was better than reality TV. Now I see why Mina chose you as godmother over us."

I smile and hold out my hand. "I'm Talia. You must be

one of Mina's childhood friends."

She nods and shakes my hand, dark brown eyes reflecting amused respect as she releases me. "I'm Laura. I've never seen anyone stand up to Isabel like that." Tilting her head toward the bottom of the stairs, she continues, "Not even Regan. We deserve second chair."

"Second chair?"

She nods. "Yeah, Mina's mother insisted that she have more than one godmother, so Regan and I get the honor of second godmother, for lack of a better term. Which basically means we get to sit upfront beside Isabel in the pew during the ceremony."

"Ah, I see," I say, offering a smile of sympathy that she has to be anywhere near Isabel.

At that moment, Mina shoulders her way back through friends and family with Sebastian in tow. Josi is giggling while her mom happily calls out, "Coming through with the girl of the hour."

Quickly passing by, Mina says to Sebastian, "Grab Talia. The ceremony starts in ten minutes, but Pastor Meyer wants us there now."

Though surprise reflects in his eyes, Sebastian doesn't hesitate to clasp my hand and pull me inside the church with them.

After the stoic-faced pastor with a bone-crushing grip tells Sebastian and me where to stand during the christening ceremony, and then turns to Mina to discuss a couple last minute details, Sebastian says, "Why didn't you tell me Mina asked you to be Josi's godmother?"

I offer an apologetic shrug. "When you invited me to come with you today, I realized that you had no idea Mina had asked me. I didn't know what to tell you. What if Mina wanted to surprise you?"

He snorts. "She certainly accomplished that."

His sharp quip makes my chest hurt. "Is it so hard to believe she would ask me?" I say, frowning slightly. I glance toward the front pew where Regan and Laura are seated next to Isabel, Adam, Gavin, and Damien. "Do you think Regan is a better choice to stand up here with you?"

"What?"

"Talia, Sebastian, it's time," Mina whispers, beckoning us.

As Sebastian and I walk forward, and then turn to the side to wait for the ceremony to begin, I catch a glimpse of Regan staring at Sebastian with heat in her gaze. When she turns to whisper something in Laura's ear, then gives me a smug look, I swallow the bile in my throat. Based on Laura's scandalously shocked expression, it's probably something kinky she and Sebastian have done.

The pastor calls us forward to stand beside Mina and all my focus shifts to Sebastian's little sister and her child. And as I watch the love in Mina's eyes as she holds a squirming Josi still for the pastor to pour water over her head, I can't help but hope for an unconditional love in my own life one day.

Do Sebastian and I even have a chance? Or were we doomed from the start, each of us carrying too much baggage for the other to handle. Cass' last words come back to me. If anyone's worth the risk of losing my heart to, it's Sebastian.

As the pastor discusses the important role godparents play in shaping the life of a child, I look at Sebastian and see him staring at me with an unfathomable depth of emotion. I smile, and just as he returns it, the pastor turns to us.

"In lieu of traditional vows, Mina has chosen a different one today." Opening the pamphlet he's holding, he continues, "These ribbons represent your commitment to Josi. Speak from the heart as you tie your bow on each wrist, binding your word and your hearts with hers. Sebastian, you take yours first."

My pulse rises as I stare at the two quarter-inch-wide ribbons, ten inches in length lying side by side in the crease of the pamphlet. One is baby pink and one is baby blue. Sebastian won't be able to tell the colors apart. *Why would Mina do this to Sebastian?*

I glance to her for help, but Josi is keeping her mom busy by working herself up to a good cry. Mina is too distracted to rescue Sebastian, so I quickly reach over and grab the pink one. When the pastor frowns disapprovingly at me for not waiting my turn, I smile sheepishly and whisper, "Sorry, I'm just so excited."

Sebastian chuckles and takes his ribbon, then gestures for me to go first.

I tie the delicate ribbon in a bow around Josi's tiny wrist now that Mina has settled her. Josi's big green eyes stare up at me as I rub my fingers through her blonde baby-soft curls. "Little Josi, you and I are going to have great adventures together. There will never be a puzzle you can't solve or a mystery you can't figure out. You will grow up smart and brave, and you'll never fear failure, because you'll know that no matter what, you're protected and loved for just being you."

Sebastian ties his ribbon around Josi's other wrist in a very neat bow. I smile at his military precision and patience despite the baby's flapping arm. Cupping her entire head in his big hand, he bends down and kisses the top of it, then says, "Josi-bean, there's no greater protector than your Uncle Sebastian. You concentrate on growing up strong-minded and fearless, and I'll take care of the riff-raff. Enough said."

As the entire congregation laughs at Sebastian's no-nonsense vow, I can't help but smile. It's so Sebastian. Watching him kiss the baby's head about does me in though. I sniff back the tears that cloud my vision. He is *everything* I want. Everything. Can I convince him to keep me—to want us—forever?

When the ceremony is over and after the photographer has taken tons of pictures of us with Mina and Josi, my heart skips a beat when I hear Adam call Sebastian's name as the crowd disperses out of the church.

"Sebastian, a word please."

I try not to stare when Sebastian walks out of the church to speak to his father, but Mina distracts me, gripping onto my arm. "I'm so horrified."

"By what?" I glance around to see where Josi is. Isabel is showing her off to some friends. Resisting the urge to walk over and snatch the baby away from her grandmother, I say calmly, "I thought the ceremony went well."

Mina looks on the verge of tears. "The ribbons, Talia. I provided a red and navy blue one to make sure Sebastian wouldn't have an issue, but the pastor is very traditional. He switched them without telling me."

I lay my hand over hers. "It all worked out. Sebastian

doesn't blame you."

"Only because you jumped in. I can't thank you enough for fixing my blunder."

I release her hand and hug her, whispering in her ear, "We're family, Mina."

She hugs me back, squeezing me super tight. "Thank you for storming your way into my life."

I laugh and squeeze her back. "I'll be waiting for an invite to that girls' night out you promised."

Pulling back, Mina smiles. "And thank you for the lovely bracelet for Josi. I especially love the heart. Your gift is coming later tonight. You'll see why."

I nod my understanding, a little sad to see she's not wearing the floating heart I gave her. Not that I expected her to wear it everyday. All that really matters was the thought behind it. Asking me to be her child's godmother pretty much solidifies that Mina trusts I'll keep my word.

"Here, she's getting fussy," Isabel says, handing Josi back to Mina. Eyeing me, she continues, "It would've been a much nicer ceremony if you hadn't been so rude to the pastor by jumping in front of Sebastian like you did. You'll never see him again, but I have to see that man every Sunday."

"Mother!" Mina looks like she's about to explode, but I put a restraining hand on her arm where she's holding Josi on her hip.

"I apologize for my overzealousness, Mrs. Blake."

She sniffs and tilts her chin up. "See that you don't teach my grandchild such uncivilized behavior. It won't be tolerated."

As her mother walks away, Mina looks at me, her eyes

full of abject apology.

I just smile. "She's exhausting, isn't she?"

Mina starts giggling and can't stop. She's giggling so much Josi starts laughing, which is the sweetest sound. I start to laugh too. Laura comes over to see what's so funny and Josi's laugh draws her in as well. We're all still chuckling as we walk into the church's entryway together. I let the girls walk out and slip into the bathroom.

When I leave the bathroom, I'm surprised to see Calder open a side Exit door instead of walking out the way everyone else has.

"Calder, right?" I call out quietly.

His broad shoulders tense and he turns to look at me, light brown eyebrows pulling down. "You're Josi's godmother, but we've never met. How do you know me?"

I approach and hold my hand out. "You met me as 'Scarlett' at that masked party for Mina a few years ago. I'm Talia."

A brief smile registers in his serious expression as he takes my hand, vivid green eyes skimming over my face. "Ah, Scarlett of the Red Hood. You're much prettier without your mask."

"Thank you," I say with a smile, then gesture to the main entrance. "Why aren't you leaving that way?"

Pain flickers in his expression for a split second before he releases our clasped hands. "I came for Mina and Josi, but I can only handle so much family time."

I tilt my head, studying his expression. The loneliness in his eyes breaks my heart. "I'm sure Sebastian would love to have a drink with you now that the christening is over."

"Yeah, he mentioned it, but..." Calder spears his hand through his short hair, then rubs the back of his neck and exhales a long breath. "I'm not...I just can't be here right now."

He starts to turn away, but then looks back at me. "Would you do me a favor though? Can you tell Celeste that I appreciated her letter more than she'll ever know, and... apologize to her for me for not writing back? My life kind of went sideways right after that party."

Did Cass send him a letter as Celeste? Why didn't she tell me? I know he's referring to his father passing away, but I don't want to bring up a painful memory, so I quickly nod. "I'll tell her." And even though I want to tell him the truth about Celeste, I don't know if he's in the right frame of mind to hear it, but I want to give him *something* that'll brighten his day. "I'll bet she'd love to hear from you. It's never too late to reconnect, Calder."

A half smile tilts his lips as he slides his hands in his suit pant pockets. "You think so?"

If he and Cass start communicating via email, she can meet him in person and tell him who she really is. The truth should come from her, not me. I lift my hands and smile. "What do you have to lose?"

He shrugs, glancing toward the church entryway where people are outside chatting and laughing. "Not much."

It makes me sad that he feels so disconnected from his family. "Would you like her contact information?"

He shakes his head. "No, I've got it. Thanks, Talia."

At least he kept it. As he opens the door, I say, "Please touch base with Sebastian and let him know how you're doing. He's been worried about you."

Calder snorts and gives me a "you really don't know my cousin very well" look. "Bash never worries."

Before I can tell him how wrong he is, he's gone, the door quietly clicking closed behind him.

When I step outside, I glance around, looking for Sebastian. Regan has cornered him outside yet again. Apparently she'd grabbed his hat from the church pew, and now she's flirting with him once more. Makes me wonder why he even brought it. The moment he walked into the church, he took it off. Then again, it is part of his uniform.

Instead of walking over and snatching the damn hat out of her hand like I want to, I decide to wait by the car. Too many uncivilized moments in a row might revoke my godmother card. Since most all the guests have already driven home, I can see our car from here. I hug Mina and Josi goodbye. While Mina's chatting with Laura, I wave to Den as he walks out of the church ahead of the Blakes, then start down the sidewalk. At least someone has cleared the snow from earlier, leaving me a clear path.

Cars zoom by, horns beeping. *Always in a rush to get around someone.* I shiver as cold air blows against my coat and turn my collar up, then push my hands deeper into the pockets. Staring at the steep pile of snow that has been pushed along the backside of the sidewalk, growing taller as I head down the street, I let my mind wonder. I would've crawled all over that as a kid and used it for cover in snowball fights. At one point, the pile of snow completely covers the three-foot brick wall that frames the small courtyards in front of the homes lining the street. I grin when I see that the mound grows to over six feet farther down. Now that would make an awesome hill for King of the Mountain.

"Talia!" Sebastian calls my name at the same time I hear his footfalls coming up behind me fast and hard. I pause, his tone is so sharp and full of alarm, I glance over my shoulder.

"Run!" he yells at the same time I see a fast moving car fully jump the curb not thirty feet behind him, racing out of control.

I start running, but the snow is blocking my way on the left and other cars are driving by on the right, completely ignoring the car careening down the sidewalk. The only path I have to run is straight ahead.

My lungs burn and running in heels is crushing my toes, but I keep pushing forward. I yelp when I'm suddenly yanked off my feet. Sebastian's arm is a steel band around my waist and we're climbing up the huge mound of snow. I try to help, but he's much bigger and faster. All I can do is touch my toes to the snow and pray he gets us out of the way.

The force of the car hitting the pile of snow, its back end jackknifing into the front of a parked car, sends us careening over the edge. Sebastian turns as we fall, taking most of the impact as we roll the rest of the way down into the snow-covered yard. When we finally stop, I land on his chest, facing him. Heavy clumps of snow rain down on us, and my forehead stings, but at least the danger is over. The brick wall and heavily packed snow stopped the car.

While I try to regain my breath, Sebastian grasps my head between his hands. "Shit, I thought—" He cuts off and swallows. "Are you okay?"

I gulp and then nod, finally regaining the ability to speak. "Are you ok—?"

The hard pressure of his warm mouth landing on mine feels so good, I instantly kiss him back, soaking in his warmth and amazing smell. He tugs me closer, and when he tilts my head, his tongue tracing along mine, seeking deeper intimacy, the snow caked on my hair seeps into my scalp, making me shiver.

Breaking our kiss, he brushes the snow out of my hair, his voice suddenly brusque. "We're not going back to the hotel."

"We're not?"

Sebastian shakes his head, then rolls to his feet, pulling me with him. Scooping me up in his arms, he carries me across the snow-covered yard. Just as he sets me down on the pavement, Den reaches us, his attention on full alert as he addresses Sebastian. "Jesus, you weren't kidding about the danger she's in." Shifting his gaze to me, he says, "Are you all right?"

When I nod, Sebastian looks over the crushed front end of the car, then peers past the broken glass and beyond the empty driver's seat. Glancing up at Den, he says, "Steering wheel is tied and a heavy brick is on the gas pedal." His narrowed gaze searches up the street where the car had to have started from, looking for the culprit. Shifting his attention back to Den, he says, "I'm taking Talia somewhere safe. I'll send some of my men here. Check out the vehicle and let me know what you learn."

"You shouldn't take the car you came in just in case." Den pulls a pair of keys out of his pants' pocket. "Take my car. It's around the corner on the backside of the church.

I'll be in touch."

Sebastian cranks up the heat in Den's BMW. I don't say anything while he makes a call to someone named Elijah as he maneuvers through traffic. But once he hangs up and we're on the highway, I say, "Sebastian..."

"Not a word," he says in a clipped tone.

His expression is intense, his hold on the steering wheel tight. I'm not sure what he's thinking, but I can't just sit here. "We should—"

He reaches over and clasps my hand. "I didn't think I was going to get to you in time, Talia."

I glance down at his big hand folded around mine. The tension in his hold says volumes. He's on-the-edge and really doesn't want to talk. Not right now. So I fold my fingers around his hand and clamp my lips closed. He'll talk when he's ready.

After we pull up to a sky rise apartment building on the Upper East Side, I glance at Sebastian as he hands the car keys to the valet. Then he tugs me through an elegant main entrance and straight into an elevator.

He doesn't release my hand. Instead he punches in a code with his free one, then hits the top floor button.

Who lives here? I wonder as we zip toward to the penthouse floor.

The moment we walk inside and low lights automatically turn on, Sebastian begins slipping the gold gilt eagle buttons of his coat free. Reaching over, he slides the silky black scarf from my throat. While he turns and sets them on a side table farther into the room, I stand in the entryway, staring in awe at the floor-to-ceiling windows that span across the entire apartment and the amazing city-view beyond.

Sebastian stalks forward, and I back up at the focused look on his face. Placing his hands on the intricately carved doorjamb on either side of me, he commands in a low tone, "Take off your coat."

"Is this your apartment?" I ask as I fumble with the buttons.

He straightens and yanks his tie off, then unbuttons the top two buttons on his shirt, his fingers moving with swift precision. "It's wet. Get it off."

As soon as I shrug out of it, he takes my coat and tosses it behind him. When it lands in a heavy heap on the polished wood floor, he steps into my personal space. His broad shoulders blocking me in. "There's only one place I want to be right now. Take your underwear off."

Stomach fluttering with anticipation, I swallow and start to speak, but his mouth sets in a determined line. "If I remove them, you won't be able to put them back on."

My heart races as I toe off my heels and then start to shimmy out of my underwear. Now that I'm barefoot, Sebastian's massive size towers over me. But he hasn't moved back an inch; he's taking up my entire personal bubble. Once I've kicked my underwear to the side, he clasps my hips and slides his hands down my curves. Bunching my skirt between his fingers, he dips his head, his husky voice vibrating against my jaw. "Unbuckle my pants, Talia. Show me that you want us."

My hands shake with my own need, but I manage to unbuckle his belt. Quickly sliding the leather out of the loops, I drop the belt to the floor with a loud clatter. When I reach for the button on his pants, Sebastian's lips mark a searing path down the side of my throat. I gasp in excitement when his hands slip under my dress to palm my bare hips in a fierce hold, warm skin to warm skin.

"Touch me," he commands, his fingers digging into my ass.

The second I push his pants and boxers down, and then wrap my fingers around his thick erection, Sebastian exhales harshly in my ear. Stepping aggressively between my thighs, he effortlessly lifts me, sliding my body along the door.

Heart thrumming, I grip his shoulders and wrap my legs around his hips, holding his serious gaze as he slowly lowers me until his cock slides just inside me. The tease shatters my even breathing. As a gust of want rushes past my lips, Sebastian closes his eyes for a second, then snaps them open. The lustful heat and yearning in them whooshes the rest of the air from my lungs. "You're soaking me, and it's sweet fucking torture. It has always been for me, hasn't it, Talia?"

Tears spill down my cheeks with my nod.

"I need to hear you say it," he says, desperate.

I clasp his jaw with both hands. "I want you to fraternize me senseless, in every way possible, Sebastian. You're the *only* man I've ever wanted."

A rumble of unadulterated satisfaction sounds in his throat and he pulls my body down over him in one powerful jerk.

As I let out a wail of shocked pleasure, he goes completely still and locks his hands on my hips, keeping me in place. "Don't move. Not one muscle," he orders.

I bite my lip, but even as I nod I can't stop my body's

reaction to finally feeling him deep inside me. Of their own accord, my lower muscles begin to contract around him, and once they start, my orgasm rushes over me. I vaguely register what sounds like wood cracking as my body is racked with pulses of intense shudders, quickly followed by chill bumps scattering across tingling skin.

Sebastian mutters colorful curse words, then drops his head to my shoulder, literally shaking. Once my body stops clenching around his hardness, I slide my fingers through his hair and clasp his head to my shoulder, whispering in his ear, "I'm sorry. I couldn't stop. I can't help how you make me feel, Sebastian. It's just too intense."

"Fuck-ing hell." His breathing continues to bellow, his back and shoulder muscles turning hard as stone. Pressing his face into the crook of my neck and shoulder, he grips my ass with both hands and takes several deep breaths. I didn't even realize he'd been holding me up with just one hand until then. Finally, he stops quaking.

A warm, steady breath rushes out, teasing my collarbone just before his grip on me tightens. Slowly withdrawing from me, he slides his thick length back inside with an erotic roll of his hips. As he moans along my neck, pressing his mouth against my skin, I twist my fingers in his hair and hold on, soaking in every breathy bit of the mounting intensity and passion between us.

He picks up the pace, this time burying himself so deep I lean my head back and relish the gratifying sensation of being so thoroughly taken. Arching, I begin to move with him, meeting his powerful thrusts with counters of my own.

Sebastian pauses and hooks one arm under my ass and

the other against my back. On a deep rush of breath, he says, "Hold on a sec, Little Red." Stepping out of his pants and boxers, he walks us over to the black leather couch.

Lifting me off him, he sets me down on my feet, then quickly turns me around to unzip my dress.

By the time I step out of my dress and slide free of my bra, he's already taken his shirt off. Tugging me onto the couch, Sebastian tucks me under his powerful body, then clasps my hands, pulling them over my head.

Our breathing ramps once more as his knee nudges my thighs apart. When he slowly eases himself inside me once more, he rumbles, "Fuck, you're perfect, Talia. Made for me." Letting out a primal sound, he dips his head and sucks one of my nipples into his mouth, then releases it. He does the same to the other, but doesn't stop increasing his mouth's pressure until I moan. As soon as I start to move my hips, he jerks his forward, thrusting hard.

I arch into the erotic sensation of his rough claiming of my body. Tugging my hands free, I dig my nails into his back, jacking his desire even more. "I want to smell like you, Sebastian, to be unable to walk tomorrow without cursing. You keep telling me I'm yours, show me why I'll always feel empty without you inside me."

"I *am* the last fucking man for you," he vows. Hooking his hand on my thigh, he yanks it high up on his hip, and a fierce roar erupts from his throat as he surges deep. His balls teasing my sensitive sex, Sebastian rocks against me, grinding his hard body along my clit, heightening my desire with just the right amount of pressure. When I squirm and gasp, my insides tightening, building toward release, he says in a low, determined tone, "There's no question you're mine. That you *will* always be mine."

The intensity of his words, mixed with the sharp edge of pleasure/pain he inflicts as his powerful frame stakes its claim on my body, puts me on the precipice, but it's the last statement he utters before clamping his teeth on my bottom lip that sends me over. "And I am yours."

The bliss and intensity of my orgasm is so extreme that my vision dims, then it blurs with tears. Sebastian captures my cries of pleasure in a dominant kiss before he follows me over. I hold him close and relish the sound of his guttural shout and the comforting sensation of his big muscular body locked to mine while he coats my insides, thoroughly marking me his.

CHAPTER SEVENTEEN

Talia

Sebastian doesn't move. Instead, he lowers his forehead to mine and stays buried. After a few seconds, he lifts his head and frowns when he brushes my hair back. "You've got a cut on your forehead."

"Ice," I explain, then touch my thumb next to a gash along his jawline. "Yours looks deeper. I wonder if you'll need stitches."

"I've had worse." He meets my gaze and slides his knuckles along my cheekbone. "What made you finally say 'yes'?"

I'm surprised by the brief vulnerable look in his eyes. Smiling, I shake my head. "I finally let go of losing you."

His brows pull down. "Are you saying you don't care if you lose me now?"

I slide my fingers through his bangs. Gripping them in a fist, I hold on tight. "No, Sebastian. I decided to stop being *afraid* of losing you."

"Is that why you kept me at arm's length all this time? Because you were afraid you'd lose me?" With a laugh, he cups my breasts, pushes them together, then buries his nose in the cleavage. Inhaling like a man starved, his deep voice rumbles against my chest. "Why would I ever leave such beautiful breasts?"

I smack his shoulder. "Oh, so it's my chest you're infatuated with now, is it?"

His eyes snap to mine, a wicked smile flashing. "How many times do I have to tell you it's my second favorite place? I guess I'll just have to show you."

He moves so fast, standing and gathering me in his arms, all I can do is wrap my arms around his shoulders, my stomach fluttering in anticipation of his plans.

As Sebastian passes the table with his jacket, an idea forms and I snag my black scarf. While he carries me into a huge bedroom with a massive king-size bed, I quickly tie the scarf around my eyes. Once he flips on the warm floodlights in the bathroom and sets me down, I turn toward him and grin when I realize I can see him through the gauzy material. Twirling one end of the scarf between my fingers, I tease, "Hmmm, bring back any memories?"

Emotion churns in Sebastian's gaze. "Actually, I have a better idea," he says as he removes the scarf. "Would you like to take a shower like I do?" he asks against my ear.

I nod, intrigued.

Sebastian flips the light switch back off, dousing the room in darkness. Then he pushes another button on the wall and skylights above the shower appear at the same time ceiling-to-floor vertical blinds begin to turn against the far wall, allowing the city lights to bleed into the room. "Is that a Jacuzzi?" I ask, staring at the huge sunken tub next to the blinds.

"We'll use it another time," he says, his voice full of sensual promise as he clasps my hand and guides me toward a huge walk-in shower.

Once he taps on a button along the outside of the shower, and water begins to pour out of the square plate in the ceiling in a smooth, steady rain, Sebastian pulls me under the warm spray.

Pressing my back against his hard chest, he wraps his arms around my waist and tilts his head back, exhaling in contentment as the water spills over our bodies.

I sigh blissfully when Sebastian dribbles shampoo on my scalp and begins to massage suds into my hair. Once he rinses the suds away, he pours body soap down the middle of my chest and as the masculine scent of the liquid slides all the way to the hair between my legs, I arch into his knowing hands, wrapping my arms around his neck while his hands slide sensually across my chest before moving down to appreciate the full weight of my breasts.

He kisses behind my ear, down my neck and then along my jaw the whole time his hands are on my breasts. Cupping them, he slides his thumbs around the areolas several times before tweaking my nipples. Just when I think I'm going to lose it all over again, his hands shift to massage along my arms.

After he turns his attention to my waist, Sebastian's fingers curve around my hipbones and meet at my bellybutton before slowly sliding down to the hair between my thighs. When his fingers dip lower, I tighten my arms around his neck and nip at his jaw, encouraging him to spend as much time in that area as he deems necessary.

His low laugh rumbles against my back before he clasps my elbows and pulls my arms down to run his hands over mine. When he slides his thumbs along my palms and then rubs each finger individually, I'm thoroughly enthralled by his attentive exploration of my body. Then I turn around and start to return the favor. But while I'm massaging shampoo into his hair and his eyes are squeezed shut to avoid the suds, he grasps my hips and rubs his erection against me. I laugh and instantly move my sudsy hands to his cock and begin to bathe him thoroughly.

Groaning, Sebastian tilts his head back and lets the water rinse away the soap in his hair. When the action also rinses the suds from my hands, I lean over and slide my lips down his erection. Taking him deep into my mouth, I suck hard then twist my tongue around him as I pull upward. I love hearing his growl of pleasure and the feel of his hand snaking into my hair, fisting the wet locks between his fingers.

"Every part of you feels so fucking good around me." His strangled words rush out on a frustrated grunt right before he uses his hold to pull me off him.

"What the hell, Sebastian!" I gasp at the sudden cold sensation of the shower wall against my back, but Sebastian presses his hard body fully against mine and captures my mouth in a devastating kiss, devouring me with a wild abandon I've never felt from him before.

As the steam between us starts to compete with the

steam in the shower, he slows the arousing sexual rhythm of his tongue against mine and breaks the kiss to murmur against my cheekbone, "I have plans that involve coming long and hard in that beautiful pussy of yours, Little Red. I want to be up to the task."

When he tilts my chin and presses a gentle kiss to my forehead near my wound, I grumble, "One of these days, you'll let me give you a proper blow job."

Hooking his thumb on my chin, his blue gaze drills into me. "I don't want to think about how you became so incredibly talented in that area, but rest assured, from the teasers I've had, I'm relishing being totally sucked in by you."

I giggle at his pun and his lips quirk. Chuckling, he turns me in his arms. As he moves us under the spray once more, I lean my head back against his shoulder and sigh my pleasure of feeling so content in his arms. Holding my hand out, I enjoy the massaging sensation of the water battering away on my palm. "I had no idea taking a shower in the dark could be so sensory."

Sebastian cups one of his hands just above mine, gathering water in it. "What do you see, Talia?"

As I stare at the pool of water, he opens his fingers and it all drains away, hitting my hand below and sliding off in clear rivulets. "I see water."

"Do you remember what my three favorite things were on your invitation to that ball at Hawthorne's?"

I lay my palm on his and fold our hands together. "They were black, red, and water."

I feel him nod behind me. "Like us, water is a favorite because it's one constant that never changes. It always remains the same. No matter what."

I melt that he's calling us, Black and Red, just as steady and constant as water, but the underlying tone of his voice sounds both frustrated yet grudgingly accepting, making me wonder what deeper meaning he's trying to convey. When he cups the water in his hand again and exhales deeply as he lets it go, I suddenly understand what he's trying to tell me.

I've been doing everything I can to get Sebastian to *tell* me about his colorblindness, while Sebastian, in his own way, has been *showing* me the limits of his vision. Taking me into the shower with him tips the first domino. And just like that, the cumulative effect of all the things he's said and done come rushing toward me, falling into place.

Water is absolutely one thing that would remain the same in a world suddenly stripped of color. He might've loved water when he was in the Navy, but now the clear liquid has an even greater significance in his life. It represents normalcy. Just like standing in evening light does. All colors turn monotone in the night's shadowy light. That's what he meant that night I walked in his dark hotel room and he said "this feels normal to me."

And he bought me that black scarf for the same reason he bought the lace mask. Sure, he can turn just about anything into a sexy object, but the way he grinned at that vendor through the black silk cloth while we were both under it, tells me that was Sebastian's way of trying to show me what life is like through his eyes. He wanted me to understand how he sees...in shades of gray and black. And red.

Even with his impairment, Sebastian sees me better

than anyone. On so many levels. Now it's my turn to tell him that I see him too.

I lace my hands with his and I fold our arms together across my chest. Bringing our clasped hands to my lips, I kiss each of his knuckles and say, "I know about your colorblindness, Sebastian. And if the reason you haven't told me before now is because you somehow feel it makes you less, you really don't know me very well. I sure as hell don't care what the Navy thinks."

He stills behind me. "How'd you—?" A heavy sigh. "Mina."

I shrug. "You've been trying to tell me, haven't you?"

He kisses the back of my head. "Colorblindness aside, I didn't belong in the military anymore. And my visual limitation isn't something I like to admit to anyone. I didn't have a choice with Mina, but thank you for saving my ass at the christening."

If not the changes in his vision, what happened that made him feel he didn't belong in the Navy anymore? I glance up at him. "The pink and blue ribbons were the pastor's traditional roots getting in the way. And of course I came to your rescue; I promised I'd be there for you. We're a team."

Sebastian shuts the water off and turns me in his arms. Water drips off his nose and down his face as he pulls me close. "You bring color to my life every day in a sea of sameness, Talia. And I'm not talking about this." He rubs a strand of my hair between his fingers. "Or this." A sexy smile cants his lips as he glances down at the bit of hair between my legs. "I'm talking about making me *feel*. I've been numb most of my life. You give me something intangible I can't explain. It's just the way I feel when I'm with you. Like I'm whole and not a damn thing is missing."

For a man who claims not to know the words women want to hear, Sebastian has managed to render me speechless. I never thought he'd say anything so beautiful and heartfelt. I wrap my arms around his neck. "You are everything I want, Sebastian. The whole package."

He folds his arms tight around my waist, his gaze tracing over my face. I can tell something is weighing on his mind, but then he flashes a smile and smacks my ass hard. "Get dried off, grab a shirt from my closet if you'd like, and then meet me in the kitchen."

The colorful pillows on Sebastian's sofa make me wonder how long he's had this place as I walk from his bedroom through the living room, toward the kitchen. Or did someone help him pick them out? He glances up from twisting a corkscrew in a bottle of wine, and a smile of male satisfaction spreads across his face. He takes his time sliding his gaze down my nipples pebbling under his light blue button down shirt to my bare legs and feet. "My clothes will most definitely be a requirement in the future."

I lift the edge of his shirt and touch the tag sewn on the inside. "While looking for something to wear, I noticed this tag: Light Blue, 3,1. The ties also listed a basic color and numbers." I tilt my head. "It's a numbering system, isn't it?"

He nods as he pulls the cork out of the bottle. "It's how I'm able to match my ties to shirts and then those to my suits."

My heart breaks just a little for how he's had to learn

to adapt to the limits of his vision. "Did you come up with it yourself?"

"Yes. It keeps me sane and helps me appear mostly normal. Otherwise, you'd only ever see me wear a black or gray suit, white shirts and gray or black ties. Every once in a while I'd go all crazy and wear a red tie."

He might sound like he's joking, but I can tell he's still dealing with his disability. The fact none of his family knows makes that clear to me. Does his BLACK Security team? And how ironically bittersweet that the injury that turned his dark brown eye mostly blue, changing his unusual two-tone eye color to matching gorgeous blue ones, also stole his ability to see in color. Life can be such a fickle bitch.

"It's very clever. I'm impressed," I say, hoping to put a positive spin on things. Running my hands up the front of his shirt, I lift the collar and inhale. "Whoever does your laundry deserves major praise. This shirt is so soft and now I know why you always smell so delicious."

Pouring a glass of red wine, he snorts. "I'll be sure to tell Teresa."

"Who's Teresa?" I ask, trying not to sound jealous.

He sets the bottle down on the black granite island and peers around the apartment. "The same woman who decorated this place, buys my groceries, and pretty much runs this place for me." He smirks and nods toward the pillows I ran my hand across as I walked through the living room. "Hopefully she chose the colors well."

I look at the bold turquoise and red pillows, and then take in all the glass, marble and chrome. "Your place definitely has a masculine feel, but your house manager has added warmth with her color choices in the pillows, rugs and art pieces. Very high-end too. Apparently being in the security business pays off."

Picking up the two wine glasses, he strolls around the island and holds the red wine out to me, keeping the sparkling water for himself. "Yes, business is good. I know you don't usually drink red, but I'd like you to try it. The wine came highly recommended. And it just seems appropriate for this toast."

"A toast?" I ask, taking the wine.

Sebastian nods and lifts his glass, his bright blue gaze full of warmth. "I was your first, and now you're mine."

I lower my glass and raise an eyebrow. "You were no virgin, Sebastian. So what *first* am I to you?"

He moves closer, and it's hard for me to concentrate with his muscular chest and six pack abs just inches from me. He's pulled on a pair of soft dark gray lounge pants that hit him low on the hips, displaying those two muscles that dip past his pants waistline…the ones that make even the smartest women lose brain cells.

Tapping my glass with his, he lifts my chin until I meet his gaze. "You're the first woman I've brought to this apartment—a place I've always considered my personal sanctuary. You're the first woman to drink a toast here with me." His voice drops to a seductive purr as his finger traces my jawline. "The first to help me christen the door, the couch, the shower, the chair, and the first to share my bed."

I choke back the emotion swelling inside, my fingers curling around the glass stem. What he's saying is so heart-stopping I focus on something else so I don't get too caught up in his words. He said some amazing things in the shower, but he hasn't professed any kind of deep commitment and he may never. "We haven't had sex in a chair or in your bed for that matter."

Sebastian releases a knowing laugh. "The night is young, Little Red. Drink your wine and tell me what you think."

I take a sip and am surprised by the rich taste and how easily it slides down my throat. I raise my eyebrows. "Mmmm, it's delicious." I take another sip and savor the intense earthy flavor spreading across my tongue. "I can tell the tannins are firm, but with its spicy notes, the combination is the smoothest red I've ever tasted."

Sebastian smiles, pride in his eyes. "It's Italian, the Primitivo grape, known for its deep color and full-bodied flavor. I'm glad you like it."

I eye him with amused suspicion. "You know a lot about wine for a man who doesn't drink."

He skims his fingers over my collarbone, his touch arousing my senses. "I've found knowing wine reaps its own benefits."

"And you just happen to have a bottle of this fabulous wine on hand for guests you never have?"

"Actually, yes and no. It ties together." He starts to say more, then pauses. "Hold that thought." Draining his sparkling water, he sets the glass down, then walks through the living room over to a black and chrome built-in bookshelf. Sliding open a drawer above a row of books, he takes something out, then turns around and dangles a pair of silver handcuffs. Eyes sparkling turquoise blue, his gaze sweeps slowly over me, primal and predatory. "All

I've been able to think about is seeing you in these. Will you let me bind you, Talia?"

While every nerve-ending jumps to life at the look in his eyes and the knowledge that he's been thinking about me wearing those in what I'm sure will be a mutually satisfying sexual experience, my brain won't shut off. Is he saying something deeper? More symbolic? Then again, who keeps wine in a place no guests supposedly ever visit? Do I even want to know about the handcuffs? Why can't my brain take a fucking break for once?

I start to confess my conflicted thoughts, but a buzzer sounds at the door. Sebastian walks over and touches a panel on the kitchen wall, saying in a gruff tone, "That you, Connelly?"

"Yeah, just delivering Talia's purse. I thought she might want it."

I set my wine on the counter and follow Sebastian to the door. I can't believe I hadn't realized that I didn't have my purse with me. I was really shaken after that near miss with a runaway car.

My face flames when I catch sight of my underwear next to the doorway. I'm in the middle of scrambling to pick up my coat, Sebastian's pants, belt, my heels, and underwear when the elevator pings. As the door slides open, I toss everything in my hands a good five feet to the left and hopefully out of Theo's line of sight.

When Theo starts to step inside, Sebastian holds out his hand. "Thanks for bringing Talia's purse."

Stepping back, Theo puts his hand on the elevator door to keep it from shutting. As he hands Sebastian my purse, he nods to me as I peer around Sebastian's shoulder. "Hey,

Talia," he says, giving a half wave. "Mina told me to tell you she put a gift in your purse." He gestures to the cut on my forehead. "Ouch. I heard it was pretty hairy earlier."

Theo has grown his buzz cut out since I saw him last. I smile at the slight curl in his light brown hair. The hair, combined with his tall height, barrel chest and thick arms, makes him look even more like a big teddy bear. I want to give him a hug, like I did every night after he walked me to my car, but since I'm underwear free, I stay hidden behind Sebastian as I gingerly touch my cut. "Yeah, it's not too bad for battling a car. Thank you for bringing my purse."

Wrapping his arm around my shoulders, Sebastian pulls me to his side and slides his arm to my waist, locking me against him. "Any news about the car that almost hit us?"

"Den gave me the rundown. The car was reported stolen a couple days ago. The owner of the car, Dwight Tucker, is a convicted felon who's out on parole. The police are looking for him now, but in the meantime they're dusting for prints other than his just in case. Nodding to me, Theo asks, "Does his name sound familiar?"

I fiddle with the collar on Sebastian's shirt to keep the material off my chest. The last thing I want to do is hi-beam Theo. "No. I try not to associate with known criminals. Uh, well, excluding the Sly Fox scenario."

"Despite the circumstances, we had interesting convos, right?" Theo says, grinning, then turns serious when Sebastian frowns at him. "Anyway, I'm going to look deeper into this Tucker guy, just in case. I'll let you know if I come up with anything."

Once the door slides closed, I look at Sebastian. "I thought Den worked for your father."

"He does," he answers simply. When I raise my eyebrows, Sebastian smiles. "Apparently you made quite an impression on Adam Blake. He doesn't want anything to happen to Josi's 'fearless' godmother, hence Den's involvement right now."

I laugh. "He said that to you?"

Handing me my purse, Sebastian hooks his hands at the base of my spine and draws me close. "He did. He also apologized to me for all the hurt and resentment he caused. He told me you're the reason he finally pulled his head out of his ass. Apparently, he never took me out of the will, but he didn't know how to tell me that." He shakes his head. "He also asked me to come work with him, but I turned him down."

I eye him tentatively, wondering at his mood. "So, you're not mad at me?"

He snorts. "For meddling? Now why would I be mad?"

When I wince, he grins. "You're adorable. An amazing contradiction of fierce warrior and peacemaker."

I wrinkle my nose. "Sometimes you have to fight for peace."

He lowers his face to mine. "Never stop fighting, Talia. Your tenacity against all odds is one of your most admirable traits." Lifting his head, his tone shifts to an annoyed one. "Apparently every man who interacts with you is destined to fall for that very quality."

My heart swelling from his praise, I gesture to the door and start to tell him to give Theo a break when my gaze lands on the doorjamb. Part of the carved wood has broken away from the main piece. Remembering the cracking sound I heard earlier, I look at him, wide-eyed. "Did you do that?"

He glances at the wood and shrugs. "You nearly broke me." Dropping a kiss on my nose, he steps back. "Why don't you open your present from Mina? She told me she had something for me as well. Maybe she put it in your purse."

I follow Sebastian into the kitchen and try not to stare at the handcuffs standing out against the island's black granite as I set my purse down next to them.

Sebastian leans on his elbows and watches me pull out the small navy box with a white ribbon tied around it and a tiny envelope. I hand him the other small envelope with Seb written on the front in swirly handwriting.

He takes his card, but doesn't open it until I tug the bow off of mine. When I lift the lid and see a gorgeous gold heart locket with a smaller, slightly tilted raised-heart incorporated into the design on the front, I smile. It reminds me of my floating heart.

"What a lovely present," I say. Setting the necklace down, I open the tiny card Mina included with my gift.

Talia,

I hope you don't mind, but I thought what better way to keep Amelia's memory alive, than to combine her heart with your promise to Josi. I'm so happy to have you as part of my family.

Love,
Mina

I lift the necklace and trace my finger over the tiny raised heart. It is the one I gave her. Mina must've had the locket custom made to include it.

"Open it." At Sebastian's encouragement, I use my nail to pop open the three-fourths inch wide heart. The picture of me holding Josi after the christening on the inside makes my heart twinge. Mina had planned everything so well. Down to getting the picture from her photographer and having it incorporated into the necklace to be delivered to me this evening. *How could her mother think she's flighty?*

Sebastian comes around the island and slides my thumb out of the way. "Don't forget the other half."

Once he moves my finger, my hands shake as I stare at the tiny "2 Lias" drawing. Tears fill my eyes as I raise them to him. "How did you get this?"

He takes the necklace from me, closes the locket, then hooks the delicate chain around my neck. "After the ceremony, Mina told me her plans of incorporating the heart you gave her into your godmother gift, and I emailed her the picture I'd taken of the drawing."

"Why didn't you tell me you'd taken a picture of it?"

"I saw you close the leather binder that day and yet had never seen you order room service. While you were in the bathroom, I snapped a picture of the drawing to study later. If it was important to you, I wanted to know why." He rests his hands on my shoulders, his fingers massaging me. "After you lost the original, I thought I'd have it printed for you, but then when I heard Mina's plans, I realized incorporating the drawing into the locket would be a perfect way for you to keep it with you." Clasping my face, he thumbs the tears away from my cheeks. "I know what it meant for you to give up that heart to Mina that night. I'm just glad she was able to give it back in a way that's equally honor-worthy."

I sniff back my tears and touch the locket with my fingertips. "It's perfect, Sebastian. Thank you both. I'll always treasure it."

He captures my lips in a tender kiss, and I wrap my arms around his hard body and kiss him back. Pausing, I glance toward the counter to look for his card. "What did Mina say in her note to you?"

He smirks. "She thanked me for wearing my uniform."

Laughing softly, I lay my head against his shoulder and tighten my hold on him.

The sound of my phone ringing draws my attention to my purse. I don't recognize the ringtone. Releasing him, I retrieve it and answer. "Hello."

"Talia! Thank goodness I got ahold of you. I've been trying for a while."

"Charlie?" The concern in his voice knocks me in the gut. "Is something wrong with Aunt Vanessa?"

"I've left messages on your phone, at your apartment, and I even called the hotel, but they said you checked out yesterday. Vanessa collapsed at dinner. We're at Mount Sinai now and they're running tests. She didn't want to worry you, but when she learned I couldn't get in touch with you, she made me promise not to stop calling until I made sure you were okay."

"I'm sorry to worry her, but I'm so glad you called. I'll be right over."

Charlie stands and hugs me when Sebastian and I arrive in the hospital waiting room. I pull back and mumble my apology for my damp coat and wrinkled appearance. At least I'd been able to tame my wavy, air-dried hair with a couple of clips from my purse.

"What happened to your forehead?" he asks, concern in his gaze.

I wave it off. "We, um, got caught up in a snow deluge. How's Aunt Vanessa doing? Can I see her?"

Clasping my hands, he tugs me down on the chair next to him. "They should be setting her up in a room now."

"Her room? They're admitting her?"

"The pain makes her a little too shaky on her feet right now. They've given her pain medicine, so I'm sure they'll call you back once she's settled."

"What kind of pain is she having?"

"Stomach and other stuff. She's been forgetting things...then she'll remember later. He shakes his head. "I'll let her fill you in on what's been going on with her medically. Would it be okay with you if I step out for a little bit? I need to call my husband and tell Stuart where I am. After I run a quick errand, I'll be back."

"Of course," I say, squeezing his hands. "Thank you so much for being here with her. I don't know why she hasn't shared this with me. Do you think this is why she lost all that weight?" When he slowly nods, guilt tugs at my stomach. "I wish she'd said something."

"As blunt and forthright as your aunt can be, it surprises

me too." Exhaling heavily, he stands. "For what it's worth, I think she planned to tell you when you two had lunch. Oh, just so you're prepared, she's fairly aggressive tonight and not quite herself. I'm not sure if it's the pain or the meds she's on, but I just want to warn you."

As I watch him walk out, the thought of something happening to my aunt squeezes my chest. She's all I have left. I do remember her being pretty aggressive with Jared at the kick off party. Then she forgot about our lunch plans. *God, what could be wrong with her? Is it cancer? A brain tumor?* Sebastian's warm hand clasps mine, bringing me out of my worried thoughts.

"Don't conjure up all kinds of horrible scenarios in that imaginative head of yours. Let's wait and see what your aunt and doctors have to say."

I fold my fingers around his and squeeze. "Thank you for being here with me."

"Hey, Aunt Vanessa. I'm here," I say, peeking my head into her hospital room once the nurse tells us we can see her.

"Talia," she calls in a low voice, waving me in.

As I tug Sebastian in behind me, my aunt frowns slightly. "Your Mr. White attends hospital visits too? Isn't the tour over?"

I'm a little surprised by the sarcasm in her tone, but I move toward her bed, keeping him close. "Sebastian has saved my life more than once this week, but he's also more than a bodyguard, Aunt Vanessa." As I reach her bedside I notice how wan she looks. Even her hair has thinned. "Why didn't you tell me you were sick?"

She completely ignores my question and stares at the

cut on my forehead, alarm in her eyes. "You acted like those threatening letters happen all the time. I thought the bodyguard thing was just marketing PR for your book. What do you mean he saved your life?"

Ugh, I didn't mean to tell her, but I didn't like her inferring he didn't belong here with me. Sebastian answers for me. "The fire at the Regent was purposefully set just inside Talia's room."

My aunt's eyes widen and she holds her hand out to me. "Is that true, Talia?"

I release Sebastian's hand and take my aunt's, sitting on the edge of the bed beside her. "Yes, it's true. I'll answer your questions in a minute. Tell me what's wrong with you. Charlie didn't tell me much."

Aunt Vanessa sighs. "Weight loss I can't explain, but the stomach pain was so bad tonight that I passed out. My luck it'll be an extreme food allergy, but further tests will need to be run." Sighing, she squeezes my hand. "I'm sure I'll be fine, but I'm very worried for you. I'm afraid your troubles might be my fault."

I snort and pat her hand. "How in the world can you say it's your fault?"

My aunt heaves a frustrated sigh. "I should've known better when she came back asking for more information."

Her? My stomach bottoms out, but Sebastian's hand settling on my shoulder gives me the strength to ask. "Who are you talking about, Aunt Vanessa."

"Paige."

I shake my head. "Who is Paige?"

"Paige Hansen." Her voice drops and she waves her hand dismissively. "She's the blonde girl I hired to derail your engagement to Nathan."

CHAPTER EIGHTEEN

Talia

I blink rapidly and try to focus on what my aunt just said, but it's like another person spoke the words that came out of her mouth. I pull my hand from her tight grip and try to keep my voice calm. "You hired someone to make Nathan cheat on me?" Horror and disbelief fill me. "How could you do that to me? I ended our relationship over a *lie*."

Sebastian's hand falls away from my shoulder, but I don't let it bother me; I'm numb with anger.

My aunt fists her hand on the bed. "He did sleep with her. Though it was after you left him. I've always told you, Talia. It's just you and me. I'm the only one who will be here for you. Who will always be here for you. When you got engaged, I knew I had to do something. Nathan would've ruined you, just like your father ruined my sister."

"You told me he left us."

She nods briskly and grips my fisted hand. "Your father left your poor mother with a newborn. Weak-willed man! Tasha was so depressed. When she tried to take her life, I was there for her. But she just couldn't let him go. I didn't stop her the next time."

I wrap my arm around my stomach, feeling ill as I try to process it. "How could you not help your own sister?"

"I didn't make her *take* the pills, Talia!" My aunt's face flushes. "You were supposed to be mine. Your father met me first, but he fell in love with Tasha and gave her a baby. Her life should've been *mine,* and yet even though she had you, she couldn't see past her own sphere."

Tears stream down my face as I stare at her in shock.

My silence must've seemed like understanding, because my aunt pats my arm. "Don't you see, I couldn't let a man destroy you the way your father did your mother. I wanted you to go places, be independent."

She heaves a sigh and waves her hand, like doing so sweeps her decades' old confession away. "It was for the best, Talia, but I didn't expect the girl I hired to fall in love with your fiancé. She called me a few weeks ago, wanting to know more about you. Since I hadn't seen much of you these last few months, I wondered if you were seeing Nathan again and that's what prompted her call, so I told her something she could use to tip the scale in her favor. If Nathan's not in your life, maybe your success as an author is what drove her to reach out to me."

"Are you saying this Paige person is the one stalking Talia?" Sebastian's tone is crisp, all business. "What information did you tell her?"

She looks at me, as if for permission. I stare blankly at her. I want to think she is having a true slip from reality, that the pain meds are giving her nonexistent memories and none of this is real. But as my mind reconciles the blonde server I almost bumped into at the kick off party with the quick image of the girl I saw messing with Nathan, and then Cass' later comment about Nathan dressing down a female server at the party, my aching heart knows that I'm finally hearing the truth. Is the combination of the meds on top of her condition bringing all this out of my aunt? Aunt Vanessa knows nothing about my past, certainly nothing that could destroy a relationship. "What did you tell Paige?"

Her gaze slides to Sebastian, then back to me. "You're okay with me telling him about the drugs?"

Blood drains from my face. I jump to my feet, my whole body quaking. "You *knew?*"

My aunt snorts. "I'm not an idiot, Talia. I needed to get us out of that situation and the fastest way was to get through nursing school. How could Walt pay for it when he hadn't worked a carpentry job in over a year?"

I jam my hands in my hair and dig my fingers into my scalp. When Sebastian grips my elbow and tries to calm me down, I jerk from his grasp and lean close to her, hissing, "So was it okay with you that Hayes got his rocks off by violating me on the side too?"

My aunt's eyes widen and her bottom lip quivers. "I didn't know, Talia. I knew you delivered bags. I would never let anyone hurt you," she says, reaching for me.

I jerk away from her, whispering, "What kind of monster are you?"

Aunt Vanessa's eyes narrow slightly. "I guess I'm the kind of monster who *protected* you." She quickly looks at Sebastian standing behind me, then returns her attention to me. "Does he know you've killed a man?"

It's bad enough that Sebastian has just learned all about my fucked up family, but now that he knows my darkest secret, I want to shrink into the floor. "It was an accident," I whisper.

"Was it, Talia?" Aunt Vanessa's eyebrows pull together. "I saw the mess you left behind in our apartment that night. I know how much you loved Amelia."

I throw my hands out. "Walt was wacked out on drugs. He shoved Amelia too hard, and the way she fell and hit her head killed her. When I wouldn't go along with his plan to say her death was an accident, because I wanted him charged for being under the influence, he threatened me. Not an hour before, he sat right there, passed out in the same room, while Hayes violated me. I was so angry that he was more worried about covering up his part in Amelia's death than mourning her that I dumped an entire container of those stupid pills on him. When he came after me for destroying their drugs, I went for the gun to protect myself."

My aunt nods slowly. "I got home and saw Amelia and Walt's bodies and the drugs strewn everywhere. Then I noticed your shoe print in Walt's blood and I put enough together to know you were in trouble. I didn't know about Hayes, Talia, I swear to you, but I knew he'd blame you for destroying his drugs, so I took care of it. I was the one who blew up our apartment. Cleaned up *your* mess...to save you. I protected you, like I always have, because you have always come first, and you always will."

My aunt's twisted mindfuck idea of protecting me leaves a heavy silence in the room. I'm afraid to even look at Sebastian, and he hasn't tried to touch me since I shook him off. Or was it since my aunt told him I killed Walt? I jump at the sound of the door swinging open. Unaware of the tension in the room, the incoming nurse looks at her watch and says, "My patient has one more test for the day, folks."

As Sebastian and I start to move toward the door, my aunt leans forward in her bed, her brow furrowed. "I was surprised when I saw Paige working at your kick off event. At the time I just thought it was an odd coincidence. Was Nathan there?" When I nod numbly, her gaze shifts to Sebastian. "Find Paige. That deranged girl has to be behind the stalking and attacks. She hated that Nathan never gave up on Talia. Have her arrested and protect my niece."

As soon as we walk into the hall, Sebastian pulls me over to a quiet spot near the stairwell. "Do you know what Paige looks like?"

I really don't want to discuss how I've seen her, but I swallow my pride. "Yes, I walked in on her messing around with Nathan once at work. That's why I couldn't place her face. I'd only seen her once."

He dips his head and looks at me. "So she was the blonde you saw at the event?"

When I nod, he pulls out his phone and calls a police contact. "We have a suspect with motive. Please have your men pick up Paige Hansen for questioning." A pause. "Yes, attempted murder of Talia Murphy. I'll meet you at the precinct. I want to be in the room when she's questioned."

He eyes me as the man's voice rumbles. "Fine, at least let me listen in. Yeah, yeah…lawyer bullshit. Just pick her up. I'm coming."

He hangs up and says, "Are you okay?"

Too many emotions are racing through me. My brain feels like it's exploding, but my body is numb. I still can't believe what my aunt did. How she destroyed my life in so many ways. I've never felt more alone. I blink, not even sure how to answer him.

Sebastian rests his hand on my shoulder. "Why didn't you tell me about shooting Walt?"

The way he asks the question, his tone is very careful. "You knew, didn't you?"

He shrugs. "I learned about the fire another way, but it was enough to help me narrow down where you lived. Once I got ahold of the police report and crime scene analysis of your apartment, I put the fact that a single bullet was found wedged into a far wall and the medical examiner noted something the size of a bullet had damaged one of the male's ribs, together with everything else you've told me since…so yeah, I figured you might have shot him." He pauses, then exhales his frustration. "Were you ever going to tell me?"

"That I murdered a man? Or how about the fact that I've done things I'm disgusted by? Does it matter that I did it to survive?" I meet his gaze and the disappointment there rips at my heart. "The condemning look in your eyes is exactly why I didn't tell you, Sebastian. I didn't want to lose you, but I guess it's too late for that."

When I start to walk away, he grabs my arm, his expression hard, furious. "You've spent all this time worrying about losing me, when you're the one who's always running. All I've *ever* wanted was for you to fucking trust me enough to tell me everything, no matter what."

"You mean like you've told me everything?" I shoot back. "You should've told me about your colorblindness, but you held back. And why did you leave the Navy if it wasn't because of your vision impairment? Did you share? You could've, but you didn't. And for the record, how am I supposed to believe that I'm the *only* one who's ever been to your apartment when you conveniently whip out a pair of handcuffs at a place I wasn't *supposed* to be, and no one but you ever visits? As much as I'd like to blindly believe, Sebastian, I guess that old saying is true; trust goes *both* ways."

He stares at me, jaw muscle jumping, then says in a clipped tone, "I'm going to the station. I think it's best if you stay here in the waiting room."

When Sebastian slams the Exit door open and heads down the stairs, I sag against the wall. *God, could I have fucked up any more with him?* How can I trust the man so easily with my life, but not with my heart? I want to bang my head against the wall for being such an idiot. The one thing I worried about the most, him discovering everything about my past, isn't what destroyed us. It was my own inability to trust him with it.

Charlie arrives a few minutes later, and when he sees me crying in the hall, he tugs me into a chair in the waiting room. I let him comfort me, because I'm truly at a loss as to why I'm crying so hard. Is it for losing Sebastian? For losing my faith and trust in my aunt? I can't explain any of my family's fucked-up scenario to the sweet man sitting next to me, so I don't even try.

While I'm dabbing my eyes with a tissue, my phone buzzes with a text from Sebastian.

> *PainInMyAss: Paige confessed to sending threatening letters and to breaking into your apartment. Still in interrogation.*

His text is cold and impersonal. Just the facts. I sniff back my tears and send him a "thank you for the update" response. Then, scroll through my contacts and type Nathan a quick text.

> *Me: I just want to say that I believe you about that intern. I don't think I ever really said that. No hard feelings.*

My phone instantly rings with a call from Nathan. I exhale a heavy sigh and send the call to voicemail, already regretting trying to absolve some of my guilt.

Patting my shoulder, Charlie says, "You've had a long week. Why don't you go home and take a warm bath. Visiting hours will be over soon. I'll let your aunt know that you'll be back tomorrow morning."

I stare at him, unsure what to say. *Will I be back? How can I even be around her, let alone trust anything she says now?* But what if the doctors diagnose her with something debilitating? What if it's something terminal? I'm her only family. Numb all over, I just nod and stand. "Thank you for being such a good person, Charlie."

He stands too and hugs me. "Don't worry, Talia. I'm sure Vanessa will pull through whatever this is. I'll see you tomorrow."

Now that my stalker has been arrested, the idea of taking a long bath in my own tub sounds instantly appealing. Even though the realization that I won't be going back to Sebastian's apartment depresses the hell out of me, I decide going home is better than the hotel. I'll definitely be taking Cass up on her movie and ice cream marathon promise as soon as she gets back.

Nathan tries to call me again as I hail a ride home. When a cab drives up, I turn off the audible alerts and drop my phone into my purse. The sound of it hitting the handcuffs I swiped at Sebastian's before we left—I couldn't stand the idea he might use them on someone else—is just another sad reminder of what Sebastian and I could've had.

CHAPTER NINETEEN

Talia

The light above the stove is on when I walk into my apartment. I'm annoyed with myself for leaving it on, but it provides enough dim light for me to kick my heels off and walk through the apartment to shut it off without jamming my knee on a table or chair.

I skirt the butcher-block island in our kitchen and just when I reach up to turn off the light, something not-quite-right registers. I slowly turn to stare at the apple peel, cut in one long, perfect spiral, sitting on a small plate in the middle of the island.

"Cass?" I call out, even though I know it's not hers. Cass' idea of cutting an apple involves a tool that slices eight perfect segments in one swoop. She never peels her apples.

I move back around the island, calling Cass' name

again, my gaze on the door. Can I get to it in time? When I take another step, a man's voice calls casually from the shadows, "Hello, Talia. You didn't write. You didn't call. It makes me think you really didn't care for me at all."

A revolting chill races up my spine at the sound of that smarmy voice; one I hoped I'd never hear again.

"You're supposed to be in prison," I say to the figure with his boots propped up on our tiny table next to a gift fruit basket. I might sound calm, but my insides are like jelly and my hands are shaking so bad that I have to grip the edges of my coat to steady them.

Flipping the light switch next to him, Hayes pulls off the knit cap he's wearing and stands. "Yeah, well…the Warden and me, we have an arrangement."

He's changed so much since I saw him last. His face is fuller and his head is completely shaved, shining under the kitchen light. Crossing his arms, he carries himself with a cocky-edginess, his body bulkier, arm muscles bulging under his T-shirt.

Stomach plummeting, I take a step back toward the island, putting it squarely between us. "What kind of arrangement?" I try to keep him talking, while I surreptitiously look for the knife he used to cut the apple.

Hayes' leering gaze sweeps over me. "I finally get that fine wine saying. You definitely have gotten better with age, Talia. It'll make watching the life drain from your eyes that much sweeter."

As soon as he finishes speaking, Hayes darts to the left of the island, the knife I'd been looking for flashing in his hand.

He might've bulked up but he still favors his ankle.

I noticed his face twitch when he first stood up. The hesitation in his step gives me time to shuffle to the left as well, keeping the big kitchen piece between us. "Is that what you did? You broke out of prison?"

We skirt two full circles around the island, him pursuing and me keeping to the opposite side each time, before he stops and narrows his gaze. "Nah, right now I'm stuck in medical, all due to this horrible flu going around." He flashes a smile. "Got to keep up my good behavior so I can get out in eighteen months."

I knew he was trying to distract me, so when he quickly feigns to the left, only to double back to the right, my heart nearly stops, but I'm ready. I mimic his moves and remain just out of his grasp once more. "Why would he help you sneak out?" I ask at the same time I reach for the plate on the island.

" 'Cause his son got in a bit of a bind with drugs a few years back, and he knows I have a score to settle." Hayes lunges forward, trying to slice me as I grab the dish.

I jerk out of the way just in time, apple peel flying. Smashing the plate over his wrist, I knock the knife from his hand.

Roaring his fury, Hayes grabs hold of the island to keep his balance, and my heart jerks when he notices it shift with his weight. *How long will it take him to realize it's not bolted to the floor?*

A couple of knocks sound at the door and we both freeze. "Talia, it's Nathan. I heard something crash. Are you okay?"

As Nathan talks, I quickly grab the knife from the floor.

"Is that your boyfriend?" Hayes asks in a low voice.

When I shake my head, his eyes taper to pleased slits. "I've learned that everything out of your mouth is a lie."

"Run, Nathan!" I yell at the same time Hayes tugs a silencer-tipped handgun from the back of his pants, then pops off two rounds right through the door.

The sound of a thump outside churns my stomach. *Oh God. Did he just kill Nathan?*

Hayes chuckles and slowly blows his breath over the tip of his gun. "One down," he says, then pulls something out of his pants' pocket.

When he lifts up the strand of black pearls Sebastian gave me, and then circles them around the gun, swinging them around, a fierce protective anger erupts inside me. "I will not let you destroy everything in my life." Screaming my fury, I throw the paring knife as hard as I can, and I'm shocked when it buries to the handle in Hayes' upper arm.

Bellowing in pain, Hayes drops the gun to grab his arm.

The second his gun hits the floor, I quickly snatch up the pearls, then kick the gun across the kitchen, hoping to give myself time to bolt for the door.

My fingers barely brush the knob when his hard arm snakes around my waist in a bruising hold and my hair is yanked back hard.

"I see you're still a deceiving little bitch!" he hisses in my ear.

Eyes watering from his painful hold in my hair, I try to claw free of him, but he just laughs and tugs the pearls from my hold.

"It'll take more than a pig-sticker to put me down. You have no idea the depth of your betrayal, but you soon will," he says right before he loops the strand of pearls around my neck a couple of times. Releasing my hair, he quickly cinches his arm over the pearls around my neck.

"Here's a preview of what's to come," he rasps as he begins to squeeze. "I'm going to squeeze this neck of yours while I fuck you until you can't help but come before you pass out."

I try to suck in air, to hiss my hatred, but I can't. My throat is closed off and my lungs spasm painfully. He chuckles, delighted by my struggles and my fear as he roughly shoves his other hand inside my dress and down my bra.

"Nice tits. Damn you've grown some great curves. Such a fucking waste. I'm going to make you pay for all your sins, Talia. Fuck and choke, fuck and choke. I'll do it, over and over again. You'll get what you deserve, and when I'm done, I will make sure you take your last breath."

I fight to stay conscious, but my vision blurs as his vengeful promises throb in my head like a death knell over and over.

A grunting sound wakes me. My throat burns and my neck and back hurt. I'm in the middle of our kitchen, where the island would normally be, and the butcher-block piece is now up against the table. I try to straighten, but I'm sitting in a kitchen chair, handcuffed to one of the arms, my ankles tied to each chair leg with cooking string.

My heart jerks at the sight of hand-smeared blood on my knees and inner thighs where my dress' skirt is ruched up. Red stains streak the edge of my coat too and along my legs. I gulp and exhale a quiet sigh of relief when I don't feel any major pain between my thighs or any other part of my body. The blood must be Hayes'.

I quickly look up as Hayes drags Nathan inside my apartment. Nathan's not moving or struggling at all. I look back down and bite my lip to hold back the wail that he might be dead.

My gaze lands on the handcuffs, and I blink when I notice some kind of swirled design on each cuff. I turn my wrists slowly so the light hits them just right.

As I stare at the custom engraved R on one cuff and then the engraved B on the other, big fat tears seep out of my eyes. I should've just trusted him. I don't deserve Sebastian. As I bow my head, thinking I brought all this on myself, Sebastian's words from earlier come back to me.

Never stop fighting, Talia. Your tenacity against all odds is one of your most admirable traits.

I glance up at the hair clip dangling in my hair in front of my face, and my heart jumps. *I'll keep fighting, Sebastian.* I lower my hair close to my hands and slip the clip from the strands, then start bending it back and forth until I break off a thin sliver of metal.

Before I can work on the cuffs, Hayes glances my way. "I see you're awake." As he laughs and drops Nathan's limp body on the floor in the living room, I tuck the piece of metal inside my fist. He approaches, his tone jovial, despite the bandage he's tied around his arm to stop the bleeding.

"Those handcuffs came in handy. Didn't take you for the kinky type. Hell, you'll probably get off on being choked. Guess I'll just beat the shit out of you each time I fuck you instead." He smiles as if the idea makes him incredibly happy. "I'll probably have to break the chair to get you into your bed. Couldn't find the damn keys to the cuffs in your purse."

When Hayes pulls up a chair to the side of mine and sits down in my periphery, holding his gaze toward the door, I blink at him in surprise. *What is he doing?*

He sets his gun on the table. "In case you're wondering. We're waiting."

"Waiting for what?"

Hayes rolls his eyes. "Your other boyfriend. The bodyguard."

A new round of fear crawls in my belly and worms its way into my chest. "What does he have to do with this?"

Hayes waves his hand. "I'm only going to explain it once. We'll just wait until he comes to rescue you so you can both hear it. It shouldn't be long now. I've made sure your phone is on so he can track it. If he knows his shit, that's what he'll do to find you."

I shake my head. "He's not looking for me. He thinks he has the stalker, but that's not true, is it? You're the one who wrote those last couple of letters, you set that fire in my hotel room, and I'll bet you're the one who tried to run me down."

He gives a slow, mocking clap. "Very good, Talia. I've been using your apartment as home base all week. Stupid doorman thinks I'm your neighbor's secret lover." Picking up the gun, he points it at me. "Death by fire or by car would've been too easy for you anyway. I figured if I couldn't get you during the tour, I'd just wait for you to come home, where I could take my time inflicting the most pain."

I'm so thankful for Cass' work obsession right now.

So very thankful. I don't want to think what he would've done to her if she'd been here. "I don't understand. Why the ruse? Why pretend to care about the book and the tour when your issue with me has nothing to do with it?"

"Answer her. Why the smokescreen?" Sebastian says calmly from the doorway, the laser on his handgun pointed at Hayes' shoulder since Hayes made sure to keep me in the line of fire.

Without looking away from me, Hayes casually says, "Come in Mr. White, Blake...or whatever the hell name you're going by today, and shut the door behind you. We've been waiting."

Sebastian quietly shuts the door and moves closer, keeping his gun trained on Hayes. "It's Sebastian Blake," he says in a curt tone as he moves forward.

"So are the rumors true that you're Adam Blake's bastard?" Hayes asks, eyes glittering with interest.

"I am."

Hayes laughs at Sebastian's response, but when Sebastian tries to move to the left slightly, Hayes puts his gun right against my temple and gently rubs my earlobe with his other hand, "Ah, ah. That's close enough. Now put your gun on the kitchen floor, then slide it over to me and back away."

"Don't do it, Sebastia—ow!" I yelp when Hayes yanks hard on my ear.

"It's okay, Talia," Sebastian says in a gruff voice as he slowly lowers the gun to the floor.

When Sebastian's attention snags on the blood on my legs, then his furious gaze snaps to mine, I quickly say, "It's not mine."

"It's my blood," Hayes grates impatiently. "Your gun, Blake. *Now*."

Sliding the gun across the tile to Hayes' feet, Sebastian glares at Hayes, then stands up once more and takes a step back. "Answer our question. Why all this elaborate bullshit?"

"It's not bullshit," Hayes barks out. Grabbing Sebastian's gun, he holds it up. Pointing it at Sebastian, he says, "Let's start from the beginning, shall we?" Nudging my temple with his gun, Hayes looks at me. "Pop quiz time, Talia. What was my old lady's name? Do you remember?"

When I shake my head, he sneers. "Of course you don't. You just came on to me, told me that you wanted more without a thought beyond your own selfishness. I left Brenna for you that night. For *you*," he hisses in my ear. "Only to come back to a blown up apartment."

Brenna? Why does that name sound familiar? I glance up at Sebastian, my gaze pleading for him not to believe Hayes. "That's not how it happened."

"She was thirteen-years-old, you pedo-assfuck," Sebastian says, his voice guttural and raw.

"Fuck you!" Hayes' snaps, then slides a covetous gaze over my hair. "It wasn't like that. Talia reminded me of Brenna when she was younger."

"Brenna wasn't your wife," Sebastian states, his tone still tight but less antagonizing. "But you had a son together, didn't you?"

"Ding, ding, ding." Hayes sits up straighter. "Give the man a star. Our boy's name was—"

"Tommy—" I cut Hayes off, suddenly feeling as if the floor dropped out from under me. Sebastian's mention of

Brenna connected all the dots in my brain. Favoring one foot over the other, Hayes is the *clompy* boyfriend Brenna's building manager described. I can't believe Tommy is Hayes' son, but now Hayes' utter hatred of the book *Blindside* makes sense. In the book, I painted Tommy as the true madman he was.

"Yes, Tommy. You *two* are responsible for killing my son!" Hayes glares from Sebastian to me. "You led me on and made me leave Brenna, Talia. God knows Brenna could be a vengeful bitch. I'm sure she didn't handle my leaving her well, but then I got sent to prison not long after the explosion. My kid had always been a bit off, but he didn't have a fucking chance against her wrath once I was locked away."

All the things Tommy said to me—blaming me for how his mother had treated him—flickers through my mind. He didn't confuse me *for* his mother. He really believed I was the cause for all his pain. His mother hated and blamed me for Hayes leaving her. I look at Hayes, guilt knocking on my chest. "I didn't know. I—"

"You took everything from me!" He raises his voice. "My business, my family, my fucking livelihood. *Everything*. And you," He glares up at Sebastian. "Stop moving, you son of a bitch. You killed my son."

"Tommy murdered several women," Sebastian says in a low, matter-of-fact tone.

Hayes shrugs. "My son might've been a nut, but he was all I had. There I was, finally working something good from prison, selling a new drug to rich college kids, and my idiot son had to go and get all obsessed with you, Talia." Hayes narrows his gaze on me. "What is it about you that makes men lose their goddamn minds?"

"You were behind the drug ring on Talia's campus?" Sebastian asks, his hands curling into fists, banked fury tracking in his voice.

"*Was* behind it until Talia went and royally fucked that up for me too. Even though my son swore up and down it wasn't you, I know you wrote that anonymous article exposing the professor running the ring for me."

I was right to question that Hayes might've been involved in the drug ring back then. I knew that "backward ampersand inside two letters" hand stamp Mina said she and her college roommate looked for to identify who to deliver the drugs to was too similar to what I'd seen when I delivered bags for Hayes.

"And you..." Hayes squeezes Sebastian's gun's grip, drawing a red circle target over Sebastian's heart with his gun's laser. "You're going to earn me the payday Talia has denied me twice now."

Sebastian adopts a cold smile. "I'm not paying you jack shit."

Hayes barks out a laugh and shakes his head. "Not you. I'm talking about your stepmother. I wonder how much she'll pay to get rid of you this time?"

"What did you just say?" Sebastian grits out each word very slowly.

This can't be happening. It can't be. Is Isabel really responsible for his mother's death? I remember Hayes talking to Walt about taking on a hit. *Holy shit! Was it really for Sebastian?* I sense an icy stillness roll off Sebastian, and I chance a glance at him, worry for his state of mind making me feel lightheaded.

Hayes shrugs. "Your stepmother wouldn't stand for you gracing her doorstep the second your mother died. She wanted you out of the Blake family picture for good. Word got around certain circles to see who'd take the hit on. They wanted a no-name for the job. I needed the money to fund my business, so I took it. I sure as hell didn't expect your mother to take all the bullets. Lesson learned on using the wrong type of gun for a hit."

"You're lying," Sebastian grates. "The guy who broke into our apartment was thin. He didn't have your body build."

"Prison changes people." Hayes smirks as he taps his gun against my temple. "Tell him what I looked like back then, Talia."

I raise my eyes to Sebastian, feeling sick to my stomach. "He was thin and had dark brown hair."

Sebastian holds my gaze for a second, then shakes his head, drilling his gaze into Hayes. "Isabel's a royal bitch of the first order, but she would never stoop to this, let alone hire the likes of you herself."

Hayes laughs. "You're right. She didn't hire me directly, but when I caught up with the guy she paid to hire me and beat the shit out of him to try and get the rest of my money, he at least told me who contracted the hit and why before I put a bullet in his head. I'm sure Mrs. Blake will gladly hand over the rest of the money now if I finish the job she hired me for. Well, unless she wants word to leak to the news what she did."

Sebastian walks straight up to Hayes and presses his heart against the gun's barrel. "You'd better fucking pull the trigger now, because the only way you're leaving this apartment is in a body bag."

Hayes snorts at Sebastian's cold fury. "If that's the way you want to go out." He pulls the trigger, and during that split second when nothing happens, right before realization hits Hayes, Sebastian knocks the other gun out of his hand. Lifting Hayes straight out of the chair, he throws him across the room, where he lands on the coffee table with a deafening crash of glass.

While Hayes scrambles to his feet to launch himself at Sebastian with a roar of outrage, I quickly lean forward and try once more to slip the small hairclip piece inside the handcuffs to free myself. This time the cuff pops open. Once I repeat the process on the other cuff, I use the toothy edge of the handcuffs to cut the thin ropes off my ankles.

I dive for Hayes' gun, since it's the closest, then roll over and lift the weapon. I've never intentionally shot a gun, and as much as I want the man dead for all he's done to Sebastian and me, my hands are shaking too much. I can't take a chance that I might accidently kill him instead of maim him. Sebastian needs him to turn in Isabel for his mother's murder.

Sebastian lands three good punches in a row, but Hayes is like a man possessed. He just doesn't go down, but instead slams Sebastian with a powerful hit. When Sebastian falls to one knee after Hayes' last punch, I call his name and slide the gun across the tile floor.

He quickly grabs the gun as Hayes thunders toward him. Lifting his arm, Sebastian pulls the trigger without hesitation, hitting Hayes dead center in the middle of his forehead.

After Hayes falls to the floor, I stumble past Sebastian

and stand over Hayes, staring at his sightless expression. As much as I want to kick his thigh and yell at him, telling him what a vile person he is, and that I'm not sorry he's gone, I swallow all my anger, then walk over to squat next to Nathan. Trying not to look at the blood oozing from the two wounds on his upper arm, I press my fingers to his throat and glance up at Sebastian, hope tightening my throat. "Thank, God. He has a pulse."

While Sebastian binds Nathan's wounds with hand towels to slow the bleeding, I call the police and request an ambulance. Once I hang up, I pat Nathan's curly hair and whisper in his ear, "Hold on, Nathan. Please hold on."

Releasing a shaky breath, I straighten and meet Sebastian's gaze as he sets both guns on the end table. "Why didn't your gun go off?"

He lifts his gun once more, showing me the grip. "It's a personalized gun, calibrated to my fingerprints. It won't work if someone else tries to shoot it."

I nod my understanding, then frown. "Why did you kill Hayes? You could've shot him anywhere and taken him down. Now he can't point the finger to Isabel for your mother's murder."

Setting the gun back down, Sebastian cups my jaw. "Hayes has already stolen so much from both of us. I wasn't taking a chance he could get out again and do even more damage. You mean more to me than anyone, and after what he did to you in the past…" He pauses and exhales sharply, trying to remain calm. "I should've emptied the clip into him in non-fatal places first, then taken him out."

"But it's not right that Isabel will get away with—"

"My mother's killer is *dead*, Talia," he snaps.

The door bursts open and Den rushes in, his gun pulled. Sebastian calmly tells him, "We're all good here, Den."

Den looks at me. "You okay?" When I nod, he lowers his gun and glances Sebastian's way, his gaze apologetic. "The sleet caused a pile up. I would've been here sooner."

"Can you wait downstairs for the ambulance and escort the EMTs up?" Sebastian asks.

When Den leaves, closing the door behind him, Sebastian slides his thumb down the side of my throat, his tender touch softening the harsh edge of his last comment. "I'll deal with Isabel. For now, all that matters is that you're safe."

I sigh, somewhat appeased. "When did you figure out that Paige wasn't my stalker?"

"The fact that last letter had your perfume on it kept bothering me. As soon as I learned Paige had an alibi for the fire, I left. That letter wasn't from her, which meant someone else had to have access to your perfume." Shaking his head, he exhales. "Paige still stalked you, Talia. Only it was for an entirely different reason. She sent those first letters because she wanted to make you edgy and nervous, like she felt. Then she tried to discredit you."

I twist my lips. "Jared told me someone dropped a note about my past on his plate while he was standing there talking to Nathan at the kick off party."

Sebastian shrugs. "Ultimately, her actions all boiled down to her trying to figure out what made you tick and what it would take to make Nathan give you up."

Shaking my head, I exhale slowly. "Did you ping my phone to know I was here?"

He nods. "On my way here to check out your apartment, I got Connelly to ping your phone after you didn't respond to my texts. Turns out Dwight Tucker had been Hayes' cellmate. I thought I was coming here to protect you from Dwight and that Hayes had sent him after you. The last person I expected to see was Hayes himself, since he was supposedly in jail."

I shudder, thinking about my close call with Hayes. "He had something on the Warden and was allowed to sneak out to seek his revenge."

Sebastian's jaw tightens. "We need to make sure the authorities know about the Warden." Pushing my hair back from my face, he continues, "When the ambulance comes for Nathan and after the police do their thing, I'd like you to come home with me, Talia."

I tuck my hair behind my ear, wondering where *we* are. "Once I know Nathan's going to be okay, I'll come. It might not be tonight."

Sebastian glances down at Nathan, then meets my gaze. "Then I'll wait with you, because I wasn't just talking about tonight."

CHAPTER TWENTY

Talia

After eighteen straight hours of grueling police interviews, then hospital visits with Nathan after his surgery, followed by talks with Charlie to learn my aunt was diagnosed with lead poisoning—which thankfully the doctors were able to trace back to an imported ceramic coffee mug Charlie suspected and brought in for testing— I'm totally beat. While I'm relieved that my aunt will be okay now that the doctors have figured out the cause of her health problems, I just can't bring myself to talk to her face-to-face. Charlie probably thinks the fact that I used him as a go-between with my aunt is odd, but thankfully he's too kind to point it out.

Stepping into Sebastian's elevator, I punch in the penthouse code, then lean against the wall and mentally go over everything I did to put my apartment back in order so Cass doesn't freak out when she gets back tonight. Satisfied I did a thorough job, I exhale my exhaustion. Apparently napping in a hospital chair isn't *good* sleep.

"How's Mina's apartment?" I ask Sebastian as I walk in and start to unbutton my coat. When Mina called in a panic about water rushing in her apartment not long after Nathan went in for surgery, I understood Sebastian had to leave, but I missed his calming presence.

Sebastian pushes my hands out of the way and quickly unbuttons my coat for me. "Between my dad and I, the pipe's now repaired. Mina hates the loud fans drying out her floors, but at least she and Josi aren't in crisis mode anymore. Did you eat something?" he says in a gruff tone, tugging my coat sleeves off my arms.

I turn and let him, too worn out to argue. "Hmm, yes… it was supposed to be steak, I think. It's hospital food, so you know…" I wrap my arms around his neck as he lifts me in his arms. "Where are we going?"

"To bed," he rasps against my temple.

I wave to the daylight shining through the windows. "It's three. I can't go to bed now."

He walks into his bedroom and hits a button on a remote sitting on the nightstand. As room-darkening shades start to lower, he sets me down on the bed to tug off my shoes. "Sleep is what you need, Talia."

I climb under the covers and when he starts to pull them over me, I clasp his hand. The room is completely dark now except for the daylight coming from the hallway. "Lay down with me for a bit?" I ask, trying not to sound as needy for his company as I feel.

He slides the covers up and then crawls in bed behind

me. Hooking his arm around my waist, he tucks his other arm on my pillow and kisses the back of my head. "Go to sleep, Little Red."

I pull his hand to my chest and kiss the curve of his thumb, saying quietly, "Another first. Sleeping in your bed."

He chuckles, his chest vibrating pleasantly against my back. The sensation makes me smile and I snuggle closer, despite the covers between us. "The first of many," he says, moving his hand to my hair.

I sigh my contentment, totally entranced by his fingers gently massaging along my hairline. "I'm glad you spent some time with your dad."

"Arguing over which wrench to use?" He snorts.

I don't bother to point out that a couple of billionaires could've called a plumbing team instead of fixing it themselves. At least Sebastian's grumbling sounds good-natured. "You only fight with the ones who matter."

"Says the woman who riles me more than anyone I know." He tucks my hair behind my ear and presses his lips against the curve. "Close your eyes. I'll be here when you wake up."

"You matter the very most," I mumble before falling asleep to the relaxing sensation of his fingers trailing to the ends of my hair.

"I'm here, Talia." My eyes fly open to Sebastian squatting next to the bed, his hand clasping my jaw.

I shiver at the feel of his cold skin against my sleep-warmed cheek, but the sensation of his fingers digging into the back of my neck is so comforting, I don't care. The shades are up in his bedroom now, letting in dim evening light. My gaze travels over his thermal athletic clothes to the snow coating his dark hair. "You went running?"

He nods. "I think that big snow storm they were calling for is finally here. Are you okay? You were shaking in your sleep."

"Old stuff," I mumble.

"You want to talk about it?" His blue gaze holds mine for a couple seconds. When I don't blurt out the nightmare I had, he nods and moves to stand.

I clasp his wrist, not ready for him to leave. "Wait, Sebastian. I want you to know what Hayes was talking about...what he said about me."

Sebastian sits on the edge of the bed, his comforting smell of all male, wintery outdoors and musky sweat sliding over me. I trace my fingers over his hand resting on the bed and tell him what happened between Hayes and me the night Amelia died.

I stand in the dark alley, hunching over the artwork Amelia and I drew to protect it from the cold rain that's starting to come down harder now. The image of her lying on the kitchen floor plays over and over in my head, squeezing my chest tight as I peer in the darkness at the brick wall, looking for the one brick that's slightly tilted. When I spot it, I quickly tug the half brick free. I have no idea how long this hiding place has been here, but I'm thankful for it now. The rain will ruin the artwork, so for now, the hiding place should keep it dry. With a sob, I quickly tuck the folded paper into the square hole, then slide the brick into place.

Patting the wall one last time, I lower my hand and start to run up the alley. Just as I reach the edge of the light near the top of the alley, I see Hayes walking past. The sound of my shoes slapping against the road draws his attention and he stops.

"Where are you going in such a hurry, Talia?"

Normally his slick-as-oil voice makes my skin crawl, but now it knots my stomach with fear. When he pivots and meanders into the alley, panic seizes me. He's ten feet away, and all I want to do is run, to get as far away from him as possible, but I'd have to pass him to do it. As he draws closer, the memory of Walt's blood spewing on me when I shot him flashes through my mind. Is it on my face? My neck?

I quickly step farther back into the alley, hoping that if the rain hasn't taken care of any blood that might be on me, the shadows will hide it from Hayes. Not that he gives a damn about Walt, but my aunt's boyfriend represents a distribution avenue that leads to money flow for Hayes' drug business, and intentional or not, I just cut that channel off permanently.

Hayes backs me up against the wall, his hand on the cold, wet bricks behind me. "I think I'm going to be spending more time at this place." I cringe when he pulls the pin holding my braid and it tumbles in a wet thump to my shoulder. "Been stock piling my drugs, saving for a big expansion I have planned. And I've been thinking..."

"What do you want?" I say. It comes out raspy as the knowledge that I've destroyed half his stockpile burns through my mind. The instinct to shove him away is so great I have to clench my hands by my sides. If I act, he'll hurt me. He's far stronger.

Hayes lifts my wet braid, flicking the wet ends with his thumb. "I've been thinking about all that studying you do. I could use someone like you in my organization. You could keep track of every aspect of my growing business with that book-smart mind of yours. And maybe, in a couple of years, you can go with me to set up new deals, really learn the ropes. What do you say?"

He wants me to get deeply involved in his drug business? To help him? My stomach drops. All I want to do is run. I'll say anything to make him move away from me. I don't plan to come back anyway. "I'll think about it." A smug smile tilts his lips, and as I watch him start to turn away, I panic. He's going upstairs now. He'll see what I've done and kill me. I need time to get far enough away.

"Send me to college."

He turns back, his gaze narrowed. "What?"

I straighten my spine and meet his gaze with a confident one. "Promise to pay for college and I'll work for you."

He steps back into my personal space once more and grasps my chin. "And what else will I get if I pay for your advanced education, hmmm?"

I gulp back my revulsion. I can tell by the leering gaze he slides to my neck and chest what he's inferring. I want to spit in his face, but I remain quiet and lift my shoulders, pretending indifference.

With a pleased laugh, Hayes says, "Let's seal the deal with a kiss, shall we?"

As he presses his mouth to mine, I stand there immobilized in the cold rain, my body numb with shock and disgust.

Lifting his head, Hayes tugs hard on my braid, annoyed amusement in his gaze. "You're going to have to work on your *technique, Talia."*

I feel sick to my stomach, but what can I do to delay him from going upstairs right now?

Just as he takes a couple steps away, my brain short-circuits to a solution that'll buy me some time. "Prove you have the money to send me to school," I say with self-confidence I don't feel.

He scowls. "I have the money. You've got a few years yet."

"Show me."

He throws his hands out. "It's not on me."

I shake my head. "I want to know you can afford to pay, or no deal."

Hayes eyes me in the darkness, his demeanor coldly assessing. "I'll get the money, along with my stuff. Go get dried off and be in your apartment when I get back." He walks away, but when he reaches the edge of light at the front of the alley, he glances my way, his gaze glittering. "You turned out to be an interesting surprise, Talia. Quite the little negotiator."

I might be thirteen, but I'm not an idiot. I know he's expecting me not to fight him touching me. When he walks out of the alley, turning in the opposite direction, and I hear his keys jingling, I know he's leaving, but he will be back.

I try to wipe the taste of his mouth away on my wet sleeve, but sickening revulsion rolls through me. I end up puking in the street with the cold driving rain pounding the back of my neck. Wiping my mouth, I exhale a shaky breath and take off running as fast as my legs will carry me.

When I'm done reliving the past, I squeeze Sebastian's hand, my chest aching. "Even though it didn't exactly happen the way he said it did, I played a part. My chest hurts when I think about the repercussions I didn't know

I caused. They're all I've thought about since I learned Tommy was his son."

Sebastian folds his hand over mine. "We've all done things we regret, but there's no way you could've known, nor should you feel responsible for how it all turned out. Hayes was a selfish, sadistic bastard whose choices were forced on you as a child. You survived a horrible situation, Talia. I won't let you blame yourself. Not now, not ever."

"But I held that gun, Sebastian. Walt died because of me. I'm still not sure if I actually pulled the trigger, or if it was him trying to grab it from me that set it off, but the fact is...I killed a man."

"And I killed four of my own men," he responds harshly.

When I just stare at him with wide eyes, he exhales and slides his fingers through mine. "You asked why I left the Navy. That day of the explosion, it was my job to scan for threats. I made the call, deemed the area clear, but the insurgents were so well camouflaged, I couldn't see them. My decision got four men on my team killed."

"Your situation was different. You were working for your country, doing the best with the intelligence you had at the time."

Pulling my hand to his mouth, he presses a tender kiss to my palm then slides his thumb over it. "The point I'm trying to make is, we can't know the impact our choices will have on others' lives, either right in front of us or down the road. All we can do is make the best decisions we can and hope the positive ripples far outweigh the negative ones."

He grows quiet, his gaze focused on the wall. I can tell

he's thinking about the men who died. "I'm sure no one blames you, Sebastian," I say, tightening my hand around his.

He shakes his head. "What's ironic, is now my limited color vision allows me to see through just about any camouflage, and my night vision is better than a color-sighted person's, but a SEAL can't be colorblind. Too many other factors on the job depend on full color sight. Even though I could remain in the military in another role, staying didn't feel right."

"Leaving allowed you to start a business where you continue to protect and help people." I reach up and cup his jaw. "Theo and the others at BLACK Security…they're all ex-military, aren't they?" When he nods, I smile. "Seems to me they trust your leadership just fine."

Sebastian clasps my hand and kisses my palm, a half smile tilting his lips. "How did this turn into you making me feel better?"

I shrug. "It's a mutually beneficial conversation."

"No, it's an honest one," he says. "The first one we've had, and long overdue."

The tension between us shifts and heat builds as we stare at each other. I lick my lips and lower his hand to the edge of the covers, teasing, "Are there any *more* firsts you have in mind, Mister Black?"

Heat sparks in his gaze and he pulls the covers back to slide his hand along my jean-covered thigh and then over the curve of my rear. "Absolutely, Miss Red."

Smacking my butt cheek, he stands. "I'm heading for the shower. Per your request, your belongings from the hotel are in the corner. I left some food and a new bottle for you on the island. Eat your fill. I expect to find you in the living room, holding a glass of wine when I get out."

His tone might suddenly be all business, but there's an underlying sensuality in his promise to join me that can't be mistaken. As soon as the shower turns on, I jump out of bed, switch on the light, then head for my suitcase.

Just like Sebastian said, I find the unopened bottle of wine on the island along with a tray of cheeses and fresh fruit. I nibble on some cheese and pop pieces of pineapple and raspberries in my mouth as I walk around the island, opening drawers to find the bottle opener I saw him use the other night. I finally find it, but my gaze snags on the card from Mina he'd apparently shoved in the drawer and forgotten about.

Lifting the small envelope, I slide the card out.

Seb,

Thank you for wearing your uniform. It meant a lot to me and Josi. As for my gift to you, she's standing right there. Talia is special in so many ways. Don't let her slip through your fingers this time around.

Mina

Setting the card on the island, I uncork the bottle. As I wait for the wine to breathe, I graze on more cheese and fruit, while Mina's note flashes through my mind on an endless loop. Why didn't Sebastian tell me everything the card said? Is he just not ready for more? The thought makes me a little sad while I pour myself a glass of wine.

As I take a sip of wine, my gaze strays to the window. The sight of the snow rapidly falling lifts my spirits. I move to turn off the kitchen light and grin when the switch I hit starts a fire in the dual-sided fireplace instead.

Glancing around for a chair that'll suit, my black silk lounge pants whisper quietly around my legs as I turn off the light, then move the piece of furniture right in front of the window. I retrieve my wine and return to the window, where I lean on the chair and lift the collar of Sebastian's jacket to draw in its amazing smell.

"What is it with you and rearranging furniture?"

Sebastian's low chuckle makes my body tighten with anticipation. I smile when he rests his hands on the back of the chair I'm leaning on, blocking me in. He smells so good I inhale deeply a couple of times.

"Watching the weather in the dark is just something I do. I find it relaxing. I'd planned to sit, but for some reason I'm too antsy, so here I stand, sipping this fantastic wine." I turn and glance up at him as understanding clicks into place. "You bought that wine specifically for me too, didn't you? Just like the handcuffs." I offer an apologetic smile. "I only saw the engravings after Hayes put them on me."

He holds my gaze for a second, then nods. "I bought a couple bottles six months ago. I meant what I said about a clean slate, Talia. I wanted you badly then, but after everything we've been through..." He pauses and slides my hair over my shoulder, tracing his thumb along my jaw. "What I feel for you goes beyond anything I've ever felt for another person. All I want to do is protect you and keep you safe. I like seeing you smile and knowing that I'm the reason for it. And even if our lives hadn't crisscrossed in the maze of fuckedupness we just discovered in the last twenty-four hours, I know our connection would still be undeniable. You bring out the best in me, and I don't plan to let you go."

My heartbeat leaps and my chest swells. That sounds pretty committed to me. I smile and fold my hand over his. "Good, because I don't plan to go anywhere."

Sebastian shakes his head, his jaw tightening. "You might one day."

Does he still think I'm going to run? Not after that speech. "Why would you think that?"

Sebastian takes the glass of wine from my hand and holds it up to the light outside. "You see that red color?"

When I nod, he turns the glass toward the darkened room. "Now what do you see?"

I squint at the wine. "I know it's red, but the color is so dark it looks black."

He turns the stem in his hand, staring at the wine moving in the curved glass. "I've had days where reds look like this, the blackest red. One day I could wake up and all I'll be able to see are shades of gray." Sebastian sets the glass on the built in bookshelf, then turns to me. Lifting a lock of my hair, he slowly runs his fingers down the strand, exhaling harshly when he reaches the end.

"I went through hell after I opened my eyes in that hospital bed and realized I lost most colors from my sight. At first, I thought it was like amnesia and that it would come back. I kept hoping. Once I realized that was my new reality, it took me a long time to get my head on straight. I don't know what I'll do if I lose the red spectrum too, Talia. I doubt I'll be a fit man to be around. You won't want to stay."

I hold his gaze. "You will never lose red from your life, because *your* red will still be here, standing right in front of you." I touch his jaw. "But if the day ever does come, where all colors completely disappear...let me be your rainbow, Sebastian. I can show you where to look."

"You—" He pauses and clears his throat, looking away.

His throat is bobbing. My tough SEAL is choking up. The second I lay my hand gently on his bare chest, he meets my gaze.

"You already are, Talia. Through your eyes, no matter the shade, all colors are endlessly fascinating."

I sniff back my own emotions and smile, adopting a teasing tone. "At the moment, red and black are my favorite colors. Though I think they're best displayed right up against each other, so you can truly see how well they complement." I unsnap the side button on the leather jacket's collar. "Would you like to see how I usually wear your coat?"

Sebastian slowly tugs the zipper all the way down. When he sees nothing but skin underneath, hunger flares in his eyes. Tracing his knuckle along the inside curve of my breast, his gaze snaps to mine. "You wear it just like this?"

I nod. "I feel safe when I wear it. The smell comforts me."

He lets out a low chuckle as he runs his finger along the inside curve of my other breast. "The smell of leather comforts you?"

I shake my head. "No, *your* smell comforts me. It always has."

He stills and his nostrils flair. "When I learned that you kept my coat all this time, yet you wouldn't let me touch you...that night about destroyed me, Talia. I haven't been able to get that evening out of my head."

I turn and place my hands on the back of the chair, then glance at him over my shoulder. "Would you like a redo?"

Sebastian steps behind me and slides his fingers along the edge of my hair. Pushing the curtain over my opposite shoulder, he rasps in my ear, "Will you let me add one variation?"

My heart is already racing, but I nod.

I stay still as he moves into the darkness of the apartment and then returns. When he steps up behind me once more and lays his hands over mine, my insides tingle with anticipation as he runs his fingers along the back of my hands.

He clasps my wrists and then surprises me by lifting them off the chair.

"What are you doing?" I ask, panic rising in my chest as he starts to draw them to my sides.

"I want you to trust me, Talia. You've trusted me in so many ways. I would like you to trust me with this."

When he pulls my arms fully behind my back, my breathing ramps. I can't help it.

"Don't think about the past," Sebastian whispers in my ear, while locking our fingers together. "Think about how all I make you feel is pleasure. Trust me, Talia. Will you let me?"

I don't know if I can. I blink several times, trying hard to focus on his words and not the fear clawing inside me. I take a deep breath and nod, hoping to convince myself I can do this. Sebastian cares for me. He would never hurt or terrorize me.

He plants a warm kiss on my neck at the same time I feel one of the handcuffs snap closed on my wrist. I gulp and reflexively try to jerk free, but Sebastian holds fast and says in a lighter tone, "At some point, I want to know how you got out of these cuffs in order to send that gun my way."

"Hairclip," I say, praying that talking will distract me from the panicked tension building in my chest.

Sebastian stops moving. "Do I want to know how you know how to do that?"

"Theo taught me."

His fingers encircle my wrist, tension in his hold. "*What?*"

I ignore the annoyance in his tone. "You can thank him by calling him Theo from now on."

Sebastian grunts before kissing the back of my head. As I smile in the darkness, knowing that means he agrees, he slowly rubs his thumb along the inside of my hand. When he adjusts the cuff, tightening it, I stiffen.

"We'll take it slow," he murmurs, then steps right up against me. Pressing his erection along my ass, he clasps my other wrist.

I keep my eyes focused on the falling snow and try not to let my mind go back to the past. Sebastian kisses my jaw, his warm lips lingering on my skin. "Your safe word is always there. I will stop immediately if you wish, but I hope your trust in me is stronger."

Trust is key with Sebastian. That fight we had in the hospital hall was all about my lack of trust in him. I inhale deeply and try to keep my body from shaking when I hear the other handcuff opening. He hasn't moved away and I find his presence covering me from my shoulders to my butt so comforting. I can only hope that I'll be able to hold on to the calm his closeness gives me once he steps away to lock my wrists together.

When he curves my left wrist around his lower back and then lifts my right wrist around the other side of his body, surprise eclipses the dread gnawing at my stomach. *He's locking us together?*

"I would never make you do it alone, Talia," he says, closing the second cuff around my other wrist. "I'm giving you control." Releasing my cuffed wrists, he slides his hands up my waist, then slowly along my ribcage. Cupping my breasts, he pinches my nipples hard and husks in my ear, "I love you, Talia. A first for me to say to anyone."

My heart jerks. *He loves me!* Blinking back tears, I whisper, "I've always loved you."

His hands stop moving on my body and he utters, "So much fucking wasted time." Pressing his lips to my temple, he whispers, "Use your power to let go of the past."

I arch into his hands, loving when he twirls my nipples then tugs just enough to make me cry out. Moisture floods my sex and my arms react instinctively, trying to tug him closer.

"Tell me what you want?" he demands, and I feel his erection slowly rub against my ass.

"Touch me, Sebastian."

While one hand twists my nipple in jaw-grinding pleasure/pain, he tugs at the string holding my pants up. Before the material even hits the floor, his fingers are tracing along the bit of hair between my thighs. He spreads the sensitive lips and then kisses the side of my neck as he slides his fingers back and forth along my clit.

I buck against his hand and gasp, loving his hands on me. The pleasurable sensations override any negative thoughts I have of Hayes and what he did to me.

"Is this enough?" he teases, barely touching my entrance. When my body floods with more moisture, he groans and grinds his erection against my ass. "God, it jacks me up how you soak for me, Talia. I can't decide what I want more...to fuck your pussy first or dine on it."

"Inside," I demand, panting.

He slides a finger into my channel from the front, rubbing along my clit. "Is this what you want?" When I whimper and rock my hips, his breathing amps. Releasing my breast, he moves his other hand down my ass, then between my thighs. "Or do you want it from behind?" he says in a gruffer tone and plunges two fingers deep inside me while moving his other hand up to tease my clit.

I gasp and moan as he builds my desire from both sides, his knowing fingers hitting crazy-level bliss buttons. But as much as my heart races and legs shake, I crave more.

His breathing elevates and his chest heaves against my back. "Fuck, I want you so much, Talia. Tell me what you *really* want."

My hands are already clutching at his pants. "You, I want you. *Now.*"

Grunting, he releases my body to yank his pants down. I moan when he flattens his hand on my lower belly and pushes me toward him. Lifting me slightly, his cock nudges at my entrance from behind. He's breathing hard, his muscular body tightly wound and straining behind me.

"What are you waiting for?" I pant out, near delirious to feel his thickness stretching my body, taking me, branding me his.

Staying just outside of me, he clasps my hips with both hands. I feel the barely leashed strength behind his bruising hold as he grates out, "Control it, Talia."

And it finally hits me what he's been saying. Turning my hands in the cuffs, I grab the top curve of his muscular ass and arch my back at the same time I pull him forward, demanding, "Fuck me, Sebastian."

Sebastian surges deep inside me, expelling a guttural groan. I shiver at the toe-curling sensations the new position elicits and the erotic feel of the jacket's silk lining rubbing against my hard nipples with our movements. Moaning, I dig my nails into his tight butt muscles, telling him to thrust harder.

He nips my neck and my body jerks with the next roll of his hips' deeper penetration. "I fucking love being inside you." His voice is hoarse as he clasps my thigh in a tight hold while his other hand slides along my clit. "Every time is—"

"Right where I want you to be," I say on a gasp, then shake all over when he tweaks the sensitive bit of skin between his fingers with just enough edge to make me keen. Biting my lip, I flex my channel muscles around him, taking us both higher.

He shudders, then withdraws and takes me hard once more, exhaling a primal roar. I feel him release, and I come right along with him, screaming as my body quivers through the powerful waves of euphoria crashing over me. I give myself fully over to Sebastian's masterful hands and strong embrace, basking in his support and love.

CHAPTER TWENTY-ONE

Sebastian

I pull my car into a close parking spot, the tightness in my chest easing when I see Talia's red hair blowing in the wind as she squats to place flowers on the grave. She'll probably be pissed I pinged her phone to find her, but I don't care. Her safety is more important. Even though she's back to her routine at the Tribune and busy working on her next book, you would think the knowledge that Hayes is gone and Paige has been arrested for stalking and harassment would settle my concern, but a part of me can't help but worry for her.

I rub my jaw, smirking. Maybe that's what love does to you. It makes you think about scenarios you never have before. I'm a prepared kind of guy, so fuck yeah, I'll always want to keep an eye on Talia. For my own peace of mind.

But I understand why she didn't tell me where she was

going. I'm sure she doesn't want anyone around while she has private time with her mother. As far as I know she's never visited her mother's grave. This is a first. I hope it helps her.

Talia and I have been great these past couple of weeks, but the sadness I see in her eyes sometimes when she doesn't know I'm watching feels like my own chest is caving in. All I want is to make her happy, to never see that sadness. But there's not a damn thing I can do about her aunt. The woman made her bed. It'll be up to Talia to decide if she wants to let her back in her life. Personally, I would like her as far away from Talia as possible.

Just like Isabel. I would prefer booting my stepmother the hell out of all our lives. My earlier conversation with Isabel before I came here still festers in my chest. She hated that I interrupted her massage, but that was by design. I wanted her at her most vulnerable.

"What are you doing here?" Isabel squawked, while grabbing a towel to cover her bare ass.

"Excuse me, sir, but you can't be in here," the young male masseuse said to me as he turned and held his hands up.

"Get out," I ordered in a low, deadly tone.

He stiffened, his lips pressing together. "I'm going to get management."

I offered a cold smile. "You're looking at him. I just bought this place. Now get the hell out. I need a word with your client."

Isabel sniffed her annoyance that he closed the door behind him without another word, leaving her naked and all oiled up under nothing but a couple of small towels.

I pulled a side chair up, unbuttoned my suit jacket and sat right down in front of her, face to face.

Raising herself up on her elbows to make sure she was above me, she tucked a towel to cover her breasts, her gaze slitting. "I see you're already spending your inheritance."

"I haven't touched any of my father's money, but then you should know all about doing your best to make sure *that* never happened."

Isabel's brow wrinkles with her frown. "What are you talking about?"

As I watched her fidget slightly on the table, I smoothed my hand down my tie, taking my time. "I would think you'd be relieved to learn that the man I shot saving Talia ironically happened to be the man you hired to kill me when I was a teen."

She had the audacity to gasp her outrage, diamonds flashing on the hand she put to her chest. "Have you lost your mind? Accusing me of such a horrific thing. I would never do—"

"Save your theatrics for those who naively believe you have a heart," I snapped, cutting her off. I leaned forward, my voice stone cold. "I could so easily snap your neck for what you did to my mother, to *me*. And you know I've got the skills to do it."

True fear briefly registered, but was quickly overtaken with arrogance. "How dare you threaten me? I'm a Blake, I can—"

"You're not fucking getting it, so let me be clear how this is going to go down, *Isabel*. Hayes Crawford admitted that you hired him to kill me, so unless you want to go to jail for murder, you're going to be the best damn mother to Mina and grandmother to Josi, the *most* supportive. No more negativity, no more snide comments to Mina, Talia, me, or anyone else for that matter. If I see you step out of line even just a little, I'll have you arrested."

She shook her head. "You're making this up to try and destroy me. You have no proof."

"The fact Hayes *knew* details about me and my ties to the Blake family is enough," I state.

"That's all you've got?" She let out a haughty laugh. "The notion that *I* concocted a plan to commit murder is ridiculous. You really are delusional, Sebastian, but then what should I expect from gutter trash."

I smiled and stood, buttoning my jacket. "This *gutter trash* can very easily make your life hell without involving the police. How do you think my father will react when he learns what you did?"

Her face contorted in true anger. "Go ahead. Take your bullshit lies to your father. You two barely speak. He knows you hate me. He'll never believe you."

My smile turned icy. "I wasn't the only one in the room when Hayes admitted what he did and your involvement. Talia was too. My father and I are working on mending a relationship that you tarnished, but he adores Talia and trusts her implicitly. One word from her and your life as a Blake is over."

When I start to walk away, her tone turned downright smug. "No one will believe you. All you've got is the word of a crazed killer who's dead. You have nothing on me."

I slowly turned back around, my smile confident. "*Now* the claws come out. I knew you couldn't hide them forever. How quickly you forget that Hayes wasn't the one you hired. Your liaison, who can easily identify you, is still out there. Give me a reason to find him. You do realize that's what I do for a living, right? I protect people. As far as I'm concerned, my family needs protection from you."

"They're Blakes! I would never hurt a Blake," she said as if that justified her actions.

I shook my head in a fast jerk. "No, Isabel, in our family, you're the only one who's *not* a Blake. Walk the straight and narrow or you'll discover just how true that is."

Hell yeah, I lied right to her face. I knew Hayes killed the man she hired, but I could tell by her suddenly wary expression she didn't know that. I wasn't above fighting dirty to protect my own. I'd do whatever it took.

"Why don't you just go ahead and ruin me, since you seem intent on doing so," she said, her eyes watering.

"The only reason I haven't is for Mina. I don't want to take her mother away from her. My brothers could handle finding out what you've done, but Mina..." My gaze narrowed. "I know better than anyone what it feels like to have my mother ripped away from me. I won't do that to my little sister unless you force my hand. So *don't* force it."

Talia looks up from the grave, pulling me out of my musings. At first I think she sees me, but then she looks back down and puts her hand on the headstone. I see her lips moving and wonder what she's saying. She still has moments where she keeps things to herself, moments like these. I understand them, but a part of me wishes she would share all her thoughts with me.

She stands and I straighten in my seat. When she turns and heads right for my car, I expel a low laugh. Of course she saw me. She notices everything. The price I pay for loving an overly observant person, otherwise known as a writer.

Cold wind whips in the car when she opens the door and sits down in the passenger seat. Her face is flushed from the brisk air as she turns her expressive eyes my way. It's times like this when I wish I could see the gorgeous green color and not just rely on memory. Holding my gaze, her eyebrow hikes.

Well, shit. Yep, not liking the pinging.

"You know…" she begins as she pulls her gloves off and drops them in her lap. "I didn't tell you where I was going for a reason."

I shrug, unrepentant. "If you had told me, I could've waited at home for you."

Talia sighs and attempts to fingercomb her windblown hair. "I'm fine, Sebastian. Really."

"It's been two weeks, Talia. Are you going to talk to your aunt?" I don't want the woman back in Talia's life, not after everything she did, but I do want Talia to have some closure. I think she needs that.

"Are you going to talk to Isabel?" she challenges.

"I have," I say curtly. "Now it's your turn."

Her eyes widen. "You have? What did you say to her? What did she say?"

"I'll tell you when we get home."

As I start the car and pull out of the cemetery, Talia quietly says, "I don't know what to say to Aunt Vanessa, Sebastian. I'm just…" She raises her hands and lowers them to her lap, her shoulders slumping.

I slide my hand in hers and fold our fingers together. "I understand how much she hurt you, but nothing is worse than limbo. If my father and I can finally have a conversation after this much time, I hope you can at least consider saying what needs to be said. Then you can move on, no matter what decision you make."

A tear escapes and she quickly dashes it away. "It's just so hard. She's my only family."

"You're part of *my* family," I say, rubbing my thumb over hers.

She smiles, her eyes lighting up. "I'd be a basket case right now if you weren't in my life."

I release her hand and trail my knuckles and thumb down her cheek, telling her without words that I love and support her. After I've turned several streets, she looks around and frowns. "Where are we going? This isn't the way home."

"You'll see."

"Wherever it is, remember I have to be back by six for girls' night out. Mina and Cass will shoot me if I'm late."

I grunt. "My sister has informed me twice about your schedule."

As I parallel park in front of a small bookstore with new and used books displayed in its front window, Talia smiles. "Ooh, I've never been to this store before." She's out of the car before I can come around and open the door for her. I quickly grab her hand just as she steps onto the sidewalk and turns toward the door.

"Wait, Talia."

"What?" She glances back at me, excitement brimming in her eyes. "Your bookshelves are too empty. I'll bet there are some classics in there."

I nod toward the window. "Do you recognize anyone

inside?"

She peers through the window and looks at an older woman talking to a man behind a register. "Isn't that the man from my book signing?" she asks, her teeth starting to chatter. "The one who brought all my books to sign?"

I fold our clasped hands and blow on them to warm her. "It is. I had Kenneth McAdams checked out after the signing. I was worried he might be a threat, because he was so into your books. He cleared, but then after your aunt's confession, I couldn't help but wonder if there was anything else she hadn't told you. I pulled some strings and got a copy of your birth certificate. It doesn't match the one you used to get into college."

Talia squeezes my hand as the old woman walks out of the store. "What are you saying?"

"Do most people ask you to sign your books to their full name?"

When she shakes her head, I nod to indicate the man who's now carrying a basket of books toward a bookshelf. "He's your father, Talia. His name was listed on your real birth certificate. Maybe the circumstances of how he left aren't exactly how your aunt described either." I shrug. "Maybe they are, but either way, you two have something in common—your love of stories. It's a place to start."

My heart thumps and I wonder what's going on in her mind as she turns and stares into the store window. All I know is...I love seeing the look of hope bloom in her eyes as she tracks his movements.

"Why don't you go in and talk to him." I lean over and open the door for her. "I'll wait out here for you."

Once she walks in, I watch Talia call out and wave to

catch his attention, then exhale on a chuckle when he turns and drops the basket of books on the floor. As Talia rushes to help him with the spilled books, I smile and slide my hands in my coat pockets, hoping that maybe over time she can get her family back. It might not be the one she started with, but family is still family, and we all want to know we belong.

CHAPTER TWENTY-TWO

Talia

This day has ended on the best note. After visiting my mother's grave for the first time and telling her how sorry I was that I never got to know her, I met my father and made plans to have dinner with him next week. And now I'm celebrating with the girls as I tap the salted rim of my margarita glass to Mina's and then Cass'. "To Fridays and happy hour!"

"TGIF," Mina says, then takes a sip of her drink. "So good. Man, I've missed this."

I smile as I watch her chat with Cass about my roommate's photography career. I knew these two would hit it off. Before I came tonight, Sebastian told me the conversation he had with Isabel. My heart aches as I look at his sister. She has no idea the sacrifice Sebastian is making for her, but at least she appreciates him dearly for everything she is aware of.

It's a tough call—deciding not to tell his father over Mina's happiness.

The truth may eventually be revealed over time if he and his father grow closer, but all I know is, the knowledge that Sebastian is choosing others' happiness over his own makes *me* love him that much more.

When my purse buzzes in my lap, I pull out my phone.

"No *men* tonight," Cass says, wrinkling her nose like the whole gender is the devil incarnate.

"If it's my brother, he won't stop until she at least acknowledges him," Mina says, snorting.

Cass heaves an exaggerated sigh, waving permission. "Fine. Appease the man who adores you, then cut him off."

Snickering at the two of them, I read Sebastian's text.

PainInMyAss: Are you ever going to change my contact info?

Me: It's perfect just the way it is.

PainInMyAss: While I admit to an endless fascination with that gorgeous ass of yours, something more personal perhaps.

Me: Maybe it should be PantyThief? Found your Talia stash today!

Even though I'm teasing him, I cried when I ran across them in a bureau drawer. He had kept every pair.

PainInMyAss: Those are Talia Trophies; hard earned and worth all that sweat. Of course I kept them.

I grin and while I'm changing his contact info, he sends a text with ideas for his new contact name.

Snorting at his outlandish suggestions, I send him a screen shot with his new name.

Me: Happy?

RainbowMaster: Exceedingly. How long does GNO last?

Me: Until it's over.

RainbowMaster: Expect to be kidnapped after four hours.

Me: What happened to that infamous control, Mister Black?

RainbowMaster: I met you, Miss Red.

"Wha—what are you doing?" I mumble as Sebastian slides a soft sleep mask over my eyes, then lifts me out of bed. I'm still slightly drunk from the night out with the girls. *Is it morning already? It feels like I just fell asleep.*

"Shhh, go back to sleep."

"The mask is a nice touch," I snicker tiredly.

"You'll see when we get there."

"Ooh, where are we going?" I ask, my mind rousing a little at the idea of a trip.

"Don't you dare wake up, not yet," he says, his tone crisp. "And if you do, the mask stays on. Got it?"

As the elevator starts to descend, I salute him. "Yes, sir."

"Smartass."

I hear the smirk in his comment. "That's me." I start to grin but end up yawning, which makes him laugh outright.

I'm shivering by the time he sets me in the leather car seat. I welcome the warm blanket he quickly tucks around me, followed by a seat belt.

"I hope you packed everything. My purse?" I'm itching to take off my mask, but I don't want to spoil his surprise.

"I've got it all covered." The car dips as he gets in and shuts the door. He presses a kiss to my forehead and orders gruffly, "Go back to sleep, Little Red."

The heaviness of sleep quickly rolls over me as the car begins to move, which makes me think he really did wake me not long after I fell asleep. Sneaky man.

Sebastian's hand slides up my thigh bringing me fully awake. I'm lying on my back on something soft, my arms above my head. It feels like a bed. Did he bring me to my apartment? What other places could he just walk into carrying a masked sleeping woman without getting arrested? I start to pull off the mask, but soft bindings tighten around my wrists.

Just as I tug, he pushes my thighs apart and slides his tongue leisurely along my folds all the way up to my clit.

I instantly buck and gasp, surprised that he goes right for my most sensitive area so quickly. "Good morning?" I ask, intrigued.

"That it is," he rumbles against my body, then moves his mouth to my inner thigh, pressing light kisses along it. "I've been thinking about ripples."

"Ripples?" I arch my back, hoping he'll kiss my sex just like that again. His mouth feels good, so warm and so very talented.

"Mmm, hmmm," he says, his thumbs parting my sensitive skin.

I swear I can feel the heated burn of his piercing blue gaze inspecting me, wondering which place to hit next. He rests his hands on my hips and places a tender kiss just above my hairline. My stomach flexes and I feel moisture sliding south, preparing for him to nip and kiss and generally drive me crazy.

"If you hadn't stumbled into my life that night all those years ago, I wouldn't have given you that watch and may never have gone to live with my uncle. Having his positive support at such a critical time in my life shaped who I became. That's one of the many reasons I love you, Talia."

Before I can respond, he goes straight for my clit with fierce intensity that has me tugging hard on my bindings. I want to say something, but I'm too busy panting and pushing closer to his mouth to say a word.

"Seb—Sebastian, stop. I can't speak."

When he lifts his head and kisses my other thigh, I gulp in air. "If you hadn't given me that watch, I don't know if I would've had the strength to keep looking forward. That night with you at the masked party was so unexpected, but I cherished it so much. I still do."

"The kind of memory to last a lifetime," he says, then moves up my body to kiss my breast.

I whimper when he sucks a nipple into his mouth and nips at it. I squirm against my bonds, wanting to touch him, while loving that I don't know where his mouth will land on me next.

He kisses my throat at the same time that he slides two fingers inside me. When I moan and arch against him, he whispers in my ear, "I held onto that night, Talia. The pureness of it helped me when I thought I'd lose my fucking mind in a mostly colorless world."

"Then why didn't you do something when you found me, damn it!" I say, frustrated by his confession.

Withdrawing his hand, he lifts my thigh and my tears soak into the mask as he slowly slides inside me. I love it. I love the way we feel together.

"Every time, Talia," he rasps. "I just can't believe how good."

"Why, Sebastian?"

He lowers the full weight of his body over mine, sliding as deep as he can go. "When I saw proof that you were engaged, I thought you were happy. I was still fucked up, not sure if or when all the color would leave my sight. I didn't want to screw you up right along with me."

"I hate that you made that decision for me. I hate—"

Sebastian kisses me, cutting off my anger. I welcome his mouth on mine, the thrust of his tongue showing me how much he loves me. I tug on the bindings and feel them suddenly slacken.

With a sob, I pull my hands free of the bindings and wrap my arms around his broad shoulders, kissing him with pent up frustration, sadness, and happiness. "I love you, Sebastian. I've loved you all my life."

He clasps my face, his mouth barely touching mine. "I know that now, Talia," he starts to say, then slides the mask off. "That's why I brought you here."

I blink until my vision comes back into focus. When I see a familiar set of windows, my gaze flies around the sparsely decorated room. It's his old bedroom at the Hamptons house. The one Isabel sold. "How...did you do this? Did you rent the house?"

He slowly shakes his head. "It's mine. Something special happened here and I wasn't about to let someone else own this place."

"You really bought it?"

He holds my gaze with a steady one. "I had a third party take care of it for me. Not even Mina knows I own it."

"She's going to be so excited!" I laugh happily and squeeze his neck, planting kisses along his jaw.

Sebastian grins and rolls his hips, hitting places that make me arch and moan. "I had a decorator take care of it, but whatever you don't like we'll switch out. For now... this weekend, we're going to christen every room in this monstrosity."

I lift my legs around his hips and smile. "How about we start with this one? I have a feeling it'll always be my favorite room in the house."

Sebastian pulls out, then thrusts deep inside me, and when I slide my fingers in his hair, he lowers his head close to mine, his voice husky with want in my ear. "I think you know now that I made love to you that night, Talia. You were special from the very beginning and you always will be."

My heart is brimming with love for him. I kiss his throat and tease, "I think I need a repeat performance. You know, just to be sure you were actually making love to me."

With a dark chuckle, he grips my thighs. Lifting them high along his sides, he begins to rock against me, a sexy smirk tilting his lips. "Are you sure you can rise to the challenge, Miss Red? Who do you think will last longer?"

He's hitting me just right and making me want to howl. Shivers of delight race along my body; it's taking everything not to lose it instantly. I rake my nails down his back and revel in the lustful hunger that flashes in his gorgeous eyes. "Who do you think, Mister Black? Life with you is like Kegels on steroids." I flex my inner muscles as he starts to pull out and smile when he pauses and expels a harsh groan. "I'm a fighter, remember? Give me all you've got."

Sebastian pulls out of me completely, a dangerous smile on his face. "Oh, it's on, sweetheart."

Before I can form a comeback, I'm on my stomach with my arms stretched over my head. Clasping my wrists with one hand, Sebastian's warmth surrounds me, his voice seductive velvet in my ear. "Raise that sweet ass of yours. *Now*."

I consider challenging him, but I'm intrigued so I hold my breath and lift my pelvis, waiting as he shoves a folded pillow under my hips.

"Spread your legs, Talia," he says as his knee nudges

mine apart.

I'm already panting as I comply. His deep voice just hits all the right notes for me.

Sebastian whispers all the ways he's going to make me come as he slides inside me, but it's the position that brings my body humming to life. Every time he pulls out and then eases back inside, his slow, unhurried motion sliding deep hits right on my g-spot.

The combination of his dirty mouth and his cock strumming my body like his own personal fine-tuned instrument turns my brain to mush. I can't close my legs. I can't buck or rock to drive him nuts. I can't move. I'm completely at his relentless mercy. All I can do is feel the sensory build-up racing inside me in time to my thudding heart.

"I—I can't take it, Sebastian."

"Have you had enough?" he rasps, his own voice strained, almost hoarse.

"Yes! Just let me come—" I scream out as he slams deep once more, but then he rolls me over onto my back and is sliding inside me in a powerful rush of primal possession.

Burying his nose in my throat, he shakes, his body tense as he groans deeply, then he hitches his hips at just the right angle and slams into me with one more aggressive thrust. I'm lost in the moment, screaming as my climax consumes me faster than it ever has. Sebastian's hold on my hair is as tight as his hand on my ass while he rocks into me, and utters a guttural rumble of pleasure through his own orgasm.

As our pounding hearts batter each other's chest, he lifts his head, a wry smile on his face. "I think we both lost that one, Little Red."

I grin and pull him close, inhaling his amazing smell. "I'd call that a major win-win."

The next morning, I tug on Sebastian's T-shirt and walk downstairs to find him sitting in a soft leather cushion chair in front of the bank of French doors that lead out to the patio and small private beach beyond. I smile at the sunrise just coming up over the horizon, its yellow beams reflecting off the water, and slide my fingers in his hair. "Why didn't you wake me?"

"I thought you might be worn out after hitting half the rooms in this place." Shirtless and wearing a pair of soft black lounge pants, he clasps my hand and flashes a cocky smile, tugging me into his lap. He nods to the folded paper in my hand, and his eyebrows shoot up. "What's that?"

I exhale a shaky breath and open it for him to read. "It's a contract. For us. I um, didn't put an expiration date on it, but I thought maybe—"

"How long have you had this?" he asks, frowning.

I squirm under his direct stare. "It's been in my purse for a week."

"And you're just now showing it to me?"

He's angry? I lift my shoulders. "I didn't want to make assumpt—"

Sebastian yanks the paper out of my hand and tosses it behind us. As I watch it land with a soft whisper, sliding across the Tuscan flooring, he slips a ring on my left hand.

"Marry me, Little Red."

I stare at the gorgeous quarter-inch wide platinum band. Its smooth polished surface is slightly concave with a band of sparkling red stones residing in the channel created by the curved design. "I didn't know if you believed in marriage," I say as I touch the stones, my throat tight with emotion.

His brow furrows. "I said that I'm never going to let you go, and I meant it. When I bought this house, I couldn't let go of an amazing memory, but I really bought it for *us*, Talia. I don't claim I'll be easy to live with...And fair warning, I'm going to be a pain-in-the-ass about some Tribune work assignments—you'll take backup on riskier cases so I don't lose my mind with worry—but I want you to share your life with me."

I open my mouth to speak, but glance back down at the ring when the band of red stones moves under my finger. Sebastian gives a wry smile and lifts my hand to turn the sparkling band all the way around inside the channel. "These are red diamonds. The rarest, just like you." His gaze meets mine. "I'll always be dominant, Talia. I won't apologize for that, but I wanted you to know that marriage to me means together, but independent."

I glance down at the ring, moved by such deep sentiment. "So that's why the red band moves?"

He slowly nods. "I'll protect you, but I'll never smother you."

I inhale a deep breath and blink rapidly so I don't start sobbing. He just makes me melt. Touching his jaw, I smile. "I love that you chose red diamonds instead of traditional ones. But if they are the rarest, maybe I should wear a replica and put this one in a vault—"

"No, you'll only wear the real deal. You're worth every penny, Talia. Every last one."

Humbled, I grasp his left hand and trace his ring finger. "Will your ring have black diamonds?" When he starts to scowl, I raise an eyebrow. "Real men aren't afraid of diamonds, Sebastian."

He grunts. "How about black platinum?"

I sigh and shake my head. "You're such a *man*. Fine, but I get to pick the design." Lifting my hand, I take off the ring and hold it out to him.

"What are you doing?" he says, scowling.

"Giving it back until the wedding."

Sebastian takes the ring and slides it back on my finger. "Hell no, I'm not waiting for that. This means you're mine. I want every man around you to know it, every last one. When we finally get married, it'll just be a formality as far as I'm concerned."

I hold up the ring, loving the way the early morning light catches on the diamonds. "Well, there is the whole legal aspect if you want me to take your last name."

"Hmm, good point. We'll have to set a date very soon." He rubs his overnight beard, contemplating. "Tomorrow works for me."

My jaw literally drops. "We can't do that."

"We can do whatever we want. That's the great thing about being adults."

"But our friends and families…"

He clasps my face, bright blue eyes peering deeply into mine. "This is about starting *our* family, Talia. They don't get a say-so in that."

I smile at the spot of brown in his left eye. When he's

intense like this, it really stands out against the blue. I adore that bit of imperfection about him so much. "Our family. I love the sound of that."

"Good, because *with me* is where you'll always belong," he says, kissing my forehead. Settling me against his chest, he wraps his arms around me. "Now let's watch the sunrise and don't skimp on any colors. I want the full, 120 box of crayons version."

Sign up/join P.T. Michelle's:

NEWSLETTER
(free newsletter announcing book releases and special contests)
http://bit.ly/11tqAQN

FACEBOOK READERS' GROUP
https://www.facebook.com/groups/376324052499720/

GOODREADS READERS' GROUP
https://www.goodreads.com/group/show/130689-p-t-michelle-patrice-michelle-books

ACKNOWLEDGEMENTS

To my fantastic beta readers: Joey Berube, Amy Bensette, and Magen Chambers, thank you for reading Blackest Red so quickly and for your spot-on feedback. I'm thrilled you loved this conclusion to Sebastian and Talia's story. You ladies definitely helped make Blackest Red a better reading experience.

To my wonderful critique partner, Trisha Wolfe, thank you for reading Blackest Red, for your fabulous critiques, brainstorming sessions and checking over all those "extra" scenes. Major hugs, girl!

To my family, thank you for understanding the time and effort each book takes. I love you all and truly appreciate your unending support.

To my amazing fans, thank you for loving my books and for spreading the word by posting reviews and telling all your reader friends about them whenever you get a chance. I appreciate every one of you and all the fantastic support you continually give!

ABOUT THE AUTHOR

P.T. Michelle is the *NEW YORK TIMES, USA TODAY,* and International Bestselling author of the contemporary romance series IN THE SHADOWS, the YA/New Adult crossover series BRIGHTEST KIND OF DARKNESS, and the romance series: BAD IN BOOTS, KENDRIAN VAMPIRES and SCIONS (listed under Patrice Michelle). She keeps a spiral notepad with her at all times, even on her nightstand. When P.T. isn't writing, she can usually be found reading or taking pictures of landscapes, sunsets and anything beautiful or odd in nature.

To keep up-to-date when the next
P.T. Michelle book will release,
join P.T.'s free newsletter http://bit.ly/11tqAQN

CPSIA information can be obtained at www.ICGtesting.com
Printed in the USA
LVOW08s1757140816

500337LV00006B/309/P